TOLL OF THE CROWNED FLAME
ORACLES OF THE GELID
BOOK TWO

OLIVIA TILDON

Copyright © 2026 by Olivia Tildon

All rights reserved.

No generative artificial intelligence (AI) was used in the writing of this work. The author expressly prohibits any entity from using this publication to train AI technologies to generate text, including, without limitation, technologies capable of generating works in the same style or genre as this publication. The author reserves all rights to license uses of this work for generative AI training and development of machine learning language models.

No part of this publication may be reproduced, distributed, or transmitted in any form or by any means, including photocopying, recording, or other electronic or mechanical methods, without the prior written permission of the publisher, except as permitted by U.S. copyright law. For permission requests, contact Olivia@OliviaTildon.com.

ISBN 979-8-9985316-3-7

The story, all names, characters, and incidents portrayed in this production are fictitious. No identification with actual persons (living or deceased), places, buildings, and products is intended or should be inferred.

Cover design by GetCovers.com.

First Edition, March 2026.

For those living through moments that remake them.
May you find courage here, and the reminder that you are not alone.

In the depths of darkness, find the flicker of your inner light, and let it guide you towards the path of freedom and survival.

CONTENT WARNINGS

This story contains moments of beauty and ferocious hope—but it also walks through fire. To help you care for yourself as you read, here are the themes and elements you can expect to encounter within these pages:

- **Violence and war**, including battles, fire, and physical injury
- **Threats of death** and high-stakes danger to main characters
- **Mentions of torture**, occurring off-page and referenced
- **Psychological manipulation** through intimidation and mental intrusion
- **Trauma responses**, including fear, panic, and emotional aftermath
- **Civilian harm and destruction** during acts of war
- **References to death and loss**, including grief and survivor guilt

This list is not meant to alarm, only to honor your autonomy. You deserve to decide how and when you engage with stories that touch on difficult themes. If you choose to continue,

CONTENT WARNINGS

I hope you'll find strength in Lyla's fire, comfort in the bonds she refuses to relinquish, and a reminder that even in the darkest moments, we are never done choosing who we become.

Take what you need. Leave what you must. And above all, may you read safely.

CHAPTER 1

I blinked, staring at the dust cloud.
A man had been standing there. He had handed me an ominous letter while shouting, "All hail Bel!" Then he choked, as if air had turned solid in his lungs.

Before anyone could move, he turned to dust. Not collapsed. Just… disintegrated.

My muscles refused to work for me. All around me, shouts rang out. Guards scrambled to secure the room. To protect the people. To protect me.

This was supposed to be my coronation, my wedding night.

Bel, the God of Death, had promised to kill me before I became Queen. He meant to stop it.

I didn't know why, I hadn't even known he existed—much less that he was walking among the people—until after he started targeting my family. My mother was first, killed with some kind of lightning strike.

Well, he'd sent someone to do it.

Just like he sent Prince Egan, of Scoria Bay, to win my hand in marriage, with the hidden motive to kill me instead.

The terror of his attack caused me to use my own magic, setting off a whole volcano near his lands. He had fled, promising to bring war to me if I had harmed his people. I could hardly blame him for his vengeance over innocent lives lost.

My mind raced while I looked down at the letter I was holding. The threat was written by Egan's hand, I recognized his handwriting, but it was Bel's words. The words swarmed in front of me, moving on the page. Had that been magic, or just my inability to focus on them? I blinked, blinked again.

Before I could try to read it one more time, Spencer hugged me—no he pulled me, shouted for me to get down. He forced me down with his arm, and I slid off my chair ducking under the table on the dais.

We needed to hide.

I could feel the paper crinkling as I clenched my hand, trying to find my balance. Amyra reached for that hand, but not to take the paper from me. Her fingers gripped my fist with quiet resolve.

Even in the chaos, I caught the scent of warm apple cider clinging to her, grounding me. Her wavy black hair fell over pale skin, the sweep of it brushing her pale blue eyes as she glanced around us. Those lips—always tasting of raspberries and honey—pressed into a thin line, holding back words.

The world was spinning.

My eyes couldn't focus on anything. My vision was blurred, the glitter from my gown sparkled, and I felt my brown hair tickle my neck as it fell from a pin that must have loosened.

I heard Ethan barking orders, his voice getting closer.

The sharp commands cut through my fog, and when he appeared, his crystal-blue eyes were bright with focus, framed by the tumble of chestnut curls that refused to stay tamed. Within moments, he was moving the chair protecting me, reaching down.

"Let's get you out of here, in case there's more conspirators. I have an escort."

The words reached me, but meaning lagged behind them. My brain was still catching up, stuck on the image of a man turning to ash.

Before I could process it, Spencer was behind me, lifting me.

Amyra was face to face with me when we reached standing. We made eye contact and I willed myself to focus on her ice blue eyes. The irises swirled as she studied me carefully, then she looked briefly behind me, then back to me.

Her mouth moved.

Did she say something?

I couldn't hear anything. Was that normal?

'*Lyla, my love, we need to go.*' Spencer's voice inside my mind finally broke through the shock. '*Walk with us, listen to Ethan.*'

Spencer's voice cracked through the fog. I was the target, I didn't have time to freeze. I willed my mind to bury the emotions, process it later.

I nodded and turned to my brother. He pointed to a group of guards standing on the stairs. "These guards will take you to your chambers."

I shook my head, shifting into action. "No, once you've handled security, go to the cave. Tell Father, Juniper, and if General Kellen is in the castle, him too."

Ethan nodded. "Be safe, above all else."

He gave me a quick hug, reaching to touch Spencer's shoulder as we separated. He nodded at Amyra too, then turned to command a different group of guards.

The first group surrounded us as we descended. I informed them of the destination, and they moved as one, keeping us fully shielded as we navigated out of the ball room. In the halls, they couldn't surround us so well, the walls too narrow. But they still kept us surrounded, forcing us to pause at each intersection while they visually checked each way.

Each second dragged as we navigated the halls to Juniper's office. The Lady was already waiting for us, breathless and still in her finery.

Gold eyes locked on mine, fierce despite the damp sheen on her dark hair. Only 27, Juniper carried her youth and authority in equal measure, a balance that made her seem both older and more unshakable than she was. "Ethan directed Emberly to send us here."

She opened the locked door, and the guards escorting us took positions around the door and through the hallway.

"Allow my father, Ethan, and the Commanding General to join us, as well as the priestesses if they arrive." I instructed before entering Juniper's office.

Once inside, Juniper wasted no time in moving to her side room, then performing the small ritual to reveal the cave door. The stone door groaned open, and we headed down the stairs, the smell of mildew and dust permeating the air. The air in the passage was damp and heavy, the stone walls closing in. And yet, it was here, in this hidden cavern beneath the castle, that I'd felt safest these last few months. It was the only place Bel's shadow hadn't touched.

It didn't take long for the group to assemble, most were in the ball room when it happened. Ethan informed us that Kellen was not in the castle tonight, but his steward was delivering a message about the events and requested that he meet with us in the morning.

Once Juniper had closed the door, I looked around at my inner circle. Ethan, my father, Spencer and Amyra, Juniper, and the head priestess, Emberly were staring back at me, waiting for me to share the letter. I unfolded the paper, noticing all the creases I had made in the moments after, when the horror had dulled my senses.

"It's in Egan's handwriting, but it's definitely a message from Bel." I explained. Then I read it out loud.

To the New Queen of Elthas,
Congratulations on your coronation. What a cute little spectacle of a wedding. Three crowns for one throne. How spoiled. It is always the indulgent who believe they can outwit the weight of history.
You still believe you have time. That you have power. But the outcome is already sealed. This war will only hurt you, and everything you claim to protect.
I offer you one path forward: bend the knee. Dedicate yourself at my Temple. Let me govern Elthas through you, and I will allow you to keep

your title — in name only. You will obey, or you will watch your people die screaming.
Their blood will be on your hands.
You have one month. I will come prepared to accept your dedication to me.

I LOWERED THE SHEET, glancing around the room. Father's face reflected stony resolve. Ethan had gone pale. Juniper and Emberly looked angry. Amyra and Spencer looked ready to fight for me.

I turned to Ethan. "Was there anyone else?"

Ethan shook his head. "When I left, they were still checking people and no one was allowed to disperse, but they hadn't found anyone.

"I don't think they will. I think he was a lone guy, sent to rattle us."

"And it worked." Amyra grunted.

"Well, yeah, it's unnerving to see someone vaporize in front of you." Ethan muttered.

"We need to focus. The plans need to move up. I need to go to the coastline so that I can help those towns survive their fleet coming here." I said.

"That's too dangerous, you can't leave when there's a war coming." Spencer said softly.

"Who else can just erect thick stone walls in a matter of hours to protect those people?" I scowled back.

Juniper stepped forward, "We can do that, and you should go. But you need to be smart. You need to travel with the military reinforcements that these towns need as well. It will be slower travel, but it will be safer."

I smiled gratefully. That was a compromise I could live with.

"We also need to plan to leave as soon as possible," I said, turning to the next fire to fight. "One month is too short to protect these towns."

"You can call a meeting in the morning," Father said. "Have

the Council approve the troop movements. Kellen will be there too."

Then his expression softened. "But tonight, my sweet daughter... you just got married. If you don't allow yourself a moment to feel that joy, then no matter what happens next, he will have stolen something more than lives. He'll have stolen your beginning."

He was right. Bel wanted to take more than my crown, more than my people. He wanted to steal the parts of me that were still soft, still human. Still capable of joy.

I turned to Spencer and Amyra, both waiting—ready to fight, yes, but also ready to love me through the storm.

I nodded slowly, a resolve settling deep in my chest. "Tomorrow, we'll prepare for war." I reached for their hands. "But tonight? I'm choosing love. Bel can't take that from me."

We reached my room quickly—my last night here before everything shifted. The next day, our things would be moved to the royal chambers, and Father settling into the suite my grandmother once used after her king died.

Relief filled me once we crossed the threshold. The rest of the night would be about me, my partners, and our marriage. I was grateful in a small way, because if that man hadn't interrupted the night, the party would still be going on—and as lovely as that might've been, this was better.

Spencer immediately headed to the bedroom to change into his nightclothes first, while Amyra and I sat down and pulled our hair free of the pins holding it in place.

"Do you think I'm doing the right thing, going to the coastline?" I asked Amyra, as we brushed our hair.

"Saving lives is always a good choice to make. Do you feel drawn to any other choices?"

I considered her question. Did I feel obligated to go elsewhere? As I examined my thoughts and worries, I felt a tug around my heart, pulling towards the coastline. I needed to go there.

"My heart tells me this is the right choice." I answered.

Amyra smiled. "It is. And we will make sure you get there."

We stood, and I reached for the crowns to place in their boxes. As I placed the box into the armoire, I asked. "Will you come with me? I don't think I could go alone."

I stood and turned to face her as she nodded. "I'll go wherever you need me to be."

We shared a small smile and headed to the bedroom, where Spencer slipped out of the bathing room and tended the fire while Amyra quietly unlaced my dress. The soft movements between us made me wonder if tonight would truly become what we all hoped for.

Freed of our gowns, Amyra and I stepped into the bathing room and found the tub already filled with steaming, fragrant water—wild roses, sweetgrass, and fir. Ivy's wedding-night blend. We exchanged a knowing look.

We slid into the heat, and it wasn't long before my mouth found hers, the kiss slowed my pulse even as my heart pounded inside my chest. Being here with her—finally—made my whole body buzz with anticipation.

When we left the bath, towels waited for us, Ivy's care in every detail. We dried each other slowly, laughter softening the weight of the night.

She dropped her towel and reached for me. Her arms wrapped around my neck, elbows straight, her body close enough to warm every inch of me. We shared a tender kiss for just a moment before she pulled away.

"My wife, you're actually my wife." She whispered incredulously.

I smiled, touching my forehead to hers. "You're my wife too."

"Let me show you what pleasures my wife gets to have every night," her eyes twinkled with mischief. Her arm slid down my shoulder, her hand reaching for the back of my head, and she gripped my hair.

I moaned, loving the way she takes control. She guided me into the bedroom, where we found Spencer.

Our husband, Spencer. Who had been sitting on our bed, waiting for us. Completely ready for what we were about to start.

Oh dear Gods, was this really my life?

Amyra and I stopped the moment we saw him. He was stunning. All dark, burnished heat, like the blackened cedar used to trim the royal chambers. Firelight kissed every line of him, each muscle shaped by years of bearing armor and training. I'd seen him bloodied, soaked, exhausted, but never like this. His quiet strength carved into every contour, his waist tapering into the sharp, deliberate lines that held an unspoken promise of power… the kind that made my pulse trip.

And oh, that power rose in such a strong, tantalizing cock, waiting for us.

I knew he was strong, but I didn't realize the beauty his clothes hid from the world.

Amyra's grip slackened in my hair, equally struck by this statuesque God before us.

"Goddess, Spencer," I whispered. "You're… wow."

Amyra let out a low whistle. "Spencer, where have you been hiding all that?"

He flushed as his hand shifted to cover his abdomen, a shy gesture that only made him that much more attractive.

"I don't know what you mean."

I approached him, a smile spreading across my face. "You know exactly what we mean. I love you, Spencer. You're all mine, and hers. You're ours."

He sat up as I reached the bed, and my fingers hovered just above his chest, wanting to touch, but hesitating. His hand reached up and pulled my hand the last distance, allowing me to touch his chest.

Amyra's hand reached for his shoulder, and we slide our hands down him. Spencer shifted to put one of his thighs between my legs as Amyra climbed onto the bed behind him.

My breath caught as Spencer leaned in to kiss me, soft and

slow. His lips were so warm, his kiss so achingly patient. I moaned into it, threading my fingers into his hair as Amyra's hands traced over his back. Her mouth pressed against his neck while mine stayed locked with his.

Spencer's thigh was still between my legs, and I rocked against it without thinking, chasing the friction. He groaned into my mouth and reached down, gripping my waist as if to anchor me through my movements.

Amyra's hand snaked around his hips, reaching for his cock. She slowly ran her hand along the length of his member and he moaned into my mouth. I felt the knuckles of her hand brush against my belly as she teased him. After just three strokes, he broke our kiss and stilled her arm.

"We need to slow down, please, or else my side will end very, very soon." He panted.

Amyra's wicked grin spread on her face as we locked eyes. She pulled away from his neck, already a deep, dark bruise visible, as she shifted her focus to me.

"My queen, you are way, way too far away from my fingers." She teased, shifting around Spencer, pulling me closer to her. I climbed onto the bed, having only just a moment before she tackled me down.

She spread my legs, quickly inserting one of her fingers as she held her other hand around my neck, gently but firmly pinning me in place. "Spencer, her nipples need your attention." She ordered.

He happily obliged, shifting to the other side of me, which allowed his lips to gently kiss each nipple before he chose one to nibble on. I moaned, feeling my back arch, shoving my breast into his mouth.

Amyra's finger curled just right, and I let out a broken gasp, my hips rising to meet her hand. Her grip on my neck wasn't tight, just enough to remind me I was hers tonight, just enough to make me want to obey her every command. The heat building in my core was already threatening to spill over, and Spencer's mouth was only making it worse. Or better. I couldn't decide.

"I love watching you fall apart," Amyra whispered, her lips brushing my cheek as she spoke. "So beautiful like this. Open. Ours."

Spencer pulled off my chest, "I need to know how good you taste."

His words made my whole body thrum.

He shifted between my legs, Amyra's fingers replacing his tongue. She leaned down to kiss me, darting her tongue into my mouth. I had only a moment to enjoy this before Spencer's breath tickled my bud, his finger rubbing my slit.

"Lyla, you smell heavenly, and you're so very ready for me." He whispered, almost worshipping. Then I felt his finger enter me as his tongue swirled around my bud. His tongue was practiced, insistent. My hips bucked into his mouth. His other hand reached around my thigh to hold me still.

Amyra shifted her kisses down my chin to my neck, and my eyes fluttered. I briefly saw the look in her eyes, raw, pure hunger, which made me clench even more.

"Don't stop, please" I gasped, my hands reaching for both Amyra's and Spencer's heads.

A moment later, the orgasm crashed through me, white flashing before my eyes. I cried out, my hips lifting from the bed, wave after wave rocking through me. Spencer moaned against my core, like I was the sweetest drink he'd tasted.

I collapsed, boneless, trembling, completely undone.

Spencer lifted himself up, a delicious grin on his face. I watched as Amyra shifted her attention to him. She grabbed her face and they kissed so intimately above me. Amyra moaned into his mouth. My hand reached up to twist her nipple, pinching and tugging at it as she enjoyed licking every last drop of my orgasm off of Spencer's face.

Amyra finally broke the kiss, her lips slick, her breath uneven. She looked down at me, flushed and glowing.

"You taste even better on him," she murmured, brushing a strand of hair from my face.

Spencer chuckled, low and hoarse, still catching his breath. "That was one of the most beautiful things I've ever seen."

I pulled him down, his heat sliding against me as his cock pressed to my thigh. I wrapped a leg around his waist, guiding him closer.

His eyes met mine—want softened by care. "Ready?"

"Yes," I breathed. "Please."

He lined himself up and eased inside, stretching me just enough to steal my breath. He paused, worry flickering.

"I'm okay," I whispered through the ache. "Go."

He pushed deeper, inch by slow inch, until he filled me completely, a shiver sparking up my spine. His forehead met mine.

"You're perfect," he murmured.

Amyra's mouth brushed his shoulder as her hand slipped between us, pinching my bud just right. I gasped, my hips rising into both their touches.

Spencer began to move, and his deep, slow thrusts fanned every ember Amyra coaxed from me. I clung to him with one hand and reached for her with the other; she laced her fingers with mine and squeezed.

"I love you," I whispered.

"We love you," she returned, then kissed the place where his neck met his shoulder.

Spencer's groan vibrated against my mouth as his rhythm quickened, his thrusts hitting that perfect edge while Amyra circled my bud.

"Come for us again, my queen," she breathed.

It snapped through me white-hot, unstoppable. I shattered, crying out as my nails dug into Spencer's back and Amyra's hand. Spencer held on through my climax, driving into me with desperate, beautiful precision, until finally he slowed, still inside me, panting.

"I... need a moment," he managed.

Amyra leaned in and whispered something that made Spencer groan and pull out. She lay back beside me, opening herself with a soft, "Come here, my king. You've cared for our queen—let us care for you."

Spencer moved to her with raw hunger, kissing her as he

eased inside. I reached for her breast, twisting her nipple just the way she loved most. She gasped and arched into him, her eyes finding mine as I slid my hand down to her bud. Her nails grazed Spencer's back, drawing a hiss. He gave her all his focus, all his intention, and it was beautiful—this man loving her with the same reverence he showed me.

A deeper stroke tore a startled gasp from her. Her eyes snapped open.

"Lyla—"

"I've got you," I whispered, kissing her cheek, her jaw, her neck. "Let go. You're safe."

Spencer shifted slightly, and Amyra made a sound I'd never heard—high, wild, breaking apart. Her thighs trembled, her telltale sign that she was right there. I bent to her nipple, my fingers circling her bud faster. She clenched around him, desperate for more.

Spencer groaned into her neck. "Gods, Amyra... you feel so good."

"Don't stop," she gasped.

"I won't," he panted. "You're perfect."

He thrust deeper, slower, drawing every ounce of pleasure from her. One more twist of her nipple—and her whole body seized. Her cry tore free as her orgasm crashed through her, thighs clamping around him, fingers digging into his shoulders, pulsing wave after wave.

It broke Spencer. His rhythm shattered as he slammed into her one last time.

"Amyra—fuck—" he gasped, going rigid.

I watched the release ripple through him—his hands gripping her hips, his body pressing deep, giving her everything. He came hard, moaning into her skin until his strength faltered and he collapsed against her, braced on trembling arms.

They stayed there, breathless, wrapped in the aftershocks together.

Amyra was glowing. Sweat slicked her brow, her lips parted as she tried to catch her breath. Her hand came up to cradle

Spencer's face, and he leaned into her touch like he needed it just to stay grounded.

"I've never—" Spencer started, voice hoarse. "That was... more than I thought it could be."

Amyra smiled up at him, then turned to look at me. "Because it's us. All three of us."

I nodded, my throat too tight for words.

Spencer slowly pulled out of her, careful and tender. He groaned softly at the loss, then settled down beside her, drawing her into his chest. I curled against her other side, wrapping one leg over both of theirs, my fingers tracing the rise and fall of her chest.

She looked between us, eyes still heavy with satisfaction.

"I love you," she whispered.

"I love you," Spencer echoed, kissing her temple.

"I love you both," I whispered.

Amyra's fingers laced with mine over her stomach, and Spencer's hand wrapped around both of ours.

And in that perfect moment, no matter what else comes, I knew. This was home.

CHAPTER 2

I woke up dreading the meeting I had to call today. While I knew that the most pressing matter was the threat in that letter, I also knew that Lord Luther would insist on fixating on my wedding, and trying to invalidate it. An upcoming war should be the highest priority. But no, this council didn't care about that. Not yet.

So I decided to keep my eyes closed, my arm over Amyra's chest, my hand resting on Spencer's arm. I could feel each of them breathing slowly. They still slept. I smiled, choosing to enjoy this peace.

That was, until Ivy knocked.

I sighed, knowing the day needed to start.

Amyra stirred, then kissed my shoulder. "I'll get it," she murmured, her voice husky from sleep.

I didn't argue. She slid out of the covers, still naked, and grabbed her night shift from the foot of the bed. She tugged it on and padded toward the door, glancing back to make sure the sheets still covered Spencer and me.

Before she reached the door, Ivy knocked again, and I could hear her sing-song voice shouting, "Good morning, sunshines!"

Amyra opened the door and Ivy swept in like a whirlwind. She precariously balanced two trays of food in her arms, a courtier followed with two more.

"Oh thank goodness you all are ok! I assumed you were, but that was just so wild last night!" She exclaimed as she waited for the courtier to set the trays down.

"What even was that," she continued, not waiting for any of us to respond. "A three way wedding? Was it legal? Like for real? Whose idea was it? I bet it was Lyla's. You never lose, Lyla. Always getting what you want. Tell me everything! How did you keep it a secret?"

She finally paused to take a breath. Amyra started explaining her plotting with Mina, but I tuned them out. Instead, I dragged a lazy finger around Spencer's chest, tracing aimless patterns into his skin. He was even more gorgeous in the light of day.

"Come on, sleepy," I murmured. "We need to start the day. Would you like Ivy to leave so you can get dressed?"

He groaned, finally acknowledging he was awake.

"No, it's fine. My pants are right here." He reached behind himself, on the far side of the bed, and slipped them on under the covers. Once done, he sat up, waiting for me to crawl out of bed first.

Ivy's sentence trailed off as I reached for my robe. I turned to see her staring, her jaw dropped. I followed her gaze to Spencer.

"That.." She started, her eyes wide. "Oh wow."

Spencer flushed as he reached for his shirt.

I growled. "Ivy. Let him be comfortable or I'll raise a wall right here to give him privacy."

She blinked rapidly, turning towards me with a sheepish smile. "Sorry, Lyla, not sure what hit me."

Spencer slipped into the bathing room with a chuckle, shaking his head.

Once we were all dressed and gathered around the small table in the sitting area, Ivy returned to her questioning with laser focus.

"Tell me everything! Don't leave a single detail out."

Amyra and I exchanged a look, and I nodded. "Go on, wife. It's your story."

Amyra grinned at me. Gods, I loved that smile. She launched into the explanation—how Mina came up with the plan, while Amyra suggested making it a surprise, and how she handled the logistics like it was a game of chess.

Ivy grilled Amyra, gleefully loving every detail. Finally, the food distracted them both, and peace returned to the room, only soft sounds of chewing remained.

The peace lasted for only a couple minutes. Ivy couldn't help herself.

"But what about Dusty, that Scoria Bay guy? What gives?"

Amyra and Spencer both looked at me, willing me to explain. I set my cup down and sighed.

"He brought a message. A threat, really. If the council hadn't already planned a meeting for today, I would've called one myself. Though honestly—"

A knock cut me off.

Ivy sprang up, opening the door to a young courtier holding a sealed note. "An invitation for the Queen, the King... and Amyra," he said, bowing, before turning to leave.

Ivy passed the note to me as she teased Amyra. "They don't know what to call you yet."

"I'm not really sure what to be called, either," Amyra admitted, her voice light with uncertainty. "Perhaps Princess?"

I didn't answer, I was already opening the seal and reading.

"They want the meeting this morning." I muttered.

I shouldn't have been surprised. Yet, my gut twisted.

Spencer placed a hand on mine. "Then let's get ready. We'll review the details while we dress."

I nodded, and Ivy began clearing dishes as we started preparing for the political battle ahead of us today.

We left the warmth of our shared morning behind and stepped into a council chamber already bristling with quiet hostility.

The long table had been rearranged awkwardly—my usual chair still at the head, but flanked tightly by two others to fit Spencer and Amyra. It looked cramped and wrong, a physical manifestation of the council's discomfort with us.

I stepped forward. "Lords and Ladies, please step back from the table."

Murmurs rippled as they obeyed. I reached inside for the ripple of magic that had become second nature, letting it shape itself to my will. The table shimmered and groaned, widening enough for the three of us to sit comfortably. New chairs also bloomed into being. I ensured they were equal in size, carved with matching crests.

"That's better," I said lightly. "Please, take your seats."

They did so, though not without glances and mutters. Ethan took his place to my right, across from Lord Luther, exactly as planned.

Luther lingered standing, his mouth pressed thin. "I will never accept magic used so freely," he muttered, but loud enough for me to hear.

I ignored him as I sat. Spencer's hand found mine under the table; Amyra's hand covered my other.

At last, Luther took his seat, striking the gavel once. His voice was stiffly formal. "Lords and Ladies. Your Royal Highness"—he nodded to Ethan—"and... Your Majesties." He all but choked on the word.

Then, instead of looking at me, he turned his gaze directly on Spencer.

"Your Majesty," he said, his tone clipped and cold, "I appeal to you as the husband and presumed guardian of our Queen. Last night's... arrangement is a disgrace to the dignity of the Crown and the moral order of Elthas. A man and a woman—that is the order sanctioned by our laws and tradition. To place a second spouse—another woman—beside you is an offense to both. I urge you to act as any responsible husband would. Compel Her Majesty to dissolve this union with Lady Amyra and send her into exile, where she cannot... further influence the Queen's judgment."

Amyra stiffened beside me. My own breath stalled, shock freezing my tongue.

Luther went on, voice still civil but laced with poison.

"Indeed, it may be prudent to open an inquiry into Her Majesty's state of mind—and moral fitness—to rule."

The room erupted before Spencer could respond. Juniper shot to her feet, indignant, while Greenhow's chair scraped back so hard it nearly toppled.

"You overstep yourself, Luther!" Juniper snapped.

"How dare you suggest banishment for my daughter," Greenhow barked, "or question her worth to this realm?"

They went at him from both sides, the air tightening with argument.

Spencer suddenly stood, his voice cutting through the din. "Enough!" The sharp authority in it made even Luther pause. "Lord Luther, the choice to wed is not yours to approve or dissolve. This marriage—" He faltered for half a beat, clearly weighing his words. "—was made in good faith and in the sight of... higher authority than this council. I will not be undoing it."

It was meant to defend me, but the phrasing landed clumsily. *I will not be undoing it.* As though it were still his decision to make.

That did it. My shock burned away, replaced by heat in my chest.

I rose slowly. "Lord Luther, I am not a ward in need of my husband's supervision. I am the Queen of Elthas, and I will not permit you to strip titles from those I love to appease your sensibilities. Amyra is not leaving this castle. She will not be exiled, and she will not be diminished."

Luther's mouth curved faintly, the condescension in his eyes sharp enough to cut. "Your Majesty, you are young. You've been on the throne for less than a day. Surely you can accept counsel from those with more... seasoned judgment."

The shimmer in Denenbaum's chair solidified into Mina, lounging like she'd been there the whole time. Her chin rested in her hand, her gaze fixed on Luther with the kind of lazy interest a cat gives a cornered mouse.

"Lord Luther," she said, her voice silk over steel, "if you

want to declare your Queen insane and unfit to rule, then you'll have to say the same about me."

Luther's eyes widened.

"Because I," she continued, gesturing languidly to herself, "am the one who joined them in marriage. Before the Pantheon. Before the realm. Before you."

The silence was heavy, every councilor frozen.

Mina's tone hardened. "So go on. Look me in the eye, and tell me I lack the judgment to bless your Queen."

Luther's throat worked, but no sound came.

She leaned forward, her smile edged like a blade. "That's what I thought. The Gelid Pantheon never dictated your marriage laws—you mortals did. And mortals can *unmake* them. I saw three people willing to swear themselves to each other without fear, without compromise, and I blessed it. That's power. That's love. If you can't stomach that, then perhaps it's your fitness for this council we should be voting on."

Gasps rippled through the chamber.

Mina leaned back again, tossing one leg over the arm of her chair. "Now, either shut your mouth about their marriage... or get ready to explain to the gods why you think you know better."

Luther swallowed hard and gave a jerky nod. "Very well. I will... support the arrangement going forward."

"Excellent," Mina said with a satisfied smile. "Now let's talk about something that actually matters."

Greenhow seized the pause. "Then perhaps, Your Majesty, you might clarify—what is Amyra's formal title?"

"Amyra has chosen to be addressed as Her Royal Majesty, Princess Amyra," I said without hesitation, meeting his gaze. "Equal in authority to myself and King Spencer. Three rulers, three thrones."

Pride softened his features. "Thank you. And when do you depart for the coast?"

That was my cue. I drew Bel's letter from my gown and held it up. "In three days. But first, the council needs to hear this."

"This," I said, holding the letter aloft, "is urgent. For those who weren't present last night, a courier from Scoria Bay delivered it to me during the reception." My tone flattened. "Immediately preceding his untimely demise."

A few councilors stiffened. Mina snorted quietly, clearly enjoying my understatement.

I broke the seal and read aloud. The words scraped the air like a cold wind. When I finished, I let the silence stretch, letting them sit with the image of what they'd just heard. A few shifted in their chairs. Others had gone pale, their mouths tight.

Good. Let it sink into their bones.

"This isn't a surprise to us," I said, lowering myself back into my chair. "We've been preparing for their attack since Mina's arrival. But this confirms it—the threat from Scoria Bay is real and imminent. Which means we accelerate our plans."

Luther leaned forward, clipped and wary. "At what expense?"

My patience thinned. "Less than the cost of rebuilding towns and raising war orphans if we delay. Do you disagree with prioritizing their safety?"

He shuffled a stack of papers, as if buying himself time. "Let's hear your proposal."

"I depart in three days with Princess Amyra and a small escort. Two purposes: introduce the people to their new rulers, and use my gifts to fortify the port towns before an attack can breach them."

Luther folded his hands. "And what 'gifts' would those be? The council has yet to receive an official briefing."

I met his gaze, slow and deliberate. "You just watched me alter this table in less than a minute. Imagine what I can do to a crumbling seawall."

Murmurs stirred the air like the first shift of a coming storm.

"I can raise stone battlements in hours. Reinforce walls that would take engineers years. And I will."

No one challenged me.

"King Spencer will remain here to manage the capital with Ethan's counsel," I continued. "I expect every one of you to support him in my absence." I swept the table with my gaze, holding it until a few councilors looked away.

Greenhow lifted his hand. "When, exactly, do you leave?"

"Three days. General Kellen will have the escort list tonight —one hundred guards, twenty-five staff."

A quiet gasp came from the far end of the table. Luther's scoff followed. "Three days to prepare one hundred and twenty-five personnel? Impossible, unless you intend to sacrifice competence."

"If Elthas is truly ready for war," I said, my tone cutting clean, "we can deploy five hundred troops in six hours. We've trained for this. Three days for one-fifth that number is more than enough."

Luther's jaw flexed. "Very well. But if the schedule slips—"

"It won't."

We held each other's gaze until he gave a short, stiff nod. "I'll see to the logistics."

"Good."

I rose, Amyra and Spencer rising in perfect sync beside me. "Then begin preparations. We leave nothing to chance."

But as the council began to shuffle out, a sharper truth cut through my resolve—outside these walls, there would be no guards thick enough, no stone high enough, to keep Bel from finding me. And if he did, he wouldn't come for my crown. He'd come for my life.

CHAPTER 3

We reached Tulaleth around lunch time on our first day of travel. The first thing I noticed was the sound. Louder than the clatter of hooves and creak of leather that had become comforting, we heard the crowd. Dozens, maybe hundreds, filled the town square, their voices a living tide of cheers and laughter. Someone had hung bunting between upper windows on many of the buildings, and the scent of fresh bread and smoked fish drifted on the wind, mingling with the sharp tang of air heavy with snow.

Amyra shifted beside me, her gloved hand tightening slightly on the reins of her horse. I turned to her just as she looked at me, her smile luminous beneath her hood.

We dismounted together and I nearly groaned as my legs protested. Apparently, even being queen didn't spare you from saddle soreness. Still, I straightened, chin high. Tulaleth might be a small town, but it was the last threshold between the rivers and the capital of Tathlamar. If Scoria Bay sent ships up this channel, this would be the last city to fall before they reached the castle.

The crowd swelled forward a step, and my guards shifted instantly, shields up, forming a narrow path towards a central building. I held in a sigh. I'd hoped for more proximity to the people, but I couldn't fault their caution. Not with Egan missing and Bel's shadow looming over us.

A man in a thick wool coat pushed through the front ranks, his pace brisk but not rushed. He had the look of a man who'd spent his life working with both his hands and the people—calloused palms, a creased face, and salt-and-pepper hair tied back with a leather cord. He dropped into a deep bow when he reached us.

"Welcome, Your Majesties. I am Hollan Windlow, the mayor of Tulaleth. It is our honor to host you today."

Amyra blushed. She still hadn't adjusted to the way strangers address us now. I smiled and extended my hand to Hollan.

"The pleasure is ours, Mr. Windlow. Please rise."

He did, beaming. "We prepared a reception in the justice hall. It's the largest gathering space in town. Warm food awaits, and we will also host your People's Court in there after you've had your fill."

"I look forward to it," I said sincerely.

Hollan turned and led the way through the bustling square. Children darted along the edges of the crowd, tossing snow balls and laughing. One girl waved a hand-painted flag bearing the royal crest. Amyra caught sight of her when I did, and offered a small wave. The little girl's face lit up and she ran off shouting in joy.

The justice hall stood like a stoic guardian over the square, its upper floors aged and crumbling, but the ground level freshly scrubbed and decorated with evergreen garlands and decorative banners. Inside the hall opened into a cavernous room with rows of chairs and two raised thrones at the front.

Hollan led us through this room, into a narrow hallway behind the thrones, and into a back room that clearly had been repurposed for the day. Twin buffet lines stretched the length of the space, each laden with roasted meats, stews, and loaves of steaming bread. The smell made my stomach clench with hunger. There was enough food here to feed the entire escort.

I nodded to one of the guards, "Let the captain know to send the men through here for food."

The woman bowed and darted off. Amyra and I grabbed plates and moved down the line. I found myself oddly grateful for a chance to stand while we ate. Sitting so soon after riding the horses would be a special kind of torture. We drifted to a high table in the corner, the kind meant to gather cocktail glasses during a social. For a moment, we were alone.

Amyra hummed as she scooped squash onto a piece of bread. "This might be the first moment of quiet we've had since the wedding."

"Mm, and I'm going to enjoy every second," I lowered my voice with a grin. "Starting with this."

There was a dab of sauce clinging to the corner of her mouth. I reached out and wiped it with my finger, then, with a mischievous gleam in my eyes, pressed it to her lips.

Amyra's breath caught. Her eyes flickered around the room, then relaxed as she seemed to remember we don't need to hide our affection any more. She parted her lips and drew my finger in, her teeth grazing gently as she sucked it clean.

My heart fluttered.

Before I could speak, she leaned in and kissed me. The connection was brief, but sent a spark down my spine. When we pulled apart, I spotted one of the courtiers staring, mouth agape, a chunk of bread lifted halfway to his lips.

Amyra spotted him too and whispered, "I think we just made his month."

I bit back a laugh. "Wanna make it the whole year?"

Without warning, she plucked a slice of apple from her plate and held it out for me. I leaned forward, eyes locked on hers, and took it between my teeth, brushing her fingers with a kiss as I pulled back.

A sharp cough came from behind us. The captain of the escort, doing an admirable job of pretending to not notice anything. His pink cheeks betrayed his efforts.

"Warning received," I murmured.

Amyra winked at the captain.

"Once we are done with People's Court," I whispered, brushing a strand of hair behind her ear, "I'll save the rest for the reception and let everyone see exactly who I belong to."

The People's Court that afternoon was long. It was a tradition my mother had begun, inviting the people of Elthas to voice their concerns in the week before the new year. Mother had created the concept, using the grievances brought to her as a way to plan her priorities for the year ahead. To her, it wasn't a duty, but a compass, lighting the path on how to meet the needs of our people. She listened with her heart, letting the people's words shape the realm's priorities for the year to come. Over time, it became one of her proudest legacies.

I thought of her now as I sat beneath the banner bearing the royal crest, her sigil still woven into the tapestry behind me. I wasn't sure I'd ever live up to her strength, but I could start by listening the way she did.

So I listened.

And what I heard wasn't surprising, but it still cut deep. So many of the concerns and grievances boiled down to the same handful of needs: more investment, more protection from the Crown, and something to look forward to. A future that felt worthy of working towards.

I'd always known life was harder outside of the capital. The walls of Tathlamar offered more than just beauty. They offered safety and comfort. But I hadn't realized just how stark the difference was. These people had been fending off pirates, especially under Scoria Bay's banners, for years, while we debated tariffs and marriage contracts over the wine they imported.

They didn't care who I married. They just wanted to see someone on the throne who listened and cared. They even seemed pleased to see three sitting on the throne. If two are better than one, then three must be better than two.

The thought made me glance towards Amyra, seated at my side. Warmth stirred within my chest. Maybe there was something sacred in threes. Although, the gods ruled with seven on their council. Well, eight, now that we know the God of Death exists. Eight was... strange. It wasn't a significant number in the religious stories. Seven was, and nine was even more significant, but eight?

'*You can ask,*' Mina's thoughts interrupted mine, clearly eavesdropping even over the distance. '*But you won't like the answer.*'

I nearly rolled my eyes. She always seemed to know when I was thinking about the gods.

'*I suppose that means you won't tell me until I'm back at the castle?*'

'*And miss seeing your face when you finally get it? Never.*' Mina's laughter echoed faintly through my mind before vanishing. Typical.

I shook her voice from my thoughts and returned my attention to the next speaker.

"My Queen," the woman in front of me said gently, her head bowed low. "Please accept my condolences for the loss of your mother. May her glory honor you."

"Thank you, miss," I said, offering a grateful nod, "please rise."

She stood and met my gaze with a warm smile. "May I also offer congratulations for your husband and wife. It's beautiful to see."

I glanced at Amyra beside me and gave her hand a small squeeze, using our code to say *I love you.* She squeezed back. I turned to the woman again. "Thank you."

"My issue is small," she continued. "Especially compared to everything this town has endured. But it's big to me. I'd like to ask for the laws to one day permit unions like yours. Whether between two women, or three people... many of us here are like you."

"Yes," I nodded enthusiastically. "The council is already working to revise the marriage laws to allow for this. When the Goddess of Peace blesses and ordains such a union, who are we to prevent it? You deserve to love openly just as much as we do."

Her breath caught, and she let out a small cough. "Thank you, my Queen. That means more than you know. May I also.."

She hesitated, as if worried she would be asking too much. "May I ask that you also provide laws that protect us from those who would harm us to try to fix us in their eyes?"

My heart stuttered. I straightened my back. "Fix you?"

She gave a bitter smile before explaining. "We're not allowed to exist as we are, not safely. People think that we just need to have our thoughts beaten out of us. Or worse. And no one stops them, because there are no laws saying what they do is wrong."

I swallowed hard. I hadn't seen reports of these attacks. I should have. Had the reports been filtered before they reached me? Or worse, had I stopped looking?

I thought to my parents, of their insistence I marry a man. Had they been trying to spare me from these ugly truths? I glanced at Amyra, and saw her jaw tick, her cheeks flushing with rage.

"I'm so sorry," I said, voice low but firm. "That's not acceptable. I want you to gather a small coalition, no more than five, and travel to Tathlamar. You'll advise the King and Prince Ethan on how to best protect you. We can't afford to overlook any of our people."

Her eyes went wide. "You mean *me*? Truly?"

"I do. You have lived through something my advisors haven't. I need your truth, so I can end this."

Another woman rushed to her side, grabbing her arm. Both were beaming, eyes watering. "I will do you proud, Queen Lyla. And Princess Amyra. I swear it."

I thought again of Mina. *'Did you eavesdrop on that, too?'*

'Yes.' The clipped reply lacked her usual tone. Then silence. A prickle of unease crept across the back of my neck. Mina seemed unsettled in that one syllable. She was in Tathlamar, was it something there? I couldn't spend time now wondering what was wrong.

"If you can stay behind for a moment, I will have one of my staff speak to you about travel arrangements."

The two women shuffled to the side, immediately greeted by one of my courtiers.

I scanned the chamber. No one else waited in the queue. I turned to the mayor seated at the far side. "Will there be more?"

He shook his head, standing to approach me. "That was the last. There's about an hour until the reception starts, so they want the room cleared to set this up. Would you like to see your accommodations?"

Amyra and I rose in tandem. "Yes, please, lead the way."

As we stepped out into the square, I let myself exhale. The air was brisk, sun already fading behind the trees, and smoke curled lazily from chimneys in every direction.

No one had spoken out against our marriage. No one protested. After what the last woman shared, the contrast rattled me. At first I had hoped it was a sign that people were more accepting than I had dared to hope, but now I knew, the ones who didn't accept were staying quiet for now.

We followed the mayor up a path just past the square, toward a cedar-shingled inn perched on a hill, its stone chimneys heavy with moss and smoke. Lantern-light flickered in the windows. The building looked old and worn, but still warm and inviting. How romantic.

I caught myself scanning the sky for green and pink streaks, but it was much too early in the evening for the northern lights to glow. When I glanced sideways, I caught Amyra looking too. We shared a soft smile, both realizing we were recalling our first night together, and I reached for her hand. We laced fingers as we stepped inside the inn together.

The innkeeper introduced himself with a flourished bow and promised that everything was ready. The mayor excused himself, saying he'd return for us in an hour. The innkeeper guided us up to the top floor, showing us to a private suite that covered the entire floor.

The room was stunning. A luxurious bed laid beneath a skylight window, draped in many warm blankets. While it was much too cold for flowers to be used as decoration, the green garlands from juniper and fir trees were adorned with shiny red berries.

The innkeeper softly closed the door behind us, and I turned to Amyra. Her lips met mine, sweet and soft as honeyed raspberries.

I cupped her jaw, feeling the familiar, grounding strength in the way she leaned into my touch. She tangled her fingers in my hair, pulling me closer until I could feel the smile curving against my mouth.

We stayed like that for a while, the kind of kiss that didn't rush anywhere, that just let time stretch between heartbeats. When she finally pulled back, it was only far enough for her forehead to rest against mine.

"It feels like forever since we had a night to ourselves," she murmured, her voice low, almost hesitant, as though saying it too loudly might make the night disappear.

I brushed my thumb along the curve of her cheek. "Too long." The firelight from the hearth flickered over her face, painting her skin in gold and shadow. "I've missed you."

Her lips twitched upward. "You've had me every day."

"Not like this." I slid my hands to her waist, feeling the way her breath caught. "Not in a way where I could show you how grateful I am for your love."

Her eyes softened, pale blue glinting in the lamplight, and she reached up to push a stray lock of hair behind my ear. "Will you show me now?"

A quiet laugh slipped from me—light, almost giddy—and I let her draw me toward the bed. We sank into the thick blankets together, the scent of juniper and fir wrapping around us. Through the skylight, the first stars began to prick through the indigo sky, cold and far away, while inside the world felt impossibly warm.

I TRACED idle circles against the back of her hand where it rested on my chest. "Do you remember that night?" I nodded toward the window. "Under the lights?"

"How could I forget?" she whispered. "You kept pretending to watch the sky, but you were staring at me the whole time."

"Guilty," I said, smiling against her temple. "I couldn't take my eyes away from the stunning beauty before me."

Her answering laugh was soft and breathless, and then she kissed me again—deeper this time, with that steady, sure pressure that always unraveled me. My fingers found the laces of her bodice, loosening them slowly, like unwrapping a gift I already knew by heart. She helped, her touch brushing my skin as she worked at the fastenings of my dress, and soon there was nothing between us but warmth and the press of skin to skin.

We moved together in unhurried rhythm, savoring every sigh, every whispered confession. The world beyond our door could wait; here, beneath the growing scatter of stars and the faint promise of northern lights, there was only us—lips and hands and the kind of love that could burn quietly all night without going out.

For the first time since the morning after our wedding, I let myself breathe.

CHAPTER 4

A knock startled me awake the next morning.

I blinked at the door across the suite, disoriented for a moment before I remembered where we were. Tulaleth. The inn with cedar shake siding and moss-covered chimneys. Amyra curled against my side, her breath warm on my shoulder, still sleeping.

Another knock, firmer this time.

I slid from the bed as quietly as I could and wrapped myself in the thick, warm robe waiting on the chair in front of me. I crossed to the door and found a castle courier standing there, out of breath and awkward, holding a sealed parcel wrapped in protective oilcloth.

"Apologies, my Queen," he said, bowing low. "This was meant to arrive earlier, but the delivery proved... complicated."

I thanked him and shut the door quietly. Amyra stirred behind me, but hadn't yet woken.

I carried the bundle to the hearth, settling into the overstuffed chair, and untied the cord. Three wax-sealed letters slid out. The one on top was in Juniper's flowing script, the second had Spencer's unmistakably sloppy handwriting, and the third bore Ethan's seal. I didn't expect his letter.

I opened Juniper's first.

. . .

I'd have delivered it to your room, darling, but my magic couldn't find your precise location. I require either a direct reply from your room or a previously cast tether. You'll need to send one tonight, or tomorrow's letter will be late as well.

Right. I had known that. I had completely forgotten.

Spencer's letter was next, the paper slightly crumpled. I smiled, remembering back to the time we spent together as kids when he always whined about writing during the lessons.

Court session went as expected. No protests, no outbursts, and a surprising amount of questions about irrigation. Most seem... fine with the marriage. A few even joked that three is a lucky number, like the divine trinity in older myths. Ethan and I held our own. I hope Tulaleth's court was kind to you. Write back soon. I miss you both.

The tension between my shoulders softened a little. He always knew how to steady me.

The third letter was shorter, and more confusing.

Lyla—there's a matter I'd like to discuss when you return. It's nothing urgent, so please don't worry. I'm only not including the details here because I want to speak about it in person. Yours, Ethan

I frowned at the page, rereading it twice. Of course I worried. Ethan didn't keep secrets, not unless he had something worth hiding. My mind leapt through several worse-case scenarios before I could stop it.

'*I know something you don't know, and it's* juicy!' Mina sang inside my mind, syrupy with mischief.

I groaned aloud as I stood to set the letters at the desk. '*You're not helping.*'

'*I'm not supposed to. But if you wanted to guess…*'

'*You still wouldn't tell me?*'

'*Absolutely not. That would ruin the fun!*' Mina's giggles echoed through my mind.

'*What's the point of talking to me like this if you're never going to share anything of value?*' I pouted as I moved to the bathing room to prepare for the day. I noticed Amyra sitting up now, stretching, the strap of her nightgown slipping down her shoulder seductively.

"No urgent disasters?" She asked, rubbing sleep from her eyes.

"Only mild mysteries and a mental argument with your favorite goddess." I said.

'*Oh, I'm not her favorite, not by a long shot,*' Mina retorted.

Before Amyra could ask for details, another knock sounded. This time it was the innkeeper, arriving with breakfast on a silver tray. Amyra helped carry it to the low table while I heated water for tea. We ate quickly and dressed for the day. Amyra dressed in a medical uniform she had taken to liking when she practiced her healing work. I dressed in a long tunic with a thick pair of riding pants, my preferred outfit for working with my harder magic as well.

Downstairs, the mayor was already waiting for us.

"Good morning, your Majesties," he said, offering a deep bow. "The princess is expected at the infirmary, and I'm ready to escort you to the seawall when you are ready."

"Let's not hesitate," I said before turning to Amyra. She nodded, adjusting her satchel. I reached for her, sharing a quick kiss. When I pulled away, her smile crinkled the skin beside her eyes, and a wave of peace washed over her face.

"I'll see you tonight, my love." She said.

"Not if I don't see you first," I replied, offering a smile back.

The mayor led me toward the coast, his boots crunching over the freshly fallen snow as the town slowly came to life around us. Tulaleth was quieter than Tathlamar, but there was a warm energy in the air, as though the townsfolk were grateful to see us, even though it was for grim purposes.

The seawall was low and crumbling, reinforced in places with scavenged wood and mismatched stones. From the bluff I could see down the river and into the open sea, scattered with fishing boats and a couple merchant ships preparing to enter the river with the upcoming high tide.

When this town was settled, the western border was against the open sea as well, but as time went on, and the world healed from The Great War, the sea levels retreated. Scholars said that they were returning to the levels they had been before the War. It felt strange to me to think that there could have been miles of land between this town and the sea one day, only the river at the southern boundary to connect it to water.

"This way, Your Majesty," the mayor said, leading me towards the western edge of the wall.

Two men waited there. One I recognized as Captain Wintershaw from my guard, dressed in the polished armor of the military. The other was in a roughspun uniform with Tulaleth's city crest embroidered on the chest. He looked more like a lumberjack than a soldier with his scruffy dark beard and weathered skin, but his eyes were sharp and his posture spoke of years of training to be alert.

"Captain Halden," the mayor introduced. "He oversees our town's security."

"Your Majesty," Halden greeted with a bow, "we are honored to have you here."

"And grateful that you're taking steps to reduce loss of life now," Wintershaw added, a wry smile crossing his face.

"Don't worry, Captain Wintershaw," I smiled faintly. "I plan to earn my keep."

We spent the next few hours reviewing defensive plans, marking weak points, and debating the best use of my skills. I set to work once we had a plan. I reshaped the sea wall, raising it and reinforcing the foundations with solid limestone. Where the original walls stood, I stretched the stones using my magic, sealing cracks. The work was draining, but so necessary. Sweat beaded at my temples by the time I allowed myself to stop.

Lunch was simple, smoked salmon and sourdough still

warm from baking. I shared my meal with a few fishermen near the docks. They were inviting and curious, and happy to share about their lives.

"Been less attacks lately," one of them said. "Might be thanks to the Crystalford ships-started escorting us around the time that volcano popped up."

"Did they?" I asked, hiding my surprise.

"Yeah, don't know why, but we're grateful. They don't even ask for money, and we've lost less boats in this water."

Frederick. Of course it was him. I made a mental note to thank him before turning to Captain Wintershaw.

"Find out what the merchants here need to stay safe on the water. Have the information ready for me by dinner. I'll send word back to the castle tonight, so they can make that happen."

"As you wish," he said, reaching for a notebook in one of his pockets.

I took a crunchy, chewy bite of sourdough and stared out onto the water, watching the wind tug at the sails around the harbor. One day in Tulaleth, and the weight of what was coming felt heavier than ever.

But, for the first time, I also felt strong enough to carry this, to see my people through to a victory.

CHAPTER 5

A few days later, we were on the road to the next town, Swyneth. The road curved along a bluff, offering a sweeping view of the town tucked against the sea. Salt-weathered rooftops leaned together like gossiping schoolgirls, chimneys exhaling the scent of hearth smoke into the gray sky. From this height, the coastline looked almost peaceful.

As we passed beneath the wooden post bearing the town's name, I felt the familiar twist of tension coil in my stomach. I tried to ignore it as I admired the evergreen boughs used to decorate the sign. Someone had taken time to make us feel welcome.

I sat taller in the saddle and scanned the horizon. Swyneth was a smaller town than Tulaleth, but far more exposed. There were no hills here to slow a landing force. No natural choke points to funnel entry. Just open land sloping straight into the waiting sea.

To protect them properly, I'd need to construct a wall nearly three times the size of the last. The scale of it stretched in my mind, heavy and daunting. As we rode into the square, I began mentally mapping how to use the terrain to my advantage.

Amyra dismounted beside me. "I'll head to the infirmary. I had received a letter this morning from the mayor here, it said they also have a backlog of patients, a bridge collapsed nearby that trapped travelers."

I reached out and gave her hand a gentle squeeze. "Come find me at lunch?"

"Always," she smiled, and brushed a wind-blown strand from my cheek before heading off down the path.

The land around here was crumbling, and not just from age. Plenty of structures had survived the Last Great War, but without proper care or access to good materials, they were starting to fail. That bridge was probably just the latest in a long line of collapses. Maybe, if we won this war, I might find others like me—strong in magic—who could help rebuild faster. But that was a future still out of reach.

I turned toward the sea, pulling my gloves off, letting the wind bite at my fingers so the magic could flow more easily. The sooner I got to work, the better. The breeze smelled of a storm, and I didn't want to battle one of those.

I inhaled deeply and closed my eyes, grounding myself in the rhythm of the waves crashing in the distance. The wind tugged at my hair and skirts, impatient. I let my magic slip free through my fingertips, calling it up from the core of me like drawing heat from a wellspring. It responded with a low thrum in my chest, eager and crackling.

The land here wasn't completely flat, but it was stubborn—rocky in places, soggy in others. I walked a few paces forward, then knelt, placing my palm to the ground. The magic coursed outward in slow pulses, mapping the texture of the terrain through my touch. I could feel where the wall would need reinforcement, where it might settle too deep or crack too easily under pressure.

I rose and started shaping the base, drawing stone from below and compacting earth until it held fast. The magic obeyed, but it was harder here. Maybe the soil was more resistant. Maybe I was just tired. Either way, this wasn't going to be easy.

I pressed on, weaving strength into the foundations and sealing weak spots before raising the outer face. Stone lifted into place under my guidance—layer after layer, thick and tall. I staggered the joins and curved the corners for deflection, just like the guards had taught me. Sweat prickled at my back. I paused only to drink, rub out the ache in my palms, or squint toward the sea to judge how much time I had left before the weather turned. Hours passed. My shoulders burned. My fingers cramped. I pushed through it all, because I had to.

The final section was nearly in place when I heard it—shouting. Men's voices, urgent and rising.

I dropped my hands, the magic faltering as I turned toward the commotion. Fishermen near the docks were pointing toward the horizon, their gestures frantic.

Then I saw them.

Three dark sails, stitched with the unmistakable emblem of Scoria Bay, slicing through the gray water like knives. They were moving remarkably fast.

Before I could react, the guards from the escort were swarming the area. Within moments, Captain Wintershaw had found me, and he reached roughly for my arm.

"You need to fall back." He ordered. "You need to get behind the wall. We can't lose you!"

"Oh no, I can help, I will help." I yelled back, already lifting my hands.

"You will be if you don't get behind this wall. Your magic won't protect you from cannon fire."

He was right, but I didn't care. My people would fall if I didn't act fast.

A crack of thunder split the air. No, not thunder. Cannon fire.

Stone exploded a dozen feet to my left, tearing into the wall and spraying shards of rock and earth. I stumbled, my heart hammering out of my chest. A second cannonball smashed into the outer edge, sending up a shockwave that knocked me back a step.

"Lyla! Go!" The Captain shouted, more concerned about protecting me than ordering his men.

"No. Go take care of your men." I gave him one last withering glance before I focused on the ship nearest to me.

I raised my hands, let the power build within me. I closed my eyes and screamed inwardly, '*Mina!*'

She didn't speak, but I could feel her listening. I let panic flood the connection. '*If I die,*' my thoughts raced wildly, 'm*ake sure Spencer knows I love him and I'm sorry. Please!*'

'*Don't you dare,*' she replied, but it was too late.

The fire ignited in my hand, hot and burning. I threw my hand back and launched at the ship. The fire left with the force, arced skyward, crackling as it hurdled towards the ship.

The fireball roared through the air and struck the ship square in the hull. A plume of flames ignited, engulfing the side and deck of the ship.

I didn't wait to see how they responded. I closed my eyes again, pulling on my magic, feeling it burn me from the inside. Please, please, please, let me save my people.

I don't know who I was pleading with, but I needed this.

The second ball formed, and I hurdled it at the second ship. Within moments, it found the mark, just below the mast, and the ship ignited like paper.

The third ship was still coming, but angled itself behind the two burning ships.

My knees shook. I felt the magic in me, dwindling yet burning. I was panting, unable to catch my breath.

The air behind me shimmered, and Mina appeared in a rush of gold and white, wind curling around her cloak.

She rushed to me, wrapping her arms around me. "Don't, you can't." She whispered.

"I can do it, I just need—"

"No, sweet Nivara, you need to stop. You'll collapse. You've drained yourself."

I hesitated, realizing what she was saying. I relaxed my call to the magic, and felt it recoil. The burning feeling in my chest started to cool. My vision started blurring at the sides.

"I've got her, stay in command," She nodded to the captain. When he acknowledged her order, she guided me down the stairs of the wall, back to safety. Amyra rushed to me, worry crossing her features. She reached for her water and a cloth, dampening it to touch to my face. Despite the frigid air, the damp cloth was welcome.

A cheer rose up from the other side of the wall. I lurched forward, to the arrow slit nearest. I saw the third ship sinking, split down the center from a hit that came from the other side.

Beyond it, a fourth ship, smaller and sleeker, pulled close to the wreckage. I noticed it had no flag.

A boat started lowering once it couldn't get closer.

"They're sending a landing party! Prepare to attack!" The captain shouted from above.

"Hold!" Mina barked. "Do not engage!"

The soldiers froze, not sure who to obey.

The captain came rushing down the stairs, angry at the contradiction.

"You don't tell me how to handle my men—"

Mina held her hand up, silencing him. "I do tell you how to handle events you need to get right. Do. Not. Attack."

Mina turned to me. "Go. They'll meet you on the central pier."

I blinked. "What? Who are they?"

Her eyes twinkled and she winked, but said nothing.

Then a tug yanked me. An invisible thread pulling me towards the pier. I tried to resist, to even ask Mina, but it hurt too much to ignore it. I moved forward.

Amyra fell into step beside me without a word. I glanced at her, about to ask her to stay, but her jaw was already set. I let it go. We walked together down the creaking planks of the pier, the icy wind pulling at our cloaks.

The boat slid closer, and my heart tugged at me harder, like it wanted me to go out there into the water. This tug was so strange, it felt urgent, like it was calling me to do something. Was this another manifestation of my magic? Why had it been tugging me toward the boat?

Four figures sat within. Three remained seated while one, a

woman, stood and jumped lightly onto the pier before the boat even docked. Her boots hit the wood with a thud.

"Hello, my Queen," she said, executing a theatrical bow that nearly made her hat fall off. "Heard rumors of a scuffle coming here, and felt it would be fun to help out."

Beside me, Amyra's posture stiffened.

I didn't respond right away. I was too busy trying to understand how someone could look so effortlessly at home on a war-torn dock. She stood taller than many of the men in my court, and was one of the most beautiful women I had ever seen. Her ashy blonde hair, almost silver, cascaded in waves around her shoulders, matching flawlessly with her navy coat trimmed in brass. A sword swung at her hip, and her hand slipped to it casually, like it was part of her hip.

I could hardly take my eyes off of her, not until her gaze found mine, sharp as a blade. She looked a bit older than us, though I wasn't sure if that was just the salty air or if she really was older. She was laughing with her eyes, even before her mouth caught up.

And then those eyes landed on me—blue, but not just blue. Silver flecks moved inside them like something alive, like starlight trapped beneath the surface of a tide pool. My magic hummed. She felt like a wave right before it broke.

"Thank you," I breathed, my pulse skipping. "I—what's your name?"

"Nymbria," she said, straightening. "Stromvik, if we're doing last names. Though I can't say I've used it much recently. Not a lot of formal invitations at sea."

"You're nobility?" I asked, before I could stop myself.

She grinned. "Once. Crystalford, daughter of Duke Stromvik. They wanted me to marry a boy who couldn't even steer a dinghy. I said no thanks and ran off with a ship I may or may not have inherited improperly."

Amyra's eyes narrowed.

Nymbria caught it and winked. "Don't worry, love, not here to steal your Queen. Unless you're into that sort of thing…"

Nymbria's eyes glanced down Amyra. I flushed.

"She's joking," Amyra said flatly.

"Usually," Nymbria said, her eyes returning to me. "But I'm not above telling the truth in joke's clothes. Besides, it's not every day you get to rescue a stunning queen from a cannonball."

I coughed, trying to recover my breath and my bearings.

'*Interesting, very very interesting.*' Mina purred within my mind.

"Why did you come here? How did you know to come help?"

"Well, I'm not exactly welcome in Scoria Bay's port these days," she said. "And word travels fast along the waves. When you have good ears and better spies, you hear things. War drums, or the sound of destiny knocking."

"Destiny?"

"I mean," she said, sweeping her arm out to the burning wreckage in the bay, "If I'd have known I get to meet you while blowing up the ships of tyrants, I'd have brought wine."

Her smile curled at the corners of her mouth like smoke.

"She's outrageous," Amyra muttered.

"She can hear you too," Nymbria replied cheerfully. "And she's brought her ship, her sword, and her crew if you'll have them."

"I don't even know who you are, why would you offer to fight for us?" I inquired.

"You'll get to know me." She said softly, and just for a moment, her bravado slipped into something gentler. "I don't know why, but I think we're meant to."

CHAPTER 6

The Captain grew sick of waiting for us to finish talking, and stormed down the pier. I could see the fury in his stride. I hadn't taken a single weapon, or any guards, to greet this boat. And, he was probably right to be upset. But, the tugging in my chest had stopped, and that felt right. I couldn't regret a decision that went well.

"Who are you and why are you landing here?" He demanded.

I twirled around.

"You will show more decorum when greeting the ship that just saved our town," I said, voice edged with authority.

Captain Wintershaw paused to consider, then nodded. "My apologies."

"This is Nymbria Stromvik, formerly of Crystalford. She heard of the coming war and came to offer her services to the Elthas crown," I continued. "We will be accepting her expertise. Prepare a missive to inform the General of the attack and offer, and I will send it this evening. You and your men will stay here to offer further protections, and the rest of us will return to the capital."

Captain Wintershaw nodded once more. "Yes, of course."

"Nymbria, would you like to invite your crew on shore for the evening? I'd like to invite you to dine with us tonight, as well." I offered. I could feel Amyra's glare at me, the tension was thick. I didn't like that she was upset, but I couldn't very well have this discussion in front of others.

Nymbria nodded. "Yes, my crew needs to dock anyway. I will have them start coming in this evening."

We shared a lingering glance, tangled with unspoken questions and the quiet ache of walking away too soon. I walked back down the pier, feeling the exhaustion of using so much of my magic with every step of the way. By the time I stepped off the wooden planks, I was leaning on Amyra immensely to be steady on my feet. Mina met us, slipping under my arm with a smirk.

"She's spicy, I like her. You're keeping her, right?"

Amyra's scowl reflected her displeasure.

"She's not that great," she muttered.

"Oh hush, you're jealous, but there's nothing to worry about," Mina retorted.

I sighed. "She's hired, we need the help. And, I need to not argue about this right now."

I didn't remember getting back to the inn. I passed out fairly hard.

I woke to the sensation of warmth at my chest and the sight of Amyra leaning over me, eyes squeezed shut, a sheen of sweat clinging to her brow. She was working hard to heal me, I realized.

"Hey love," I whispered.

Her eyes flew open, and tears threatened to spill. "Don't do that again, Lyla, promise me. You almost burnt out. Mina has spent the last hour telling me how dangerous this is."

"How long have you been working on me?" I frowned. I felt fine, even better than I had when we arrived in Swyneth.

"It's almost time for dinner. We have just a few minutes to get ready." She replied. "It's been two hours since you collapsed on the street."

I groaned. Amyra helped me to sit up, her hands trembling as they steadied my shoulders. I hated that I scared her. I hated that this war demands so much from me.

"I'll be more careful," I said softly. "I promise."

She didn't answer right away, choosing to rest her forehead against mine instead. Her hand slid down to rest over my heart.

"We need you. This war is pointless if you sacrifice yourself. Bel wins if you die. Don't let it happen, please." She pleaded.

"I didn't have a choice, my love." I murmured.

"There's always a choice. You need to choose yourself first."

That landed like a punch to the ribs. I couldn't deny the truth, but I couldn't see any other way we would have won that battle.

I kissed her, just a gentle press, to apologize for what I couldn't put into words. She sighed into me, not melting but not pulling away.

"Get dressed," she whispered after a moment. "We have a dinner to attend, and I need to find it in me to be nice to your new biggest fan."

Amyra stepped to the bathing room to wash up. As I got dressed for this dinner, I could feel my magic pulsing faintly under my skin, finishing Amyra's work. While this pulsing was becoming more and more familiar, I realized I still had so much to learn about how it worked within me. I wondered if the priestesses had ever experienced this, and could help me figure out how to avoid this burn out again. Or maybe this was something Mina would have to help me with.

We made our way down the dining room at the inn. This innkeeper had set aside a table for us, overlooking the town's bay and pier. On any other day, the view would have been breathtaking. The sun was setting behind Scoria Bay's jagged silhouette, painting the water in gold. But tonight, debris drifted and plumes of smoke scarred the horizon.

Amyra and I took our seats with our backs to the wall, and awaited service. Nymbria hadn't arrived yet, but I hoped she would soon. In the meantime, one of the courtiers was sitting with us, reviewing the plans we had for returning to Tathlamar. Captain Wintershaw had requested that we try to find a way to travel light on our return so that we could leave as many supplies as possible for the troops.

Just as our meals were set before us—a steaming bowl of chowder paired with sourdough croutons and some roasted winter root vegetables—Nymbria strode in, taking the remaining empty seat. She had a second person with her, I assumed her second in command. He was a little shorter than her, but still tall compared to Amyra and me. He had long curly hair and an equally long beard, both inky black, though well combed. He dressed similarly to Nymbria, wearing dark colored trousers and tunics, clothes that must work best for the daily life on the ship.

Our table only had four seats, but Nymbria just instructed him to grab a chair and join us. He dragged a chair over with a screech of wood on wood and swung it around to straddle it backwards. I caught Amyra's expression—one eyebrow raised, the slow blink of barely restrained judgment.

"Nymbria, thank you for joining us." I offered graciously.

She nodded, looking around the room, and waving at a waiter when she spotted one. "Of course, my queen," she said distractedly. "You asked for me to come."

Her friend cleared his throat, waiting for the introduction.

"Oh! That's right, he was left on the ship." Nymbria said. "Queen Lyla and Princess Amyra, please meet my second in command, Finnian Locke. We call him Finn for short."

He nodded with a flourish of his hand, expecting one of us to put ours in his. "It's all my pleasure," he assured. Despite the odd choice in posture, he clearly had been trained in formal settings.

I offered my hand first, which he accepted with a kiss to my knuckles. Then he waited for Amyra's hand and did the same.

"Uh, thank you," I said, hesitating. I genuinely couldn't decide if I liked him or wanted to slap him.

I caught Nymbria's smirk.

"He grows on you, promise." She winked at me.

"So, are we here to talk war battles?" He wiggled his eyebrows at me. "Or can we talk about the far more interesting battles here?"

"Far more interesting battles?" Amyra raised her eyebrow skeptically.

"Oh love, you know the kind, they involve the sheets that cover you at night." Finn growled before laughing.

Amyra's mouth fell open, and she gave him a look so sharp it could cut wood.

"Charming," she deadpanned. "Do all male pirates court their executions this boldly, or is it just you?"

Finn held his hands up, grinning. "Only when the company's worth dying for."

I coughed into my hand, fighting back a laugh. "Finn, perhaps you could… behave like we're handling official business?"

"Of course, Your Majesty," he said with a wink as he moved his hand to his heart. "But don't pretend that wasn't the most fun you've had all day."

Nymbria slapped his arm.

"Quiet, fishface." She scored him. "They're clearly not into men. Lay it off or I'll promote Ryxan over you."

Amyra's eyes lit up. "You didn't tell us about that nickname. Fishface suits him so much better." Her lips curled with mischief.

Finn scowled but quieted down.

"Now, my ladies, how may I be of service to you?" Nymbria asked. She stole a chunk of potato from Amyra's plate, which was met with a scowl and jab of her fork. Nymbria winked back at Amyra.

"We need all the help on the sea that we can get," I answered, ignoring the antics between the two. "But, I am familiar with how pirates in this Sound work. What costs are attached to your assistance?"

Nymbria's face softened as she smiled. "Normally, any services my fleet provides to governments would come at a steep cost. I'm not a fan of stuffy bloated bureaucracies, you see. But for this? I came to you, and other than providing supplies for ship repairs and the crews, I don't intend to charge anything."

I narrowed my eyes. Why would a pirate provide assistance

in a war effort for free? She could lose ship within her fleet. She will definitely lose people. "Why would you be so generous?"

Nymbria paused, as if shocked that I would question this. "I think you know," she whispered, her tone so serious.

The tug. She was feeling it too. I was suspicious earlier, but that confirms it.

"What does it mean?" I asked. Amyra's eyes darted between us, not understanding what we were talking about.

"I don't know. I've never felt it before, but it's been happening for days, and I had no choice but to follow where it dragged me." Nymbria admitted.

Our eyes locked, and the silver flecks in her icy blue eyes swirled.

"Do you have a gift of the sea?" I asked.

Nymbria's eyes darted down towards her lap. "I don't know what you mean."

Either she didn't have magic, or she had been taught to hide it. Perhaps that was why she fled her betrothal?

"You seem to be quite a talented captain." I offered a cover.

Nymbria looked up, and I could have sworn I felt her gratitude within me.

"Yes, I've been leading a ship for almost a decade. Have three in my fleet these days." She offered up.

I noticed Amyra's gaze was fixed on the sea. She looked serene, but distant, like she was seeing something I couldn't.

"Are you alright?" I asked softly.

She blinked, as if she had forgotten where she was. She offered a small nod, but didn't elaborate.

"Was just thinking of the tides," she murmured, "and how fast they turn."

I wasn't sure if she meant the water or the conversation.

Nymbria studied Amyra for a moment, then folded her hands over her lap.

"I'm not here to steal your queen, if that's what you're worried about," she said plainly.

Amyra's lip twitched. "I'm not worried."

"Good, you shouldn't be," Nymbria replied genuinely. "I

know what it's like to love someone you'd fight the gods for. I'm not here to test that."

Amyra's brow lifted. "Then what are you here for?"

Nymbria's glanced at me again. "I'm still trying to figure that out."

I let the answer hang for a breath before changing the topic. "I need to head back to Tathlamar, but I need to leave my caravan here. Are you willing to take my crew with you? I will have twenty seven of us to transport."

Nymbria's lips curved slightly, the question grounding her back with us. "We can do that. We had intended to restock here and move on, but it's just a few hours up the river bend, we can grab supplies there and figure out the next moves."

I shook my head, reaching across the table, though her hands remained in her lap. Her eyes darted to Amyra, a quick, uncertain movement. I withdrew my hand, resting it on the table instead. "If you need supplies, get them here. The merchants could use the coin. I will go with you in the morning to inform the shopkeepers to send the bill to the castle."

Nymbria nodded. "We would need a day to get the boats resupplied, we could leave the day after 'morrow."

I nodded. "That's very doable, how long would it take to get up the river to the capital when we leave?"

"With a strong tide? Half a day, maybe less. Leave at sunrise, dock by noon."

We lingered at the table until our bowls were scraped clean and plans had been sketched in broad strokes. Nymbria and Finn rose first, offering casual farewells before heading back to the docks. Amyra and I followed the quieter path upstairs, the creak of the wood beneath our boots the only sound between us.

Back in our room, I settled at the small desk tucked beside the hearth, the fire now reduced to glowing coals. I dipped my pen into ink, scrawling a quick letter to the castle. The motions felt mechanical-outlining our return timeline, requesting a council session, including Wintershaw's battle report. I sealed it with wax and whispered the spell to send it to Juniper, just like Mina had taught me before we left.

Behind me, Amyra sat on the edge of the bed, one leg tucked underneath her. She watched me in silence as she finger-combed her hair free of its styling.

"She gets to you," she said, her voice low but not accusatory.

I blinked, caught off guard. "Nymbria?"

Amyra nodded slowly. "There's something between you. I can feel it. The way she looks at you, how you... seem pulled to her."

I moved to the bed, reaching for her hands, kneeling so we were eye to eye. "There's a pull, yes. A literal one. Something inside me is tied to her. It started before I ever saw her face, and it's led me to every major choice for a couple of weeks now. I don't know what's happening. But it doesn't change us."

Her gaze flickered, searching mine. I threaded my fingers between hers.

"You are my heart, Amyra. My anchor. No magic, no mystery, no war changes that."

She exhaled, some of the tension easing from her shoulders. "I know," she whispered, her eyes cast downward. "I just hate how easily she flirts. And how easily you... respond."

I smiled, soft and sad. "I'll try to do better, to make sure you never wonder where you stand with me."

Amyra leaned forward, resting her forward against mine. "Don't let her storm drag you under, Lyla. I can't bear the thought of losing you."

"I'm not going anywhere," I murmured.

CHAPTER 7

The morning air was crisp with the bite of salt and mist when Finn appeared at the inn, bringing his charm and theatrics. He swept into a bow so deep it looked like he might kiss the floor.

"Please let me offer my Captain's apologies, Your Majesties," he said, straightening with a grin that didn't quite reach his eyes. "She's currently bound to the helm. Figuratively, of course, unless…"

He trailed off, winking at Amyra. She rolled her eyes and crossed her arms.

He let out a chuckle then continued, "I've been sent to escort you aboard and ensure every last soul of your party is accounted for before we cast off."

We followed him to the docks, where the ship waited like a beast at rest, sails tucked in. As we stepped onto the deck, the change in atmosphere hit me immediately.

Nymbria stood at the center of it all, boots braced wide, one hand casually resting on her hip while the other cut through the air, pointing while she commanded. Her voice rose above the creak of wood and slap of rope, loud but precise.

A teen boy scurried to adjust a sail just as she called for it. An older crew mate reached for a knot as soon as she shouted. It was like watching a conductor mid-symphony, every move anticipating the next, every rhythm falling into place as it was signaled.

She never glanced at a chart or paused to think. She just knew what was needed. And the crew responded with the confident efficiency of those who trust the one giving the orders.

I stood still, momentarily forgotten, caught in the effortless power of her presence. No wonder she commanded fleets. No wonder she had survived, battle after battle. With Nymbria at the helm, even chaos seemed to bend to her will.

As the final ropes were untied and the ships all began to drift from the dock, the other two following the one we were on, I felt a familiar tug in my chest. This wasn't the magical tug tied to Nymbria, but the ache of leaving people behind, who might not survive this war I got my kingdom in. The townsfolk had gathered along the pier to wave us off, a few shouting blessings. I lifted my hand in return, heart tight, hoping that our departure wouldn't bury them.

The ships surged forward with the morning tide, sails snapping to life above us. Amyra stood beside me at the railing, her eyes on the horizon, hair pinned but already loosening in the breeze.

"Not bad for a bunch of spoiled princesses." Finn's voice broke the moment. "You even boarded on time. I was half expecting a dramatic farewell on the pier and tearful pleas."

Amyra didn't turn. "You're projecting."

"Am I, darlin'?" He drawled. "Because I saw the way you were staring. Very wistful. It reminded me of a tragic novella."

I snorted despite myself. "Do you talk like this all the time?"

"Only when I'm conscious," he retorted, slinging an arm over the nearest post.

Nymbria approached from the helm, wiping her hands on a cloth tucked into her belt. "Ignore him. He gets chatty when he's nervous."

"I'm not nervous," Finn protested. "I'm just delighting and entertaining our company."

"Delightful people don't refer to the queen's departure like it's a scene from *Love and Low Tide*." Nymbria shot him a look, then turned to us with a grin. "He had been rehearsing that one all day yesterday."

Amyra crossed her arms, turning from the railing. "And that's still the best he could come up with?"

Finn gasped while Nymbria chuckled. "Wounded! Gutted. You see this, Captain? Our royal guests are icy."

I raised an eyebrow. "Don't mistake caution for cold. Something you may want to learn before putting your foot in your mouth around foreign dignitaries."

"I never just put in my foot," Finn said, winking. "I dive in head first, and always leave 'em satisfied."

Amyra gave him a flat stare. "How do you have any teeth left? Surely, you must get punched more frequently than you land in bed with others."

Nymbria groaned. Finn guffawed before replying, "I don't start fights that don't end with immense pleasure. Wanna see?"

"Hush, you, or you're gonna fight for your life over that railing, and I won't be helping." Nymbria scolded him.

Finn threw his hands up in mock surrender. "Alright, alright! No more teasing. Gods forbid I drown around these lovely ladies."

Nymbria rolled her eyes. "You'd joke through your own funeral."

"Do you still promise the open bar, and a little bit of scandalous fun?" He winked.

Amyra turned to me, "Is it too late to switch ships?"

"I'm afraid so," I replied grimly, my smile betraying my tone.

"Aw, you'd prefer a ship without all the built-in nobility?" Finn didn't seem to know when to stop.

Nymbria shoved him. "Shut. Up. Now." Her tone was firm and threatening. "Isn't there a bilge that needs cleaning?"

"Surely the deckhands have that under control." Finn protested.

The look Nymbria gave him a look that could have shattered a diamond. "It needs your personal attention. Now."

Finn realized the line he crossed and nodded. "Aye, aye."

He couldn't resist winking at Amyra and me before he left.

Nymbria watched him descend, then turned to us. "My apologies, Your Majesties. He's normally more capable of toning down the remarks."

"I can imagine he's tense with the knowledge of what's to come." I offered.

"So, tell me, what's the capital expecting when you return with a pirate escort?" Nymbria asked, leaning against the same post Finn used to brace himself earlier.

"A miracle," I admitted. "And maybe some chaos."

Nymbria smiled. "Then it's a good thing we specialize in both."

I let the wind carry her words as I turned toward the horizon. The river narrowed ahead, and I caught the first glimpse of the capital spires piercing the morning sky like blades. Home was waiting.

A cluster of figures gathered at the docks, banners fluttering in the breeze. My heart gave a quiet stutter when I spotted Spencer's dark curls and Ethan's familiar stance, arms crossed like he was already judging the ship's rigging.

As we pulled alongside the pier, the crew surged into motion. Nymbria barked commands with sharp precision, and the chaotic dance of docking began—ropes tossed, sails furled, boots pounding across the deck. The same choreography we'd witnessed in reverse that morning unfolded like a well-rehearsed finale.

Finn appeared at our side, nodding toward the gangway as it groaned into place. "Ladies first," he said with a grin that didn't quite mask the flicker of pride in his eyes.

The moment my boots touched the wooden pier, a cheer broke out—scattered at first, then swelling into something jubilant. Townspeople lined the end of the dock, waving handkerchiefs and shouting blessings. Somewhere, a bell began to ring.

Amyra and I walked down the pier, hand in hand.

Ethan was the first to break from the crowd. "That's quite the entrance," he called as he approached, eyeing the ship behind us with a skeptical lift of his brow. "I assume there's a story."

"Oh, several," Amyra muttered under her breath.

Spencer didn't speak at first—just met my gaze and reached for my hand as I stepped onto solid ground. His fingers curled gently around mine, grounding me more than the dock ever could. "You're safe," he murmured, too low for anyone else to hear. Then, with a glance over my shoulder, he added dryly, "And you brought pirates."

Nymbria strode down behind us at that moment, her coat flaring in the wind like she'd staged the moment. "Privateers," she corrected cheerfully. "Though we've been known to dabble."

Ethan stared. "You're Nymbria Stromvik."

"In the flesh." She swept a bow far more graceful than expected. "And you must be the brother. Ethan, is it?"

He blinked. "We... thought you were dead."

"Most people do. It's the best way to stay interesting." She winked, then glanced at Spencer. "And you must be the only man this Queen was willing to settle on?"

Spencer narrowed his eyes, clearly unsure what to make of her. "We'll discuss logistics inside."

"Oh, he's going to be fun," Nymbria whispered under her breath.

I didn't answer. The ship was behind us now, and with it, the relative freedom of the sea. The castle's weight settled on my shoulders with each step toward the gates.

As the heavy doors of the castle shut behind us, the air warmed by fire was a welcome shift from the wintry winds of the docks. An attendant hurried towards us, curtsying deeply.

"Your Majesties, shall I escort your guests to their quarters?"

I nodded. "Please see that they're shown to their rooms and where lunch will be served. And assign an escort to take them through the castle and gardens as they please. They've earned a warm welcome."

"Yes, Your Majesty." She turned to Nymbria and Finn with

a courteous gesture. "Right this way, Lady Stromvik and Lord Locke."

Nymbria dipped her chin. "You've got good manners for a palace dog."

The poor girl flushed but smiled and motioned for them to follow. Before they completely departed our company, I informed them, "We will see you at dinner. Formal attire not required."

Finn winked over his shoulder. "Do you believe we even own formal attire?"

Amyra smirked. "You wouldn't clean up well in a good suit, anyway."

The four of us—Spencer, Ethan, Amyra, and I—headed through the familiar halls towards the royal chamber's dining room. The moment we entered, Ivy leapt to her feet.

"Gods, finally. I've been stalking the windows for half the morning waiting for you!"

She threw her arms around me. The warmth of her hug helped release tension I hadn't realized I was holding.

We sat around the circular table as courtiers brought in trays of warmed bread, stew with roast game, and spiced wine. I ate slower than usual, enjoying the food I had missed while we had been away.

Spencer cleared his throat. "People's Court went well, all things considered. The major concerns brought up mostly surrounded the upcoming war. Merchants and fishers alike requested extra patrols, both from piracy and from the increased presence of the Scoria Bay fleet in the sound. But…" His expression sobered. "The biggest concern was morale. People are worried that we are fighting a losing war."

I frowned. "And the council?"

A muscle in his jaw ticked. "No major issues."

He didn't meet my eyes. I didn't press, deciding to save that for later.

I turned to Ethan. "Your letter said there was something urgent to discuss. What was it?"

Ethan stiffened. "I'd.. rather speak to you privately about that, Lyla."

"Oh?" I lifted an eyebrow. "Can you at least tell me what it pertains to?"

His face turned crimson. "It's... personal." His eyes begged mine to not press.

Amyra leaned forward, grinning. "Have you finally found a lady to court?"

Ivy choked on her wine and fumbled for her napkin, waving off the attention. "Wrong pipe."

My eyes flicked between her and Ethan. I sipped my wine, scheduling the meeting with Ethan for after the one with the council.

Duty called, so we quickly wrapped up our lunch. We left the warmth of the dining room behind, quickly moving to the Council's meeting.

By the time we had arrived to the meeting room, the chamber was full. The long table gleamed under the light of the daylight's dwindling sun. Mina was here for this meeting, claiming Denanbaum's chair once more.

Once the formalities were done, I stood and gave the battle report—honest and unembellished. I detailed our defense of Swyneth and the pirate fleet's assistance that might have saved the city.

"So you used your magic again." Luther said, his voice clipped.

My back stiffened. "Yes. Of course I did. I defended our city."

"And what are the consequences of this magic? What if you cause damage you don't intend? Casualties? We should discuss a process to authorize—"

"I don't need authorization to defend my people," I snapped.

He raised an eyebrow. "And how are we to trust that you understand the magic you're wielding?"

Something in me snapped. I slammed my first onto the table, the sound echoing like thunder. "Either you trust that I am learning from a literal goddess who will ensure that I use it well, or you submit your resignation now, Lord Luther. I was not crowned queen to have my every move second guessed by someone who doesn't even understand this power I have."

Gasps and murmurs circled the room. I began to realize, too late, that I was not handling this well. Luther's face reddened.

"You do not have unilateral authority—"

I flicked my wrist. Vines of a woody ivy shot up from the arms of his chair, coiling around his wrists, thickening around his chest. A final strand stretched across his mouth, silencing him. His eyes bulged in fury.

I turned back to the others, voice calm and deliberate. "I am happy to answer genuine questions, ones asked in good faith. But I will *not* entertain any efforts to constrain what the gods themselves have come to teach me. The power that runs through me is older than our kingdom. It demands reverence and responsibility. I am giving it both, with Mina's guidance."

I glanced at her, and her smile gave me the strength to continue. I took a slow breath, and let it out. "Now. Has anyone prepared a proposal for improving waterway security?"

Not a single hand rose.

"Very well, I have a two-part plan to propose. First, we partner with mercenaries personally vouched for by Captain Stromvik. She has already sworn her allegiance to us in this war, and knows her kind better than any of us could."

I paused, noting that respect was on the faces of some of the councilors. Juniper and Lord Greenhow both looked exceptionally pleased with me.

"The second part involves sending a request for assistance to Crystalford. They have a strong naval fleet, and since they had sent Prince Frederick for the ball last summer, I hope they're interested in becoming allies in this matter."

Lord Greenhow cleared his throat. "I agree. Their admiralty has long been respected, and they have reasons to support us."

Murmurs of assent spread across the table.

I turned to Luther. With another flick of my wrist, the ivy

dissolved into harmless curls of bark. "Do you understand my powers better, Lord Luther?"

He nodded wordlessly, still angry. He rubbed his wrists as he flexed them.

"Do you have any contributions towards the proposal I offered?"

"No, Your Majesty." He hesitated, then added. "Shall I draft the message to Crystalford?"

"No," I met his gaze coldly. "I'll write it myself."

I let the silence settle, then said, "There's another matter—one unrelated to the war, but no less urgent. On my recent visit to Tulaleth, I learned of a series of hate-driven crimes against citizens in same-gender relationships and those raising families outside traditional norms."

The room went still.

"I want to know—has anyone been tracking these incidents?"

Greenhow cleared his throat again, slower this time. "My office receives such reports. I compile them and forward them to Lord Luther with recommendations for how to proceed."

My gaze cut to Luther. "And why," I asked, voice quiet but sharp enough to draw blood, "have they never once reached this council with a proposal for action?"

He shifted in his chair, fumbling for words. "These… matters… were not pressing. I believed our resources were better spent elsewhere."

Rage boiled up, clean and cold. "You didn't think the safety and dignity of our people was important enough to act on?" I turned back to Greenhow. "From now on, you may submit those proposals directly to the council. No one will stand between these reports and my desk again."

Greenhow straightened, a flicker of relief in his eyes. "Yes, Your Majesty. Gladly."

"Good. And I am trusting you to meet with the delegates I've invited to the capital. Work with them on amendments to our laws—stronger protections against these crimes, and full rights to marriage and building families. This kingdom will not tolerate hatred."

Greenhow's expression warmed with genuine pride. "It will be my honor to see it done."

I nodded once. "Then we are finished here. Prepare to act on both matters at once—the war effort and these reforms will proceed together."

The council murmured their assent, and Luther—silent now—gave a curt nod. The meeting adjourned.

I wasted no time leaving the chamber. Ethan was waiting, and his urgent matter was next. Whatever it was, I had the distinct sense it would not wait.

CHAPTER 8

I settled at my desk in the royal study, the afternoon light slanting through the windows. The ink hadn't even dried on the draft of the letter to Crystalford when a knock sounded at the door.

"Come in," I called, straightening the paper.

Ethan lingered near the door longer than necessary, fingers drumming against the frame as if he were debating whether to come in at all.

"You're hovering," I said, looking up from the stack of letters on my desk. "Either you've come to tell me something important, or you're here to steal the last of my tea biscuits. If it's the second one, you'd better run before I sic Spencer on you."

A ghost of a smile tugged at his mouth. "It's... important."

I leaned back in my chair, arching a brow. "Important like, 'Elthas is under siege,' or important like, 'I've adopted a stray animal and need you to pretend it was your idea'?"

He snorted, shifting his weight from one foot to the other. "Neither. And I haven't adopted anything in years, thank you."

We shared a grin. I couldn't help but remember how mother had screeched when he pulled a timid little field mouse from his pocket, declaring that this was his new pet named Edward, and would be joining us for dinner that night.

"Then spit it out before I start imagining worse scenarios."

He hesitated again, eyes flicking toward the window as though hoping the view might rescue him. "I was wondering if... well, I've been thinking, and I'd like your... blessing. Or approval. Or whatever it is you give when—"

"Ethan." I cut him off before he could trip over himself completely. "Are you asking for permission to date someone?"

His ears went a little pink. "Court," he corrected. "Properly. Not just—"

"Who?" I asked, my curiosity already sharpening. "Because the last time you looked this nervous, you were twelve and had just put a frog in the royal bath."

He let out a quiet groan, running a hand through his curls. "Ivy."

I blinked. "Our Ivy? My handmaid, my best friend Ivy?"

He met my gaze squarely, shoulders squaring as though bracing for impact. "Yes. She's... remarkable. And I don't mean just because she can braid hair faster than anyone alive."

A slow grin spread across my face. "You're serious?"

"I am."

I studied my brother's face, seeing it in a new light. His face held a hint of a glow, one I recognized from when Amyra and I first acknowledged our feelings to each other. "You're in love with her."

His eyes widened and he tried to backpedal. "I didn't say—I mean, it's too soon to—"

He blew out a breath. "Fine. Yes. Maybe. Probably. She just—"

His mouth twitched into an almost-boyish smile, the kind he used to wear when he'd sneak pastries from the kitchen. "She makes the air feel lighter. Like I can breathe easier when she's near."

"Oh, gods, you've got it bad," I teased, leaning my chin into my hand. "Head over heels, tripping over yourself, next you'll be writing her poetry."

"I would never," he said, far too quickly. Then softer, "Well... I wouldn't share it with you."

I laughed, shaking my head. "You don't need my permission to court her, Ethan. But you do need to promise me you'd treat her with the same respect you'd give any princess in the realm."

His expression sobered instantly. "More than that. I'll treat her like she's my guiding light."

"Should Amyra and I start planning the wedding now or do I get a few weeks' notice? She's got a knack for stunning surprises."

He rolled his eyes, but the corner of his mouth curved up. "I was hoping for months at least."

"Mm-hmm," I said, drawing out the sound. "I'll give it a fortnight before you're ready."

"That implies I'm not already," he muttered, then froze when he realized what he'd admitted.

I let out a laugh that probably sounded far too pleased. "And there it is."

He groaned, rubbing a hand over his face. "You're impossible."

"You're in love," I sang.

"Are we done with this interrogation?" he asked, though there was no real heat in his tone. His cheeks were the color of roses.

"For now." I smiled, leaning back in my chair. "But I expect updates."

He glanced to the window, taking a moment to calm his flustering emotions, then asked, "Do you know Nymbria's history?"

I shook my head, "Only the little she's let slip."

Ethan leaned back in his chair, folding his arms in thought. "She's infamous on the sea. Tactical brilliance, legendary escapes, a reputation for sinking warships without losing a single crew member. Sailors swap her stories the way children trade sweets—half of them sound impossible, but after watching her fleet unload at the docks, I'm starting to think they might all be true."

"That doesn't surprise me," I said, resting my chin on my hand. "She moves like someone who's used to winning. I saw her give three different sets of orders without raising her voice once, and everyone obeyed immediately."

He gave a small huff of agreement. "What do you know about her?"

I folded a slip of paper and carefully tucked it into my pocket, then joined Ethan on the sofa.

"She's from Crystalford. Said she fled a betrothal she didn't want."

Ethan's brows lifted. "Do we know who it was to?"

"I didn't ask," I said, shaking my head. "But if she ran this far, I'd guess it wasn't someone she trusted."

He tapped a finger thoughtfully against the arm of his chair. "Or maybe she just wanted the sea more than she wanted anything else."

A faint smile tugged at my lips. "If that's true, she found the right life for herself."

We rose together, still talking—trading small observations about her crew, her ships, the way she seems to have an unshakable hold over both—as we navigated the halls to dinner.

We were the last to arrive.

The dining room was already filled with energy, and not all of it was pleasant. Amyra sat rigid, her expression frosted over, fork poised like it might become a weapon. Spencer looked like he was suppressing a sigh every few seconds, his jaw ticking in that way I knew meant he was holding his tongue. Meanwhile, Nymbria and Finn looked maddeningly at ease, both wearing wide, unbothered grins as though they were at a seaside tavern rather than a formal dinner.

"I take it we missed something," I murmured as we crossed the room.

Ethan gave a low whistle. "What did we walk into?"

"Finn is showing off," Nymbria said dryly, though her eyes sparkled with amusement. "He thinks wearing formalwear makes him more tolerable."

Finn leaned back, grinning like the cat that had eaten the canary. "You said I didn't have a proper suit. I corrected that oversight. Now you can enjoy my company and my tailoring."

"You could've stopped at 'company,'" Spencer said, voice smooth but edged, as he slid into his seat opposite Finn. "The suit's not making up the difference."

Finn's grin only widened. "I'd say the difference is sitting right in front of me."

Spencer's eyes narrowed slightly, and a ripple of tension went through the table.

'*Jealous already?*' I sent the thought toward him.

His gaze flicked to mine for the briefest second, and I felt his answer slide into my mind, '*Not jealous. Just not in the mood for peacocks tonight.*' The warmth in his mental tone deepened a shade. '*You're much more interesting to watch.*'

Heat curled low in my belly at the implication, and I caught myself smiling before turning my attention back to the table.

Dinner passed with a veneer of politeness, though the undercurrent was anything but. Finn and Spencer traded remarks that could almost be mistaken for compliments if you weren't listening closely.

When I mentioned the letter to Crystalford was finalized and would be sent in the morning, the mood shifted.

Nymbria's expression dimmed. Her hands stilled over her plate, and she glanced away from the table.

Ethan, oblivious, leaned toward Spencer. "You think they'll send Frederick? Would be quite the reunion." He elbowed Spencer in the ribs.

Spencer raised an eyebrow. "You're assuming I'm the jealous type."

"You're not?" Ethan teased.

"I keep both my wives very satisfied," Spencer replied smoothly, raising his glass in a toast that somehow still felt like a challenge. "They have no need to look astray. Do you, my queens?"

Amyra and I shared a knowing glance. "There's absolutely nothing we are left wanting," I said, my tone light but deliberate.

Nymbria's eyes flicked to me. "Frederick. The one from the tournament?"

Amyra answered before I could, her voice clipped. "Yes. He stayed here for a while, was one of the final contenders."

"He never said much about sailing," I added, keeping my tone neutral, "but he's a logical choice for sending as a diplomatic liaison, since he was here recently and knows Elthas."

Nymbria nodded, though her expression tightened further. She poked her food without eating, the earlier playfulness gone. Finn, for once, kept quiet—his eyes on Nymbria, his easy smirk replaced by something sharper, more protective.

As the laughter faded and conversation moved on, I studied them both. That nerve I'd seen strike between them wasn't small, and it wasn't nothing. And it left me wondering—just who had Nymbria been supposed to marry before she vanished into the sea?

After dessert, the table began to empty with the lazy ease of old friends—though there was nothing lazy about the way Spencer and Finn sized each other up.

Spencer pushed his chair back, eyes still on Finn. "I could use something stronger than tea. How about we see if the parlor still has that billiards table?"

Finn leaned back with that same infuriatingly calm grin. "I'll play. Always good to see how landlocked royalty handles a cue."

Spencer's mouth curved, but it wasn't a smile. "Better than a sailor handles losing."

"Guess we'll find out," Finn said, standing. "Ethan, you're in. Every game needs a witness... or a referee."

Ethan groaned good-naturedly as he rose. "I'm only going to watch you two try not to kill each other."

"Then keep your eyes open," Spencer replied, brushing past Finn toward the door.

As they turned for the parlor, Spencer tossed me a look over his shoulder—half tease, half warning—and brushed my mind with his voice: *Behave.*

I sipped my tea, letting the heat curl in my chest. *You first*, I shot back, picturing his smirk as the door closed behind them.

The sitting room settled into a gentler kind of quiet, lit only by the fire's glow. Shadows moved lazily across the pale stone walls, and our teacups steamed in our hands as we sank into deep chairs. For a time, none of us spoke.

Amyra, who knew every inch of me, curled to my left, tucking her feet under her as she leaned into me. I welcomed the chance to cuddle. Nymbria, still guarding her presence despite the battle we'd fought together, occupied the chair across from us.

I studied her for a moment, then let my voice slip into the calm. "You handle a ship like it's an extension of yourself. I can't help wondering… is it only skill, or something more?"

Her eyes flicked to mine, then away. "Skill can take you far enough."

"Far enough for most," I said softly. "But you go farther, don't you?"

A long pause. She took a slow sip of tea, the steam wreathing her face, and I could see the calculation in her eyes. She was weighing what to say, what to keep locked away.

Amyra broke the tension without a word. She lifted her cup, held her hand above the surface, and coaxed several droplets of tea into the air. They hovered there between us, glistening in the firelight like tiny amber pearls.

Nymbria's gaze tracked them, curiosity sparking but no shock.

"You're not the only one with something to guard," Amyra murmured.

I tilted my fingers toward the hearth, coaxing the flames into the silhouette of a swishing-tailed cat before letting it dissolve into sparks. "Magic runs through all of us here," I said quietly. "Amyra's is water. Mine, land and fire. It's connected to eye color. And yours…?"

I let the words trail, studying the stormy blue-gray of her eyes. "They're close to Amyra's."

Nymbria's lips pressed together, her knuckles whitening around her cup. The silence stretched until I thought she'd stay silent altogether. Then she set the cup down with care. "I can move water," she said at last, voice barely above the crackle of the fire. "Not drops. Tides. Swells. Waves that can send a warship spinning or hold mine steady when the sea tries to break her. I've shielded my crew in storms that should have ended us."

Amyra leaned forward, interest and respect plain on her face. "Does your crew know?"

"Only a few," Nymbria said, her tone turning guarded again. "Most sailors wouldn't sail with someone like me. Pirates are superstitious. They'd rather fear the waves than know someone could command them."

Amyra gave a small, warm smile. "Or maybe they'd rather not admit they'd envy you."

Something in Nymbria eased at that—just slightly—but it was enough for me to see.

I let the quiet settle again before asking, "Is that why you left your betrothal?"

Her gaze dropped to her tea. "Part of it. He was a good man. Kind, in his way. But his world was inland—gardens, stone halls, no sea in sight. And he saw me in a shape I'd never truly fit. I tried to imagine living there, and all I could hear was the silence. No waves. No salt air. The pull in my chest to chase the horizon going unanswered until it broke me."

Her voice softened, tinged with something wistful. "He might have been the right choice for someone else. But not for me. I'd have drowned there—not from water, but from the lack of it."

Amyra reached across the small table, her fingers curling gently over Nymbria's hand. "Then I'm glad you didn't let yourself sink."

For a moment, the room felt smaller, warmer. Nymbria's eyes shifted between us, some unspoken calculation settling into something closer to trust.

"I didn't just run," she said finally. "I carved a life. The sea... she loves me back."

I wondered if the sea understood her more honestly than any person ever could. I leaned in. "And you don't have to hide that, not from us."

The fire cracked softly. Our tea had gone cold. Yet when Nymbria excused herself for the night, boots whispering against the rug, the warmth she left behind lingered.

When the door shut, Amyra let out a small sigh. "She's... different than I thought."

"Different good?" I asked.

Amyra smiled, still looking at the door. "Different good."

Amyra and I lingered in our chairs after Nymbria's departure, the firelight softening the edges of everything we'd just shared. The scent of juniper garlands and cooling tea hung in the quiet. For a while, neither of us spoke, letting the new thread of trust settle into place.

Amyra's gaze met mine, her thumb brushing over my knuckles in a silent question. I squeezed back, answering without words. Whatever had shifted tonight wasn't just between Nymbria and me—it was between all three of us.

A log in the hearth cracked, breaking the spell. "We've been gone a long time," Amyra murmured.

"And there's someone else we both need to see," I said, rising.

The walk back to our chambers was hushed, the corridors dim but warm, the faint hum of conversation from other rooms fading as we neared our door.

We'd barely crossed the threshold before Spencer was there, closing the distance in three long strides. His hands came up to frame my face, his eyes searching mine as though to make sure I was real.

"You're home," he said, his voice low.

I smiled faintly. "We're home."

Amyra slipped past me into his arms, and the way he caught her—like she might disappear if he didn't hold tight enough—made something ache deep in my chest. He pressed his forehead to hers for a long moment before pulling her into a kiss that was slow, certain, and threaded with all the things letters can't say.

When he finally drew back, his gaze found mine again. "You both look like you've been through hell."

"We won," I said, though the word felt heavier than it should.

His mouth quirked. "And you came back to me. That's all that matters."

He guided us toward the hearth, his arm settling around my waist as Amyra's fingers laced with mine. We sank down onto the couch, and Spencer pulled me into his lap without ceremony, his hand immediately finding its familiar place at my hip. Amyra curled against my side, draping her arm across both of us so that her hand rested on Spencer's thigh.

For a moment, the three of us just stayed like that—no titles, no court, no war—just warmth, and the soft press of bodies that knew each other as well as their own.

"I hated being so far from you," Spencer admitted, his thumb brushing lazy circles over my hip. "Every letter I sent, I kept wondering if it would reach you before the next battle."

Amyra's voice was quieter. "I hated knowing he wasn't there to see you work, Lyla. To see how you command." She glanced at Spencer, a faint smile tugging her lips. "You'd have been proud."

"I'm already proud," he said simply. "Of both of you."

I leaned into him, feeling Amyra do the same from the other side. The fire painted everything in shades of gold, and for the first time in weeks, I let myself stop thinking about the next step. We were here. Together.

Spencer pressed a kiss to my temple, then turned to do the same for Amyra. "Tonight," he murmured, "there's nothing else to do but rest. The three of us."

Amyra's hand tightened over ours. "I like that plan."

We stayed like that for a while, wrapped in the fire's glow, until Spencer's thumb brushed the inside of my wrist in a slow, thoughtful circle. The touch was light, almost absentminded, but it sent a ripple through me. Amyra must have felt it too; her gaze met mine, warm and knowing.

No one moved in a rush. The world outside could keep its noise and demands—here, we could take our time.

Spencer shifted first, drawing me from his lap only to rise

with me in his arms. Amyra followed, her hand finding mine again as we moved toward the bed. The covers were cool when we slipped beneath them, but between the three of us, warmth bloomed quickly.

We didn't speak. There was no need. Spencer's lips found mine in a kiss that was unhurried, tasting of relief and homecoming. Amyra pressed against my back, her arm curling around my waist, her breath steady against my neck.

I felt Spencer's hand slide down my spine, felt Amyra's fingers twine with mine again. It wasn't urgent—it was an unspooling, a quiet reknitting of the space between us after too many nights apart.

When clothes finally gave way to skin, it was with the same unhurried care. Gentle touches, soft sighs, the steady rhythm of hearts finding their way back into sync. Spencer's mouth traced a path along my collarbone; Amyra's lips pressed against my shoulder. I turned to kiss her, and her hand came up to cradle my cheek, holding me there as if she might keep me from slipping away again.

The firelight reached only so far, leaving us in a cocoon of shadow and warmth. We moved together in the slow, quiet way of people who knew each other's bodies like familiar roads—every turn expected, every touch welcome.

When the last tension eased from my body, it wasn't with sharp edges or gasping breath, but with the deep, steady calm of belonging. We stayed tangled in each other's arms, the night settling heavy and safe around us.

For the first time since we'd left the capital, I slept without dreaming of battle.

CHAPTER 9

I sealed the final draft of the letter to Crystalford with a press of wax. The courier waited just outside my study, already equipped for the long journey. "Please hurry, and wait for the reply," I instructed. "Don't return until you have one in hand."

He bowed low. "Yes, Your Majesty."

As his footsteps faded down the corridor, a breath left me that I hadn't realized I'd been holding. There was nothing to do now but wait.

We fell into a rhythm in the days that followed. Meetings in the morning, defensive planning in the afternoon, and magical training with Mina in the evening. And, increasingly, Nymbria at my side.

The first day I invited her, she hesitated, caught between intrigue and suspicion. But when I explained that Mina herself had asked to meet her, curiosity won out.

We met in the eastern training courtyard, where the walls were charred from my past sessions. Mina stood at the center in her strange form of preferred clothing—weird blue pants and a fitted, short tunic. Her hands were folded, expression unreadable. But when Nymbria approached, Mina's lips curved into a smile so sharp it felt like it should have drawn blood.

"Captain Nymbria Stromvik," Mina said with a hum of satisfaction. "You've come far. Good."

"Far enough," Nymbria replied carefully.

Mina tilted her head, eyes glinting. "You and the Queen... a pairing that will terrify Bel."

My spine stiffened. "Why?"

"You'll see," Mina said simply, and gestured for us to begin.

I conjured a flame in my palm and flung it toward the target dummy across the yard. It exploded on impact, sending cinders into the air like fireflies. Nymbria raised an eyebrow, then turned to the barrel I'd constructed from stone and heat-fused earth. With a single flick of her fingers, water frothed and surged inside, responding to her command like a trained beast.

She pulled it upward in a spiraling stream, shaping it into blades, then spears, then ribbons that sliced through the air with impossible precision. Her control was breathtaking—fluid, deliberate, lethal.

"You've done this before," I said.

"Every storm," she replied, not meeting my eyes.

As Mina drifted between us like smoke, her hands light on my shoulder, then Nymbria's wrist, she murmured phrases I barely processed—"alignment of intent," "resonance in motion," "opposing forces with mirrored rhythm." Her voice was a hush under the crackle of flame and the churn of water, more feeling than instruction.

I braced to cast again, rolling a fireball between my palms, when I caught Nymbria shift in the corner of my vision. She was circling the barrel now, coaxing a thick rope of water into the air, its end tapering like a whip. I inhaled, timed the beat of her movement, and flung the flame in a tight arc—not at her, but beside her, letting it pass through the spray she'd conjured.

The fire hissed and vanished midair.

Her eyes snapped to mine. "Was that intentional?"

"Was it too close?"

"It was perfect." Her lips quirked. "Again?"

This time, she moved first. The water danced upward like a ribbon pulled by wind. I followed instinct, shaping a ring of flame around it, letting the heat curl without touching. Her hand twitched; mine mirrored it. Her pivot—precise and sharp—gave me the cue to pull back, then step left. I did, and we turned in a half-circle, not choreographed but completely unbroken.

Mina clapped once, sharply. "There. That's it. Don't question—feel."

Nymbria laughed under her breath. "We're going to make people nervous."

I met her eyes, my breath shallow from the pace, but not tired. Not at all. "Good. Let them be nervous."

She extended a hand, summoning a crescent of water that spiraled toward me like a coiled blade. Without thinking, I raised my arm and the flame flared into a curved shield. The steam that burst between us was warm and soft—like breath, like trust.

We were circling again before either of us gave the order, steps aligned, movements counterbalanced. My fire darted where her water curved. Her strikes closed the gaps mine left open.

"You feel it too, don't you?" I asked quietly.

Nymbria nodded, her smile tinged with something almost reverent. "I don't think I've ever felt anything like this."

"I've been feeling it since before we met," I said. "A pull. A... tugging. Every choice I made that led me to you felt like it wasn't really mine."

Nymbria froze, the water dropping back into the barrel with a splash. She looked at me, truly looked, and said, "I've felt it too."

I turned to Mina. "What is it?"

The priestess smiled like a cat watching birds. "The call."

"That doesn't explain anything."

Mina only folded her hands. "For now, just accept it and follow when it tugs. It will make sense once you embrace your destinies."

A strange hush settled over us. Even the wind seemed to

still, the chill air falling flat against my skin. The usual creaks of wood and distant gull cries faded, as if the world itself had drawn a breath and was holding it, waiting.

Destinies. Mina had said it so nonchalantly, but the word rang in my chest like a bell struck underwater—muffled and vast, the ripples spreading deep.

I turned to Nymbria slowly, pulse flickering behind my ribs like flame struggling for air. She was already looking at me.

Our eyes met, and something passed between us that had nothing to do with training, nothing to do with Mina's cryptic riddles. A pull, taut and humming, like the moment just before a storm split the sky open. It wasn't just awareness. It held recognition. Shared awe. Shared fear.

She blinked first, but only just. Her breath misted in the air between us, caught in the slant of light from the setting sun. "You felt it too," she said, barely louder than a whisper.

I nodded. "Since the day you saved my town."

Her fingers tightened at her sides, and I noticed the water she'd left suspended in the air had stilled, no longer flowing—it was just floating there, motionless and perfect. My flame had gone out entirely, but I hadn't even noticed.

"Do you know what it means?" I asked.

"No." Her voice was rougher now. Honest. "But it's not just magic."

Mina said nothing. She stood at the far edge of the courtyard, head tilted, watching us with the inscrutable calm of someone who knew the shape of the ending but refused to spoil the story.

"We were meant to meet," I said, the words surprising me even as I spoke them. "Meant to stand together."

Nymbria inhaled like she'd been holding her breath for hours. "And if we're meant to fall together?"

I didn't have an answer. But I reached for her hand, and she didn't pull away.

Mina stepped forward and raised her hand. "Again," she said.

So we obeyed. Fire and water. Push and pull. The Queen and the Captain. And something deeper woke between us, unseen but undeniable.

CHAPTER 10

The courier returned just past dawn, almost a month after he had left. He bowed low, almost sweeping at his dew-soaked boots, weariness lining his face but pride in his voice.

"I bring news from Crystalford," he said, offering the sealed letter.

I broke the wax and read quickly, scanning the fine looping script. My breath hitched as I read, they requested a meeting at Lummi Island, the Crystalford-owned island closest to each of our territories. They wanted to discuss naval strategy face to face, on the day of Lupercalia. They were sending a battalion of five hundred ground soldiers as a gesture of good will, and wanted to discuss what more they could offer, if anything at their fort on the island.

Lupercalia. Two weeks from now.

Too far. I closed my eyes and pressed my fingers to my temple. Two weeks felt like an eternity in this war. The God of Death could strike at any time.

"They're really coming?" I asked quietly, eyes still closed.

The courier shifted. "Yes, Your Majesty. They should arrive within days. They're camped just north of Skageth now, moving steadily."

I nodded and offered my thanks in a dismissal, already spinning towards my desk.

I wrote to the council immediately, pen biting into the page as I apologized for missing their meeting. *Training must continue without interruption*, I explained. *In light of Crystalford's arrival, I ask that we deploy five hundred of our soldiers to the coastal towns, to show the realm we stand ready. Theirs can stay here to train and learn our methods.*

When I finished, I pressed the wax seal hard, feeling the heat of my magic catch along the edges. Then I headed to the training grounds.

Mina met me as she always did: casually leaning against the wall, inspecting her nails, like I was boring her to death.

I launched into the routine, sending fireballs into the waiting wall. I didn't even wait for her to greet me, I needed to feel the burn, to have the fire catch in my bones. If this war had been sparked just to harm me, then I wanted my fury to be the blaze that consumed his cruelty. Let them choke on the smoke of a queen who would not fall.

I launched burning fire over and over, practicing my targeting. Mina sauntered over, waiting for me to be ready to speak. Finally, I paused.

"How's Nymbria's training going?"

Mina's brow arched, the corner of her mouth twitching into something not quite a smirk. "She's busy, back at sea, protecting the merchant routes. Very competent, and very wet."

I snorted despite myself.

"She's been joining me for drills in the mornings." Mina added. "She's clever, her magic is more practiced than yours, though less varied. I suppose that's not a surprise, she's been using it for almost a decade to protect her crew. She can take down a ship with a whirlpool, use currents to shield her own, and ensure that no one is lost in their battles."

"She told me that was the only magic she had." I said.

"Because she limited herself to what she thought was possible. She never imagined to try more." Mina replied. "Just like you, she didn't know she could send objects long distance, and never thought to try."

I paused. "And why can we do that? Juniper said only people with golden eyes could manipulate distance like that."

Mina's eyes glittered like sunlight on water.

"Juniper was speaking of priestesses, the witches that were given magic by the gods." She said. "You and Nymbria are not merely priestesses."

A knot twisted in my chest. "Then what are we?"

Mina turned away. "You already know that answer. You just don't like it."

Seriously? She was going to play with this cryptic game again?

The fireball I had launched twisted midair, stalling as if it hit invisible resistance. The flames convulsed, curling inward until they formed a new shape. A dragon, wings outstretched, body twisting, its mouth open in a silent snarl.

It snapped at Mina once, just once, before banking in a lazy arc around her like a predator circling its prey.

I didn't mean to do it, not that way, but it matched the energy I felt as I shouted at her.

"I'm tired of the riddles! Of destinies and half truths and cryptic smiles. I'm out here breaking myself open every day while you keep hinting at these plans the gods have for me. Just tell me already!"

The dragon's wings flared, flinging sparks like embers from a forge. I was breathing hard, vision blurred from heat and fury.

Mina remained still, arms folded across her chest, utterly unbothered. Only when the dragon flew high above our heads, she summoned a slip of paper from thin air.

She held it up and recited the prophecy on it.

When the Queen of the realm binds her fate to a King who sees the depths of souls, she shall cause the land's heart to bleed flames into the sky and will herald a change in the realm itself.

When the earth trembles and rivers of fire reshape the ocean, the Gods will wake from their celestial sleep. Amidst the tumult and the awe-inspiring spectacle, they shall bring life into a new Goddess, born not of flesh but of magic, destined to weave balance into the very fabric of existence.

She will destroy the way of life, her steps resonating with power older than time itself. Through her touch, greed and envy will find their match, and the realms shall know an era of unparalleled enchantment.

Thus, the ancients foretold, their voices a whisper carried on the winds of destiny, for in the union of Queen and King lies not just the union of hearts, but the awakening of powers that shall reshape the world.

Every word wrapped tighter around my chest, like the vines I used to toy with Luther. By the time she reached the final line, I was trembling. The dragon overhead faltered, light splintering off its wings as it disintegrated into ash and ember.

"I'm the goddess." I whispered. The words tasted foreign.

Mina's lips curled into something between pride and sorrow. "At last, she's connecting the dots."

My gaze snapped to hers. "But what about Nymbria? That pull between us—it's real. You said destinies. Plural."

"She is part of yours," Mina said gently. "Her fate is connected with yours, yes. But you, Lyla—you are the Goddess of Balance reborn. You are the axis the world forgot it needed. The source of magic's return, the harmony after destruction. You are what the old gods feared and what the new age demands."

I dropped to my knees, hard, the stone courtyard rising to meet me like a blow. The air thinned. My hands trembled in my lap.

Not Queen. Not even human, not entirely.

Goddess.

The word settled into my bones like molten gold—luminous and heavy and unbearably hot. I had always felt something burning beneath my skin. I thought it was fury. Or grief. Or love. But it was this. It had always been this. I'd just been too afraid to give it a name.

Mina crossed the courtyard, and knelt beside me. "You are not alone in this. You never have been. But you must stop fearing the truth of what you are. The world cannot afford your denial any longer."

The weight of her words cracked something open inside of me, some hidden place I had spent years ignoring. The idea that I could be… *divine* was too vast. I had always feared I'd never be enough. And now… could I be too much?

This didn't feel like clarity. It hollowed me out. Everything that kept me tethered to my humanity—my grief, my longing, the fragile hope that I could have a family and keep my kingdom prosperous—suddenly felt paper-thin. The pieces of me that I was clinging to no longer held the truth of what I was. Who I was.

And yet… it all fit. In an uncomfortable, almost painful, yet perfect way.

I was a Goddess.

I had always been one.

And that meant that I was the only one that could effectively fight this war.

I sat in silence, the courtyard stretching wide and stilling around me. Somewhere nearby, the embers of the training fires snapped and hissed. I was vaguely aware of Mina crouching nearby, waiting patiently.

"Wait… why is Bel coming after me?" I shifted my body to face Mina directly.

Mina sighed, and settled into a seated position.

"I cannot say for certain. But I suspect he knows you are Nivara reborn—and that terrifies him."

"Why?" My voice trembled over the syllable.

"She was the only one strong enough to imprison him. The only one strong enough to bind any of us."

"Imprison him? What did he do?" I whispered.

Mina's voice dropped. "He caused The Last Great War."

The words hit like a blow. A god capable of nearly ending humanity once before… and now, hunting me. Preparing for another war.

And somehow, I was supposed to stop it.

CHAPTER 11

I needed to get my mind off of this revelation. That night, I turned to Spencer and Amyra for that.

They each were late coming back to the royal chambers, but I didn't care. I sat on the sofa, staring into the fire as I toyed with it, forming various animals and shapes. The alone time left me thinking long and hard about how I needed to change my role in this war. I couldn't afford to stay behind front lines. If I did, people would die. I wondered if I could afford to be in the same battles as Nymbria. If she was a goddess too... No. Wait. No more wishy-washy. She *is* a goddess. And since she is, maybe we were meant to fight this war on two different fronts. I had the land; she had the sea.

A knock on the door interrupted my thoughts. Ivy entered, offering a warm greeting. I barely acknowledged her, watching my fire puppy chase a fire fox around the coffee table in front of me.

"Ah!" Ivy exclaimed. "Lyla, I know you control fire, but can you, uh, keep it more contained?"

I glanced at her finally, seeing her wince behind a tall chair as the bird fluttered too close for her comfort. I giggled, and let both animals vanish.

"Will you want your meal here, or will you join the rest in the dining hall?" Ivy asked.

"The dining hall? Did I forget about plans?" I started to panic, moving to the vanity, checking my appearance in the mirror. I certainly looked like I had been playing with fire all afternoon. I moved to the bathing room to clean my face and arms of the soot.

Ivy followed. "There was no planned dinner, no, but the other two have chosen to take it there. Ethan is there too."

I looked at Ivy as she mentioned my brother's name. She blushed as I caught her eyes. Had he made his move? What kind of sister was I, to not know what my brother and best friend were doing?

"Why would you be blushing, Ivy?" I teased.

"Oh, you know how things go," She tried to dismiss. She moved behind me to brush through my hair and pin some of it off of my face.

"No, Ivy, I don't. Enlighten me," I prodded. "What has Ethan said to you lately?"

"He asked you first, didn't he?" She accused me, a smile spreading across her face.

I feigned innocence. "Asked me what? I know nothing."

Ivy giggled, "OK, well, my clueless friend, Ethan has asked if he could start courting me."

"Annnnd?" I reached for a fresh dress.

"And, I think I said yes?" Ivy seemed like she was asking me, rather than telling.

"You think you did?" I raised an eyebrow. "I hope you did."

She exhaled a sigh. "I did, but then I worried about how you'd feel about it."

"Ivy, please, if he excites you, then I enthusiastically encourage you to allow him to court you."

She swept behind me, adjusting the dress and fluffing my hair.

"Really?" She asked.

"Really, really." I replied, calling back to our childhood.

Ivy hugged me from behind. I held her hands close to me.

"Thank you, Lyla," she squealed into my shoulder.

I laughed as I turned to her, gripping her shoulders. "Ivy,

chase your happiness, please. I don't want to lose you as my Lady, but I absolutely will happily bear that burden if it means you get to be my sister in law."

She pulled away, and squealed as she hopped from one foot to the other. I laughed, her excitement was infectious. After she spun in a circle, she stopped and grabbed my hands. She took deep breaths, then said, "OK, I need to collect myself, so that I can face this dinner tonight."

I nodded, so glad to see her happy. I really hoped both find their happiness in each other.

"Let's go see what the others are up to." I said, moving towards the door. By the time we were ready to leave, Ivy was just as composed as always.

We quickly arrived in the dining hall. I felt my smile reach my eyes as I laid eyes on my stunning wife, who seemed to be enjoying the story that my handsome husband was telling. Neither noticed us, and it filled me with such joy to see them enjoying each other's company together. I was glad to see that even with the stress and worry of this war happening all around us, they could carve out time to be happy. It gave me hope that the future could be one of happiness.

I must have slowed down a bit, because Ivy was starting to tug me as much as she could politely tug. I looked at her, and saw her staring with affection as well. I followed her gaze, and almost laughed, realizing that I had missed Ethan sitting right next to my spouses at the lone table sitting on the small dais. Only two seats remained empty.

We reached them, and as we sat down, two courtiers brought over a plate of food for each of us. I glanced at it, roasted lamb with winter root vegetables and a crusty bread. It smelled incredible, and I made it a point to savor the food, knowing that war can change these details.

"We were wondering if you had forgotten us," Spencer teased us. His hand reached behind my back, gently rubbing with his fingertips. I leaned a bit back into it as I turned to give him a smile, my mouth full with my first bite.

"You smell like a bonfire, must be training hard." Amyra said, stealing my attention.

"I was just making some friends in the hearth," I said lightly.

"She let her fire-fox try to attack me," Ivy announced as she shared a quick look with Ethan.

Ethan's brow creased. "It didn't actually burn you, did it?"

Ivy grinned. "No, but it tried. I only got scorched feelings."

His lips twitched like he wanted to scold her, but instead, he shook his head with a fond exhale.

The three let Ivy and I eat while they continued their conversation. The moment felt like that rare kind of peace, too precious to disturb. I let the sounds of their laughter and excitement wrap around me like a blanket.

I could see too clearly what I had to lose. How this table, my family here, could all be harmed if I failed in this mission.

"So," Ethan's voice interrupted my thoughts. "Anyone wanna talk about what that pirate did this week?" A mischievous glint sparkled in his eyes.

"You mean Nymbria?" Amyra asked just before sipping on her wine.

"Yep, that's the one. Heard she tore open a whirlpool under a ship from Scoria Bay, swallowed them whole without a second thought."

Spencer snorted. "If only Egan was on that ship."

"You know, I met a sailor once who swore she seduced an entire fleet into crashing on the rocks. Said her voice is terrifying if you've angered her." Ethan continued.

Ivy leaned into him, "Is that true?"

Ethan shrugged. "No idea. Seems a stretch, even with the magic we know about. But who knows?"

Amyra reached for my hand, squeezing her worry into mine. I looked at her, and could see the unspoken question on her face. *Is she safe enough to trust?*

I cleared my throat. "She didn't get to the position of leading multiple ships in a fleet by the age of 30 by looking pretty and batting her eyes. She's a fierce sailor and knows how to use her water magic. That's all."

I hoped I sounded more convincing than I felt.

"She scares me a little," Ivy admitted softly. "She's beautiful, but she always seems one step away from cutting someone with her blades."

"She's cut plenty of people, though she doesn't seem the type to strike without cause." Spencer added.

"Did you know her? Before she joined us?" I asked.

He shook his head. "No, not exactly. But something feels familiar with her."

"Initially, it felt like she had come to take you from me," Amyra added quietly. "Now I can see that's not her intention, but something between her and me feels different. When I work with the other priestesses that can use my type of magic, we feel a kinship with each other. But with her, it feels different."

Amyra paused, like she wasn't sure how to say the next part. "I almost feel compelled to bow to her, to swear allegiance to her."

I felt something twist in my gut. Amyra's voice was calm, but I could hear the tremor beneath. The idea of her swearing allegiance, or feeling the need to worship her, or me... it felt wrong. Unbearably wrong.

I turned to her, hearing the quiet fear she didn't want to say. "She is different. She's like me. We're different in the same way."

"Wait a minute," Ivy said, leaning in. "Like you? Is she part of that prophecy?"

I felt the weight of their eyes. The conversation was teetering on the edge of something I knew shouldn't be shared around so many people. Not yet anyway.

I sighed. I hadn't wanted to get into this discussion tonight. And definitely not here.

"Let's... let's go back to the royal chambers," I said, maybe a too quickly. "There's some Vondalon rum—Spencer's family sent it as a late wedding gift."

Spencer caught the shift in my voice, and without a word, reached for my hand as he stood. I never felt more grateful that they understood what I left unspoken.

CHAPTER 12

Back in the chambers, I let the others drink and talk and laugh, let their voices blur into something soft and distant. I sat near the fire again, knees drawn up to my chest, watching the flames curl and flicker, like they had something to tell me. I didn't play with them, didn't want to upset the others.

Goddess.

The word kept echoing, reshaping all I thought I knew about myself. About the war. About what it would take to win it.

It wasn't just about armies, or ships, or strength. It was about the ancient feeling, buried deep within me.

It terrified me. If I'm the one meant to stop Bel, if I had done it before in a past life, then I needed to understand how.

What had happened in that war? What had I done?

What had it cost?

I waited until the fire burned low and the others said their goodnights. I waited until Spencer and Amyra were in bed, and I could hear them sleeping. Then I pulled on my cloak and quietly slipped away.

I meant to walk the gardens, to let the crisp wintry air help me think. But somehow, my steps led me to her.

Mina was already there, seated in the gazebo like she'd been waiting all night. A small flame flickered beside her, keeping the chill at bay. She didn't turn as I approached.

"Come," she said simply, patting the bench.

I sat, crossing my legs, and staring into the fire. We were silent for a few minutes, watching the flames dance.

"Go on," she said at last. "Ask."

"I need to know what happened." I said it so quietly I wasn't sure she heard me. "In the Last Great War."

She sighed in that way that told me she was about to tease me. "Didn't they teach you anything in school?"

I turned my head, offering her a half smile. "They taught me nothing. You haven't noticed?"

She chuckled, "Glad to see my humor is rubbing off on you. Veluna will be *delighted.*"

Veluna, the queen of the Gods.

Oh gods. I'd need to meet all of them. The thought felt heavy.

"Not just meeting them, you'll be responsible for bringing them out of their sleep. Or guiding the resurrected ones, much like you and Nymbria were."

I hated when she read my thoughts.

"Tell me what happened." I whispered. "Before. In the war. How did it end?"

"If I share this, be prepared. It's heavier than what your people teach. It will not sit well for a while yet. You're not supposed to be ready for this." Mina warned.

I considered her warning. I was already carrying so much more than I could bear. But really, what's a little bit more?

I nodded. "I need to know. I need to know how to defeat him now, and I don't have anywhere else to turn."

Mina looked at me then, truly looked. And for the first time, I thought I saw something like sorrow in her eyes.

"Alright," she said. "Then listen."

Mina didn't speak right away. She watched the fire for so long, I thought she might have changed her mind. Then, softly, she began.

"The Last Great War was the final time all nine of us were all awake. It was the last time we were among your ancestors."

She tilted her head, the light from the flames dancing in her eyes.

"Bel was the cause. He'd grown envious. As the God of Death, his power came from endings. When people die—especially those with magic—their energy flows to him. But it wasn't enough. He wanted more. He always wanted more."

She exhaled slowly, and the weight of it made my spine feel heavier.

"So he began to sow discord. He whispered to the mortals without magic, promising them power if they hunted those who had it. He made them afraid. Told them magic was dangerous, impure. Worth destroying. And they believed him."

I felt a shiver trace down my arms, even with the fire beside us.

"He turned cities into weapons. Encouraged enslavement, torture, executions. All to feed himself. It didn't take long for him to realize, war brings more death than fear ever could. So he pulled Varek into it—his twin. The God of War."

Mina's voice hardened with regret.

"Varek didn't need much convincing. Chaos is his birthright. But Bel twisted him, stretched the war long and wide, until the world bled endlessly. Every death fed him."

She glanced at the stars, at the streak of color lighting up the sky. The northern lights were back—ethereal, watching.

"When we discovered the truth, it was already too late. Nymbria was the first to rise against him. She summoned the tides to drown his armies, hoping to cut off his power source. But those deaths only fed him."

Mina's hands clenched in her lap.

"We had to trap him. That was the only way. Nymbria, Lysira, Halric, and Nivara—you—all agreed. You created a prison in the sea. Nymbria shaped it. Nivara—you—wove the spell to keep him asleep. Only you would have the power to wake him again."

Her voice broke, just slightly.

"We believed it would work. Veluna, Rhathren, and I went to put Varek to rest, to ensure he was contained. Then we went to our own, to rest ourselves. We thought you would join us. We thought the plan would work."

Her hands shook.

"But, it didn't. Something happened, inside the prison. Just before the lock sealed. He killed you all."

Silence filled the air.

"I should have known." Mina whispered. "I should've waited. I should have stayed awake to make sure."

Her voice cracked, stripped bare by grief. "I'm so sorry."

I looked at her, and could see the horror. The failure she carried, the regret that etched every line on her face. The Goddess of Peace, burdened by a war she couldn't stop, friends she couldn't save.

I didn't know what to say.

But in the quiet, deep inside me, in my chest, I felt my purpose growing. A fire building, slow and relentless.

I understood what I needed to do. I had to finish what they started. I had to stop him.

But I didn't know how to reach the power buried within me. And I didn't know what it would cost me to use it.

Mina sat still for another breath, then blinked quickly, brushing the back of her hand across her cheek like she could erase the tears away.

She cleared her throat. "It's late, time to head inside," she muttered more to herself than me, "no sense in missing sleep yet."

She rose stiffly from the bench, the firelight casting long shadows behind her. Her blanket slipped slightly from one shoulder, and she tugged it tighter as she turned back to the castle.

"I'll see you at first light," she added, her voice low but steady. "Try to rest, your training needs you strong."

I nodded, not sure I could bear the thought of going inside yet.

The fire crackled beside me, a reassuring sound, reflecting

the fire I could feel wanting to burn within me. The night pressed in close, wrapping around me. I looked up, seeing the northern lights, the same colors and dances that they had that one night, long ago, where Amyra and I confessed our love for each other. It felt like they watched me as I grappled with how to change the future.

I stayed there for a long while, watching the lights until they faded and only the stars shone.

In the end, it was a guard patrol that found me, and encouraged me inside.

CHAPTER 13

The corridors of the palace were quieter than I expected for the hour, the air still scented faintly with the roast and spices from dinner. I rounded the corner toward the library, intent on fetching a map I'd left there, and stopped short.

Through the open double doors, I saw them.

than and Ivy sat on the couch near the far hearth, angled toward each other, their knees nearly touching. A decanter sat open on the low table between them, two glasses catching the light. They were speaking in low tones, the fire popping softly in the pauses.

"…and you didn't even hesitate," Ivy was saying, her voice warm with admiration. "You just—stepped in front of me like it was nothing."

Ethan shook his head, smiling faintly. "It wasn't nothing. It's never nothing." He reached over, brushing an errant curl from her cheek. "And I'll do it again. Every time. You don't need to think twice about that. Taking care of you… it makes me better too."

She caught his hand before he could pull it away, turning it so she could press a kiss to his knuckles. "You make it very difficult not to think about you," she murmured.

He chuckled quietly, leaning closer. "Good. I'd hate to think I wasn't on your mind as much as you're on mine."

The smile that spread across her face was pure, unguarded joy.

Ivy laughed softly, the sound carrying like a little bell through the quiet room. Ethan was leaning forward now, elbows resting on his knees, listening with that intent focus he usually reserved for strategy meetings. She reached out, smoothing the lapel of his coat where it had folded back on itself, and he caught her wrist in a light hold, his thumb brushing absent circles against her skin. It was such a small thing, but it told me more than words could. The comfort, the trust, the ease between them. I hadn't seen Ethan like this since... maybe ever.

It was such an intimate little moment, I felt like an intruder just for witnessing it. I slipped away before they noticed me, continuing on toward the library with a strange, buoyant warmth in my chest.

Inside, the air was cooler, touched with the scent of paper and ink. I found the rolled map where I'd left it earlier, but before I could head back, Juniper emerged from between two tall shelves, her arms cradling a stack of books.

"Your Majesty," she greeted with a small nod, then glanced at the map in my hand. "Planning another excursion?"

"More like refining one," I said, tucking the map under my arm. "We'll need better coastal references for the next leg of the journey."

Juniper smiled faintly. "Good. Forethought will serve you better than bravado out there." She adjusted the stack in her arms. "And try to get some sleep before you go. I have the distinct impression you've been letting your thoughts run you ragged."

"You're not wrong," I admitted with a wry smile. "But I'll manage."

Juniper's gaze flicked toward the library doors before she returned to me. "I saw your brother earlier. Looked... lighter. Happier. It suits him." Her tone was casual, but the knowing curve of her mouth made me wonder how much she'd noticed.

"Ivy's good for him," I said simply.

"Mm," Juniper murmured, shifting the books in her arms. "Sometimes, the right person does more for a kingdom than an army."

She studied me for a heartbeat longer, then gave a little hum that might have been approval. "Good night, Lyla."

"Good night, Juniper."

I decided to take the long way back to my chambers—just in case Ethan and Ivy were still in the sitting room. I didn't want to chance interrupting them.

When I finally stepped inside my own rooms, Ivy was already there, perched at the edge of one of the chairs, still in her dinner gown. Her cheeks were flushed, her eyes bright.

"Have a good evening?" I asked, closing the door behind me.

She laughed softly, leaning back in her chair. "He's... gods, Lyla, he's wonderful. I don't even know where to start."

I crossed the room and sank into the chair opposite hers. "Start anywhere."

Her smile widened, shy but unable to be contained. "He wants to take me to my parents' estate. Said it would be nice to see where I grew up before things... change." She twisted the skirt of her gown in her hands, then released it with a small, giddy sound. "I think he's going to ask my father for permission to marry me."

"Permission?" I teased. "That's old-fashioned of him."

She shrugged, though the grin didn't fade. "It's Ethan. Of course he'd do it properly. I think he likes the idea of having my father's blessing. And—" she leaned forward, lowering her voice conspiratorially, "—I think my father might actually like him better than me by the end of the visit."

I laughed, shaking my head. "That would be a disaster."

"A disaster," she agreed solemnly, before the two of us dissolved into laughter again.

When it finally quieted, she gave me that wide, dreamy smile again. "He's so... thoughtful. He notices things. Like when I've been standing too long, or if I don't finish my tea. He's patient, and he listens."

I rested my chin on my hand, studying her. She looked happier than I'd ever seen her—lighter, even.

"I'm so happy for you," I said softly.

Her eyes shone. "I know you are."

I smiled back, warmth blooming in my chest.

I could almost picture it — Ivy leading Ethan through the gardens she'd grown up in, introducing him to the old oak where she'd once hidden contraband novels, her father watching from the veranda with that grudging approval only a man meeting his daughter's match can have. The image was so absurdly domestic that it made me grin. We'd be family in truth then, the lines between court and home blurring until they were one and the same.

It was a strange thought, but not an unwelcome one.

If someone had told me a year ago that my best friend and my brother would fall for each other, I would've laughed and said it was impossible. They were so different—or at least I thought they were. But watching them now, it made sense in a way that went deeper than reason. They balanced each other, drew out the best in each other without even trying.

And maybe, I thought, that kind of love had a way of making more than just the two people in it stronger.

CHAPTER 14

The day had finally come to head to Lummi Island. The ships had been readied at dawn, sails unfurled like teeth against the wind, and by midday, we were cutting across the blue-black waves under a steel sky. Nymbria stood near the bow, speaking quietly to Finn. Her posture was rigid, and she hadn't spoken much since we boarded.

The castle on Lummi's western cliffs came into view just after the sun began to dip. Pale towers rose from dark stone, trimmed in the blue-and-gold of Crystalford. I stood beside Amyra as we approached the docks, watching the figures gather along the pier.

Frederick was there. Even from a distance, I could recognize his stance. The same careful control I found so comforting last summer. How much has changed since then. It felt like a lifetime ago, like I was a child compared to now.

Nymbria moved to my other side, but said nothing. Her hands, usually steady, flexed open and close at her sides. I thought I saw her mouth something to herself.

Was her broken betrothal really to Frederick? She was so tense. She said nothing about it when we told her about this meeting. She didn't joke like she normally would, but she didn't oppose going either.

We docked, only the deckhands shouts heard. The ramp lowered.

Nymbria bowed, "After you, Your Majesties."

She was so stiff, so formal.

I glanced at her, uncertain. "You don't have to—"

"I do," she said, too quickly. Her voice was steady but she couldn't raise her eyes to mine. "Go, please."

Amyra and I descended the ramp together, boots clicking softly against the worn planks. The air was cold, and smelled of brine and pine smoke. I could feel the connection to Nymbria again, tugging harder the more distance separated us.

She needed to be here, on the land, with me.

Frederick stepped forward alone, leaving his men behind him in a practiced show of diplomacy. His winter coat was clasped neatly, the Crystalford crest pinned high at his collar.

He bowed low. "Your Majesties."

His eyes lifted to mine first, reflecting warmth and a cautious curiosity.

They paused only briefly on Amyra before shifting past us. His eyes widened for a moment, a small spread of shock that left his face almost as fast as it hit him.

I heard Nymbria behind me, her cloak swishing as she bowed. "Prince Frederick." Her voice was clipped.

Frederick cleared his throat. "Nymbria, hello."

Amyra's browed pulled together, but she said nothing. I didn't either, not sure how to bridge the frosty gap between these two. I would be even more shocked if this wasn't her former betrothed.

Frederick stared at her, frozen, for what felt like an eternity. I ended up clearing my throat. "Uh, yes, we have hired Captain Nymbria and her fleet to assist us with our naval response. It seems you two already know each other?"

Frederick blinked a couple times, and then shook his head, as if needing to clear his thoughts.

"Yes, my apologies, Lyla. We have." He replied. "Please, follow me, we will head inside. We've prepared a meal, and my admiral is already inside. We can speak after you've rested. "

And with that, we walked down the pier towards the gates to the castle.

AFTER THE MEAL, a soft knock on our door informed us that the meeting would take place in a couple of hours, giving us time to freshen up. The quarters we'd been assigned had a shared sitting and dining area, two bedrooms branching off opposite ends. Amyra and I were to share one; the other had been prepared for Nymbria.

As we stepped inside our respective bedrooms, Amyra hung her cloak up and gave me a look.

"You're going to ask her, aren't you?"

I hesitated. "I need to."

Amyra sighed, not out of disapproval but understanding. "Fine. I'll take my time washing up."

I caught her wrist gently before she turned away. "Thank you."

Her hand lingered in mine a beat longer, then she disappeared into the bathing room, shutting the door behind her.

I settled into one of the armchairs in the sitting area and absently picked up the book left on the table. The book was thicker than I expected, its cover worn smooth by use. "A History of Worship in the Realm of Crystalford" sounded like it would be dull, but something about the table of contents pulled me in. One chapter title in particular caught my eye: *The Moonborn and the Trials of Shifting Grace*.

I flipped to the page, skimming the dense script. It read more like folklore than scripture, describing tales of ancient stewards who claimed to be born beneath the moon and granted a gift of duality. Beasts in form, but human in heart. There were trials, it said, meant to test whether their loyalty belonged to the gods or to their own kind. There was no mention of which gods had created them. Or if the stories were meant as metaphor, parable, or something more.

I turned the page, but before I could read on, a heavy sigh drew my attention.

I looked up. "You alright?"

She gave a tired half-smile. "Define 'alright.'"

I closed the book and let it rest in my lap. "What happened out there? On the dock."

Her eyes flicked to mine, wary. "Are you asking as my queen… or as my friend?"

I offered a small, rueful smile. "Your friend."

She looked away, the muscles in her jaw tightening. "Then don't use this against me later."

"I won't."

She studied me, searching for something in my face. Then, finally, she said, "It was him. Frederick. He was the man I ran from."

I kept my expression soft, hoping to invite more of an explanation.

Nymbria frowned. "You already knew."

"I suspected," I said gently. "But I figured you'd tell me when you were ready."

Her posture loosened a little, but not much. "I didn't think I'd see him again. I didn't expect it to feel like that."

"Like what?"

She hesitated. "Like a closing door I already locked… being forced open again."

I nodded slowly. "What made you leave?"

Her gaze drifted toward the fire. "A marriage to him would have ended everything. No more ship. No more sea. Not even a chance to be on the docks. My parents told me as much. And the keeper assigned to me, after the betrothal was formalized— he made it clear. Being his wife meant being a princess in the palace. Polished. Presentable. Grounded."

She spat the word like it tasted bitter.

"Did you ever talk to Frederick about any of that?" I asked.

She blinked at me. "No. Why would I?"

"Because it might not have been true."

"Maybe. But it wouldn't have changed the risk. Princesses

don't get to be pirates. And pirates don't get to keep their crew alive if the crown has enemies." She gave a slow shake of her head. "I loved my people too much to put them in that danger."

I watched her for a moment. "If he had said he'd let you stay on the water… would you have married him?"

Nymbria didn't answer right away. Her fingers traced the stitching on the arm of the chair. "No. I don't think I could have. I would've resented him. And being a princess, even one with permission to sail, wouldn't have given me what I needed. It would've always come with a leash."

I let the silence settle between us.

"I'm happy now," she added, softly. "Or… content enough. I wish I'd found someone. But I have my freedom. My ship. My purpose. And that matters more than a title or a ring."

The door creaked open, and Amyra stepped out, dressed and ready. She paused at the threshold, reading the mood of the room, then crossed to stand beside me.

Before she could speak, a knock sounded at the outer door.

A courtier stepped in with a polite bow. "Your Majesties, Captain, the Prince is ready to receive you."

I stood, brushing my hands along my skirts. Nymbria rose as well, her expression unreadable again.

As we followed the courtier down the corridor, I could feel the tension coiling again behind her quiet steps. This wasn't over.

But for now, diplomacy waited.

We reached the conference room and were immediately struck by how bleak it was. The floor was laid with dull gray stone, cold and uneven beneath our boots. The walls were rough-hewn planks, aged to a lifeless beige that offered no warmth or charm. Even the table—a long slab of pale wood—looked more like something salvaged from a storeroom than meant to host diplomats. The whole room felt like it had been drained of color, of spirit. It was hard not to feel like it was draining us, too.

I nearly turned to Nymbria to ask if this was typical for

Crystalford. I couldn't imagine choosing to rule from a place so devoid of life. But she was unreadable, and I let the thought go.

Frederick rose as we entered, his men following suit in crisp formation. He greeted us with a shallow bow, and waited for us to take our seats before he and his party did the same.

He met my gaze, composed but watchful. "Tell us what you need."

I kept my voice measured. There was no mention of gods or prophecies, just tactics and numbers. I requested naval support by way of ships along the coast and within the sound to intercept any approach from Scoria Bay. I asked for troops as well, to reinforce the garrisons stationed at our river mouths and key coastal towns.

The admiral—a graying man with sharp eyes and a voice like wet gravel—narrowed his gaze. "What kind of support? Patrol routes? Blockades? Escort vessels for your supply lines?"

Before I could answer, Nymbria spoke. Her tone was sharp and assured, each word chosen with care. "We'll need rotating squadrons posted along the northern mouth of the Sound, keeping watch for any fast-moving vessels. Scoria Bay favors speed over bulk—scouts first, then raiders. If we miss the scouts, we won't see the full fleet until they're already on our shores."

She stood and moved to the table, clearing some glasses to spread out a map from her coat. "We've identified three primary approaches: here through the Strait, this line skimming the western shoals, and this deeper route through open water. We'll station Elthas's ships in tighter formation here"—she pointed—"but your ships have more long-range capability. I recommend putting your galleons at these two points for crossfire coverage. If Scoria tries to break through, they'll find themselves in a trap."

The admiral leaned in as she continued.

"We'll also need escort vessels for merchant runs between these towns. Food, weapons, medical supplies—they won't reach the front lines if pirates or rogue Scoria ships intercept them. Your presence will serve as a deterrent."

She paused, scanning the room, then added, "And we'll

need to coordinate signal systems. Elthas is using red flare spells for ground-to-sea alerts. Your ships should be able to see those from five miles out if we time them with high elevation and dusk patrols."

The admiral listened, his expression unreadable, then gave a slow, considered nod.

"We can commit half our fleet," he said. "Two squadrons to the Sound, one for patrols and merchant escorts, one held in reserve at our deepwater port. We won't move into your rivers, but we'll stay close enough to provide cover fire and reinforcements if needed. And we'll engage only if provoked."

He tapped the map once with a calloused finger. "We'll follow your formations, Captain. Just send us the final routes."

Nymbria gave a crisp nod, her posture flawless. "You'll have them by morning."

Then Frederick, ever the prince with good intentions and poor timing, leaned back and sighed. "Part of me wishes I'd taken Egan out during that tournament. Might have saved us all a lot of trouble."

The admiral shot him a look sharp enough to draw blood, but said nothing. Amyra, not missing a beat, quipped, "Well, it certainly would've made my life easier."

A few low chuckles followed, but I didn't join them. Because deep down, I knew it wouldn't have changed anything. Not really. The war was never just about Egan.

As the others shifted their attention to maps and supply estimates, I let my gaze drift to Nymbria. The way she moved, the quiet authority in her voice, the ease with which she took control of a room full of military men. It was more than impressive. It was like the sea itself had risen to speak through her.

She didn't rule from a throne. She didn't need velvet or gold. She had the song of sirens in her bones and spoke the language of the tides. She was made for this, I thought.

And then, like an ember sparking in my mind—

'You realize you sound exactly like that when you're commanding your court,' Mina's voice slid into my thoughts, dry and amused. *'It's a*

goddess thing. You'll get used to it.'

I resisted the urge to roll my eyes. '*Great. Another reminder I'm divine and under-qualified.*'

'*Fake it till you smite it, sweetheart.*'

I clenched my jaw, trying my best to hide my smile. My eyes caught Nymbria's, and the twinkle in her eye tells me Mina is being just as snarky with her. She winks at me, and I smile.

Then Amyra's hand reaches for mine as Nymbria returns to the planning.

HOURS HAD PASSED. The war table sat cluttered with half-empty goblets and maps that had been shifted and re-shifted so many times the edges curled. The air was thick with the mingled scents of wax and wine, the warmth of the council chamber at odds with the chill wind hissing beyond the shutters. Even Frederick had loosened his stance, one arm slung over the back of his chair while Nymbria traded a ribald sea story with one of his Crystalford officers.

I was just beginning to feel the tension in my shoulders ease when I saw it.

A streak of fire split the night. For a heartbeat, my mind told me it was a falling star, but the arc was wrong. Too deliberate. Then it hit—slamming into the deck of a Crystalford ship with a crack that shook the air, flames blooming high enough to illuminate the panicked faces along the rail.

"No!"

Chairs toppled as everyone surged to their feet. Frederick's voice was already ringing out—sharp, clipped, practiced—"Admiral, get our men to the ships!"

Nymbria's command cut across his like a whip cracking. "Wake the crew! Everyone—move!"

The room exploded into motion. I didn't wait for anyone. My boots hit the corridor stone hard and fast, my breath burning in my throat. The cold night air slammed into me as I burst through the doors, the tang of salt and smoke already stinging my eyes. The docks below were chaos—sailors spilling from the gangways, rigging creaking as crews scrambled into position, the first tongues of fire licking at the sky.

The sea was a black void, the enemy invisible except for the brief, murderous flares that came with each cannon shot. When one flashed, I struck back—hurling fire into the dark, willing it to find a target.

Another blast. A cannonball screamed past, close enough that the air itself seemed to tear. It struck the pier ahead with a force that ripped the world open—planks exploded upward, shards of wood whistling through the air.

Something hot and sharp punched into my side and arm, the force like being struck by molten stone. My breath vanished in a violent gasp, my knees buckling as the pier lurched under me. I hit the wet boards hard, the impact sending another spike of agony up my spine. Cold water soaked through my clothes, but it did nothing to numb the pain—it only seemed to sharpen it. My vision tunneled, the world dimming at the edges, the roar of the sea dulling to a low hum in my ears.

"Lyla!"

Amyra's voice, high and ragged, cut through the muffled chaos. A moment later she was there, skidding to her knees so fast the wood splintered beneath her. Her hands pressed hard to my ribs, glowing faintly, the magic sluggish at first, like it was fighting through mud.

"Stay with me, please gods, just stay with me," Her words came in a rapid, uneven rush, as if she could hold me here by sheer will.

The warmth from her palms spread, but not fast enough. I felt every heartbeat in my wound, each pulse threatening to drain the life from me. Her magic began to stitch deep within, but the process was excruciating—threads of fire weaving under my skin, knitting muscle with painful precision.

Amyra's breathing grew harsher. Sweat beaded on her brow, sliding down her temple as she poured more power into me. My side began to steady under her touch, the blood slowing... but my arm—gods, my arm—was a white-hot scream of pain.

She touched it, and her mouth tightened instantly. "The bone's shattered," she said, almost choking on the words. Her magic hesitated there, as if afraid to touch the break. "I can't set it, my magic won't touch it, what is going on?"

Her voice wavered, but her hands never stilled. She ripped a strip from her cloak with her teeth, binding my arm against my body so tightly my vision flashed white.

"You're not leaving me," she whispered fiercely, as if daring the gods to take me anyway.

The roar of cannon fire came again, rattling the pier beneath us, but all I could hear was Amyra's voice—low, urgent, unyielding—pulling me back each time the darkness tried to close in.

Boots pounded toward us. A Crystalford medic dropped to my other side, scanning me quickly before nodding. "We'll get her back to the castle."

Amyra didn't let go until she had to, her eyes locked on mine like she could anchor me with the sheer force of her will.

As the medic guided me back towards the safety of the stone wall, somewhere closer to the water, I heard Nymbria's voice—low but cutting through the chaos—calling to the sea. A wave rose, immense and terrible. I stopped and turned to see her end this, but her wave faltered before it could crash into the shadowed enemy. The answering barrage came too quickly, forcing her back.

The battle became a series of violent fragments—blinding flashes on the horizon, the shudder of impact underfoot, the acrid smoke burning my lungs. Every moment was guesswork. We fired toward the darkness, praying we hit more than open water. The smell of burning tar and wet rope clung to everything.

Then, in the lull between volleys, I heard it. That oily, tinny voice belonging only to one insufferable god.

'Better to yield than burn. Better to kneel and survive than cling to a doomed crown.'

My breath caught. My gaze darted across the yard, but no one was close enough to speak.

The water quieted down, the fighting seemed to be over, the enemy ships no longer firing at us. The crew immediately began to clean up and rescue others who had been hurt.

Nymbria appeared at my side, her face drawn tight. "You heard that too?"

I swallowed, forcing my voice steady. "I'll tell you later."

Her eyes narrowed, but she didn't press—not with the night still burning around us.

I stood, despite the medic's protests, and went to assess what I could. Two of Nymbria's three ships were gone, swallowed into the dark. Half of Crystalford's fleet was crippled, their masts jutting like broken bones into the smoke-laden air. And the horizon still felt wrong—like something out there was smiling.

At dawn, Frederick came to see me in the healer's quarters. He looked older than he had the night before.

"My lady," he said quietly, "this harm was done to you at my castle. I swear to you, Crystalford will give the full might of our army and navy to your cause. You will have our steel and our sails until this war is done."

Gratitude swelled in my chest. "Thank you, Frederick. I promise, whatever aid you need in turn, I'll give it. We'll stand together in this."

He shook his head firmly. "Unnecessary. I feel called to offer you all the protection I can, and I will do my best to see no harm ever comes to you again."

Amyra, seated at my bedside, inclined her head. "Your oath honors us, Prince Frederick. Thank you."

He offered a faint smile, then took his leave.

The door hadn't fully shut when Nymbria slipped in. Her hair was still damp from the sea, the faint scent of brine clinging to her clothes. She lingered near the threshold, voice low. "I heard what he said. I always knew he was a good man... and I hope he finds someone better than me for his wife."

She didn't wait for me to respond before stepping closer, her expression tightening. "I wasn't... at my best last night." She hesitated, eyes darting briefly to Amyra before settling on me. "I lost the second ship because I lost focus. When you fell, I felt something. Not just the bond—pain. Sharp enough I thought you'd been killed. I didn't know if it was real or my mind playing tricks, but it rattled me. I couldn't hold the water. Couldn't think. And then it was over."

I reached for her uninjured hand, squeezing lightly. "You were fighting in the dark, against an enemy you couldn't see. You still saved lives. That matters."

Amyra's gaze softened. "It scared all of us. But you were there when it counted. Don't let what happened keep you from being ready next time."

Nymbria gave a single, almost imperceptible nod, but her eyes didn't quite match it. They were shadowed, unsettled, as though something about the night's events still clung to her in ways she hadn't spoken aloud.

CHAPTER 15

We reached Tathlamar in the last blush of daylight, the harbor washed in streaks of orange and violet. I expected only the dockhands to notice our return, but movement at the edge of a nearby tavern caught my eye. Spencer stepped into view, scanning the pier as if searching for a missing treasure.

His gaze locked on us—and sharpened. Even at this distance, I could see the restless energy in his shoulders, the way his hands flexed and released at his sides. He'd been waiting, counting each hour we were late.

The gangway thudded into place. Nymbria's third, Ryxan, appeared first, her presence impossible to overlook. Loose braids threaded with bits of shell and bone framed her face, and her dark eyes held the weight of storms at sea. Layers of sea-worn fabrics clung to her tall frame, smelling faintly of salt and strange herbs. She moved with an unhurried but purposeful grace as she offered her arm, guiding Amyra and me down from the deck.

Salt wind tugged at my hair as Spencer started toward us, brisk steps breaking into a run when he spotted the sling holding my arm.

He reached Amyra first, pulling her into a quick embrace before his attention snapped to me. His arms came around us both, warm and steady, and the familiar scent of nutmeg and cinnamon curled around me like the memory of winter nights by the fire.

"I was so worried," he murmured, voice rough. "Lyla—your mental shields blocked me out so completely I still can't feel you."

Heat rushed to my cheeks. I hadn't even realized I'd shut him out. A flicker of thought, and the wall dropped just enough for the thread between us to hum warm again. His relief brushed against my mind like the first sip of mulled wine on a cold night.

"What happened?" His fingers hovered near my bandaged arm without touching, jaw tightening. "Who hurt you?" The last words came out as a low growl.

"We were ambushed in the night—likely Scoria Bay." My voice was steady, though the memory of the dockside barrage still burned behind my eyes. "I tried to launch an attack from the pier, but they followed the light of my fireballs and aimed straight for me. I won't make that mistake again."

His mouth hardened into a line. "I will kill them all."

Something in his tone made my pulse jump, though I wasn't sure if it was from feeling his protectiveness or from a concern about what that promise could look like.

He slid an arm around me, careful to keep my injured one cushioned against his side, and guided us toward the end of the pier. Amyra stayed close on my other side, her hand brushing mine in silent reassurance.

"We'll call a meeting tonight," Spencer said, already steering me toward land. "Authorize an attack. I'm done waiting for them to come to us."

I stopped at the edge where the pier met stone. The boards shivered under my boots with the tide's pull, the scent of brine curling between us. "No. We'll meet in the morning. I need a physician first. Charging into an offensive attack because I got hurt is reckless. That's how we lose more lives—and I won't spill blood recklessly."

His head snapped toward me, eyes bright with anger. "Lyla,

you're the queen of this kingdom. Letting this go unanswered makes you look weak. Right now, your strength, your ability to lead, is under question."

The heat of him pressed into the air between us. I could feel the worry behind the steel, could almost taste the pulse of his fear through our bond—but it came wrapped in the sting of a public challenge. Dockhands had gone still nearby, glances flicking toward us from behind crates and coils of rope.

I kept my voice low but edged. "And it doesn't help that we're having this argument in front of everyone, where you lead the questions about my abilities. Every word you speak out here says we're divided."

Amyra moved closer, tucking herself under his arm as if to calm him. "Come inside. Let her get treated, then we'll—"

"Why haven't you healed her?" Spencer's tone sliced through hers. "Why let her travel all this way in pain?"

Amyra stiffened, stepping back from him, chin lifting. "Do you think I didn't try? That I'd leave her suffering because I couldn't be bothered—"

"That's enough," I cut in, sharper than the crack of a snapped mast rope. My good hand closed on Amyra's elbow; my gaze pinned Spencer. "Both of you, stop. Now."

The gulls overhead filled the silence that followed, their cries harsh and distant. My pulse pounded as I turned away, pulling Amyra with me toward the archway of the castle. She stayed close at my side, and after a few strides, I slid my arm around her waist, a silent reassurance that I stood with her.

Behind us, Spencer's footsteps followed—slower now, quieter—but the air between us still hummed with words unspoken. I could feel eyes on our backs all the way to the gate.

The corridors swallowed the noise of the docks, leaving only the echo of our footsteps. My arm throbbed with each heartbeat, the pain sharp enough to curl my fingers into my palm.

We reached the physician's door, and I rapped my knuckles against it. After a moment, the door cracked open to reveal his weathered face, eyes still heavy with sleep. He took one look at my arm and straightened.

"Absolutely, Your Majesties. I'll meet you in my office in a moment."

He closed the door, and Amyra guided me toward the small adjoining office. The scent of dried herbs clung to the air, mingling with the faint tang of disinfecting spirits. I'd barely settled into the cushioned chair when Spencer strode in, his expression a mix of worry and stubborn pride.

"Not a word," I told him, keeping my voice even but leaving no room for argument.

He stopped just inside the threshold, jaw working, eyes never leaving my face.

The physician arrived moments later, his sleeves rolled to the elbow. "Tell me how it happened," he said as he examined the wrappings.

Amyra spoke before I could. "The bone has been shattered. I tried to heal it on the island—over and over—but it wouldn't take." Her voice stayed steady, but her hand was fisted at her side.

Spencer's gaze flicked to her, lingering just long enough for me to feel the tension tighten again.

The physician nodded, then looked at me. "I'll need to reset it. Pain will be... considerable. I'll give you a tonic first."

The liquid was bitter, the burn of alcohol chasing it down my throat. I clenched my jaw as the physician positioned himself at my side.

"Amyra, be ready with your magic when I give the word," he instructed. "Spencer—hold her good hand."

Spencer stepped forward without hesitation, his palm wrapping mine. His grip was firm, steadying, the familiar warmth of cinnamon and nutmeg curling into my senses.

"Now," the physician said.

A sharp, brutal jerk—white-hot pain tore through me, and my scream broke the air. I crushed Spencer's hand in mine, nails digging in, until Amyra's magic washed cool and steady into the break.

When my vision cleared, Spencer was flexing his hand with a faint wince.

"Sorry," I said, though my voice held the ghost of a smirk.

"I deserved it," he admitted, the corner of his mouth lifting despite himself.

Amyra kept her eyes on my arm, jaw tight as the glow in her hands began to dim. "It's not taking," she said at last, frustration threading her voice.

I reached with my good hand to touch her cheek. "Then we'll talk to Mina in the morning. You've already done more than anyone else could."

She nodded, but I saw the disappointment still shadowing her features.

The physician rewrapped my arm and handed me another vial of tonic. "If Mina can't help, come see me tomorrow afternoon, and I'll set you up with the rest."

We left in silence, the three of us moving together down the corridor. Amyra stayed close, keeping my injured arm between us. Spencer walked just behind, his presence a constant weight against my back. I could feel him trying to brush my mind again, probing for a way in. I kept the shield up this time.

Some things needed to be said aloud. And when they were, Amyra would be there to hear them.

The royal chambers were warm when we entered, the fire in the grate snapping softly. I shrugged off my damp cloak, the smell of salt and sea still clinging to my skin. Amyra and I crossed the room without a word, each step weighted with the quiet aftermath of the pier.

We stripped out of our filthy clothes, the fabric heavy with briny sea water. The bathing room steamed faintly, and I stood under the spray until the water ran clear, the salt rinsed from my hair and the tension loosened from my shoulders. Amyra quietly helped me to dry off, making sure my arm stayed still enough to not hurt more.

I pulled on a soft nightrobe, the belt cinched tight, hoping to signal the distance I needed. Spencer was at the hearth when we emerged, stoking the fire and pouring tea. The scent of cinnamon and nutmeg curled into the air, warm and familiar, settling low in my chest.

He turned when we approached, eyes shadowed. "I'm sorry," he said, voice quieter than I'd heard all day. "To both of you." He looked to me first. "I shouldn't have argued with you in public." Then to Amyra. "And I shouldn't have accused you of not trying to heal her."

He stepped forward, taking both our hands — mine in his uninjured grip, Amyra's in the other. "I saw you were hurt, Lyla. In pain. And I... lost my mind. I didn't think. Please forgive me."

I didn't answer. Not yet. My gaze slid to Amyra.

She straightened, shoulders square. "I will always love her," she said, voice low but fierce. "And I will always do everything I can to keep her safe. She almost died in my arms on that island. I was covered in her blood while I tried to hold her together. I don't know why my magic won't fix this, I tried for hours." Her breath caught. "I'd never let her suffer if I could stop it."

She turned to me, eyes glass-bright. "I'm sorry, Lyla. I wish I could do more."

"My sweet, sweet love." I cupped her cheek, brushing a damp lock of hair behind her ear. "You have never failed me. You fought for me when I couldn't fight for myself. That's all I could ever want."

Her mouth curved into the smallest smile. "That doesn't mean you get to keep charging into battles like that."

"I know," I said, and meant it.

Only then did I face Spencer. "You weren't wrong to be protective. But you were wrong to make it an attack on her — and to do it where others could see. You can't let your love for me turn into a weapon against the people I love."

His jaw tightened, but his eyes softened. "You're right." His fingers squeezed mine, once. "It won't happen again."

I poured tea for all three of us, the steam curling between us like a fragile truce. Spencer cradled his cup but didn't drink, eyes still fixed on me.

"There's something else," he said finally. "We can't just patch you up and pretend nothing happened. We need to hit them back, hard. Show them they can't touch you without consequence."

I exhaled slowly, keeping my tone even. "First, we see Mina in the morning. If she can heal my arm, we'll all breathe easier — and I'll be able to defend myself if it comes to that."

His gaze didn't waver. "And after?"

"After," I continued, "we'll meet with the council in the afternoon. We give them the good news, about Crystalford's help, and the bad. Let them hear the full account, and then we decide our next move together."

Spencer leaned forward, elbows on his knees, the firelight catching in his eyes. "Our next move should be offensive. Drive them back before they have the chance to strike again. Waiting only gives them the advantage."

I sipped my tea to give myself a moment. "We'll see where the council stands."

"That's not a yes," he said.

"It's not a no, either." I kept my tone measured, though inside, unease coiled tight in my chest. I could already picture him if the council voted to hold — pacing the war room, jaw tight, finding ways to work around them.

Amyra shifted beside me, her fingers brushing my knee under the table. "Let's not plan our fight until we know we can win it," she murmured.

Spencer sat back but didn't argue. The flicker in his eyes told me the conversation wasn't over — just postponed.

Amyra shifted beside me, her fingers brushing my knee under the table. "Let's not plan our fight until we know we can win it," she murmured.

Spencer sat back but didn't argue. The flicker in his eyes told me the conversation wasn't over — just postponed.

We finished the tea in companionable silence, letting the heat from the fire sink into our bones. When the cups were empty, we drifted toward the bed without speaking, the weight of the day pressing us together.

Amyra slid in first, curling close to my uninjured side, her warmth a balm against the deep ache in my arm. Spencer lay behind me, his chest a solid wall against my back, his arm draped protectively over both of us. His scent of nutmeg and cinnamon wrapped around me, grounding me, holding me here.

I let my eyes close. The fire's glow painted the inside of my eyelids, and for a moment, it was enough — the safety of their bodies, the quiet rise and fall of their breathing.

'You're not safe.' The voice crackled into my mind, tinny and warped, like a voice carried on a broken wire. The sound reverberated against the inside of my skull, making my teeth ache.

'Do they know,' the words hissed with static, *'how close I came during that battle? How easily I could have ended you, broken your little kingdom before your reign has even begun?'*

My breath caught. Spencer's arm tightened instinctively, but he couldn't hear the echoes skittering in my head.

'I will, Lyla.' The tinny distortion deepened, each syllable buzzing against my bones. *'And when I do, they'll fall with you.'*

The warmth of the bed seemed to leech away, replaced by a cold that crawled down my spine. I forced my breathing to stay slow, my body still, unwilling to let Spencer or Amyra know just how deeply Bel's voice had sunk in.

CHAPTER 16

The courtyard lay hushed under a brittle crust of snow, the bare apple trees stretching black limbs toward a pale winter sky. My breath puffed white in the stillness as I slowed under the archway. Nymbria's voice carried easily in the cold air, low and raw.

"...lost more men in one night than I have in my whole career."

She sat hunched on a weathered stone bench, elbows braced on her knees, gloves forgotten in her lap. Her bare fingers — red and chapped from wind — twisted the frayed edge of her sleeve until the threads curled loose. Her shoulders trembled once, quickly stilled, as if she'd caught herself in the act. "I've never failed like this. Never had sailors I couldn't bring home."

Her gaze stayed pinned to the frost at her boots, eyes glassy. "And without their bodies…" Her voice caught, splintering. "I can't give them to the god of the sea. I can't even give them that." She swallowed hard, jaw tightening, like the effort of holding herself together was a battle of its own.

From the bench's far end, Mina stood with arms folded, her expression unreadable. "You've led them well. You're still leading those who remain. That's the weight we carry — not the loss alone, but the living who need us to keep moving."

Nymbria's laugh was short and brittle, the kind that left a

bitter taste in the air. "Moving toward what? More battles? More bodies?"

"That's the work," Mina said simply, each syllable falling like a stone. "And soon you'll face decisions harder than this."

Nymbria flinched at that, barely, but I saw it. The sting of it made me pause in the archway a moment longer. I'd known her only a short while, yet the sight of her bent low under grief — Nymbria, who strode into battle with the tide at her back — made something in my own chest ache.

I stepped forward, my boots crunching against the frost. Nymbria's head didn't lift, but Mina's eyes cut to me, sharp and assessing. For a heartbeat she studied me as if deciding whether I'd help or hinder.

"Today's lesson will be different," Mina said at last. "Something to clear her mind and focus her magic."

"I'm not in the mood," Nymbria muttered, shaking her head. Her voice had gone flat, the fire in it smothered. "You don't want me anywhere near a spell right now."

Mina didn't answer — she simply held that steady, unblinking gaze.

I eased closer, the cold biting through my skirts. "Maybe that's exactly why you should. The battlefield doesn't care if we're grieving. Being able to hold control when the worst is in front of you — that's the difference between winning and surviving."

Her eyes flicked toward me, stormy and ready to snap — but instead she looked to Mina. "Then tell me this," Nymbria said, her voice low but tight, as if she were holding back something sharper. "Why did I feel her pain?" She jerked her chin toward me. "When she was hit, it was like the shot went through my own body. I couldn't breathe."

Mina didn't blink. "Because your paths are woven together." Her tone was so carefully even it might have been carved from stone.

A shiver crawled over my skin. "And if one of us dies?" I asked. My voice came out quieter than I meant, the question tasting like metal on my tongue. "What happens to the other?"

Mina's gaze didn't soften. "There are truths you can only understand by living them."

The words scraped raw against my nerves. My chest tightened, unspooling images I didn't want. I could see so vividly Nymbria crumpled on the deck of her ship, bleeding out as seawater pooling dark around her, my own body collapsing at the same moment, lungs filling with that same brine, feeling both her painful end and mine until the world went black.

Heat rose in my chest, sharp and restless. "That's not an answer," I said, the edge in my voice barely leashed.

Her eyes shifted away for the briefest moment, far-off, as though she were watching something in another lifetime.

I pushed, my heart thudding. "Did you feel anything when Bel killed the gods before?"

"No," she said at last. It was the kind of no that left the air colder, like the truth was still locked behind it.

The silence that followed scraped like grit in my teeth. Nymbria's jaw flexed, the muscle twitching once before she turned to me with a sharp inhale, as if bracing herself. "Give me your arm."

I slipped my arm from the sling, the cold air biting the skin where the fabric had kept it warm. Nymbria's fingers wrapped around my wrist, firm but not unkind.

She closed her eyes, jaw set, and the first wash of magic rolled into me — a deep, bone-chilling cold that pushed against the break like icy waves shoving at a damaged hull. Pain flared so sharp it scattered my breath, left me clenching my teeth to keep from crying out.

She tried again. And again. Each time the cold pressed deeper, the pain gnawing through my arm until my fingers tingled. Every failed attempt left her breathing harder, muttering curses under her breath.

After the fourth, she yanked her hands away and raked them through her hair, pacing a short line in front of the bench. "I can't—" She stopped herself, then spun back toward me. "I can't heal anything when I'm so broken. All I can see is their faces. All I can hear is the sea swallowing them whole." Her voice cracked, and she dug her nails into her palms. "I'm supposed to protect them, and I didn't."

Mina, who had been silent through it all, finally spoke — her voice clipped, each word like frost snapping underfoot. "You need to get a grip on your emotions. Or you'll fail again when it matters most."

The words seemed to hang in the cold between us, stinging as much as the pain in my arm.

Without waiting for a reply, Mina turned and strode across the courtyard, boots crunching through the snow. Her dark coat flared with each step until she vanished into the grove of leafless apple trees, the sound of her retreat swallowed by the wind.

Nymbria stayed where she was, head bowed, shoulders rigid, as if bracing against a wave only she could see coming. The weight of her grief wasn't just beside me on the bench — it seemed to press into the air itself, heavy enough to make my chest ache.

I lowered myself to sit beside her, awkward with only one good arm, the cold of the stone seeping through my skirts until it reached my bones. The wind teased loose strands of hair across my face, stung my cheeks, carried the faint tang of salt from the harbor. She stared down at the frost-dusted cobblestones as though they might rearrange themselves into the answers she couldn't find anywhere else.

We didn't speak. The silence between us wasn't empty — it was weighted, thick in the lungs, the kind that left no room for easy words.

Finally, I reached across the gap and set my hand over hers. Her skin was chilled, fingers slow to curl around mine, as if even that small act of connection took effort. I traced slow circles against the back of her hand, offering the only tether I had.

She let out a slow, unsteady breath, and something in her seemed to crack. "I've never lost sailors before," she said, her voice frayed to threads. "Never. Not one."

Her gaze stayed locked on the ground, as if looking at me might splinter her completely. "I don't even know all their families. I don't know where to find them to tell them their son, their father, their brother died with honor." Her voice caught, and she swallowed hard. "And without their bodies..." Her eyes squeezed shut. "I can't give them to the god of the sea. I can't even give them that."

Her grip tightened suddenly, desperate, nails pressing into my skin as though she could anchor herself through me — keep from drifting into the same emptiness that had claimed her men.

I searched for something, anything that might help. I could imagine the sting of losing someone in battle, the hollow left in their absence. But the weight of being responsible for lives lost at sea, of traditions left undone, of families waiting for a truth she couldn't give them... that was a wound I had no salve for.

We stayed like that for a while, her hand locked in mine, the cold biting at our skin. Somewhere in the distance a gull cried, the sound thin and lonely in the winter air.

"Lyla!"

The call cut across the courtyard, startling us both. Nymbria's grip loosened, and she drew her hand back quickly, swiping at her eyes before the voice's owner rounded the corner.

Ethan jogged toward us, cheeks flushed from the cold, his easy grin in place as though it had been there all morning. "How's the arm?" His gaze flicked to the sling.

"Still attached," I said dryly.

He chuckled, then glanced toward Nymbria. "Mind if I steal her for a moment?"

"I need to take a walk anyway," she murmured, already pushing herself up from the bench. Her voice was flat, and she kept her head down as she headed toward the castle, shoulders hunched against the wind.

Ethan offered me a hand up. We fell into step together, boots crunching over the frost as we cut toward Mother's garden. Winter had stripped it bare, leaving only the lattice of branches against the pale sky. The evergreens still stood tall, their needles whispering in the wind, and the air smelled faintly of cedar and distant woodsmoke.

When we were far enough from anyone else, Ethan's whole

expression shifted. The casual mask dropped, replaced by a warmth so real I could almost feel it in the cold air.

"I'm in love with her," he said without preamble, voice low but charged. "Ivy. Completely. She's... gods, Lyla, she's the kind of person who sees the worst in me and makes me want to be better anyway."

The unguarded joy in his eyes tugged a smile from me despite the heaviness still sitting in my chest. "I'm glad," I said softly. "When did you know?"

He huffed a laugh, rubbing the back of his neck. "It was the night she stayed up with me after that council meeting—remember the one where Denenbaum tried to trap us in the grain tariff mess? I was furious, ready to burn the whole chamber down. She brought me tea. Didn't say a word about politics, just sat there until I'd stopped pacing... and then told me I was wrong about half of it." His grin went crooked. "And she was right. I realized I didn't just want her around when things were good. I wanted her there for all of it."

"I can hear the decision in your voice already," I said.

"I want to go with her to her estate," he admitted. "Speak to her father. Ask for his blessing to marry her."

I arched a brow. "You don't need his permission. Ivy can accept a proposal without anyone's blessing."

"Oh, trust me, I know," he said quickly, the grin fading into something more thoughtful. "But I'm next in line for the throne. That paints a target on her and her family. Political rivals, foreign agents, anyone who'd rather see me compromised... they'd all see her as a way to get to me. I need to make sure her family is prepared. Protected. I want them to know what could come."

Something in me eased at the care in his words. "Then I'll pledge what I can to help. But Ethan — don't you dare accept a dowry if they've prepared one for her."

"I'll refuse it," he promised. "But if they insist, I'll set it aside. Keep it for their family, or for our children, or her nieces and nephews. It'd feel more insulting to refuse if it matters to them."

I studied him, catching glimpses of the manners and quiet strength our mother had worked so hard to instill. Gone was the careless playboy he once played at being. "Mother would be proud of you," I said softly.

Color touched his cheeks. "I'm just doing what I think is best."

The doorway to the castle opened, and muffled sounds of laughter spilled from the dining hall ahead of us. For a fleeting moment, I let myself imagine a world where this was all there was — family, peace, a winter without war. But the vision dissolved as quickly as it came, and the cold wind at my collar reminded me it was only that: a vision.

Color touched his cheeks. "I'm just doing what I think is best."

The muffled sounds of laughter spilled from the dining hall ahead of us. For a fleeting moment, I let myself imagine a world where this was all there was — family, peace, a life without war.

We lingered at the edge of the garden path, the faint glow from the dining hall windows spilling across the snow like a promise of warmth.

"I'll speak to her tonight," Ethan said, glancing toward the castle doors. "I'd like to tell her before I leave."

"You're sure?" I asked.

He gave a small, almost amused huff. "I've never been more sure about anything in my life. If she says yes, I'll ride out within the week."

"Then I'll clear your schedule with the council," I said. "That way no one can claim you're avoiding duty."

His grin widened, boyish again. "Always thinking three moves ahead, sister."

I watched him go, his tall frame cutting through the cold, the warmth he'd left behind fading far too quickly. The moment the door shut behind him, the chill in the air seemed sharper — the night too quiet, as though the world was holding its breath.

Tomorrow would be a long day. Mina wanted an early meeting, and my arm still throbbed in its sling, each pulse a reminder that Nymbria had tried and failed to heal it. The council would have to hear both the good news of reinforcements and the bad of our losses, and Spencer... I didn't trust him not to push for an immediate strike before we were ready.

The thought followed me up the steps and through the archway into the castle's main hall. The air was warmer here, scented faintly of cedar and candle wax, but the weight in my chest didn't lift.

I'd have to keep my footing. Between Mina's riddles, Nymbria's grief, Ethan's announcement, and Spencer's temper, one misstep could tip us into chaos before the war even reached our gates.

And chaos was exactly what Bel wanted.

CHAPTER 17

The three of us walked in silence down the council hall, our footsteps echoing against stone and banners swaying faintly in the draft. The weight of what waited on the other side of those doors settled heavier with each step. Spencer kept pace at my right, shoulders squared too tightly, his hands flexing and curling at his sides as though itching for something to grip. His gaze stayed fixed ahead, unblinking, the faint muscle in his jaw ticking every few moments. Amyra walked on my other side, her eyes forward, shoulders squared as if she'd decided that if she couldn't stop the storm, she'd at least stand through it without flinching.

I didn't need mind-speak to feel Spencer's mood pressing against me. He was still set on pushing an attack today. I'd already decided not to lead with my own opinion, thinking it better to watch the room, measure who spoke up, and step in only when I had to. If I said it too soon, he'd only hear it as me telling him no.

The corridor narrowed toward the council chamber, torches throwing our shadows long over the polished floor. I found myself thinking of the boy Spencer used to be, the one who never let a rule stand in his way if it didn't suit him. Back then, his stubborn streak had been almost charming. It had led to midnight races across the castle roofs, forbidden dives into the lake, once even sneaking into a merchant's barn just to rescue a trapped kitten. I'd laughed then. Now, the same refusal to accept limits only tied my stomach in knots.

The chamber doors opened, and we stepped into the hum of voices. The air smelled faintly of parchment and smoke from the hearth. As soon as the clerk called us to order, Nymbria took the floor. She stood like stone in her fancier dress cloak, her voice steady as she delivered the battle report. She detailed the losses at the docks, the deal struck with Frederick's admiral, the expected arrival of more ships.

Spencer waited only long enough for Nymbria to finish before leaning forward, elbows braced on the table like he was ready to lunge across it. His voice cut through the chamber, sharp and certain.

"Then we take the fight to Scoria Bay. Not a small little group, the whole fleet. Straight to their capital. We burn it to the waterline."

The room seemed to still around his words. Lord Greenhow's reply came fast, almost clipped. "No. That much death and destruction makes us no better than them. We need to wait until Crystalford arrives. Coordinated strikes win wars, not rushed heroics."

Nymbria gave a short nod, her mouth tight. "He's right."

Spencer's chair screeched against the floor as he shoved it back. "You're all content to let them rebuild?" His voice rose, echoing off the high stone. "To wait until spring, when their fleets double in size and they march inland to burn every city between here and the mountains? We end this now, before they—"

"We go on the offensive when we're ready," Greenhow cut in, his tone final. "Not when you're upset that your wife got hurt."

Spencer's hand slammed down on the table, rattling inkwells and scattering a stack of parchment. "Fine," he bit out. "Then send a small unit. Find Egan. Kill him before he kills more of our people. Make him an example."

Lord Luther leaned back, folding his arms. "This isn't one

of your games, boy. In the real world, far more people die when you play these games."

The air went razor-sharp. Spencer's glare locked on Luther, so dark I half expected him to leap across the table. I knew that look — the same one he'd worn as a teenager just before breaking every rule he'd been given. My stomach knotted.

His head turned slowly toward me. "Lyla. Back me up."

Every pair of eyes in the chamber swung to me. The weight of it pressed at my ribs, but worse was the look in his — daring me to deny him. If I told him no here, in front of them all, I didn't know what he'd do when the door shut behind us.

"We plan nothing until Crystalford's fleet is here," I said, keeping my voice even, each word deliberate. "Then we move, and we move together. We can't win without their help. But we can start shaping the plan now, so the moment they arrive, we act."

His jaw clenched, the muscle twitching once, twice. He didn't argue, but the fury in his eyes said this wasn't over, he wouldn't stop until he got his way. The muscle in his jaw jumped again. For a heartbeat, I thought he might argue in front of everyone. Instead, he leaned back, staring at me with an anger that burned just beneath the surface.

No one spoke at first. The silence in the chamber wasn't relief — it was the brittle kind that comes when everyone is holding their breath, waiting for something to crack.

Lord Greenhow's gaze shifted between us, assessing. Luther's mouth was pressed into a thin line, but there was something smug there too, as if he thought he'd "won" this round. Nymbria's eyes stayed on Spencer, her jaw set, as though measuring whether she'd need to intercept him before he did something reckless.

Spencer's stare was still on me, unblinking, burning with the same stubborn fire I'd seen a hundred times in our youth — when he'd scaled the palace walls against orders, when he'd slipped away from escorts to chase some thrill in the city. Back then, it had been trouble contained within a night. Now, the stakes were measured in blood, in the lives of my people.

Finally, he leaned back, slow and deliberate, like a predator deciding not to strike at this moment. The scrape of his chair legs on the stone was the loudest sound in the room.

"Fine," he said, the word brittle enough to snap.

But I didn't believe him. Not with the way his hands curled into fists beneath the table. Not with that too-quiet tone that never meant surrender. He was counting down to something. Whether it would be in hours or days, I couldn't tell — but I knew that if the council refused him again, he'd find a way to act without their blessing. Without mine.

The meeting lurched forward into other matters—provisioning, coastal patrols, trade routes—but the undercurrent remained. Spencer's silence wasn't withdrawal. It was a loaded pause, and every beat of it set my pulse a little faster.

When we finally adjourned, the scrape of chairs and shuffle of papers sounded too loud, too ordinary, against the weight still pressing down on me.

Spencer lingered only long enough to murmur, "Need to speak with Juniper about my magic. I'll meet you for dinner." His eyes swept over me and Amyra in a way I couldn't read. His look was slow and deliberate, like he was committing us to memory.

Amyra waited until we'd cleared the chamber and the heavy doors had closed behind us. "He didn't take that no," she said quietly, her voice pitched low for only me. "Not really. He was too—" she hesitated, searching for the word "—coiled."

I gave a small nod, my gaze fixed ahead. "I know." I tightened my mental shields without thinking. "But that's a conversation for later."

We didn't speak again until we reached the physician's quarters, the familiar scent of dried rosemary and camphor meeting us as we stepped inside.

The physician, an older man with hands that always seemed to carry the faint stains of tinctures, looked up from his worktable. "Let's see it," he said, motioning me to sit.

I sank into the chair as he unfastened the sling and carefully peeled back the wrap. His fingers probed lightly along the length of my arm, his brows pulling together.

"It certainly wasn't a clean break," he murmured. "Not the worst I've seen, but the angle is tricky. The bone needs to set right or you'll lose some range of motion."

"That won't happen," Amyra said quickly.

He glanced at her, then back at me. "That's the hope," he allowed, his tone making it clear it was far from a promise. "Magic might not be able to do anything until the bone has started knitting on its own."

I caught Amyra's frown in the corner of my vision, but the physician pressed on. "I'll give you something stronger for the pain. Keep the arm elevated whenever possible. And no lifting. None. Even if you think it's light."

I let out a short breath. "Understood."

He replaced my sling with a sturdier wrap, the fabric pulled snug, then pressed a small packet of pain tonic into my hand. "Drink half with water before bed tonight, the rest in the morning. It should help you until the pain calms down."

Finally, he turned to Amyra, his voice firm but not unkind. "Keep trying. Even if it's only for a few minutes each day. Sometimes…" He paused, "…sometimes it surprises us."

On the walk back, I decided to change the subject to something lighter — something that wouldn't leave either of us staring down a knot of worry we couldn't untangle until we saw Spencer again. Still, we kept our voices low, pausing more than once to glance over our shoulders before speaking of Ethan's plans.

Amyra's eyes lit when I told her he wanted to marry her. "I've never seen Ivy so happy. We'll make her wedding a day she'll never forget."

We traded ideas like conspirators passing stolen notes. Amyra suggested commissioning a song from one of the royal court's traveling bards — something written just for Ivy and Ethan, to be performed the night they returned from her family's estate. I countered with the thought of a carved wooden keepsake chest inlaid with silver filigree, each panel etched with their favorite places around the capital.

By the time the castle's familiar corridors closed in around us, the weight from the council chamber had thinned just enough to let me breathe a little deeper. But the air shifted again the moment we stepped into our rooms. No firelight spilling from the inner door. No shadow of Spencer waiting.

We delayed dinner as long as we could, pacing the length of the sitting room while the servants tried to keep the food warm and the wine from losing its bite. At first, our questions were casual — musings tossed between bites of bread and sips of cooling wine.

"Maybe Juniper kept him talking," Amyra said, breaking apart a piece of crust. "Or he's gone to the stables again. You know how he gets when he needs to think."

"Maybe," I said, though the word tasted thin. "Or maybe he's just... cooling off."

But as the platters cooled and the wine dulled, our idle guesses dwindled. The silences between them stretched longer, heavier. I found myself glancing at the door more often than my plate, and caught Amyra doing the same.

Neither of us said it aloud — the thought that he might already have done something, set some plan in motion without us. But it sat between us alongside the extra place at the table, silent and waiting.

When his food was beyond saving, we let the servants clear it away. We changed for bed without speaking, the unasked questions trailing us like shadows.

That night, as I lay with Amyra's steady breathing beside me, my thoughts kept circling back to the look Spencer had given us in the council chamber — the one that felt too much like goodbye.

CHAPTER 18

Morning light pressed dimly through the frost-clouded windows, pale and cold. I reached for the space beside me and found only cool sheets.

Spencer hadn't come back.

The thought jolted me fully awake. I sat up fast, the motion tugging at my arm, and my gaze snagged on a half-folded scrap of parchment on the table near the hearth. The edges were creased and soft, as though it had been handled too many times in too few hours.

I was out of bed before I registered moving, bare feet chilled by the stone floor. The scrawl on the outside stopped me mid-step — Juniper's handwriting, hurried and tight. My fingers fumbled over the fold.

Behind me, the blankets rustled. "What's going on?" Amyra's voice was heavy with sleep, rough at the edges.

I didn't answer until I'd broken the seal. "It's from Juniper," I said, my own voice strange to my ears.

Amyra pushed herself upright, hair mussed around her face. "Read it."

I swallowed and began.

LYLA,

I tried to stop him. He wouldn't hear it. He threatened to leave alone if I didn't help him. I told him it was reckless — he didn't care. He's going to Scoria Bay.

I agreed to go with him rather than let him die alone. He insisted I use my gift to winnow us closer. I stalled as long as I could, but we left while the northern lights were still burning, so it was early yet in the night. I'll try to winnow slowly to give you a chance to catch us, but I can't promise it will be enough.

— Juniper

By the last line my breath had gone uneven, every word tightening around my ribs like a noose.

I looked up, the letter trembling in my hands, and met Amyra's eyes. For a heartbeat, neither of us moved — fear holding us in place. Then Amyra flung back the covers. "We have to send people after them, now."

I nodded sharply, forcing my feet into motion. We barely remembered to grab our dressing robes before yanking the door open. My voice came out sharper than intended when I told the guard, "Find a courtier. Quickly."

We were still in the sitting room when Ivy arrived with a tray, the steam from the tea curling into the chilled air. Amyra and I exchanged a silent agreement to say nothing. The fewer who knew the king was gone, the safer he'd be.

But Ivy's eyes swept the room and landed on the empty space beside me. "Where's Spencer?"

"He's—" I started, but the word faltered.

"He had a meeting," Amyra tried, but her voice wouldn't have convinced anyone she believed that lie.

"You're being cagey," she pressed, setting the tray down with more force than necessary. "What's happened?"

Amyra's lips tightened, but under Ivy's stare, she cracked. "He's gone to Scoria Bay. Retaliation."

Ivy's face went pale. "Alone? He'll—"

I stepped in, my tone low and firm. "You can't do anything.

You can't tell anyone. If word spreads, his life is in even greater danger."

The room seemed to close in, the air thinning — and then Bel's voice slid into my head, tinny and metallic, echoing as though it rattled inside my skull. *'Your king makes it so easy, little queen. Walking right into my grasp. You've done me a kindness, letting him go without you.'*

I tried to block him out, but his voice curled tighter, pressing against the back of my mind like cold iron.

'I could crush him before he even sees my shore. Snuff him out like a candle. But I'm feeling generous.'

'You won't touch him,' I thought fiercely.

A low, grating chuckle echoed between my temples. *'Give yourself to me now — bend the knee, swear your will to mine — and I'll keep him breathing. Refuse... and I'll let him watch while I burn every piece of your pretty little kingdom.'*

'No.'

'Then I'll take my time. Draw it out. I want to see the look on his face when he realizes there's no saving himself. I want him to know what fun a god of death can have.'

The words scraped like metal shavings against bone. My nails dug into my palms, my breath gone ragged.

Amyra's voice cut through, sharp with concern. "Lyla? Is he —Bel's talking to you, isn't he?"

I managed the smallest nod, still fighting the echo bouncing inside my head.

Amyra turned to Ivy. "Go. Get Mina. Bring her here."

Ivy nodded quickly, grateful for a task, and slipped out the door.

The moment the door shut behind Ivy, the control I'd been clinging to shattered. My hands shook so badly the letter crumpled in my grip.

Amyra's arms came around me, solid and warm, but they couldn't stop the tremors running through me. "We'll get him back," she murmured, though the strain in her voice betrayed the fear she was trying to bury.

I pressed my face into her shoulder, breathing in the faint

scent of apple cider clinging to her skin. "Gods, Amyra... what if we don't?"

Her arms tightened. "Then we don't stop until we've torn the world apart to try."

I wanted to believe her. But Bel's words still echoed inside my skull, tinny and grating, like they'd been carved into bone. I'll take my time. Draw it out.

Every passing second felt like another mile between me and Spencer. My mind kept conjuring images I couldn't chase away — his ship under black skies, the sea curling up like claws around the hull, shadowed figures waiting on the shore. Bel's pale hands on his face, holding him still.

Amyra shifted just enough to cup my cheek with one cold hand, her thumb brushing at tears that wouldn't stop coming. "Don't do this to yourself. Not yet. Not until we know."

But my voice shook when I whispered, "We already know. He's gone into Bel's reach."

Outside, the corridor was silent except for the occasional snap of a torch. Inside, the fire in our hearth popped and hissed, but it couldn't touch the cold pooling in my chest.

Amyra pulled the blanket from the foot of the bed and wrapped it around us both, keeping me tucked against her. We sat like that on the edge of the mattress — the world narrowed to the two of us and the too-loud beat of my heart in my ears.

Every small noise in the hall made me jerk, half-expecting it to be Ivy... or a messenger with worse news than we'd already had.

The minutes stretched until they felt like hours. I focused on Amyra's breathing, the slow rise and fall, trying to anchor myself to it. If I let my mind drift too far, it went straight to the thought of Mina arriving too late — of ships already ash on the tide.

Amyra pressed her lips to my temple. "Hold on. Just hold on until Mina gets here."

I nodded, though the motion felt hollow. Holding on was all I had left.

A soft crack split the air, sharp as lightning through the

walls, and Mina winnowed straight into the chamber with Ivy clutched in one hand. The sudden displacement made Ivy stumble forward, one palm pressed to her stomach as she caught herself on the nearest chair.

"Could have warned me," she muttered, sinking into it with a wince.

Mina didn't even glance her way. Her focus locked on me, and in two strides she was there, her hands warm and unyielding on either side of my head.

"Show me," she said, her voice low and even but edged with something harder.

A sob caught in my throat. I nodded, closing my eyes as her magic slid into my mind, cool at first, then probing deeper. She sifted through my thoughts with precision, pulling the memory of Bel's threats to the forefront. I lived it again, tinny and echoing in my skull, each syllable scraping like metal on bone. *'Can't wait to meet your king... show him all the fun things a god of death can do.'*

When the last word faded, Mina withdrew, and I forced my eyes open.

The color had drained from her skin, her gold eyes darker now, shadowed as though the light behind them had gone out. Her jaw tightened, a single muscle twitching before she could still it. For all her practiced composure, I could see the crack in the armor. Fear.

It slammed into me harder than Bel's voice had. If she was afraid, then I was already standing on the edge of something I didn't know how to survive.

That broke something in me. My breath hitched into ragged sobs, the control I'd fought for crumbling. Amyra was there instantly, wrapping me in her arms, her hands smoothing down my back in silent reassurance.

Mina straightened, her gaze sharp again as she turned toward Ivy. "Get Nymbria. Now."

Before Ivy could move, the courtier I'd sent for earlier appeared in the doorway, bowing slightly. "Your Majesty—"

"What is it?" Mina asked without missing a beat.

The young man hesitated, then shrugged helplessly. "I was told to come at once. No message given."

AMYRA'S VOICE cut across the room, firm and decisive. "You need to find General Kellen and bring him here. Immediately. And not a word to anyone but him."

The courtier's eyes widened, but he nodded sharply and darted away down the hall. Ivy followed quickly behind him.

The door clicked shut. Mina spun back toward Amyra, eyes narrowing. "Why are you involving more people?"

Amyra didn't flinch. "Because someone has to go after them. Spencer and Juniper are out there, and every second we waste is another second they're in Bel's reach."

Mina's lips pressed into a thin line. For a moment, the air between them was tight enough to snap. Then she gave a single, deliberate nod. "Fine. I can work with that."

"I need you to take us to them." My voice was raw, the words scraping out before I could think. "Now. Before they get themselves killed."

Mina didn't move. She simply watched me, then reached past the untouched tea to tear a chunk from one of the rolls Ivy had left behind. "It won't save them." She leaned her hip against the table, chewing with the same measured pace she used when delivering bad news in council.

The dismissal lit something sharp in my chest. I started pacing, every turn in the carpet wearing my thoughts thinner. "Then we'll cut them off at the coast — ride through the night, meet them before they can board. Or—" I stopped mid-stride. "No, the ports. We send messengers to every harbor master in Elthas to bar them from boarding anything. Pay them if we have to."

Mina swallowed, took another bite.

I dragged both hands through my hair. "Or pirates — yes,

bribe the captains to—no, no, that's hopeless. Someone will always take more coin."

Again and again, I stopped in front of her, every plea feeling more desperate than the last. "You can winnow. Just do it, Mina."

She stayed maddeningly still, the golden calm of her gaze unmoved by my storms.

By the time my legs gave out and I sank into the sofa, my breaths came hard enough to make my ribs ache. Mina strolled over, set a plate in my lap. "Eat," she said simply. "A weak and hungry goddess will make foolish choices."

I glared at the bread and cheese but picked at it anyway, chewing around the tightness in my throat. Between swallows, my mind kept clawing back to escape routes and interception points.

Halfway through the plate, I shoved it aside and pushed to my feet. "I'm done wasting time with food. I need to act."

Mina's eyes flicked to my rumpled shift, then to Amyra's. "Then dress for it. Both of you."

I blinked at her. "Now?"

She rolled her eyes. "If you do it quietly enough, I can sift through enough possibilities to see the path we need. Otherwise you'll just keep interrupting."

I didn't bother arguing. Amyra and I slipped into the adjoining chamber, steam rising from the copper tub where the servants had left fresh water. The heat sank into my bruises, but it did nothing for the ice in my chest. We scrubbed, dressed, and bound my arm back in its sling with brisk efficiency, both of us knowing this wasn't preparation for the day — it was preparation for bad news.

When we returned, Ivy was guiding Nymbria inside. The pirate's shoulders were stiff, her gaze darting between us and Mina. The four of us took our seats at the dining table. None of us spoke.

Mina sat perfectly still, eyes closed, her breathing slow and deliberate. For a long moment, nothing happened — then the smallest movements began. The muscles in her jaw flexed and released, almost in rhythm with an unseen pulse. Her fingers tapped twice against the tabletop, stilled, then curled tight into her palms. A faint tremor rippled across her forearms, like she was holding on to something just beneath the surface.

The quiet stretched until the air felt too thick to swallow. My own heartbeat thudded in my ears, but still she didn't open her eyes.

Finally, the tremor eased, her hands flattening against the wood. She exhaled, and when she spoke, her voice carried the weight of certainty. "You're not going to like what is needed."

I shook my head hard. "If it saves them, it's worth it."

Mina's eyes opened at last, gold irises catching the morning light as though they'd been polished. Her lips curved, the faint tightening of someone bracing to give orders. "Then listen closely," she said, low and deliberate. "And do not deviate from this plan."

CHAPTER 19

Mina had been right, I hated this plan. Every step of it scraped against my instincts. But the glint in her eyes when she'd laid it out, the way she'd said all other paths ended in disaster... it was enough to keep me in line.

The council was already in session when I shoved open the tall double doors, Nymbria at my side. The warm scent of ink and hot candle wax met me like a wall, the air inside thick with clipped voices and shuffling papers. Heads swiveled.

Luther was the first to recover, and his bark cracked through the chamber like a whip. "Your Majesty, how dare you disrupt the council without summons? This is not your time on the agenda, and your presence here is a breach of—"

The sound was so familiar, so perfectly Luther, that a strange steadiness slid into me. I let him finish his tirade without flinching, meeting his glare with the faintest quirk of a smile. Let him see I wasn't rattled. Not by him, at least.

I stepped forward, skirts swishing in the charged silence that followed. "Spencer left last night with Juniper," I said, voice pitched to carry, "using his authority to coerce her into aiding him on a direct course to Scoria Bay for a mission he will not return from if we do nothing."

Luther leaned forward like a wolf scenting blood. "Then we call for his arrest immediately."

For a heartbeat, I almost took the bait. But Mina's warning sat heavy in my chest. That way lay ruin. I steadied my breath and said, "Not possible. By the time the order reached the coast, he'd be long gone. We need another approach."

Greenhow's weathered hands clasped together, knuckles pale, but his gaze was clear and unwavering. "Then tell us the approach, Your Majesty. You've come in here with purpose — let us hear it. You wouldn't interrupt unless it was the right course."

The murmurs that had started around the table thinned to silence. Even Luther's eyes narrowed, measuring rather than dismissing me. The shift was small, but I could feel it — the room tilting, waiting.

I drew in a breath. "I've consulted with Mina," I began, letting the name hang for a moment, "and Nymbria and I will take one ship, light crew, to intercept him where he's most likely to cross the sound. We'll board, retrieve Spencer and Juniper, and bring them home."

Several councilors straightened, the idea taking root. I pressed on before Luther could sour it. "Nymbria's command of the sea will let us slow their vessel and force them to comply. It's the only way to reach them before Scoria Bay does."

Greenhow gave a short nod, decisive enough to carry weight. "You have my support." His eyes swept the table. "And unless anyone here has a faster way to bring back the king alive, I suggest you give her yours."

A few reluctant nods followed, but Luther remained still, his jaw tight. At last, he exhaled sharply through his nose, like the words tasted bitter. "Fine. Do it your way, but if this fails—"

I cut across him before he could finish, my voice cold enough to frost the air between us. "If it fails, I lose my husband, and you only lose a king. Don't pretend the cost is the same."

The chamber went still, the weight of the words hanging between us. Luther's lips thinned, but he didn't argue.

The moment the council dismissed us, Nymbria and I were

already moving, our footsteps echoing down the marble corridor. The castle air smelled faintly of ink and candle smoke, but as soon as we pushed through the outer gates, the sharper tang of saltwater hit me, biting against the morning chill.

By the time we reached the docks, the tide was cresting, the water lapping high against the pilings. Nymbria's crew moved with crisp precision, ropes coiling, sails ready to catch the wind. The ship waited like a predator at rest, and for the first time since dawn, I felt a sliver of hope.

The crew moved quickly, lines snapping into place, the slap of canvas filling the air as we caught the wind. The tide favored us, and with Nymbria's magic in the water beneath our hull, the river carried us faster than nature alone could manage.

I kept glancing at the sun, trying to will it to stay high, to keep us from chasing shadows. Every minute we lost felt like one Spencer and Juniper might not have.

The first hour passed with the sun hard against my eyes, its reflection flashing like molten coins off the water. The rooftops of Tathlamar fell away behind us, the spires shrinking to thin strokes of shadow. I kept telling myself that if we were already out of sight of the city, we were making good time.

By the second hour, the banks had closed in — tall firs leaning over the water, branches whispering in the wind. A heron took flight ahead of us, wings cutting the air in slow, deliberate beats before it vanished upstream. The smell of salt was faint but there, enough to make my heart twist with urgency.

We didn't talk much. The hours blurred into a rhythm of creak, snap, and splash, broken only by the occasional shout from the crew. I paced when I could, circling the deck like a caged thing, counting the pull of the oars and the stretch of the sails. Once, a sailor offered me tea from a dented tin cup, and I took it just for something to do with my hands. It was bitter and too strong, but it kept them warm.

By the fourth hour, shadows had started to lengthen. The forest pulled darker across the banks, and the wind rattled the rigging with a sharpness that made me flinch. Nymbria's gaze kept sweeping the horizon, jaw tight, the lines around her mouth deepening as the light began to fade.

By the fifth, the gold was bleeding from the sky, clouds bruising purple. The air turned colder, the salt sharper, until I knew without looking that we were close to the mouth of the river. I hated that night was coming. Night meant cover for them, for whoever else might be out there. Night meant we'd be hunting blind.

The sky was burning gold at the edges when the last line of trees gave way to the wide open dark of the sound.

"Want me to light the sky?" I asked, thinking it might help us find them faster.

She shook her head. "Keep everyone off my back and I can find them without it."

Nymbria moved to the rail, waiting for the next spray to break over the hull. When it did, she closed her eyes, the sheen of saltwater glistening on her skin. The deck quieted around her as if the crew knew instinctively not to break her focus.

I stood a pace away, fists tight at my sides, counting heartbeats. The minutes stretched, heavy and elastic, until my jaw ached from clenching it.

Her eyes snapped open. "Got them." The words came with a flash of certainty that unclenched something in my chest.

"Why didn't you tell me you could do this back at Lummi Island?" I asked, a little sharper than I meant.

Her smile was quick and sad. "You ran off before I could."

Heat climbed into my face. I looked away before she could read it.

She shouted the new direction to her crew, and the ship heeled as we caught a fresh angle of wind. Thirty minutes of tense, silent sailing later, the horizon ahead blurred with the deep green of land. My stomach knotted.

She called for another splash, another reading. I watched her brows furrow, her mouth set in a line that was nothing like the earlier confidence.

"Problem?" My voice was thin, too high.

She didn't answer — just barked for another course correction. We swung hard again, sails snapping, the crew moving fast. I stayed at her side, scanning the horizon until my eyes watered. Still nothing but waves and the dark line of distant shore.

The third time she reached for the water, the wind caught her hair and tangled it across her face. She stood absolutely still, eyes closed, listening for something I couldn't hear. Then, so softly I almost missed it, she whispered, "Something's wrong."

I followed her to the stern, my heart already hammering in my throat. She leaned over the rail, telescope up, scanning every inch of the horizon like she could force the ship to appear through will alone.

"The water's lying to me," she said finally, and her voice cracked. "It's not working. Mina was wrong."

Panic hit like cold water. '*Mina.*'

'*Why isn't it working? What went wrong?*' I hurled the words into the bond between us, sharp and frantic.

Her reply didn't come fast enough. I stood there on the deck, every wave slapping the hull feeling like a countdown.

Then her presence slid into my mind, steadier than my own pulse. '*Bel is interfering. He's already found Spencer and Juniper. Head back to Elthas and stay on land overnight. It's not safe to be in the sea tonight. He will send ships for you.*'

I turned to Nymbria and saw in her face that Mina had told her the same thing. She nodded once, the motion brisk and pained, and shouted for a new course.

"We will find him," she said to me, low but fierce. "I promise."

The harbor lights bobbed against the dark as Nymbria guided us toward shore, the briny wind carrying the sound of gulls settling for the night. Our ship had barely brushed the dock before a broad-shouldered man in a patched coat stepped forward, waving both arms.

"No mooring here," he called over the creak of ropes and wood. "We've no berth for you—"

I stepped to the rail before he could finish. "I am Queen Lyla of Elthas," I said, voice carrying sharp across the water. "Your berth is ours for the night. Name your price for the inconvenience, and it will be met."

He hesitated, eyes darting between the crest on our flag and the steel at the crew's belts. "Well... aye, Your Majesty. If it's just for the night—"

"Thank you," I said, letting some of the steel in my voice soften. "I know this is unexpected, and I appreciate your help in making room for us."

His shoulders eased, and with a quick nod, he stepped aside to let the crew secure the mooring lines.

"Now," I added, "send for your police chief at once."

By the time the uniformed man arrived, coat buttoned high against the chill, my command was ready. "Tonight, your watch will double at the docks. Any uninvited ships attempting to make landfall will be turned away... or detained."

The chief's brow furrowed. "Trouble coming, Majesty?"

I met his gaze. "If we're lucky, it'll pass us by. But I won't gamble lives on luck."

Something in his expression shifted—concern, yes, but also resolve. He gave a sharp nod. "Then we'll be ready. I'll put my best men on it myself. We've a hundred new soldiers arrived by land earlier today. Docks will be sealed tighter than a coffin lid."

"Good," I said. "Now, point us to the nearest inn with rooms to spare."

The man led us a few winding streets inland, past shuttered shops and oil lamps swaying in the evening wind, until we reached a squat stone inn with warm light spilling from its windows. Inside, the innkeeper lit up at the sight of us, bowing so deeply his apron nearly brushed the floor.

"Of course, of course, we'll find room for Your Majesty and her party. Only—" he wrung his hands—"we don't have many rooms open tonight. Trade season, you understand."

Nymbria and I exchanged a glance before he handed over a single brass key.

When we reached the room—a small, tidy space with one

low bed draped in a faded quilt—Nymbria's mouth curved in a teasing smile. "Looks like we'll be cozy."

I shook my head, pushing the door open wider. "It's fine. We'll both sleep here."

She leaned on the frame. "I could take the hammock back on the ship. I'm used to it."

"A good night's sleep will matter for whatever comes tomorrow," I said firmly.

Her brow knit in gentle challenge. "Still, I wouldn't feel comfortable, knowing that the king and princess aren't my biggest fans."

I turned to her fully. "Please. I don't want to be alone if he…" My throat tightened, but I forced the words out. "If Bel reaches out again."

Her eyes searched mine for a long moment, whatever argument she'd had softening into something else. "Alright."

Later, when we lay down, the mattress dipped under her weight, the faint creak loud in the quiet room. I faced the wall, listening to her shift once, then twice—until her arm slid around my waist, her body a warm, steady line against my back.

"It's going to be all right," she murmured, the low rumble of her voice sinking into me as surely as her touch.

I meant to keep still, to keep the space between us, but the steadiness of her breathing and the strength in her hold coaxed me to ease back into her. She began to hum—a deep, resonant note that vibrated through her chest and into my spine. The sound curled through me like the tide pulling at the shore, stirring something I didn't dare name.

With anyone else, I'd have worried this might slide toward something charged, something tangled with unspoken want. But with Nymbria, I wasn't sure if it was our shared godhood, or something else entirely. All I felt from her was a comforting warmth, as if she were a long-lost older sister, holding me steady while I fought to keep my fear for Spencer from swallowing me whole.

My skin prickled under the sound, my pulse falling into rhythm with hers. The warmth of her hand spread through the thin fabric of my nightdress, the faint brush of her thumb just shy of absentminded. I wasn't sure if she knew she was doing it.

I let my eyes close, letting the scent of salt and wind from her hair mingle with the quiet promise in her touch. For tonight, I allowed myself to lean into it—to let her hold back the night for me.

CHAPTER 20

I woke to the dull gray of an overcast sky spilling through the inn's shutters, the air heavy enough to press on my ribs. Pulling the blanket tighter, I closed my eyes and reached for Mina the way I had half the night—sending thoughts like pebbles into still water, waiting for the ripple of her voice in return. *Mina... where are you? What's happening?*

Silence.

We took turns in the washroom, steam curling into the hall between our comings and goings. Each time the door clicked shut behind her, I found myself staring at the floorboards, listening for some whisper from Mina that never came. The silence was its own answer, and it chilled me.

Across the room, Nymbria was tugging on her boots. "Any luck?" I asked.

When Nymbria emerged, her damp hair clinging to her cheek, I asked, "Any luck?"

Her head shook once, slow. "No. I've been calling to her since dawn." She glanced toward the shuttered window, jaw tight. "Feels like shouting into the wind."

By the time we made it down to the shared dining room, the smell of fried fish and buttered bread clung to the air, heavy as the fog still pressing in on my mind. Mina's silence hadn't lifted, and every step felt like moving through a dream where sound didn't quite reach me.

The moment we stepped through the doorway, conversation faltered for just a brief moment before the room erupted. Chairs scraped back, boots scuffed against the floorboards, voices tumbled over each other. A handful of people surged toward me, hands darting out with plates, cups, folded napkins.

"Allow me, Your Majesty—"

"Here, let me carry that—"

"What can we do for you today?"

The heat of their bodies, the scrape of their voices—it all pressed in, too loud, too close. I forced my smile into place and kept my tone steady. "I'm here on military business. I'm afraid there isn't anything you can help with."

It should have been enough. A few retreated, murmuring their disappointment, but two stayed rooted at my elbows, expectant, as if waiting for me to name a task that could turn them into heroes. Their silent, hungry stares made the back of my neck prickle. I wondered what they saw, was there an omen in their queen's unannounced arrival, a shadow of bad news without the words to name it?

I'd barely taken three bites before a man in a lieutenant's uniform cut through the crowd. The weight of his boots carried over the low murmur of the room, and when he stopped at our table, he inclined his head with the rigid precision of military habit.

"My apologies for the interruption, Your Majesty. What business can I assist with?"

I exhaled slowly, the pieces clicking into place. The ones who'd slipped away earlier must have gone straight to the garrison.

"I appreciate your attention," I said, glancing toward Nymbria. She only shrugged, lips tugging into a faint, knowing smile, as though the fuss amused her. "But I'm with the naval vessel here. We'll be departing this morning."

The lieutenant's jaw tightened. He gave a short nod and left without another word.

Nymbria pushed her chair back. "I'll get the crew ready."

"I'll come."

We walked the short distance to the docks, the wind sharper than yesterday, tangling my hair and threading the air with the faint salt of the tide. My stomach felt as unsettled as the water—every step toward the ship another reminder that Mina still hadn't answered us.

Once aboard, I found Nymbria watching the crew make ready. "Can you show me to a desk with pen and paper," I said, my voice tighter than I meant. "I need to send Amyra a message. Even if they can't reply, they should have updates."

She led me to her quarters, the low cabin smelling faintly of oil, brine, and the hemp bite of sea-worn rope. Without a word, she left me at the desk.

I sat, fingers hovering over the blank page for a long moment. So many things I wanted to say, but each thought pulled me too close to the fears I'd been holding back. Amyra didn't need my dread weighing on her, not while she was at home, waiting, even more helpless than me. I tried to imagine her morning. Would she walk the gardens to settle her nerves, perhaps sit with Ivy over tea, or pace the corridors listening for footsteps that won't be coming?

The words I finally put to paper were the safest I could give her: *Nothing yet. I hope you're safe. My arm's improving—Nymbria will try to heal it daily. I'll write again soon.*

The sentences looked thin, pale shadows of everything I felt. But at least they wouldn't keep her awake at night, staring into the dark like I had.

I sealed the page with wax, whispered the incantation, and watched it vanish from my palm. One more piece of myself gone into the unknown.

When I stepped back onto the deck, the town was already shrinking against the coastline, the sails taut with wind. I found Nymbria at the helm, her posture rigid, eyes pinned to the horizon as though daring it to change.

"What course?" I asked.

Nymbria's gaze swept over me, sharp as a captain inspecting

a deck. Then she shook her head. "Your energy's all wrong. These sailors will insist I should toss you overboard with your fears. If you can't mask them, best you hole up in my office so they don't catch on."

I nodded, forcing a deeper breath past the knot in my chest. "I don't know how to shift the energy. Suggestions?"

Her dark brows rose, then dipped in a mischievous wiggle. Without warning, she threw her head back and launched into a shanty, her voice rich and rolling like the tide:

Hoist up the sail and let her fly,

We'll chase the sun 'til it falls from the sky!

One more wave and the shore's in sight,

Sing, lads, sing, through the salt and night!

The deckhands roared their approval, catching the verses without missing a beat. Soon the air throbbed with stomps and laughter, the rhythm of boots on planks keeping time with the slap of the waves. The joy in it was infectious, and though I didn't know the words to half the refrains, I found myself smiling before the second verse was done.

It didn't take long for the ship to cross the sound, wide as it was. The wind had shifted in our favor, carrying us faster than I wanted toward the jagged silhouettes of the Scoria Bay islands. Each passing minute pulled them closer, dark shapes rising from the water like teeth. My pulse drummed higher, each beat loud in my ears.

Then—his voice slid into my skull, slick and poisonous.

'*I have your darling husband. He's so quiet, though. At least, he's trying to be.*' A low chuckle curled through the words, mocking. '*But gods, he can be such a screamer when I really get him going.*'

My stomach heaved, bile rushing to the back of my throat. I clenched the rail hard enough my knuckles burned white, fighting the urge to retch over the side. Nymbria glanced at me once, sharp-eyed, but I shook my head. Not here. Not in front of the crew.

A shout broke across the deck. "Ship on the horizon!"

The crew snapped to life, boots pounding against planks

as men rushed to their stations. Cannons groaned into place. Nymbria was already at the rail, spyglass raised, her jaw tight.

"Scoria Bay colors," she barked. "Battle positions!"

I felt the crew's energy spike like flint to steel. Powder horns uncorked, steel drawn, the air thick with readiness. My own magic flickered at my palms, the ghost of fire begging to be loosed.

Then, movement. The enemy ship hoisted a white flag.

Nymbria lifted her hand. "Stand ready, but hold."

The crew froze in place, weapons raised but waiting. The Scoria ship glided closer, sails fat with wind, until its hull swung broadside. A line of small, square flags unfurled along the rigging—nearly two dozen in a row, bright blocks of color snapping against the breeze.

"What do those mean?" I asked, voice low.

"Flag code," Nymbria said, already calling out, "Ryxan!"

The first mate hurried over, slate in hand, eyes already fixed on the pattern. Nymbria leaned close to me, her tone clipped. "It's how big ships talk. Short messages, simple instructions, all by color and shapes."

Ryxan scribbled quickly, then straightened. "It spells out: We will escort you to Blyn."

Nymbria's expression didn't ease. "Cannons away, but keep men at the ports," she ordered. Her voice cut sharp through the wind. "Appear friendly, but do not trust."

The Scoria Bay ship took the lead, setting its course for shore. Nymbria's crew mirrored every turn, keeping their distance like a shadow refusing to touch its source. My skin prickled with every yard we closed.

By the time the harbor rose before us, flags waved from the pier, signaling us inward. The escort slowed, guiding us into the central dock. But no one waited for us there. Not a single official, only a handful of dockhands. Just empty planks stretching ahead, still and silent.

Enemy territory should never welcome us so quietly. Not in the middle of a war.

Finn appeared then, moving with the kind of controlled urgency that made my pulse jump. He'd kept his distance for the whole voyage, as if his proximity might set me off, but now his voice was low and firm. "No one steps off this ship until we have a full escort. I don't care who's shows up to greet us."

Nymbria didn't argue, only gave a single nod. I stayed silent too, my skin prickling as the unease crept higher. Something was coming. I could feel it in my bones, and none of it felt right.

It took twenty long minutes, but Finn rounded up six of the biggest men on the crew. They came bristling with weapons, blades glinting, rifles slung loose at their shoulders. Finn ordered three down the gangway first. Then Nymbria and I followed, his presence a wall of heat at my back, the last three closing in behind us.

Once on the pier, the formation tightened. The three men ahead carved the way forward, while Nymbria and Finn flanked me, close enough I could feel the brush of their shoulders. Every angle of me was covered, every step shielded. For the first time since we'd sighted the Bay, I felt the smallest flicker of gratitude, that maybe I wasn't walking into this alone.

But the docks themselves were deserted. No bustle of laborers, no patrols, not even a single fisherman mending a net. Only the creak of wood and the faint slap of water against pylons. The silence pressed down, suffocating.

We kept moving, boots echoing hollow on the boards until they struck the firmer dirt road beyond. A handful of buildings huddled there, weathered and sagging, their shutters hanging crooked. Beyond them, a squat fortress crowned the hill—stone darkened by salt air, its narrow windows staring down like watchful eyes.

A door banged open. A man stepped out, uniform stiff, decorations flashing dull in the gray light. His face was carved with lines that spoke of years in service, but his posture carried the sharp arrogance of someone who believed he already owned us.

"Only three continue from here," he said, his voice clipped, carrying easily across the thin stretch of land. "Her Majesty may choose. You will meet your host in the castle."

The word host lodged sharp in my chest. My mind spun with possibilities I didn't dare give voice to. Was it him, waiting in those stone walls? The one who had whispered in my mind, taunted me with Spencer's screams? My stomach twisted. Every instinct screamed to turn back, to flee to the safety of the ship. But Finn's glare was already burning at the man, and Nymbria's hand brushed my arm, steady and wordless. I forced my chin high, though my pulse was racing so hard I thought they'd hear it.

"We don't leave our guard behind." Finn sneered at him. "If you want a meeting, you'll take all of us through those gates."

The officer didn't flinch. He only shrugged, lips curling in mock sympathy. "Then we'll slit the throats of the Elthians we've already taken. No burden to us." His eyes locked on Finn, sharp and daring. "Your choice, sailor."

My mouth went dry. I could feel Finn's fury vibrating off him, his glare promising violence. And yet, when his gaze slid to me, I only managed a small shake of my head. Please, don't push this.

I should have spoken. I was queen. My word was law. But standing there on enemy soil, the weight of their power pressing in, I felt stripped of it—like a child in borrowed finery, out of place and far too small. My tongue held still, my silence its own betrayal.

Finally, I found enough voice to rasp, "Nymbria. Finn. You'll come with me."

The others stiffened, unwilling to leave. Nymbria didn't give them a chance to argue. "Back to the ship," she commanded, each word clipped as steel. "No one leaves it without Ryxan's order."

Reluctance dragged in their feet, but one by one they obeyed. I watched them retreat down the pier, one man walking backward the whole way, his eyes locked on me until the fog swallowed him. The ache in my chest tightened.

The officer's gaze lingered until the last man vanished from sight. Only then did he turn back, satisfaction gleaming in his weathered face. "Follow. Now."

He pivoted, boots striking the stone road with a clipped rhythm. We fell in behind him, his pace unrelenting. The climb came steep and fast, a staircase cut into the rock itself, each step echoing like a drumbeat.

My legs burned almost immediately, breath dragging too shallow in my chest. I forced myself to keep stride, chin high, praying Nymbria and Finn wouldn't notice the strain in my steps. A queen should climb without faltering. A goddess should never pant like a novice soldier.

But I wasn't thinking only of myself. With every step, images shoved their way into my mind—Spencer bound somewhere in this fortress, teeth gritted against pain. Juniper too, though my mind struggled to picture her enduring this as stoically. Was she even alive? Did Bel keep her breathing just to bait us here?

The higher we climbed, the tighter my chest grew—not only from the steep ascent but from the thought that I was walking willingly into his hands, each step pulling me farther from the chance to save them.

The fortress loomed closer, its black stone walls jagged against the gray sky. Shadows seemed to deepen in its cracks, swallowing what little light the day still offered. My pulse thundered in my ears. I stole a glance at Finn's jaw, locked tight, at Nymbria's measured stare on the officer's back. They looked unshaken. I could not let them see how close I was to unraveling.

So I straightened, hid the tremor in my breath, and climbed.

CHAPTER 21

The gates groaned as they opened, the iron grinding like a warning. Beyond them stretched a courtyard too neat, too polished—the hedges clipped into precise shapes, the paving stones swept clean of even a fallen leaf. Empty. That was the most unsettling part. A fortress in wartime should have been alive with soldiers, with clangs of steel, with footsteps echoing against stone. Instead, the silence pressed on my ears, unnatural as a held breath.

We followed the officer, walking three abreast as soon as the path allowed it. My boots rang against the cobbles, too loud in the hush. I risked a glance toward Nymbria. Her brow knit faintly, her gaze sliding over the windows above us as if she expected a crossbow to jut out at any moment. Our eyes met, and though neither of us spoke, the worry passing between us was as sharp as a blade.

The heavy doors to the keep groaned open just before our guide reached them, slowly swinging inward as though unseen hands had been waiting for us. My skin prickled.

I'd kill to know what she's thinking, I thought, heart thudding.

'*Funny you say that…*' The voice slid into my skull like oil, slick and cold. Bel. '*She's just as terrified as you are. Delicious, isn't it? To feel how small you are? Mina can whisper about destiny all she wants. It won't save you when I finally face you.*'

My stomach lurched. Without thought, my fingers shot out, clutching Nymbria's hand like an anchor.

Her head snapped toward me. She searched my face, brows lifting in confusion. No fear crossed her features, just confusion.

"What is it?" she breathed, low enough only I could hear.

I tapped my temple, too rattled for words. Understanding flickered in her eyes. She squeezed my hand. "We will find him," she murmured, steady as stone. "I promise."

Her quick embrace was brief but grounding, and when we broke apart, the cold still clung to me. But at least it didn't feel quite so suffocating.

Inside, the air was worse.

The corridor swallowed us in shadow, lined with tapestries so dark I couldn't tell if they were meant to be this dark, or were just drowned in soot. The stones seemed to sweat grime, the carpets worn thin and greasy underfoot. A smell of damp rot clung to everything, undercut by something sharper—old blood, I thought with a shudder. Did anyone actually live here, or had this place become little more than a tomb that hadn't realized it yet?

I strained my ears with every step, desperate for some sound. A muffled cry. The scrape of chains. Anything to tell me Spencer and Juniper were here. Instead, the silence pressed harder. My stomach rolled with the thought of what they might have endured already—days, maybe weeks in captivity. What state would they be in when, if, we found them?

Breathe. Just breathe.

The officer stopped before a narrow door and shoved it open. "You will wait here," he said, voice flat. The chamber beyond was a study, the air stale with ink and mildew. Shelves sagged with books, their spines curling, and papers spilled across a desk like discarded feathers.

He fixed us with a look sharp enough to cut. "Do not leave this room for any reason. If you do, you may share the fate of those who came before you."

The words sank like stones in my chest as he left, shutting us in.

I sank onto a low sofa, clasping my hands together so tightly my knuckles ached. If I let myself think too much, I'd lose what little was left of my breakfast.

Nymbria and Finn didn't sit. They split the room between them in silence, a soldier and a captain falling into their own rhythms. Finn began rifling through the desk, pages rasping as he tossed them aside one by one. "Useless," he muttered, jaw tight, before stalking to the far wall to search again.

Nymbria drifted along the shelves, her fingertips brushing the spines as though she were idly browsing. But her gaze was too sharp, lingering a half-second too long on the warped leather of a binding, on the seams where dust gathered thicker than it should have. I watched the way her shoulders stayed taut, the way her head tilted ever so slightly at the glint of a lock on a cabinet drawer. To anyone else, she looked calm. I knew she was hunting.

I sat rigid on the sofa, hands clenched in my lap until the nails pressed crescents into my palms. The silence pressed heavy, deeper than I thought stone walls should allow. No footsteps. No clatter of armor. No voices bleeding through the door. It was as if the castle itself held its breath, waiting for us to break first.

'*Mina?*' I sent the thought like a flare into the dark, holding it until my temples throbbed. Nothing. Was she too far to hear? Or was she watching and choosing not to answer?

I pushed harder, trying another path. '*Spencer?*' I closed my eyes, reaching inwards the way I had before, hoping for even the faintest trace of him. Some spark, some thread. Was he thinking of me? Did he know I was here? Or had he already given up, convinced I'd never come? The thought turned my stomach, Juniper's desperate face flashing in my mind. Had she told him she'd sent word? Or had he been left in the dark, not even knowing a rescue was possible?

A wet warmth touched the back of my hand. I startled, glancing down. A teardrop glistened on my skin. Another followed, and another, pattering against my sleeve. I hadn't even noticed the tears slipping free. My throat burned as I swiped at my face, smearing the damp into the coarse fabric of my sleeve.

I kept my eyes fixed on the door, willing it to open, praying it wouldn't.

The sofa dipped under a sudden weight. I blinked, startled, and found Finn lowering himself beside me, his bulk crowding the space without apology. His eyes stayed on the far wall, but his voice came low, barely a whisper.

"Don't let them see you break," he murmured. His hands rested on his knees, knuckles scarred from too many brawls, but I felt the warmth of his shoulder pressing against mine. "That's what they want."

I swallowed, the tears blurring my vision again. "What if we're already too late?" The words scraped out, brittle as glass.

Finn tilted his head, the faintest shake. "Spencer's too damn stubborn to go out without a fight. If he's in this place, he'll hold. He'll fight. You've got to do the same."

A breath shuddered out of me, half a sob, half a laugh at the rough certainty in his tone. I dared a glance at him. His jaw was set, but when his eyes flicked to mine, there was a softness there I'd never noticed before, along with an unspoken vow, fierce in its simplicity.

"We'll get him back," he said, so quiet it was almost part of the stone itself. "Both of them. You're not alone in this."

I pressed my sleeve to my face again, nodding because I couldn't find words. But I let myself lean into the heat of his arm, just a fraction, the smallest tether in a room that felt like it was trying to unmake me.

The door creaked open.

I froze, heart pounding against my ribs. Damn it—I should've kept listening, should've felt the shift in the air before the hinges groaned. Footsteps crossed the threshold, unhurried, confident.

And then he was there.

Egan.

I surged to my feet, the breath tearing sharp from my lungs. "You've got a lot of nerve—" My voice cracked with rage, my hands trembling despite how tightly I balled them.

He lifted his palms in mock surrender, a grin spreading too

easily across his face. "Whoa there, Lyla. Easy now. No need to get so serious, remember?"

The words struck like a lash. Frederick's words. Twisted. Claimed. My vision went white-hot for a heartbeat, that dinner flashing back—the lightning, the smell of charred flesh, Frederick crumpled on the floor. I drew in long, shaky breaths, every inhale a battle not to hurl myself at him, not to give him what he wanted.

Nymbria's voice cut in, cool and sharp. "Who are you?"

Only then did Egan's gaze flick lazily over my companions, like he'd only just noticed them. "Prince Egan, son of King Jerome of Scoria Bay." He offered a shallow bow that mocked the gesture more than honored it. "I was sent to greet our... distinguished guests. Extend an olive branch, perhaps. End this nasty little war."

My laugh came out bitter, sharp as glass. "End it? You started it, you little shit stain." My words snapped before I could leash them. "All because your fragile pride couldn't handle rejection."

He scoffed, tilting his head like he was humoring a child. "Is that truly what you think? Come now, Lyla. Be honest with yourself."

He strolled toward the desk, every step a performance, and slid into the chair like it was a throne. With a flick of his fingers, he stacked the scattered papers neatly, as though tidying up a stage.

I spat, the glob landing inches from his hand.

Nymbria's grip found my good arm instantly, firm but kind. "Hey." Her voice dropped low, urgent. "I know. I know. But we need to handle this right."

I didn't tear my gaze from him. "Where is he?" The words were a growl.

One brow arched in feigned puzzlement. "He?"

"My husband," I snapped. The word cracked through the air like a whip.

"Oh." His grin widened, serpentine. "Yes, I'm right here, my dove." He spread his arms like an actor playing to an audience. "Though I must say, you're looking a bit worse for wear. That arm..." His eyes lingered, hungry. "Why don't you come closer, let me have a look?"

Finn moved before I could, his bulk interposing like a wall. His hand came back, palm raised to keep me behind him. A shield and a promise.

I didn't need it. I had no intention of stepping near that snake.

Egan leaned back in the chair, a flicker of irritation breaking through his polished mask. His grin sharpened, wolfish. "Ah. The guard dog." His gaze swept Finn slowly, deliberately, as though measuring whether he'd snap or heel. "Brave enough to stand in the way, but never smart enough to know when he's outmatched."

Finn didn't flinch, didn't even blink. His stance only widened, steady as bedrock.

Egan's eyes narrowed, voice dropping to something quieter, more intimate—and far more dangerous. "Careful, sailor. You keep blocking my view, and I might start wondering what I'll carve out of you first."

The threat slithered through the air, cold and heavy, settling like iron in my chest. I clenched my fists, the fire in me surging, barely restrained.

But Finn never wavered. He stood rooted, a wall of flesh and will, and in that silence, his refusal said more than any words could.

Egan leaned back in the chair, the smirk returning, though thinner now, sharpened. He tapped two fingers idly against the polished wood of the desk, as if weighing what piece of us he wanted to play with next.

"Well then," he drawled, eyes sliding past Finn to land on me again, "since your hound won't step aside, I suppose I'll just speak over him. Tell me, Lyla—how many nights have you lain awake wondering what your precious husband sounds like when he screams?"

The words hit like a knife under the ribs. Heat flared in my chest, rage and terror colliding until I couldn't tell which was which. My nails bit into my palms as I lunged off the sofa, desperate to get to him, to inflict physical pain that matched the emotional pain coursing through me. I could almost feel the crackle of fire waiting in my blood, begging to be unleashed.

Nymbria's hand brushed mine, subtle, grounding. "Don't give him what he wants," she murmured, so low only I could hear.

Egan's grin widened, seeing the struggle. "Ah, there it is. The flicker behind your eyes. Bel was right—you're so easy to rattle. One mention of the little consort, and you're already halfway to burning this whole room down."

I forced a breath through clenched teeth. "Where. Is. He?"

Egan leaned forward, elbows braced on the desk, chin resting in his hands as though he had all the time in the world. "Still breathing," he said smoothly, "for now."

And then—

The sound hit me, deep inside my head. Spencer's voice, jagged and raw, echoing with the same tinny distortion Bel always carried when he wormed his way into my mind. A scream dragged through pain, cracking into silence, then another, louder, broken.

My chest seized. My body rejected breath. Bel. He's actively torturing Spencer.

My knees buckled. The world tilted, blurred. A sob ripped out before I could choke it down.

Nymbria caught me before I hit the floor, arms firm, pulling me close as we sunk back into the sofa, as though her steadiness could shield me from the assault. My nails dug into her sleeve, clinging, but the sound kept tearing through my head, Spencer's agony replaying until I thought I'd shatter with it.

Finn stepped forward, a snarl rumbling low in his throat, his glare locked on Egan. "Enough."

Egan's eyes glinted like polished steel, cruel delight curving his mouth. He rose from the desk with unhurried grace, smoothing his coat as though nothing in this room carried consequence. His steps echoed too loudly against the stone floor as he closed the distance.

"Show me the arm," he said lightly, almost bored.

Finn shifted instantly, his body blocking mine, his shoulders squared like a barricade.

Egan tilted his head, smirk sharpening. "Careful, guard dog. Do you really want to make him scream again? All because you won't let me look?" His words slithered toward me, the threat weighted and undeniable.

Another jagged echo of Spencer's voice lanced through my mind, fainter this time, but enough to make bile rise in my throat. I swallowed hard and forced myself to lift my chin.

"It's fine," I rasped, nodding once to Finn. My throat burned with the lie, but if enduring Egan's scrutiny spared Spencer another shred of torment, I would.

Nymbria's hand found mine, her grip firm, grounding, and I clung to it with everything left in me. With my good arm tight in hers, I let Egan see the other.

I lifted my bandaged limb, holding it stiffly between us. My pulse thudded against the wrappings, and every instinct screamed at me to pull back, to run. But I stood my ground, nails biting into Nymbria's palm as Egan's shadow fell over me.

Egan crouched slightly, his eyes sweeping over the wrappings with surprising focus, his grin fading into something sharper, intent. "It's worse than I thought," he murmured. Then, softer, almost intimate: "May I?"

The question sent a shiver down my spine. He didn't reach. Just waited. His gaze flicked up, pinning me, patient in a way that was somehow worse than demand.

My lips parted, no sound coming. I didn't say yes, didn't say no. But I didn't pull back either. The smallest nod slipped free before I could stop it.

His mouth curved, satisfaction flickering across his face. Slowly, he lifted one hand, laying it over the bandages with almost reverent care.

Heat bloomed instantly, a radiant pulse spreading from his palm into my bones. It wasn't the searing agony of battle wounds or Amyra's tentative, searching mending. This was whole, precise. I felt the shards of bone knit themselves together, each thread fusing, nerves soothed, muscle smoothed clean. My breath caught as strength returned with unnatural ease. No pain. No struggle. Just… wholeness.

When he drew his hand back, I flexed instinctively—curling fingers, twisting wrist, rolling elbow. Perfect. Entirely restored, as though the injury had never been.

The marvel of it lasted only a heartbeat. Then I lifted my gaze, meeting his eyes with all the fury I could summon, my whisper cutting the air like a blade. "What are you?"

Egan's smirk returned, darker this time, curling with pride and something fouler beneath. "Wonderful things happen," he said, his voice silken with blasphemy, "when you pledge your soul to Bel."

A sharp scoff broke the air. Nymbria straightened at my side, her hand tightening around mine as if to anchor me. "Wonderful?" she echoed, her tone laced with disdain. "That's the word you use for shackling yourself to rot? For letting him crawl inside your skin like a parasite?"

Her eyes narrowed, cold and cutting. "I've seen men beg for scraps of magic from the depths before. It never ends with wonder. Only ruin."

Egan only tilted his head, amused, as though her contempt were nothing more than music to his ears.

I lifted my chin, my voice steady even as the fury inside me threatened to boil over. "I have no reason to pledge my soul to him," I said, my words low but sharp. "He's the one threatened by me, remember?"

For the first time, his smirk faltered. Just for a heartbeat—but I saw it. A flicker in his eyes, a tightening of his jaw. He leaned closer, too close, as if proximity might restore his advantage.

Finn's growl cut through the space between us, low and dangerous. He shifted forward, the bulk of his body sliding back into Egan's line of sight. "Step back, princeling," he said, voice rough as gravel. "Or I'll happily remind you what happens when a dog sinks its teeth in."

His smile was slow, deliberate, curling like smoke. "Ah, but that is precisely the game, isn't it? You'll know when you're allowed to know. Until then..." He spread his hands, mock-innocent, as though he were the very picture of a gracious host. "Their comfort, their treatment, depends entirely on you. Be gracious guests in my castle, as I was in yours."

The words struck something raw in me. I remembered how uneasy I'd felt with his presence in Elthas—every moment of it. The way the air had tightened around him at dinners, how my skin crawled at the thought of the would-be assassin sharing my roof while we scrambled for proof of his treachery. Worst of all, the tournament. I could still see him in the ring, his sword held over Spencer, the violence in his grin burning into my mind. I had lain awake that night, listening to the silence of the castle halls, knowing he was somewhere within them, sleeping safe and unpunished, and hating every second of it.

He leaned back against the desk now as though he owned the room. "Do you have any idea how much I despised Elthas?" His tone sharpened, venom bleeding into every syllable. "Paraded through your halls like a prize ox, forced to prance about in some ridiculous tournament—like I was meant to smile and preen, a pretty little trinket to hang on your arm. You." His gaze raked me, and the hatred in it was enough to make my skin crawl. "Me, reduced to that. Do you know how demeaning it was? How beneath me?"

Finn's voice cut in, low and biting. "You'd never rise high enough to be one of her toys, let alone her consort."

The words landed sharp as steel. But before I could even take in the barb, Nymbria turned on him with a glare that could've flayed skin from bone. It wasn't the time to cut into Egan's pride, not when every breath in this place might tip us into ruin.

Egan only sneered, clearly savoring the exchange. "And there it is. A dog barking for its master." His gaze swung back to me, colder, hungrier. "You don't understand, do you, Lyla? You've never understood. Why do you even think you should stand as my peer? My equal? You, a pretender queen, daring to believe yourself above men."

He straightened, eyes glittering with some inner spark, and then paused. His lips curved slowly, like a snake coiling before the strike. "Do you remember when we danced together? I knew, even then, how I would have loved to break your spirit." His head tilted, his expression sharpening with cruel delight. "Would you like a taste of what that might have been like?"

He took a step toward me, and instinct carried both Nymbria and Finn between us, shields of flesh and fury.

Egan clicked his tongue, the sound almost playful. "Careful now. Bel does so hate to be kept waiting. If you don't step aside, perhaps he'll find a little fun with your husband. Or Juniper. Tell me—do you really want to test how far his imagination goes?"

CHAPTER 22

My pulse hammered so loud it drowned out thought. Everything was unraveling too fast, too sharp—I couldn't keep hold of it. I needed space, just a breath to think, to find a way forward. But there was no room here. No air. Only the gnawing knowledge that Spencer and Juniper weren't near enough for me to hear them, that Bel had to force Spencer's cries into my skull. Gods, were they even in this fortress at all?

I dragged in a breath, steadying myself. "Egan," I said, forcing steel into the plea, "be reasonable. What will it take for me to see Spencer? To know he's alive?"

His smile was too quick, too practiced. "I could ask for that. It will take time." He let the pause linger, enjoying the hook. "Are you willing to pledge your loyalty to Bel?"

The word slammed into me like a trap snapping shut. "Is that the only way to see them freed?"

Egan tilted his head, as though tasting the thought on his tongue. "It's the only way I can offer."

Hope flickered, thin but sharp. If his only offer came from Bel's leash, then maybe… maybe there was another path. A way to cut the chain instead of bowing to it.

"So," I said carefully, eyes locking on his, "you swore your loyalty to him?"

Egan's chin lifted, pride swelling in his throat. He nodded once.

"And tell me," I pressed, voice cooling, "do you prefer being his toy instead of mine?"

His eyes widened, the mask cracking just enough to show the bruise beneath. "He does not treat me like a toy."

Nymbria's laugh cut the air, sharp as broken glass. She leaned back against the desk, every movement deliberate, as though she were the one holding court. "Are you sure? Because Bel sent you here to speak for him, didn't he? Surely this wasn't your idea—to rot in a dingy little castle, tucked away like a message boy." Her gaze swept down his body, her lip curling. "It's so… small."

A muscle jumped in Egan's jaw.

She tilted her head, voice dropping low, almost kind. "If you weren't a toy, you wouldn't have to ask him for permission just to let us see Spencer."

The words landed like a knife between his ribs, and I saw the flicker in his eyes—anger, shame, a flash of doubt he tried to smother.

The mask cracked. Egan's hand slammed against the desk, the sharp crack making me flinch. "Tell me, Lyla—have you degraded yourself so far that your only companions are pirates and Crystalford's castoffs?"

The words struck like arrows. Finn's jaw clenched hard enough I thought his teeth might shatter, while Nymbria's fingers tightened at her side, a flicker of unease crossing her otherwise calm face.

Egan's smile slithered back into place the instant he saw it. "Ah. I've struck a nerve." His gaze slid between them, savoring the discomfort like wine on his tongue. "Funny, isn't it? How quickly the truth crawls out when the right stone is overturned. The runaway bride, the loyal dog who followed her. Did you think Bel wouldn't whisper your little secrets to me?"

He leaned forward, elbows on the desk, eyes bright with cruel delight. "Tell me, how does it feel to have your king and queen's safety resting on the backs of two people whose very names are poison in their homelands?"

My blood surged hot. Before Nymbria could open her mouth, I stepped forward, fire snapping at my fingertips.

"Enough." My voice cut sharper than a blade. "You don't get to sneer at them, not when you've pledged yourself as Bel's pet." I took another step, my glare locking on his. "Nymbria and Finn have stood beside me when it mattered. They've bled for me, fought for me. What have you done, Egan? Other than hide behind Bel's shadow and call it strength?"

The words left me shaking, but I held my ground, refusing to let him see even a flicker of doubt.

Egan's smile cracked. "Bel's shadow?" he snarled, voice rougher, ragged at the edges. His hand twitched, and before I could move, a searing spark flared from his palm. Light burst across the room, catching the papers on the desk in a sudden whoosh of flame.

I jerked my arm forward on instinct, the fire within me leaping to my command. Heat slammed against heat, and the flames guttered, smoke curling as the blaze faltered. A second later, a hiss cut through the air—Nymbria flicked her wrist, a ribbon of seawater snapping into being from nowhere. It drenched the desk in a rush, smothering what embers remained.

Egan's jaw tightened, fury twisting his face.

Nymbria only smiled, slow and sharp, the kind that could cut. "Oh dear," she said sweetly, eyes never leaving his. "I do hope those weren't important. Paper tends to warp so dreadfully once it's been... soaked."

Her faux apology dripped with venom, her smirk daring him to try again.

Egan's glare flicked between the three of us, his jaw tight enough that the veins in his temple stood out. For a moment I thought he might lunge, might let the storm in him break loose right here. Instead, he sucked in a breath that shuddered through clenched teeth.

"You think this little game is clever?" His voice cracked with the effort of restraint. "You think mocking me makes you safe?"

His hands twitched at his sides, sparks still whispering across his fingertips like the last breaths of a dying flame. He leaned closer, his words low, guttural.

"I'll make you regret this."

The promise in it was jagged, ripped from somewhere raw and festering inside him. Then he whirled toward the door, flung it open hard enough that the door slammed on the wall. A guard straightened at once in the hall.

"Don't let them leave," Egan snapped, his voice shredding on the order. He didn't wait for a reply, just slammed the door with such force the shelves rattled, leaving the threat of his vow hanging in the dark room like smoke.

CHAPTER 23

For a long moment after the slam of the door, none of us moved. The echoes of Egan's boots bled into the walls, then faded, leaving only the hush of our breathing. My pulse was still drumming in my ears, sharp as drumbeats before a charge.

Nymbria broke first. She stepped into me without hesitation, arms firm and steady as iron bands. I leaned into her, the salt-and-smoke of her coat grounding me, and she whispered fiercely, "We will figure this out." The certainty in her voice made my throat ache.

Finn didn't waste a breath. He was already at the desk, yanking open drawers that screeched on their tracks, rifling through parchment and quills with rough hands. "Useless," he muttered, tossing aside a ledger before dropping to his knees. The chair scraped against the stone floor as he shoved it back, ducking under the desk, his curses muffled as wood thudded beneath his fists.

Nymbria's gaze tracked him, her brow furrowing. She pulled away from me just enough to turn. "You've had more training than me," she said quickly, eyes sharp on mine. "Can you sense anything here? Magic? Traps? A hidden door?"

I blinked at her, thrown. The room was just stone and

shadow to me. "Like… what exactly am I supposed to be feeling for?"

"Anything," she pressed, already sweeping her palms along the spines of books, tugging one, then another. "Hidden levers, compartments—some clue."

"I—no, nothing like that," I admitted, frustrated by my own uselessness. "But I can help search. Tell me what to look for."

"Anything out of place," Finn grunted, standing again, his shoulders tense with frustration.

"That's vague and unhelpful," I shot back, but still moved to the nearest wall, running my fingers along the cold stone, pressing into the seams.

For a time, the only sound was the scrape of leather boots and the thud of books reshelved. My eyes blurred against the gloom, and the silence in my head became unbearable. I swallowed hard. "Did you hear him too?" I whispered. My voice cracked. "Or was that just me?"

Finn's answer came flat, matter-of-fact. "We didn't hear anything." His jaw was tight. "I assume they were making Spencer scream, putting on a show for you."

The air in my lungs turned to glass. I couldn't force the words out, so I only nodded.

"We will find him," Nymbria said, low but certain, not looking up from where she dragged her fingers along the mortar cracks.

"I don't think he's here," I admitted. My hand trembled as I pressed against the wall. "If Bel has to push his voice into my head, then he's not close. They've taken him somewhere else."

Nymbria shook her head. "The water said he was here last." She tapped her temple lightly. "He's on this island. Somewhere."

The problem was, Scoria Bay's main island sprawled outward like a beast. Too much land. Too many places to hide.

I rubbed my palms together, trying to steady the shake. "The mountains here—how hard would it be to cross to another town overland?"

"On foot? Days," Nymbria said grimly. "Even on horseback, you'd be crawling. Treacherous ground."

"So where then?" My voice rose despite myself. "They're not stringing him up in the woods. Where could he be?"

Finn straightened, his eyes hard. "First task is our own freedom. Hate to say it, Lyla, but we're not much better off than he is right now."

The thought hollowed me out. I pressed a hand to my chest, meeting them both in turn. "Don't let them take you from me," I begged, my voice raw. "Either of you. I'll do whatever I can to stop it—but promise me we won't split up."

Nymbria's sea-blue eyes softened, and Finn's roughened hand clenched into a fist. They answered in unison, their voices overlapping like an oath.

"We won't."

Eventually the search dwindled into silence. Books sat skewed in their shelves, the desk lay gutted of its drawers, and not one hidden latch or whispered secret had revealed itself. Defeat pressed heavy as stone.

We gathered at the sofa, slumping into the sagging cushions. Nymbria slid between us, the heat of her shoulder brushing mine on one side and Finn's on the other, as though she could anchor both of us by sheer will.

"How do we get free?" The words tumbled out before I could stop them, brittle as glass. "We can't even leave this room without walking into danger."

Finn's gaze flicked to Nymbria. He gave her the smallest nudge with his elbow, and the look they exchanged was sharp and silent, an argument passing between them without sound. I sat frozen, caught outside of it, my stomach churning with the knowledge that there was something they weren't saying.

At last, Nymbria exhaled, long and heavy. "We've got daylight through that window." She nodded toward the narrow slit high in the wall, where a pale ribbon of sun stretched thin across the carpet. "I'll wait until dusk starts to settle. If they don't bring food, and if no one comes to talk, then…" She hesitated, jaw flexing. "…then I'll do it."

My heart skipped. "Do what?"

Finn answered for her, his voice rough with a dangerous kind of satisfaction. "The water gifted her. And blood is water." His eyes glimmered, a predator's twinkle barely leashed.

I stared at Nymbria, my lips parting. "Wait—you can…" I couldn't even finish the thought.

"I can reach inside them." Her voice was steady, almost too calm. "I can stop them cold. Or worse, if I have to."

The room felt smaller, the air thinner. I bit my lip hard enough to taste iron. Then I shook my head. "Not like that. Don't kill them."

Her head snapped toward me, shock flashing across her face. For a heartbeat she looked betrayed.

"We don't know why they're here," I pressed on. "If they're forced. If they've got families. We can't become monsters—not like him."

Nymbria's sea-colored eyes went glassy, the sharpness softening into something that hurt to look at. Slowly, she nodded. "Only what's necessary."

The silence thickened, stretching long enough that the scrape of fabric against the sofa felt deafening. Dust motes drifted in the dying shaft of light slanting through the narrow window, their slow spin marking the hours slipping past.

When the sky began to bruise with dusk, I pushed to my feet, drawn to the slit of stone like a moth to flame. Pressing close, I watched the last ribbons of sunlight dissolve into shadow. My palms flattened against the cold sill. It felt like standing at the edge of something irreversible.

Behind me, Nymbria's voice broke the stillness. Low, quiet, but steady. "Are you ready?"

My throat went dry. I forced myself to breathe, slow and deep, and then gave a single nod. When I turned back, her eyes had already begun to shimmer, faint glimmers catching the dim light—like moonlight refracting on water.

The air shifted. A pressure pressed against my ears, the same way it did before a storm rolled in. Outside the door came muffled thuds—soft, sudden, and heavy. Bodies.

My mouth opened. "What—"

"Shh." Both Nymbria and Finn hushed me at once, their attention locked on the corridor beyond. We held our breath, listening. No shuffle of boots followed. No shouts. Only silence.

At last, Nymbria gave a small nod to Finn. His hand went to his thigh, and to my shock, a knife slid free from a hidden sheath stitched into his trousers. The blade caught what little light remained, a whisper of steel against the gloom.

Finn moved first, every step deliberate. The door creaked as he eased it open. He glanced left, then right, shoulders tight, before gesturing us forward. The hall was clear.

We slipped out, shadows gliding into deeper shadows. At the end of the corridor, a staircase loomed, spiraling into unknown depths above and below. Finn paused, knife angled low. "Up, or down?"

Both he and Nymbria turned to me. My pulse stuttered. "I've never done a rescue mission," I whispered. "You're the ones that seem to know what to do. You tell me."

Nymbria's mouth curved, not quite a smile but close enough to soften her sharp features. "Down," she decided.

She led, her steps so precise the stone barely whispered under her boots. We followed, hugging the outer curve of the wall, cloaked in the staircase's shadows. Each turn of the spiral tightened my chest, the air cooler, damper, the weight of the castle pressing down.

At the bottom, the stairwell ended in a narrow landing and a heavy door barred with iron. We stopped. The silence here was thicker, oppressive, as if the walls themselves were holding their breath.

"Can you sense anyone out there?" Finn whispered, voice a ghost.

Nymbria closed her eyes. Her lashes fluttered as if stirred by an unseen current, her skin faintly luminous where the water magic brushed through her veins. Then she shook her head. "No."

Finn's jaw flexed. He pressed his palm to the handle and,

with painstaking care, pushed the door ajar. Hinges groaned in protest, the sound far too loud to my ears, though no alarm followed.

A dank hallway stretched before us, narrow and low-ceilinged, the stone damp with years of neglect. The air smelled of mildew and rust. Definitely a basement.

One by one, we slipped through. Finn closed the door behind us with a slow, deliberate pull, the click of the latch echoing like a gunshot in the dark.

The hallway stretched before us, yawning into two directions—one straight ahead, the other veering off to the right. Both ran far longer than the castle's footprint should have allowed. The stone corridors were too wide, too long, like the belly of something ancient pretending to be fortress walls. My stomach turned at the thought.

The air hung still and damp, carrying only the faint tang of rust. No torchlight, no footsteps, no distant voices. Just silence, so heavy it pressed on my ears.

Nymbria broke it with a murmur. "Lyla. Can you feel him?"

I swallowed hard and closed my eyes, reaching with my mind, the way Mina had taught me. *Spencer...?* I tried to send the thought outward, but nothing answered. No tug at my chest, no familiar warmth sparking in the bond we'd shared since our vows. Only emptiness. I shook my head, throat tight.

Nymbria didn't speak again, only gave a firm nod. Finn glanced between us, his jaw set, then lifted two fingers and tapped once toward the path ahead, once toward the right—hand signals between soldiers. Nymbria's chin dipped in acknowledgment.

"Stay here," Finn ordered, voice low but leaving no room for argument. He crouched, picked up a pebble from the floor, and let it fall. It clattered against stone, the echo running on and on, too loud in the hollow space. He nodded once, as though the sound had told him something.

He pressed the stone into my palm. "Keep an eye on us. The moment you lose sight of either of us—or if anything feels wrong—drop this. We'll come back, unless we're already trapped."

My fingers closed tight around the pebble. Cold. Solid. Useless. Still, I nodded.

I watched them split off, Finn to the right, Nymbria straight ahead. Their movements were silent, methodical. They checked doorways with quick, practiced glances, sometimes pressing flat against the wall before continuing. Every so often one of them would freeze for a long moment, listening for something I couldn't hear. My heart climbed higher in my throat each time they vanished further down their corridors.

The pebble in my palm had grown slick with sweat. They were so far now that the shadows nearly swallowed them. My breath hitched, and for one terrible heartbeat, I thought I might drop the stone just to bring them back before I lost them completely—

'And where did you run off to, little Queen?'

The voice coiled through my skull like smoke. My lungs seized. The pebble slipped from my trembling fingers, striking the stone floor with a sharp clink that rang too loud in the silence.

Both shadows snapped toward me instantly. They sprinted back, silent but fast, like hunters breaking cover.

I folded, collapsing to the ground, curling in on myself with my knees pulled tight to my chest. The air wouldn't come—my chest locked, throat closing, the edges of my vision speckling black.

Bel's laughter rippled through me, sticky and cloying. *"Cowering in the dark, are we? Such a fragile little queen. Shall I amuse myself with your consort while you play hide and seek?"*

I choked on a sob, my breath breaking against the vise of my ribs. My pulse thundered so hard it blurred every sound, every thought. Dizzy, sick, I pressed my forehead against my knees, clawing for any anchor.

Nymbria hit the ground beside me in a blur, sliding into place. Her arms wrapped me up without hesitation, firm and steady, her heartbeat thudding against my temple, the clean tang of salt on her coat filling my nose. She pressed her cheek to my hair, grounding me, willing me to find the rhythm of her breath instead of the chaos of my own.

Finn crouched low in front of us, knife in hand, eyes sharp and frantic, scanning the shadows like he could carve Bel out of the air itself.

The voice turned vicious. *"Very well. If you won't come to me, I'll send guards. And every second of your obstinance will cost your precious Spencer."*

The sound shredded out of my head as suddenly as it had arrived, leaving silence that pressed heavier than stone.

"Breathe, Lyla." Nymbria's voice was low, steady against the storm inside me. She shifted me in her arms so her forehead pressed to mine, her eyes catching mine even through the blur of tears. "With me. In—" She inhaled slow and deep, holding it. "Out." She exhaled through her nose, soft and controlled. "Again."

I clung to her, forcing my chest to follow hers, ragged at first, then steadier as her rhythm anchored me. Her hands rubbed small circles against my back, her murmurs threading through the panic. "That's it. You're here. You're not his to break."

Finally my lungs loosened enough for me to speak, though the words cracked in my throat. "He... he can't see us. He didn't know. That's why he's angry. He said he'll... he'll hurt Spencer until the guards find us."

Nymbria's jaw tightened. She looked over my head to Finn, who was crouched nearby, blade still in hand. They shared a grim silence that said more than words.

Finn nodded once. "My hallway's almost cleared. One door left. I'll check it." He pushed to his feet, muscles coiled.

Nymbria pulled me closer as he disappeared back down the corridor, her hand never leaving mine. Her voice softened, almost conspiratorial, a rasped comfort meant just for me. "We've done stupider things than this, Lyla. Finn and I once sailed blind through a fog thick enough to choke a man, just to steal a ship twice our size. We lived." A faint smile flickered across her mouth. "Finn became my second not because he's clever, but because he's too damned stupid to stop following me into danger. And somehow, it works."

Her mouth curved in a wry smile, though her eyes stayed hard. "Now we've got two goddesses and one fool who doesn't know when to die. If Bel wants a fight, he picked the wrong trio to trap in his dungeon."

Despite everything, a broken laugh escaped me, catching on the last of my sobs. Her thumb brushed the damp from my cheek.

Footsteps thundered back toward us. Finn rounded the corner, breathing hard, his face set in frustration. "Dead end. Nothing there."

Nymbria helped me to my feet, steadying me as my legs trembled. Finn sheathed his knife with a sharp motion.

"Then we don't waste more time," Nymbria said, voice firm. "We take my hallway, straight to where I turned back."

The three of us pressed close together, hearts aligned to one rhythm, and started forward into the shadows.

They reached the next door Nymbria had marked in her sweep, and all three of us froze. The air felt tighter here, as though the stones themselves were bracing for what came next. Without a word, Nymbria slid to one wall, Finn to the other, their hands brushing the wood and iron fittings as they tested the first set of doors. Locked. Their eyes met across the hall, grim but unsurprised.

We moved again, footsteps measured, every creak of the floor feeling like a shout in the silence. At the next door, Nymbria's latch gave. The faint scrape of metal releasing echoed far too loudly in the hushed corridor. She nudged it open, the black space beyond yawning like a throat.

Finn was already in motion, stepping in front of me, his broad frame blocking any line of sight from whatever might lurk inside. My pulse raced.

Inside lay another stairwell, narrow and steep, the air colder the moment we crossed its threshold. The hallway behind us still stretched on and on, as though the castle were bigger inside than out, a labyrinth designed to swallow trespassers whole. We exchanged a single glance—Nymbria's lips pressed thin, Finn's jaw tight—and then descended.

The stairs were an endless spiral downward, each step heavier than the last. By the time we reached the bottom, three flights in all, the stones underfoot gave way to packed, stamped earth, dark and damp, its smell seeping into my nose, metallic and sour. A place made to bury secrets.

Another door waited for us there. Heavy wood, banded with iron. Its silence felt expectant, like something on the other side was holding its breath. Nymbria touched the door, closing her eyes.

"This is probably where he is," Finn said quietly, his voice stripped of all pretense. He angled his body toward me, broad shoulders tense. "We don't know what we'll find. Nymbria is checking now. Whatever she senses—stay behind us. Don't speak. Don't move unless we move you. No matter what you hear."

Terror wrapped around me like chains, but I nodded, throat too dry for words.

Nymbria closed her eyes, lashes trembling, her features softening as her gift reached out. For a moment, the air shifted—like a current brushing over my skin—and then her eyes snapped open, brighter than before.

"There are bodies," she whispered. Her voice cracked like ice. "A dozen. Maybe more. Three of them hurt."

Her gaze found mine, sharp as a blade. "This is it. Spencer and Juniper are inside."

Finn's eyes flicked between me and the iron-bound door. His knuckles whitened where he gripped the stolen sword, the muscles in his jaw working. Finally, he bent close, voice rough and low.

"We go when you are ready."

The words struck me harder than if he'd simply given the order. It meant the weight of it—Spencer's fate, Juniper's fate, maybe all of ours—rested squarely on my shoulders. My lungs refused to work for a beat, my heart a frantic hammering in the silence.

I forced one breath in. Another out. The air tasted of damp soil and rust, thick enough to choke on. My hand curled tight around Nymbria's sleeve, and I nodded.

"Do it."

Nymbria didn't hesitate. She surged forward, palm lifting. Her eyes shimmered like liquid silver as the air itself seemed to condense. A rush of unseen force struck the two guards braced by the door—water inside their veins snapping to her will. They dropped without a sound, like puppets with their strings cut.

I stared too long at the slack faces, the stillness of men who might never stand again. The horror lodged in my chest like a stone, but Nymbria and Finn were already moving.

Finn crouched, quick and efficient, stripping their bodies of their short swords. He pressed one into Nymbria's waiting hand, kept the other for himself, then turned to me. From his boot, he drew the knife I'd seen him rely on since the ship. He pressed it hilt-first into my palm, his gaze hard.

"Only use it when you mean it," he said, voice clipped, urgent. "And don't hesitate, it'll give them the moment they need to stop you."

The weight of the blade seemed impossibly heavy in my hand. My fingers clenched around it, clammy, trembling. I nodded once, unable to find words.

Nymbria was already several paces ahead, her movements a predator's grace. Another guard rounded the corner, and her hand snapped up. The man convulsed, a strangled cry tearing out before he crumpled.

The cry echoed, jagged and loud, bouncing down the corridor like an alarm bell.

Finn swore, bolting after her. He caught the arm of another guard just short of him hitting Nymbria, taking her out.

And me? I stayed in the doorway, knife biting cold into my palm, every instinct screaming to run even as my feet locked to the dirt. The chaos was breaking loose ahead, the thrum of boots pounding in answer to the cry.

This was it. There was no going back.

I dragged one breath deep into my chest, the air stale with dirt and iron, and forced my legs to move. No more standing frozen. If I stayed behind, I'd be nothing but dead weight.

I plunged after them, the ground trembling beneath the weight of boots and bodies. Nymbria was a blade of water and fury ahead, Finn a wall of muscle close at her side. I trailed just behind, knife clenched so tight my palm ached.

Cells lined the corridor, the bars black with rust and filth. As we passed, hands shot through—thin, skeletal fingers clawing for us. I glanced in, heart twisting. One prisoner slumped against the wall, breath shallow as a whisper. Another lay curled, unmoving, his skin a map of bruises. A third lifted her head, eyes wild, lips moving in a prayer that broke into sobs.

One. Two. Three. Four. Five.

Five broken souls who should have been dead already but weren't—kept alive just enough to suffer.

Behind me, voices rose—hoarse shouts, begging, fists rattling the bars. The sound followed me like a tide. But I couldn't stop. Not yet.

Please, not yet.

Ahead, Nymbria's water lashed, dropping another guard with a sickening crack. Finn's stolen blade caught the torchlight, red already painting its edge. Together they cut a path through the last line of steel and flesh.

And then I saw it.

A cell where the shadows weren't empty. Chains snaked from the wall, iron biting into bruised wrists. Blood stained the stone beneath her, dark and half-dried.

"Juniper!"

Her name ripped from my throat, too loud, too desperate. I couldn't swallow it back.

Her head jerked up, dark hair matted to her face, eyes wide and glimmering with fear. For an instant, she looked at me like she wasn't sure I was real, like I was just another cruelty her mind had conjured to torment her.

But then her lips parted, the faintest of gasps escaping. Fear shone clear in her gaze, but so did the spark of something else —recognition.

"Keys!" My voice cracked as I spun toward Nymbria and Finn. "We need keys!"

They scattered instantly. Finn yanking belts off fallen guards, shoving hands into pouches, checking every body with furious precision. Nymbria rifled through another, curses hissing between her teeth as coins clattered uselessly to the floor.

Behind me, Juniper's throat worked. Her lips moved, but only a rasp scraped out, too dry and broken to form words. Her eyes, wide and wild, begged louder than her voice ever could. She jerked against her chains, the iron biting deeper into bruised skin, a choked cry tearing free at last.

"Don't worry," I whispered, though my pulse was galloping. "We'll get you out."

I pressed inward with my mind, reaching for that familiar tether, the warmth I always felt when Spencer was near. '*Spencer?*' I pushed, hard, desperate.

Nothing.

Empty silence.

My chest clenched. I twisted back toward Finn and Nymbria. "Anything?"

"Nothing!" Nymbria's voice was sharp, frantic. "None of them have keys!"

Juniper lurched at the bars, chains rattling. A strangled cry burst from her, raw and terrified. Her bound hands clawed toward me like she thought I might vanish if she didn't hold on.

"I know," I choked, heat rising in my throat. "I'll get there. Just—just hold on."

The bars. Solid iron, dark with rust. My fire flared before I even thought it through, roaring up my arms until the air shimmered. I pressed both palms against the metal.

The stink of burning filth filled my lungs. The bars sizzled, glowing red where my fingers touched, then white. I shoved harder, teeth gritted, feeling them soften under the heat until they gave like wax.

With a cry, I wrenched them apart. One bar cracked and

sagged, molten edges dripping to the ground with sharp hisses. Another peeled away with a shriek of metal.

Wide enough now. Enough.

I stumbled forward, knees slamming stone as I fell in front of her. Juniper's chains rattled as she shrank back, then surged forward, her whole body shaking with relief.

"I'm here," I whispered, reaching out though I couldn't touch her yet. My voice broke on it. "I'm real. You're safe now."

I reached for the chains anchoring her to the wall. The iron links clinked dully as she shifted, wrists raw and blistered where the cuffs had rubbed her skin. There was no key, no clean way to free her, only my fire.

I pressed my hands to the links nearest her cuffs, willing the heat to build. Sparks spat, metal glowing until it bled orange and then white. The stink of scorched iron stung my throat once more. I held the fire tight, careful, *'not the cuffs, don't burn her, don't burn her,'* until the first link sagged and split. One by one, I worked along the chains, severing them close to her restraints.

I shoved the melted ends aside, heart hammering at every hiss as iron struck stone. I wouldn't leave her clinking like livestock if we had to run.

"We're here," I whispered, voice trembling. My fingers hovered over her bruised wrists, aching to soothe what I couldn't yet. "I've got you. It's okay. We'll find Spencer, and then we'll go home."

Her head lifted weakly, eyes glassy but sharp with despair. Her lips cracked as she forced the words out.

"Sweet girl... don't save me." Her voice was a rasp, barely more than breath. "They won't let me leave. They already took Spencer. And they never meant for me to see daylight again."

Her words struck like a blade to the gut. My thoughts scattered, spinning out. Took Spencer? Where? Never meant—my mind whirled so violently I thought I might shatter with it.

"No." The word ripped out of me, harsher than I meant. I tightened my grip on the hilt of Finn's knife, forcing my voice to steady. "We are getting you out. Now. I'm here, and so are Nymbria and Finn. Can you walk?"

I looked her over, really looked. The blood crusted on her skin, the bruises painting her arms, the slackness in her shoulders. And her eyes—gods, her eyes were worse than all of it. Empty, hollowed out, the light I'd always seen snuffed down to an ember. Rage tore through me, hot and wild, clawing at my ribs, pulling my magic to the surface until the air shimmered with heat. My hands trembled, my breath came ragged. My rage threatened to steal my control.

I forced the fire down, sucking air between my teeth until the edges of my vision stopped pulsing.

To her credit, Juniper tried. She pressed against the wall, forcing her body upright. Her knees buckled but she caught herself, swaying. I stepped under her arm, bracing her weight against me.

"Any food? Water?" My voice was sharp, desperate.

Her lips cracked, voice barely a whisper. "No. Nothing. You... you need to leave me here. He's not here anymore, and they left me to die. If they think you've got me back, they'll hurt him more. They'll break you."

"No." My answer snapped out before I thought, tight and feral. I wrapped my arms around her, chains clinking between us. I pressed my cheek to her hair, willing her to believe me. "You're coming with us. We'll find Spencer. We'll go home. I won't leave you here to rot."

Nymbria and Finn skidded into the cell's doorway, weapons slick with blood. "No keys," Nymbria hissed, her eyes darting down the corridor. "Can you widen it?"

I NODDED, guiding Juniper to lean against the wall. "Hold there. I'll get you through."

I turned back to the bars. My palms pressed flat against the cold iron, fury spilling through my veins until the heat surged up my arms. The metal trembled under my touch, dark iron paling to red, then to a searing white glow. The stink of scorched metal filled my throat.

Slowly—carefully—I eased two bars aside, their softened

ends sagging without a sound. I guided them down, letting them slide against the stone until they rested in silence. The middle ones bent under my hands, the heat pliant as wax, until the opening gaped wide enough for a body to pass through.

"Come," I said, rushing back to her, taking her arm. Finn was already straddling the doorway, reaching to catch her as she stumbled forward. Nymbria stood a few paces off, her head cocked toward the corridor, listening, listening—her hand tight on the hilt of her sword.

Juniper staggered out, and the three of us turned as one.

"Did you see anything when they brought you down here? Anything that might help us?" I asked, hope clinging to my words.

She shook her head, shame clouding her face. "They blinded me. No light, no sound. I'm useless. And they are going to punish you for this."

My throat tightened, but I forced the words out steady. "You're worth the punishment. Spencer would say the same. We don't discard people—that's what he does."

Finn and Nymbria traded a glance, grim and silent. He gave her a nod. She closed her eyes, her breath slowing, skin shivering faintly with the pull of her magic. After a heartbeat she lifted a hand and pointed to the corridor opposite the stairs.

"Fewer people that way," she said. "Could be a dead end. Could be the way out."

They both turned to me. The weight of it pressed down until my lungs ached. I drew a deep breath—

—and Juniper's body sagged, collapsing into me.

We hit the ground together, my cry ripping out before I could choke it back. My hand slapped the stones, the sound sharp and awful in the silence. I clapped my palm to my mouth, holding in the rest, but the first shriek had already gone.

We froze. Every muscle locked, ears straining for the sound of boots, the scrape of blades being drawn. The silence stretched until it rang in my ears.

I closed my eyes, whispering prayers in my head. *Please, don't let them hear me. Please, give us a path out. Let us get back to the ship. Let us live to find Spencer again.*

Something tingled under my palm. The stone shivered faintly, warmth blooming into my skin. My magic surged—different this time, stranger, clearer. My vision went white, then filled with a map, a pull. The way out. I saw it—twisting corridors, a passage leading back to open air without the endless climb.

I gasped, eyes flying open. My chest still heaved, but the path blazed in my mind.

Finn had lifted Juniper effortlessly while I was down, settling her against his chest, his voice low but certain. "Faster this way. I'll carry her. Just keep me out of the crossfire."

Nymbria's eyes locked on mine.

I swallowed, then pointed down the way she'd indicated. "I know the way out."

Nymbria insisted I go first, her hand firm at my back, while Finn wedged himself between us as we slipped down the narrow stairwell. The walls pressed close, damp stone brushing my shoulders. Each step downward echoed too loudly, though we tried to place our feet soft against the grit.

At the bottom, I pressed my palm to the wall. The stone hummed faintly beneath my skin, the same tug I'd felt before, guiding with an urgency. It pulled at me the way it had when I first found Nymbria. My chest tightened as I rubbed the spot over my heart. When I glanced at her, she gave me a quizzical look—no hint that she felt it too.

The door ahead loomed heavy in the dark. I eased it open the way I'd watched Finn and Nymbria do all night: slow, steady, holding my breath to keep the hinges from betraying us.

The daylight was long gone. Beyond lay a corridor drowned in pitch black, the kind of darkness that felt like water you could drown in.

Nymbria's face hovered close, her whisper brushing my ear. "A little fire. Just enough to see."

My magic kindled small in my hand, a flame no larger than a candle's tongue. I flung it forward, my heart seizing at the thought of it catching—but it fizzled harmlessly against the far wall, casting a brief glow. Only one door waited in this hall.

"It's safe to go," Nymbria breathed.

I nodded and crept forward, the shadows swallowing each step. Another spark in my palm leapt to the sconce beside the door. Flame caught and spread a dull glow, painting the stone in amber light.

"I think this is it," I whispered. My voice felt too loud, scraping against the silence. "That door should open into an alley. We'll be out of the fortress, but the streets…" My stomach clenched. "Anyone could see us before we reach the ship."

Finn bent to Juniper, his voice gentled. "Do you think you can walk?"

She sagged against the wall, shaking her head. "Not on the hills out there."

"You can't carry her," Nymbria hissed, her eyes sharp in the torchlight. "Bloodied, bound—it will draw attention."

"What if one of us goes ahead?" I offered, my throat tight. "Fetches two from the ship. They could bring fresh clothes. Something cleaner, less likely to attract attention."

Finn and Nymbria traded a look, one of their silent conversations that made my skin crawl with its certainty. The unspoken words hung between them, louder than mine.

"It's risky," Finn said finally, grim resolve hardening his features. "But better than anything else."

Nymbria sighed, the fight slipping from her shoulders. "Fine. Go. We'll wait here. This passage is safer—they won't expect us to be here."

And then Mina's voice ripped through my head, a shriek that made me stagger. '*NO. Go together. Don't leave anyone behind.*'

Nymbria jolted beside me, her hand clutching the wall. She'd heard it too.

"Do you trust that?" she whispered, her eyes sharp on mine.

"Always." My answer came without thought, a weight of faith sinking into my chest. "That's her gift. She sees what we can't."

"Then together it is," Nymbria said, firm.

Finn's mouth opened in protest, but she cut him off, steel in her tone. "No. I'm pulling rank—and so will your queen. We don't split. Not now."

My hands shook as I reached for the door. I drew one last breath, bracing for whatever waited beyond. The latch clicked beneath my fingers.

And then we stepped through.

CHAPTER 24

I had never been so grateful for twilight. The world lay draped in shadows, deep enough to hide us but not so dark that we needed flame to see. The air smelled of salt and fish guts, thick enough to choke, and every sound—the scuff of our boots on the stones, the rasp of Juniper's uneven breaths—felt too loud, as though the whole city might be listening.

Juniper limped between us, her weight heavy across my shoulder. Each step dragged, her breath hitching sharp with pain, but we matched her pace, unwilling to leave her behind. Finn took her other side, his arm banded firm around her ribs, while Nymbria glided ahead, her head tilting now and then like she was tasting the air. The shimmer in her eyes told me she was listening through the water, searching for danger before we stumbled into it.

We turned down a narrow street, the walls pressing close, when Nymbria's hand shot up. No signal to follow this time, just a clipped, urgent whisper: "Stop."

My pulse lurched.

She flicked a glance back the way we'd come, then pointed at a recessed entryway half-hidden beneath a torn awning. "There. Now."

Before I could move, Finn scooped Juniper up in a bear hug,

her arms dangling limply around his neck. He half-carried, half-dragged her as we stumbled for the cover. The alcove was shallow—too small to hold all of us. Nymbria shoved me and Juniper inside, her body blocking half the space. She and Finn stayed outside in plain view, backs hunched, their voices rising in a sudden argument.

"I told you it's mine!" Nymbria snarled, holding up a glint of gold she'd pulled from her pocket.

"Like hell it is!" Finn snapped back, snatching at her hand, the two of them circling like sailors brawling in the street.

I pressed Juniper against the cold wall, every muscle rigid. Boots thudded against the cobblestones. They must be the patrol. Shadows moved past the alley mouth, steel catching faint light. My lungs burned as I forced myself not to breathe, my hand clamped over Juniper's mouth to stifle her broken sobs.

The guards' voices rumbled, low and indistinct. Then they passed. No barked orders, no sudden clash of steel. Just the steady tread of boots fading away.

Finn's eyes flicked down once, subtle as a dropped coin. He gave the smallest nod. Safe to move.

We emerged from the alcove, reassembling around Juniper. Nymbria darted ahead, her body low, pausing at the corner until she could confirm the patrol hadn't doubled back. She waved us across, and we hurried after her, boots scuffing on uneven stone.

The alleys blurred together—twisting, narrow, reeking of sewage and old fish—but no more patrols crossed our path. Relief swelled when the salt tang sharpened, the murmur of the tide growing louder. The docks.

We skidded to a halt in the last stretch of shadow. At the pier's entrance, torchlight glinted on rows of spears. Half a dozen guards stood at the choke point, blocking the only way through to the ships. Their uniforms caught the firelight, stark and merciless.

Juniper sagged against me, trembling. My stomach knotted.

We crouched back into the darkness, trading silent looks. None of us knew if this was routine or a trap laid for us. The ghost town we'd arrived in gave no answer—and the longer we lingered, the more the silence pressed, heavy with suspicion.

"We can't just march past them," Finn whispered, his voice low and rough "One look at Juniper and we're done. Probably the rest of us too."

I LEANED against the damp wall, staring as if I could see the guards through the stone. My mind spun. A half a dozen ways this could end, all of them ugly. A blade at Finn's throat. Shackles slamming around all our wrists. The sound of the alarm bell, and then the whole city on us.

My eyes drifted down the alley, and stopped. A cart sat half-collapsed against a wall, one wheel sunk in muck. A tarp sagged over its frame, corners drooping, and beneath it rotted fruit stank sweet and sour in the night air. The plan clicked together before I even thought.

"There." My hand shot out, pointing. "Put Juniper inside. Cover her with the best of what we can find in this fruit." I gestured towards the food discarded next to it. "Then the tarp goes over. Looks like cargo headed back to the ship."

Nymbria crouched, her hand lifting the edge of the tarp, testing its weight, its stink. She inhaled through her teeth, weighing it. "Hard to sell," she admitted, "but maybe. Dark hides the worst of the blood on us." Her eyes slid to me. "You lead. Grip the arms of the cart, head high. If they hassle us, you'll have the best chance to barrel through."

Her tone sharpened, decisive. "If it goes wrong, you run. Straight to the ship. Shout 'Strovan' as you approach. They'll know it means reinforcements."

I shook my head hard enough my braid whipped. "No. I fight too."

Nymbria's gaze cut into me, fierce and unyielding. "Juniper can't fight. If they find her, it's over. They'll raise the alarm before we can cut them down. This is the only way."

My chest tightened. She was right. My blade skills were nothing compared to theirs, and this city's guards were bred for this work. Reluctantly, I nodded. "Then I'll bring reinforcements back."

"No." Nymbria's voice cracked like a whip. "You'll get on that ship and stay there. You may be queen here, but I rule that ship. And I won't face Amyra and Spencer both and tell them I let you get yourself in over your head again."

A laugh bubbled out of me, sharp and brittle. "Like we aren't already in over our heads?"

That won her grin. "Exactly. No heroics. Just run."

I swallowed hard. "Strovan." The word tasted heavy on my tongue, like a stone I'd swallowed.

We crouched in the dark a while longer, watching the guards. No holes in their stance, no laziness to exploit. Nymbria's mouth tightened. No better plan.

Juniper winced as Finn and I eased her into the cart. I bent close, whispering, "Sorry. I know it's rough." Her lips quirked, faint and weary, as if she appreciated the apology more than the comfort.

We layered her over with stale loaves and soft fruit that squelched under our hands, pressing the tarp close to keep them from rolling. I tucked the edges in tight, my fingers trembling as I worked, praying no one would think to look too closely.

The cart's arms were cold in my grip, but lighter than I'd feared. My shoulders squared. Each step forward brought the sound of the sea sharper, the torches brighter, the line of guards closer.

We moved toward the docks.

The cart's handles were rough in my grip, the wood biting into my palms. Each step forward carried us closer to the line of torchlight, the shadows thinning until every movement felt exposed. My face was damp, but whether from heat or nerves I couldn't tell—and I prayed the guards wouldn't notice the traces of blood and grime I hadn't managed to hide.

I dragged in a breath, steadying it just before they could

hear the tremor. Chin high, I forced my shoulders square, faking a confidence I didn't have.

"Halt." A guard's voice cut sharp through the night. Two more stepped forward, steel spears crossed to block the cart. "What's in the load? And which ship?"

Finn slid in, his tone hard as hammered iron. "Heading to that one there. Last delivery for the night."

The guards didn't move. One narrowed his eyes. "Never seen one brought this late."

Another's gaze dropped, lingering on Nymbria and me. "And never seen women crewing a vessel like that."

Nymbria didn't blink. "We're paying passage. This is part of our fare. The last of our food stores, to help feed the voyage."

One of them leaned over and pinched back the tarp. My grip tightened so hard on the cart handles my arms shook.

"Ugh," he grunted, shoving a rotting orange aside with the tip of his spear. "Half molded? Really?"

Finn's jaw flexed. "Our cook will sort it. Waste isn't your concern."

The man dropped the tarp with a shrug. "Your loss if he doesn't."

Relief caught in my throat. I edged the cart forward, breath finally starting to rise—

"I didn't say you could go."

The sneer cut me like a blade. My feet froze.

The guard's eyes raked over us, dark with suspicion. "Papers? There's an alert out, on a group about your size. Can't let them leave the city."

Panic slammed into me, hollowing out my chest. Papers? We had nothing. My eyes snapped to Nymbria over my shoulder

Her lips shaped one word: *Go*.

My body moved before my mind did. I twisted hard on the cart handles, eyes locking on the steel tips of the spears barring my way. I willed them to melt, to twist, to fall—

Flame leapt instead.

The wood shafts burst alight, fire racing up them in a flash.

Guards cursed, dropping their grips, waving their weapons wildly as fire licked their hands.

I ducked low and shoved, the cart rattling hard over the stones. Shouts rose behind me, heavy boots pounding, but I didn't look back. My lungs burned, my legs pistoned forward.

"Strovan!" My cry ripped raw from my throat. "Strovan!"

The sound echoed off water and stone. Then voices answered, shouting it back, until the docks roared with it.

Six sailors bolted down Nymbria's gangway before I even reached it, blades flashing in the torchlight. Relief threatened to knock me off my feet.

I dared a glance back—no one followed.

I dropped the cart, tearing at the tarp until Juniper's pale face showed beneath the bread crusts and rotting fruit. Six crew swarmed us.

"Four of you!" I gasped, voice shaking but sharp. "Help your Captain. Two with me—get her on board."

They didn't hesitate. Two men lifted the tarp clear, helping Juniper get out of the cart. "Sorry, ma'am," one muttered as he hoisted her over his shoulder, already running. "Faster this way—can't risk a shot fired."

Behind us, steel clashed hard against steel, the shriek of blades scraping filling the air. A man shouted in pain, followed by Nymbria's fierce snarl of command. The crack of wood splintering—someone thrown into a crate. Boots pounded on the dock, shouts multiplying as more guards converged.

I sprinted up the gangway behind him, my chest tight, legs rubber. We crashed into the ship's narrow passageways, ducking into the medic's closet, the air thick with the bite of herbs and seawater.

Once the medic had Juniper settled, I forced myself back to the deck. I couldn't rest, not until I saw Nymbria and Finn with my own eyes.

The night air hit sharp, salt stinging my nose. Ryxan stood at the rail, spyglass to her eye, her posture rigid as a drawn bowstring. At the gangway, sailors waited like hounds straining at a leash, their faces turned toward her, waiting for the word to move.

I dragged my boot against the deck so she'd hear me approach. "How is it looking?" My voice came out thinner than I wanted. From here the shadows on the docks were too blurred, the clash of steel too distant to read.

"They're cutting down the last guard," Ryxan said, not lowering the glass. Her tone was cool, flat. "If no more rush in, they'll hold."

I swallowed, throat dry. "Did we lose anyone? I sent four. Are they all—?"

"I know," she cut in, the words clipped.

The telescope stayed fixed on her eye, shutting me out. I clenched the rail, staring hard into the dark. Shapes blurred into motion, then steadied into figures. One, two, three, four, five, six. My chest cracked open on a breath I hadn't realized I was holding. All of them, gods be thanked—all of them were running back.

Ryxan tracked them until even my eyes could follow without the glass. Then she lowered it, snapping it closed with a sharp motion before setting it back at the helm.

"Fucking reckless," she muttered, her mouth curling, at me. She stalked off toward the gangway, her stride taut with judgment.

Her tone left me rooted where I stood. Relief pulsed through me, hot and dizzy, but it couldn't wash away the chill she left in her wake. I stayed at the rail, keeping my eyes pinned to the docks, waiting for some sign the nightmare wasn't finished.

Around me the crew broke into motion, ropes creaking, boots hammering across planks, voices sharp with orders as they prepared to cast us off Scoria Bay's cursed piers.

CHAPTER 25

The water stretched black and endless behind us, Scoria Bay's shoreline shrinking to a jagged line of shadow. Only when the sails caught steady wind and the last torchlight faded from view did Nymbria finally cross the deck to me.

Her boots thudded soft against the planks, her voice low but direct. "Where do we go now?"

My fingers tightened on the rail. I could only shake my head, the words caught like stones in my throat. When they finally scraped free, they came thin. "I don't know."

Nymbria studied me, her expression unreadable. Then, gentler: "Close your eyes. Look for him. Where does your heart pull?"

The salt wind brushed my cheeks as I obeyed, eyes slipping shut. I stretched out, groping for that familiar tether in my chest, for the heat of Spencer's presence in my mind. Empty. Nothing but the creak of timbers, the rush of waves. '*Mina?*' I tried, desperation sharp in my thought. The silence pressed harder.

"I can't feel him anywhere." My voice broke, thinner than I meant. "Maybe... maybe if we reach land outside a city, I can try again. Touch stone. See if that map thing—whatever it was—will show me another path."

Nymbria tilted her head, sea-light glinting in her eyes. "What was that, anyway?"

"I don't know." I let out a shaky laugh, more breath than sound. "I didn't even mean to do it. I just—prayed. Begged for a way back to the ship. And then the vision hit. A map burned behind my eyes, dragging me forward. Like the stone itself demanded we take that path. I couldn't have chosen anything else." I blew out a long breath, turning toward her. "If I can touch stone again, maybe it'll work."

She didn't answer right away, only looked past me toward the looming silhouettes of Scoria Bay's islands. Her mouth flattened. "Landing without a dock will be hard. But not impossible."

Before I could press her, she was already moving. Her coat snapped in the wind as she crossed to where Finn and Ryxan stood with a cluster of crewmen. I watched her speak, her hand cutting through the air as she laid out what must have been the new course. Heads nodded. Orders rippled outward.

And Ryxan's gaze found me.

Her glare cut across the deck like a blade—accusing, heavy, cold. She didn't speak, her silence said enough.

I gripped the rail harder, the wood biting into my palms, and fixed my eyes on the water instead.

Nymbria found me back at the rail, her face unreadable in the starlight. "We'll be making landfall just before dawn," she said quietly. "Get some rest while you can."

I stopped and turned back. "Nymbria?"

She was already striding toward the helm to give her orders. At my voice she paused, glancing back, her expression cool in the dim light.

"Will you come with me? Try to heal Juniper?" I asked. I tried to keep the hope out of my voice, but it slipped through anyway, thin and insistent. My brows lifted with the plea before I could school them.

Her mouth opened as if to refuse, then closed again. She studied my face for a long beat, before finally saying, "I make no promises. But I'll try. Let me set course, and I'll meet you there."

I turned to the infirmary, hopeful that we can help.

The little room smelled of salt and herbs, a faint sharpness of alcohol lingering in the air. Inside, Juniper lay propped on the narrow cot, her hair combed clean, her body dressed in simple linen. Her face was still gaunt, but her skin no longer gray with filth. Relief broke through me like sunlight. My lips pulled into a genuine smile before I could stop it.

"I told you we'd save you," I said softly, almost teasing.

Her eyes filled at once, tears trembling on the edges. "I really believed him," she whispered, voice raw. "Bel. He told me I'd never see the light of day again. I thought..." Her throat closed, her hands twisted into the blanket. "I thought he was right."

I eased down onto the cot beside her, the wood frame creaking under the shift. "He said that out of fear," I murmured. "He's scared of me, Juniper."

Her head snapped up, shock breaking across her bruised features. "You? Why?"

Across the room, the medic glanced at us. Something in my face must have warned him off, because he busied himself gathering the soiled linens. "I'll... take these to launder," he muttered, retreating quickly.

The door clicked shut, leaving the air thicker, heavier.

I struggled with the words, fumbling for a way to untangle them. "Mina told me..." My tongue caught. I swallowed, forcing it out. "I'm... a goddess. One of the lost ones."

Juniper blinked, lips parting. "A... a lost goddess?" Her brows pinched. "Like a minor one, you mean?"

I shook my head slowly. "Do you remember Nivara?"

She nodded at once, the name stirring recognition.

"I'm her," I said, the truth still strange in my own mouth. "Or—reincarnated. I don't even understand it all myself."

Her hand trembled under mine when I covered it, grounding both of us. "But Bel didn't want Nivara's powers to stir. So he tried to kill me. I think that's why my mother was killed. And when that didn't work…" My throat closed. "Egan was sent. And when he failed…" I let the thought unravel into silence.

Juniper's breath caught, eyes wide. "The prophecy. Nivara. Lyla—" Her voice broke into a whisper. "You're the goddess of balance."

The words hung there, vibrating in my chest like a struck chord.

Then her mouth twisted, sudden fire lighting her face. "That's why Luther hates you so much. That misogynistic asshat can't stand the thought of you bringing balance between men and women."

A laugh burst out of me, unexpected, too sharp but real. "The feeling's mutual."

Behind me, a throat cleared. Nymbria had slipped into the room, arms crossed, watching us. She stepped closer to Juniper's cot, her voice level. "Let me try something."

Juniper's eyes widened, but she nodded. Nymbria laid her hands gently along Juniper's wrists, her touch steady but unyielding. A shimmer passed through her fingers, like light catching water. Juniper gasped. Her head eased back against the pillow, eyes fluttering shut as the tension drained from her body. The glow softened, then faded, leaving her face calmer, her breathing smooth.

When Nymbria drew her hands away, she stood straighter, a faint pride lifting her chin. "You're healed," she whispered.

Juniper blinked, testing her fingers, then her arms. Color flushed faintly into her cheeks for the first time since we'd found her. "I—thank you," she whispered, voice breaking.

Relief swelled in me. I grasped her hand. "Then come with us. Please. I can't leave you here."

Juniper's gaze dropped, shame shadowing her features. "I'd only slow you down. I have no strength, no use. Better to stay."

"No," I said quickly, tightening my grip. "You'd be everything I need. If not for magic, then for me—for my heart. I can't do this without you."

Nymbria's eyes softened as she stepped closer, her voice

firm. "And your magic would be of use. More than you know. I'd welcome another set of hands on this expedition."

Juniper looked between us, torn, her lip caught between her teeth. Finally, she gave a small, reluctant nod. "If you both believe it… then I'll come."

The words sent a fragile, fierce relief through me, steadier than breath, lighter than the weight I'd carried since leaving Elthas.

We left Juniper in the infirmary, letting her rest on the cot. It wasn't much, but it was steadier than a hammock swaying with every pitch of the ship. A second hammock had been slung in the captain's quarters for me.

She lingered at the door, telling me she had more to do before she could sleep. I warned her not to overwork herself, and she smiled faintly, the kind of smile sailors gave when they knew storms were ahead but pressed on anyway. "There's always more to do when we sail," she said, and then she was gone.

The next thing I knew, she was shaking me awake. My body ached, but I'd slept deeply, soothed by the rhythmic slap of waves against the hull.

"It's time," she said. Her eyes were bright, steady.

On deck, the anchor held us in a bay that looked almost unnatural. It was perfectly round, its edges abrupt and sharp, as though carved by a giant's blade. I stared too long, and Nymbria caught me.

"The land here was scarred in the Last Great War," she murmured, her voice low, reverent. "The weapons they used could change the very earth."

The words sank like lead in my gut. My gaze roamed the smooth curve of the cliffs, the still water heavy with silence. The place felt haunted, as if the souls crushed here still lingered, pressing down on us with invisible weight.

I climbed into the rowboat beside Nymbria, Finn, Juniper, and the three men who'd followed us out of Blyn. It lowered, ropes creaking. The oars hit the water, pulling us closer to shore where a sheer cliff rose up, fifteen feet high, water gnawing at its base. I wondered if the war had carved that too.

By the time we found a path up, the sun was breaking pale light across the horizon. The climb left my hands raw, but the higher we rose, the heavier the air grew, thick with an unease none of us voiced.

AT THE TOP, overlooking the bay, I couldn't hold it back any longer. I sank to my knees, pressing both palms to the stone. The rock was cold, rough beneath my skin.

And then I prayed.

Please. Show me where he is. Show me how to reach him. Give me a tether strong enough to follow him to the ends of the world.

Heat flared beneath my hands, a tremor that wasn't just the stone but my own power bleeding into it. White light burst across my vision, so blinding I gasped, before it shifted, shaping into images.

Woods. The glow of a fire. Spencer—*gods, Spencer*—lying broken but alive, bruised and bloodied, sleeping in the dirt. My breath hitched.

I strained to see more in this wooded area, spotting a wagon nearby, its wheels sunk deep in carved roads. The stamp of horses behind me. A tent of black fabric shuddering as it's occupant started stirring.

Then it ripped open.

"Who's there?" a voice bellowed. Not tinny, not echoing in my skull like before—but real, heavy, present. Bel.

The vision shattered like glass.

My arms gave out. I collapsed onto the stone, sobs breaking loose before I could stop them. Salt stung my lips. "I saw him," I choked out. "He's here—traveling. Alive, just barely. Bel sensed me. He knew I was looking."

Silence followed, sharp as a blade. Then movement—Finn swore under his breath, the word guttural, bitten off like he couldn't stand to give it sound. Juniper's hands clasped in front of her chest, knuckles white as she whispered a prayer I couldn't hear. Behind them, one of the sailors crossed himself, another spat over his shoulder to ward off bad luck. Even the wind seemed to falter.

I pushed myself upright, every muscle trembling, and locked eyes with Nymbria.

"I feel him," I whispered, raw. "He's tethered to me."

Her own eyes shone, water brimming like the sea itself. She gave a single, fierce nod. "Then we have our heading."

CHAPTER 26

Finn unrolled the map on a flat stone, the parchment creased and weathered, corners curled from damp air. Inked lines showed rivers and ridges, but the villages were old names, smudged with time. Still, it gave us bearings. I pressed my finger against the spot where the tether in my chest pulled tight, marking the southern bend of the island's U-shaped curve.

We had landed at the inner tip of the eastern arm. To reach him, we'd need to march the long curve down to the base. The ship could have carried us closer, but the ports along this bay were too exposed. Better to vanish inland than sail into waiting nets. Orders were given to the crew: flee for the capital at the first sign of Scoria Bay's ships. The words left a hollow pit in my stomach. If we returned and found them gone… I pushed the thought aside, clinging instead to the one thread of hope—that when we came back, Spencer would be with us.

We struck south, boots crunching against a road that had long outlived its builders. The stones were half-swallowed by moss and grass, the kind of road men had abandoned after the Last Great War. Our footsteps echoed in the stillness, ghosts of armies long buried.

But through it all, the tug in my chest thrummed steady, as though an invisible cord pulled me forward. It kept me upright, kept my breath even. He's alive, he's waiting. I prayed Spencer could feel me too—that he knew I was coming.

An hour passed beneath the canopy of skeletal trees, the trail narrowing as the morning light sharpened. Shadows that had stretched long and thin at dawn now pulled tighter underfoot, jagged patches between the sunlit gaps. The air grew warmer, the silence heavier, every birdcall too sharp against the stillness. Just when the rhythm of marching had begun to dull the edges of fear, the silence inside me split open.

'*You're not helping your little boytoy here, girl.*' The voice slithered through my skull—tinny, jagged, scraping like iron dragged across stone. My knees faltered. The sound wasn't just heard; it rasped against bone, worming into every hollow of my head.

"Lyla!" Juniper's voice cracked as she lunged toward me, her arm hooking under mine before I pitched fully to the ground. Her presence anchored me, pulling me back from the edge.

"I'm... I'm fine," I stammered, though my voice shook. "It's just Bel."

The tinny rasp slid back into my skull like a blade slipping between ribs. '*You might be, but your king isn't. Can you hear him now?*' The sound that followed hollowed me out. A whip cracked and Spencer's scream tore through my mind, raw and ragged. My stomach lurched.

"Stop!" The word ripped from me before I could swallow it. "Please, he hasn't done anything to deserve this!"

My plea rang out into the morning air, naked and desperate, and I didn't care that the others heard me begging a god they couldn't see.

"Gods..." Finn muttered under his breath. He took a half step forward, his hand hovering near my elbow like he might drag me back to my feet by force if he had to. His eyes burned, not at me, but at the unseen tormentor he couldn't touch.

'*Hasn't he?*' Bel's voice oozed with false sweetness. '*Wasn't he the one who came running to confront me? He got exactly what he asked for... don't you think?*'

Another crack split my head, another scream followed—

Spencer's voice breaking into something less human, the sound of flesh giving way. Tears blurred the path before me. My legs froze; I couldn't make them move forward.

Lyla, look at me." Nymbria's voice cut through, sharp as steel drawn from a sheath. She crouched in front of me, her hands braced on my shoulders. Her silver-blue eyes searched mine, fierce and steady. "He's trying to break you. Don't give him the satisfaction."

The tether in my chest ached, stretched tight as though it might snap.

'You can end this,' Bel whispered, tinny and jagged, yet coaxing. *'Swear your fealty. Bend the knee, and it all stops. Don't you want to know what we could do together?'*

My breath came in shallow bursts. I could feel Finn's presence looming behind me, a wall against the world, and Nymbria's and Juniper's touches grounding me in the now. But Bel's voice wrapped tighter, a noose in my head, each word heavy with temptation.

My breath steadied, ragged gasps hardening into something sharper. Nymbria's fingers pressed firm into my arm, her grip an anchor; Juniper's touch carried its own kind of courage, proof that even the broken could still stand with me. Finn's shadow loomed at my back, a wall of flesh and steel. Together, they braced me, and I felt the fire surge.

"I will never," I spat, the words ripping out before Bel could coil another taunt around my mind. "And you know this. Bring him to me. Now." My voice shook the air, raw and certain, born from their strength as much as mine. "If I have to claw my way to him the hard way, you will regret my wrath."

Bel's response was a laugh—cold, hollow, scraping through my skull like broken glass. Laughed at me. But Spencer's screams faltered, thinning to a ragged hush.

'Girl,' Bel sneered, tinny and sharp. *'You're in over your head. You couldn't win even if you tried.'*

I straightened, refusing to let the words take root. He could hiss in my skull, gnaw at my bones—but he couldn't touch the fire burning in my chest. "Are you so sure?" I challenged, my voice low, steady, defiant. "Every day I grow stronger. And you —" I drew a breath, felt the tether in my chest pulse like a heartbeat, "—you run like a coward because you know it. If you thought you could win, you'd be here already. You'd face me. Right now."

BEHIND ME, Finn hissed under his breath at the provocation, but his hand clamped down on my shoulder, grounding me.

I held my breath, bracing for what might come—half terrified he'd take the challenge, half daring him to.

The silence stretched until it scraped at my nerves. My mouth opened, ready to suggest we keep moving, when the word slid into my skull—thin, dismissive. '*Fine.*'

The tether to Spencer vanished. One instant it thrummed like a lifeline; the next it was gone, ripped from me. My chest hollowed. My hand flew to my sternum as if I could catch it, clutch the cord back into existence. A sound tore from me, half-cry, half-wail, raw enough to burn my throat.

The air in front of us shimmered in a black glitter, reminding me of the same ash cloud that courier dissolved into the night of my wedding. Within it, four beings came into focus.

Spencer knelt before Bel, shackled and broken, blood smeared down his temple, chains biting into his wrists. His head slumped forward, his body trembling under its own weight.

Gasps erupted around me. Even Finn muttered a harsh, guttural "Fuck." But their voices blurred into nothing. I couldn't look away from Spencer. My knees buckled with the instinct to collapse at his side, to gather him into my arms, shield him from all of this.

"Spencer!" His name ripped from me like a prayer.

Nymbria's hand clamped hard on my arm. Her whisper cut like a blade. "Up. Look."

I forced my head to lift. And saw.

Bel towered above us, an impossible wall of flesh and fire. Eight feet of muscle corded beneath skin so dark a red it seemed to swallow the sunlight. His hair writhed like living flame, heat shimmering in its glow. But it was his eyes—gods, his eyes—that froze me. Two perfect ovals of black. No whites. No pupil. Just endless void staring back.

My jaw sagged. Air stuck in my throat. This was what had stolen the breath from the others, not just Spencer's broken body, but this.

His massive hands flexed once, fingers curling as if he could pluck me from the earth like a child's doll. His scowl was carved deep, every line of his face radiating fury.

I had taunted him. Dared him. And now, standing at half his height, I understood the sheer scale of my arrogance. Terror licked up my spine.

'*Mina?*' My plea shot outward, panicked, desperate.

Her reply came faint, far away, like a voice shouted across a canyon. '*You've got this. Don't back down. I can't come.*'

She abandoned us.

My hand fumbled sideways until it caught Nymbria's. She turned her grip, sliding one palm firm against my back, the other enclosing my shaking fingers. Her presence held me upright where my own body might have folded.

Bel smirked as though he had all the time in the world, as though my horror amused him. "Still feeling confident, child?" His voice rolled low, mocking, the word child barbed to pierce.

"Are you releasing Spencer to me?" I forced the words out, squaring my shoulders, spine stiff, summoning a confidence I did not feel. My chest trembled with each breath, but I raised my chin anyway.

Bel chuckled, a sound that shook like stones grinding together. "Prove you have what it takes to take him from me." He lifted his hand, examining his nails with idle interest, then buffed them against his chest as though I were no more than a passing nuisance.

The sheer audacity made my blood seethe.

Fire would be useless—his very hair burned. So I reached for the earth beneath us. Basalt answered, surging upward in a wall between him and Spencer. Stone groaned, the air split with the sound of rock grinding on rock. I raised it higher, steeper, the backside pitched so sharply that Bel would be forced to topple as the ground bucked beneath him. The wall climbed twenty feet into the sky before I sank the earth where he and his men stood, swallowing them in a pit of my own making.

"Now!" I gasped.

Two of Nymbria's sailors rushed forward, dragging Spencer's limp body behind our line. Nymbria dropped beside him, her hands already glowing as she pressed them to his battered chest. Finn slid into her place, squaring himself against the pit's edge.

For a heartbeat, I dared to believe it had worked.

Did I just win?

Then the ground trembled.

At first, only pebbles danced across the dirt. Then gravel. Then the entire earth quaked beneath my boots. The sound deepened into a guttural roar, the kind the world itself might make as it split open.

"No…" My voice faltered.

The pit cracked wide, and the air shimmered with heat. Lava surged upward, molten stone vomiting from the earth, red-gold and blistering. The basalt wall glowed where the heat licked it.

"Run!" My voice broke into a scream. I grabbed Juniper's arm and shoved her forward. "Run!"

The sailors bolted, hauling Spencer between them. Finn was already moving, barking at them to keep pace.

The lava spilled over the lip, hissing, rolling downhill after us. Each step I took, the heat chased harder, a living tide of fire.

"Faster!" I screamed, but my own feet stopped. Lava was something I could command.

I spun, thrusting my hands forward. The molten wave thundered toward me, a wall of liquid rock. I dragged at the heat with my power, willing it out, stripping it from the stone. The air crackled, scorched. The lava hissed, hardened, then cracked apart as more seared through, boiling over.

The harder I pulled, the faster it came, spewing upward, geysers of molten rock spraying skyward.

"Fuck!" I hissed, sweat stinging my eyes. A massive bubble surged, split—and hurled itself toward me in a blazing arc.

I stumbled backward, heart slamming, the roar of heat filling my ears.

Then a rush of wind slammed against my back, shoving me to my knees.

Juniper.

Her hands lifted behind me, eyes fierce. Air whipped into a wall, the currents colliding, holding fast between me and the molten spray. The lava struck it, hissing, splattering harmlessly across the rock before cooling to black crust.

The wall I'd raised shuddered, then sagged, crumbling as Bel's heat bore down. Flames licked through the fractures. When the last slab fell, he was there—Bel, towering and unbothered, his men at his shoulders, all of them waiting like executioners.

"Juniper…" My voice cracked, low and urgent. "We need to go. Now."

Her jaw clenched. "You first, Lyla."

"No." I shook my head so hard it hurt. "I leave no one behind."

"Lyla!" she screamed, her voice sharp with terror, arms trembling as she held the roaring air-wall against the molten tide. "Go! My magic won't hold this forever."

I got to my feet, tugging at her elbow. "We can retreat together. Just come with me."

Her eyes met mine, wide and wet, despair flickering behind the fight. "If I let this go—if we both turn—neither of us walks away."

The words punched through me. In front of us, the wind shrieked against the advancing fire, the heat searing my cheeks. Bel's grin spread, cruel and patient. He didn't need to strike. He only had to wait and let me choose which of us burned.

My mind raced. The basalt wall was gone. The air shield was weakening. And she was right—once it failed, the lahar would consume us both before we took two steps.

"No," I whispered, desperate. "Not like this."

I stretched my hands toward the earth, yanking life from the soil. Ivy ripped upward, vines tangling thick, thorns bristling, brush exploding into a wall. I packed it dense, forcing every tendril to weave itself into a barrier behind her air. It wasn't stone, but it was something.

"Back," I urged, my voice breaking. Together we staggered one step, then two. Juniper's lips trembled as she let out a small, strangled sound. "I can't—"

"Run!" I shouted.

We turned as one. The roar behind us deepened. Heat surged as the air shield collapsed in an instant, the sound of rushing flame chasing our heels. My ivy wall kindled with a whoosh, crackling, firelight flaring at the edge of my vision.

I clamped my hand around Juniper's arm, dragging her with me as we sprinted after the others. My lungs burned with every breath, heat blistering the skin of my neck.

And then her weight vanished.

"Juniper!"

She had stumbled, face in the dirt, her hands clawing the ground. I skidded to a halt, reaching for her.

But the fire was faster.

The wall of flame bore down, devouring everything in its path, a living tide.

"Juniper!" I dropped to my knees beside her, the heat blistering my skin. I clawed for her arm, desperate to haul her up, but she caught my wrist instead. Her grip shook, frail, yet somehow unbreakable.

"No," she rasped, coughing against the smoke. Her eyes locked onto mine—wet with fear, yet fierce, alive with a light I'd never seen in her before. "You have to go."

"I won't!" My voice cracked, the words raw with panic. "I won't leave you!"

"You will." Her fingers tightened, digging crescents into my skin with her last strength. "Lyla… you're the goddess of balance. You must live. You must fight. Save him. Save Elthas. Don't let me burn for nothing."

Tears poured hot down my cheeks, blurring the fire into

waves of orange and gold. I shook my head, choking on sobs. "I can't... gods, Juniper, I can't do this without you!"

Her lips curved into a fierce warrior's smile. "Yes. You can. Because you're not just a queen. You're more than him. More than Bel. You are the fire that will end him."

The flames roared closer, sparks raining down. She shoved me hard, forcing me backward, her eyes blazing brighter than the inferno itself.

"Run!" she cried, voice rising above the roar. "Run, and burn the world brighter than me!"

And then the fire took her.

The smell hit hard, flesh and hair searing, a stench so sharp it scalded my throat, turned my stomach. The scream I tried to hold back ripped free, raw and ragged, as her silhouette dissolved in the blaze. One heartbeat she was there, skin and soul alight with defiance. The next, she was gone, consumed utterly, her voice the only thing that remained.

Her words rang through me, searing into my bones. *You are the fire that will end him.*

I staggered once, then turned and ran, tears streaking my face, every step fueled by the echo of her last battle cry.

I ran and ran, though the fire no longer chased me. I ran down this road to the ship, blind from grief, each sob a knife in my lungs. I ran to ignore Bel's taunts coiling through my skull, smug and cruel, '*I told you that you would lose. You can never defeat me.*'

For a moment, I wanted to believe him. But Juniper's fire burned inside me now, and with every step I knew. I had to believe in myself. I needed to get stronger, strong enough to bring him down. Strong enough to avenge her.

CHAPTER 27

I stumbled into the clearing at the cliff's edge, lungs burning, vision blurred with tears. The ship bobbed in the bay below, right where we'd left it. Relief surged hot through me, almost dizzying.

And then I saw him.

Spencer. Upright, though swaying, his face pale, his body still battered. But standing. Alive.

I broke.

I crashed into his arms, clinging to him with every ounce of strength I had left. The sobs came hard, tearing out of me as I buried my face against his shoulder, his scent of cinnamon and nutmeg breaking me open. Grief spilled free with the tears—the loss of Juniper, the terror of nearly losing him, the unbearable relief that I hadn't.

Behind us, boots scuffed hard against the earth. Finn and two sailors darted past, eyes scanning the tree line, weapons ready. I tried to speak, to tell them Bel hadn't followed, but all that came were gasps and sobs against Spencer's chest.

Nymbria was suddenly there, her hand pressing to the small of my back, steady, grounding. "I'm so sorry," she murmured, her voice low enough that only I could hear.

When Finn returned, his face told me he already knew. Still, he asked. "Juniper?"

My throat closed. I could only shake my head, the motion jerky, violent, my whole body trembling with it.

The silence that followed was heavy. Then Spencer's voice —rasped, but certain—cut through it. His first words since I'd reached him.

"He never would have let you get us both." His eyes found mine, weary but steady. "He wants you weakened. He wants your grief."

I drew a long breath, the kind that burned all the way down. "He's the god of death," I said, voice steady though my chest still shook. "He feeds on it—on grief, on what it does to us. We fight back by refusing to let her death mean nothing."

My arm tightened around Spencer. I couldn't let go—not after almost losing him. Turning to Nymbria, I forced the words past the knot in my throat. "Can you bring the boat up here? Get us back to the ship?"

She didn't hesitate. A flick of her wrist, a narrowing of her eyes toward the water, and the surf answered. The waves surged, climbing the rocks until the row boat scraped up onto the cliffside, dripping foam. We piled in, Spencer leaning heavy against me, and with a backward pull of the tide, the boat shot away from shore. Spray lashed my face as the water propelled us forward, Nymbria's magic pushing us faster than any oar could.

The whole way back, my hand never left Spencer. Fingers curled in the fabric of his tunic, clinging as though if I let go, Bel would rip him away again.

By the time we clambered onto the deck of the ship, the weight of exhaustion made my knees tremble. We retreated to the captain's quarters, though with three of us inside it felt stifling, the air close with salt and sweat. I turned to Nymbria, voice raw. "I need to send word home. They have to know we're coming."

She nodded and pulled a satchel from the desk, sliding ink and paper toward me. "We'll make landfall tomorrow, second high tide," she said as she handed me the satchel.

I bent over the paper, staring too long before the words

came. *I found Spencer, and we are returning immediately. We'll be home by tomorrow's evening high tide. Please don't let them celebrate our return.*

I prayed the last line carried the truth I couldn't bring myself to write, that Juniper would not be with us.

ONCE THE INK DRIED, I whispered the spell, watching the letter dissolve into sparks that vanished on the air. Then I tucked myself back under Spencer's arm and led him to the infirmary, hoping the medic might give him something more than my presence.

They cleaned his wounds, wrapped what little still needed tending, but it was Nymbria's hands that drew real healing into him. Her magic worked patiently, the glow ebbing and flowing like the tide, knitting flesh and bone, smoothing bruises to faint shadows. By the time she finished, his body was nearly whole.

But when his eyes closed, his shoulders still flinched. His breath still caught, as though expecting another lash of the whip. And I knew that no magic in the world could ease the kind of scars Bel had carved into him.

As much as I couldn't bear to look at the sea or at the silhouette of Scoria Bay shrinking behind us for another moment, Spencer asked to stand on the deck, to watch our way home. I couldn't leave him alone, not yet, so I went with him.

We leaned against the rail at the bow, the wind tugging at our hair, the sun warming our backs. For a moment, it was almost peaceful, the kind of quiet I thought none of us would ever have again. Which meant, of course, Finn couldn't leave it alone.

"Looking better, brother," he called, striding up and giving Spencer a hearty slap on the back.

Spencer stiffened, eyes going distant for a breath, and I almost snapped at Finn for it. But Spencer blinked, found his bearings, and turned with a nod. "I appreciate you coming for me," he said, extending a hand.

Finn clasped it, smirk tugging at his mouth. "Yeah, well, next time maybe loop us in before you decide to launch a one-man suicide mission? We've got a perfect record with those—haven't lost a single one yet." He winked.

Spencer arched a brow, deadpan. "That's not exactly a record you want to tempt."

"Tempting fate's the only thing I'm good at," Finn shot back easily.

"You're good at running your mouth too," Spencer countered, but there was the ghost of a smile there.

Finn grinned wider. "And you're still better at brooding than anyone I've ever met. Gods, you two would make a matched set on deck—him glowering, you fuming, and the rest of us wondering if we'll survive the storm."

I rolled my eyes, biting back a laugh. Spencer shook his head, but his lips curved despite himself.

By the time they traded a few more barbs—Finn boasting about how he'd singlehandedly scouted three guards during the rescue, Spencer needling him about exaggerating—they had settled into something almost easy. A rhythm of words like sparring blows, quick and light, but with respect growing in the spaces between.

I hated that it had taken all this pain and sacrifice to break down the wall between them. But I was grateful all the same, watching Spencer let someone other than me or Amyra or Ethan in, if only a little.

Nymbria strolled over then, her braid dark against the wind, expression cool but eyes glimmering with amusement. "Careful," she said dryly, "keep this up and you two might start liking each other."

Nymbria's smirk curved sharper. "Though I should warn you—if you get too friendly, Finn will start bragging about his knife tricks, and no one deserves to sit through that again."

Finn clutched his chest in mock outrage. "Again? Please. Every time I've done it, people beg for more."

"Begging you to stop," she shot back.

Spencer chuckled under his breath, shaking his head. "Sounds about right."

"Traitor," Finn muttered at him, then turned his wounded

expression back on Nymbria. "You just don't appreciate artistry."

"Artistry?" Nymbria arched a brow. "Last time you tried, you nicked your own boot. You nearly pinned yourself to the deck."

"That was strategy," Finn insisted. "Theatrics. Sell the danger, get the crowd invested. You wouldn't understand—captains don't know the meaning of fun."

"Oh, we understand fun," she said smoothly. "We just prefer ours without blood loss."

Spencer laughed outright at that, the sound rusty but real. Finn pointed between them, as if to prove something. "See? Even the brooder's laughing. You're outnumbered."

"Not a chance," Nymbria said, folding her arms with mock severity. "I always win."

I couldn't stop the laughter that bubbled out of me, catching on my breath until I was doubled over against the rail. Spencer's arm slipped around my waist, steadying me as his own quiet chuckles rolled through him. Even Finn looked satisfied, smug grin tugging at his mouth while Nymbria tilted her chin in triumph.

For a fleeting moment, the four of us stood there together, the sound of our laughter carrying out over the sea.

And then it hit me. The guilt.

Juniper's face rose in my mind, her last words swallowed by fire. My throat tightened around the echo of it, my smile faltering even as the warmth of the moment lingered. How could I laugh so freely when she would never laugh again?

I turned into Spencer's side, pressing my cheek against his shoulder, letting his arm anchor me against the sudden ache. For now, I let the others' laughter cover mine, the joy stinging bittersweet on my tongue.

CHAPTER 28

The towers of the capital rose against the horizon exactly when Nymbria had promised, the sunlight catching on the stone as if the city itself glowed with welcome. My chest ached at the sight of the docks. Busy, ordinary but alive. No celebrations.

The gangway struck wood, and Spencer and I were the first down it. His steps were unsteady, mine too quick, but the moment my boots hit the planks I could not breathe until I saw her.

Amyra.

She stood just beyond the gates, winter light soft on her dark hair, her hands clasped tight as if she had been holding herself together by sheer will. When our eyes met, the air rushed from my lungs and my legs carried me forward before I even thought.

I collided with her, arms wrapping so tight it was as if I could keep her forever. My face pressed against her neck, drinking in the scent of apples and woodsmoke that had always meant safety. My whole body shook as I clung to her. "I've missed you so much," I whispered, the words breaking apart.

Her arms crushed me back, her breath warm in my hair. "I thought I'd never see you again," she admitted, voice trembling. "I even called Ethan home. He and Ivy will be back tomorrow."

The sound of uneven footsteps pulled me back just enough. Spencer.

Amyra and I both opened our arms, pulling him into us, and the three of us held on to one another with everything we had left. The world blurred around us. There was only this moment, this proof that against every trial, every trap, every cruelty of Bel, we had come back together.

Amyra's voice wavered as she tried for levity. "Don't you ever run away again."

Spencer gave a broken laugh, the sound raw with feeling. "Oh, love. I may have learned the hard way, but I will never leave you two again." His arms locked tighter, pulling us so close that I felt his heartbeat against mine, steady and real.

Joy swelled through me, almost unbearable in its intensity. The grief still lingered like an ache, but in that embrace, it was eclipsed by something brighter. Relief. Love. The kind of joy that steals your breath and leaves only tears behind.

After a long while, Amyra loosened her hold, swiping at her cheeks as she glanced back toward the docks. Nymbria and Finn were weaving through the crowd, their strides steady, their faces set. The last of the unloading must have been finished.

"Juniper?" Amyra asked, her voice catching, the single word enough to hollow my chest all over again.

I shook my head. My throat closed, tears already burning.

Spencer's hand brushed Amyra's arm, steadying her. His voice came ragged, low enough I almost missed it. "She gave everything. She made sure Lyla could get away from Bel. She... she saved us."

Amyra broke then, tears falling as freely as mine, and we folded back into each other, the three of us knotted together, leaning into the grief and the comfort in equal measure. I clung harder than I meant to, as though if I let go, the weight of it all would crush me where I stood.

When we finally peeled apart, Amyra sniffed and forced herself upright, her spine straightening with quiet resolve. "Come," she murmured, voice still thick but determined. "I had dinner sent to our chambers. I suspected you wouldn't want to be around everyone."

We made our way through the halls, servants bowing and stepping aside. No courtiers. No nobles. Just staff who kept their heads lowered and didn't ask questions. Relief loosened something in my chest. The gods had given me this small mercy, at least.

Thinking of gods…

I reached inward, searching for Mina.

Her voice came at once, soft and certain. *'Here, my Nivara.'* A pause, then, *'I know. I watched it all. I'm sorry. I'm here when you're ready.'*

Her words slipped into me like cool water on a burn, but the calm only fanned the spark of anger under my ribs. She watched. She let me scream, let me beg, let Juniper die. She just watched.

I clenched my jaw, too raw to hold the argument now. Too wrung out to demand answers.

'Of course you're mad,' she added lightly, as though she could taste the heat in me. *'But grief's a storm, not a straight line.'*

Infuriating. And yet, threaded with something almost playful, like she knew I'd spit fire at her if she pushed harder.

I swallowed it down. Not tonight. Not yet.

I wish I could say I remembered dinner. Plates came, voices murmured, wine warmed my throat. But it all slid past me in a haze, my mind too battered and my body too heavy to hold on to any of it. I only knew the steady presence of Spencer and Amyra at my side, the anchor of their nearness. By the time we reached our bed, I barely managed to crawl beneath the blankets before sleep dragged me under.

When I woke, sunlight was already high and pouring across the bed, bright and merciless. The space beside me was empty, the sheets cooled where Spencer and Amyra had slept.

For a moment, I just stared at the hollow prints their bodies had left, my chest aching with two conflicting truths. Relief that they had let me sleep, that I was finally safe enough to collapse. And frustration that they had gone without me, that I hadn't even stolen a morning's worth of their company after all we had endured.

I forced myself up, dragging on the first gown I could reach, tugging a brush through my hair only long enough to braid it loosely over my shoulder. The reflection that met me in the glass was someone wrung out, stripped down, not quite queen, not quite goddess.

'*Where are you?*' I sent to Mina, my voice sharp even in my own head.

'*Same place as always,*' came the reply, calm as a stone dropped in water. '*With Nymbria.*'

That was enough. I shoved aside the lingering fatigue and hurried through the halls, skirts whipping at my ankles, heart thrumming with impatience. The courtyard—our training ground, our crucible—waited, and with it, whatever answers Mina was finally ready to give.

I all but flew down the corridors, skirts hiked in my fists, my pulse hammering faster than my footsteps. Servants stepped back against the walls as I passed, their murmurs a blur of sound I didn't bother to catch. No one dared to stop me, though I caught the flicker of movement behind me. Two guards trailed at a distance, their boots sharp against the stone. A hollow laugh rose in my chest. If Bel himself appeared, what could they do? But fine. Let them follow. Let whoever assigned them this patrol think their presence meant anything.

The courtyard opened before me, the winter air sharp in my lungs. Mina and Nymbria moved in practiced rhythm across the packed dirt, the sweep of water answering Nymbria's hand as Mina barked some quiet correction. It was almost graceful, almost ordinary. My anger shattered it.

"Why didn't you tell us? Why did you leave us?" The words ripped out of me before I could leash them, echoing hard against the stone walls.

Mina turned at once. The look on her face was one of gentle pity, like I was a child lashing out. It made something hot and ugly burn in my chest. "I'm so, so sorry," she said softly. "I set you on the path of least pain. I promise."

"Least pain?" My voice cracked, raw and furious. I spun, pacing, unable to stand still as rage lit through me. Sparks snapped at my fingertips, bright against the overcast day. "This was the least pain?"

Her expression never shifted, maddeningly calm. "You weren't meant to face him. Most outcomes would have ended with your death, Lyla. You can't stand against him until you've accepted who you are. And you haven't. Not fully."

Her words cut deeper than I expected. "I haven't accepted who I am?" My breath came fast, uneven, magic prickling down my arms, begging for release. "I know who I am. You wouldn't let me escape it even if I wanted to."

Mina shook her head slightly, eyes steady. "Knowing isn't the same as embracing. You still hold a thread of disbelief like a shield. Until you let it go, you'll never be strong enough to face him."

"What is there to let go of, Mina? What am I supposed to embrace, to grasp that I haven't yet understood?" My voice cracked, half fury, half plea.

Mina's gaze didn't waver. "Goddesses aren't queens, Lyla. You can't do it all. You can't be it all." Her whisper carried like a knife against stone as she stepped closer, closer than anyone should dare. "You need to choose."

A bitter laugh broke from me. I spun from her, raised my hand, and let fire rip from my palm. The target across the courtyard exploded in the center, embers scattering like angry stars.

"I need to lead this country," I snapped, chest heaving. "There's no one else who could save people like me."

"No one else is like you in your country," Mina countered, her voice maddeningly calm. "But Ethan can save people like Amyra."

I whipped back toward her. "Ethan doesn't want this! He wouldn't take it. Mother didn't want it for either of us—Father made sure we knew that."

Her eyes softened, though her words didn't. "But that doesn't mean it isn't what's needed. Your mother didn't know who you are. She wouldn't want you shackling your power for the sake of what you think she wanted."

Her tone was meant to soothe, but it scraped raw instead. I felt my throat tighten, my breath trembling out. "You let Juniper die," I hurled at her, the words tearing like glass. "You could have saved us. You could have winnowed in, pulled us out, left before Bel could blink."

Mina didn't even flinch. "She could have too," she said quietly. "She had the same gift. But she knew Bel wouldn't stop chasing until he had a death. She gave him that death so you could return safely."

The truth of it landed like a hammer blow. My knees gave way, and I dropped onto the cold dirt. Dust clung to my skirts, bit at my skin, but I didn't care. I folded in on myself, head in my arms, the weight of it crushing down.

I hated her words. Hated that they were true.

Nymbria crouched beside me, her palm firm on my back, rubbing slow circles that steadied the ragged shake of my breath. Grief leaked out of me in hot tears, soaking into my sleeves, spilling into her touch as if she could carry some of it for me. Her presence was an anchor—salt, steel, and sea.

When I finally lifted my head, her eyes caught mine. "You are strong, Lyla. You are so incredibly brave," she whispered, her voice low, meant only for me. "You stood in front of that monster. You didn't falter. You thought on your feet. You saved us."

My chin trembled. "I didn't do enough."

Her grip tightened, grounding me. "Then we train. We sharpen you until Bel can't lay a finger on you. Because he will come again, and again, until you break or until he's killed. So we make sure it's the latter."

A rough, scratchy breath rattled out of me. My chin wobbled with the exhale, but I nodded. I needed to be better. I would be.

I spun suddenly, searching for Mina, so fast my balance nearly gave way. "Why didn't you tell me he would look like that? That he'd be so vile?"

Mina's mouth curved in a grin too wide for the heaviness of the moment. "Would you have believed me if I had?"

Despite myself, a thin, brittle laugh broke through. I shook my head. "Are the other gods like that too?"

Mina tilted her head, thoughtful. "The ones who sleep have a more humanoid look, but the ones who need to be resurrected, like you?" Her smile thinned into something sly. "I don't know. I've seen some differences already."

Her gaze flicked sideways to Nymbria. Nymbria caught it, stiffening, but Mina's eyes slid away before she could pin her down.

I stood up, dusted myself off. "What can I do to get stronger for Bel? How do I outsmart him?"

Mina smiled. "There's my girl. Let's get to work on that."

CHAPTER 29

The day slipped by in sweat and silence, Mina pressing me harder with each drill until my arms trembled and the air around me hummed with heat. No messengers had come to drag me back to the council. Whether Amyra and Spencer turned them away or the lords were simply too afraid to face me after our return, I didn't know. I only knew I was grateful. I wasn't ready to sit in that chamber and see Juniper's empty seat.

By late afternoon, the sound of hooves in the courtyard broke the rhythm of training. Ethan and Ivy. I dropped the stance Mina had me holding, chest heaving, and crossed to the edge of the courtyard just in time to see them exiting the carriage they had taken. Relief stirred beneath my ribs at the sight of them whole and well, cloaks dusty from travel but faces bright.

Servants hurried past with baskets of produce and bottles of wine, the scent of herbs and roasting meat drifting from the kitchens. A small feast was already being prepared for their return. My stomach tightened with a careful, cautious hope that the news they carried would be as warm and welcome as the food smelled.

I hurried forward, catching Ethan in a fierce hug before

pulling Ivy into my arms. Both of them were grinning so widely it was impossible not to smile back.

"Well? Don't make me drag it out of you," I pressed, searching their faces.

But they only laughed, the kind of laughter that carried fun secrets. "At dinner," Ethan said, eyes sparkling.

I groaned dramatically, hand to my chest. "So my own brother doesn't think I deserve to know first? The betrayal."

Ivy nudged him, her cheeks flushed with excitement. They shared a glance that was far too full of light to be casual, and the little bit of irritation I felt melted into something softer. Whatever news they carried, it was good—so good they could barely keep it contained.

"Fine," I sighed, feigning defeat. "Keep your secrets. I'll wait a few hours longer."

We parted ways to prepare, servants bustling around us with fresh towels and steaming water. When I stepped into the royal chambers, Amyra and Spencer were already half-dressed for the feast, their laughter and low conversation spilling into the room like music.

Amyra was fastening the last hook of her gown when I slipped inside the chambers, her reflection catching mine in the mirror. She smiled faintly, eyes soft, and came to press a kiss to my cheek before smoothing an unruly strand of my braid back into place.

Spencer sat at the edge of the bed, rolling his sleeves, movements slow and careful. When I crossed to him, his hand rose instinctively, curling around my wrist. The warmth of his touch steadied me, and when I leaned in, he brushed his lips over my knuckles, his breath feathering against my skin.

"Thank you," he said quietly, voice hoarse but sure. "For running after me."

I didn't have words, so I only squeezed his hand. Amyra slipped in behind me then, her arms looping around my waist, chin resting on my shoulder. "You're not allowed to make a habit of that," she teased, her voice playful but her eyes glistening.

Spencer's mouth curved, half-smile, half-grimace. "Noted. But... if I'm honest? Knowing you stormed a fortress for me?" His gaze burned into mine, unflinching. "Gods, Lyla—it's the hottest thing I've ever known."

Heat rushed to my cheeks, and Amyra snorted softly against my shoulder, swatting his arm. "Trust you to nearly die and still make it about your fantasies."

He caught her hand and tugged her closer, his grin wicked and unrepentant. "I'm alive. That's grounds for indulgence."

Her laugh was real this time, a sound that loosened something tight in my chest. She leaned down to kiss his temple, and when she straightened, her lips brushed the corner of mine in the same motion, a spark that lingered.

Spencer tugged at my hand, pulling me closer until the three of us were tangled together. Amyra's fingers skimmed my back, Spencer's palm settled warm at my hip, and desire hummed low between us. For a moment, everything negative—the war, Bel, Juniper's absence—faded. All that remained was our playful teasing, touches that lingered a little too long, the reassurance of bodies pressed close, a reminder that even broken things could be whole again in the right embrace.

Eventually I rose, the pull of their warmth lingering as I stepped free. My clothes were still dusted from the courtyard, smudged with ash and soil from hours of practice with Mina and Nymbria. They clung to me with the weight of training and loss alike. Amyra was already reaching for the gown laid across a chair, a sweep of soft violet silk that shimmered faintly in the lamplight. She held it out with a little flourish.

"Always thinking ahead," I murmured, smiling as I let her slip the worn dress from my shoulders. The cool air kissed my skin, followed quickly by her careful hands guiding the fresh fabric into place.

"Someone has to make sure you don't show up to dinner looking like you've wrestled in the fireplace," she teased, fastening the last clasp with a deft touch.

I turned, smoothing the skirts. "I saw Ethan and Ivy arrive

just before I came up," I told her, a small spark of warmth breaking through the heaviness of the past days. "They were glowing, the both of them. They wouldn't tell me a word until dinner, but... gods, I think we may finally have a betrothal to celebrate. A wedding, even, when the war allows it."

Her smile softened, hope flickering in her pale eyes. She reached to adjust the fall of my braid, fingers brushing my cheek as if to seal the moment. "Then let's hold onto that. Something waiting on the other side."

Before I could answer, Spencer came up behind us. His arms slipped easily around both our waists, pulling us close until his chin rested on my shoulder. "You two look radiant," he murmured, the warmth of his voice smoothing the frayed edges of my nerves. "If everyone doesn't already know how lucky I am, they will tonight."

Amyra laughed, leaning back against him. I covered his hand with mine, squeezing tight, unwilling to let go of the comfort of their touches.

For one rare, precious breath, the war felt far away.

Then, together, we stepped out of the chambers and into the hall, ready to face whatever awaited us at dinner.

We slipped into the hall just before the last of the crowd, our footsteps muffled by the rush of silk and murmured voices already filling the chamber. The chandeliers above gleamed with a hundred points of firelight, casting everything in a golden haze. I stole a glance at Spencer beside me. His posture was flawless, his face calm, even pleasant, but I knew the memory of his ordeal still clung to him. He wore the mask well, but I knew how fragile the edges might be.

The air hummed with greetings and laughter, lords and ladies gliding from one knot of conversation to the next. We were folded into the current almost immediately. I found myself smiling, nodding, speaking words I barely registered, each group drifting away only for another to take their place. Every lull was patched over before it could stretch, and I realized my cheeks were aching from holding the expression. Somewhere beneath it all, my stomach growled at the teasing waft of roasted meat and honeyed bread drifting from the kitchens.

Then the doors opened again, and the room shifted. Ethan entered with Ivy at his side, both of them radiant, their smiles so wide they seemed lit from within. Conversations thinned, eyes turned. Ethan raised his hand to address the crowd gathered in his honor, his voice carrying easily over the hush.

"THANK you all for joining us tonight," he said, steady and warm. "I am honored to share that I have received permission from Ivy's family to marry her. We look forward to setting a date when Elthas has won this war, when we may celebrate as a kingdom."

The cheer that rose felt like sunlight breaking through cloud. For the first time in weeks, the celebration didn't feel hollow.

They joined us at the head table just as the servants swept in, silver lids clattering open to reveal roasted pheasant, glazed roots, and loaves of steaming bread. The scents made my mouth water, but Ivy barely seemed to notice. She leaned forward at once, her eyes alight, cheeks flushed pink with excitement.

"You won't believe it," she began breathlessly, her hands clasped under her chin like she could barely hold the words in. "He sent my cousins to fetch me, said they wanted to take me walking—just like we used to when we were little. They wouldn't tell me where we were going, of course, just kept grinning like fools. And then—" She pressed a hand to her heart, her voice dropping to a conspiratorial hush, "we came to the grotto."

Her gaze went soft with memory. "It hadn't changed. The same arch of stone, the creek was frozen, of course, the snow caught in the branches above. And there—" She laughed, unable to help herself. "There he was, standing right in the middle of it all, waiting in the cold like a stubborn statue. And the ground—oh, Lyla, Amyra—you should have seen it. Roses scattered everywhere, deep red against the snow. Like spilled wine."

Amyra gasped, her hand flying to her lips. "That's beautiful," she said, her voice trembling with genuine delight. "Ivy, that's—gods, that's like something from a ballad."

I felt my own smile tug wider, warmth pressing against my chest. "That's exactly what you always dreamed of, isn't it? You told me once you wanted roses in the snow, even if no one else believed it possible."

Ivy's eyes shimmered, and she squeezed my hand across the table. "And I thought he'd simply ask me after supper like a practical man. But no—he gave me all of it." She lifted her hand then, the firelight catching on the ring Ethan had slipped onto her finger. Gold, delicate, with a stone that caught the light like a star.

Spencer let out a low whistle. "Careful, Ivy, you'll blind us with that thing."

Ethan laughed, leaning back in his chair with a grin. "Good. Let them all know she's mine."

Spencer tipped his head, smirk tugging at his mouth. "Roses, speeches, jewels—you really went for the whole swooning romance bit, didn't you? Didn't think you had it in you."

Ivy swatted lightly at Spencer's arm, though she was giggling. Ethan only arched a brow, pulling her closer with an easy arm around her shoulders. "She deserved all of it."

Amyra smiled softly at that, her hand brushing over mine beneath the table, like she knew I was cataloging every detail of this rare, perfect happiness.

Spencer chuckled, not letting it go. "I mean, a grotto, Ethan? Snow and roses? If you keep this up, half the women in Elthas are going to start expecting poetry at breakfast."

"Then let them," Ethan shot back, his grin sharp as he raised his glass. "But you—" his gaze flicked to Spencer, teasing—"you'd better hope your wives don't start taking notes."

Spencer barked a laugh, conceding the strike, and for a

moment the four of us laughed together, the sound rising above the clatter of dishes and the hum of the hall.

I couldn't help my smile. This was Ivy's dream—romance wrapped in finery, love dressed in grandeur—and Ethan had given it to her with all the sincerity in his heart. For once, the world had aligned something perfectly.

CHAPTER 30

The council chamber felt heavier than usual that morning, as though the walls themselves remembered what had been lost. Spencer and I took our seats side by side, the scrape of the chairs echoing too loudly in the stillness. Juniper's chair stood empty across from me, her absence louder than any sound. My eyes snagged on it, refusing to move until Spencer's hand slipped over mine. His other hand tipped my chin toward him, gentle but firm.

"Look at me, Lyla," he whispered. His eyes shimmered, damp at the edges.

I swallowed hard, forcing myself to meet his gaze. His grip was steady, his lips barely moving as his voice brushed against my thoughts. '*I love you. We'll get through this together. She won't be forgotten.*'

The tears threatened to spill. I pressed a tissue to my eyes, breathing deep, trying to steel myself. When I looked back, Juniper's chair was no longer empty.

Emberly sat there, posture straight but her gaze soft with understanding.

'*I'm sorry I didn't warn you, her thought brushed into mine. But she wouldn't have wanted you to face this alone. She always made sure to be at these meetings with you.*'

'*Thank you,*' I replied, my throat tightening. '*I'm glad you're here.*'

She gave the faintest nod, then lowered her eyes to the notes before her.

I forced myself to glance around the table. Denenbaum's chair remained empty.

The great doors shut, and Luther cleared his throat with the self-importance of a man already certain of victory. "At last," he began, his tone oily, "our runaway king has deigned to return. Tell us, Your Majesty, how it serves Elthas for its crowned head to slip off in the night like a reckless child—dragging the Lady Mallard to her end and risking capture that would have doomed us all."

My jaw clenched. Spencer didn't move. He sat straight-backed, hands resting on the table, but I felt the tension radiating from him like heat from a forge. His jaw worked once, a visible grind of teeth.

Before he could answer, Luther leaned forward, spittle flashing in the light. "What were you thinking, boy? Charging into enemy territory as if it were some tavern brawl? Do you know how close you came to collapsing the throne itself?"

The chamber rustled with discomfort, a few councilors whispering. My cheeks burned, but before I could open my mouth, Lord Greenhow stood.

"Lord Luther," his voice cut cleanly through the room, sharper than any blade, "your concern is noted. But I suggest you recall to whom you speak." His weathered face remained composed, though his eyes burned with a rare heat. "This is your king. Not a child in need of a scolding. Perhaps if you—and others here—had treated him with the respect of his station, he might have trusted you enough to ask for counsel rather than act alone."

The chamber stilled. The weight of his words rippled, landing like a blow. Gasps fluttered around the table. Mine was among them.

Gratitude surged in my chest, and I caught Greenhow's eye.

He gave me the barest flicker of acknowledgment before returning to his seat.

Luther sputtered, color rising high on his cheeks. His lips worked as though chewing glass before he finally muttered, "Very well. If my tone was... ill-suited, then allow me to restate. My concern, Your Majesty, is not to belittle you but to demand clarity: why risk everything on such folly? What assurance can you give us it will not happen again?"

I stared at him, astonished. Luther conceding—even partially—was a rarity I had never thought to witness. And I hadn't even needed to tie him to his chair to make it happen.

The chamber held its breath. Spencer didn't answer at once. He set both palms flat on the table, as if he meant to steady not just himself but the room, drew one long breath, and lifted his chin.

"You're owed clarity," he said. His voice was low, even. "I acted brashly."

A stir rippled along the benches. He didn't look away.

"I believed speed could end this—cut the throat of the war before spring. I thought a hard strike, or a face-to-face, might force their hand. I hoped I could reason with them, or maybe trade, threaten, bargain, anything to keep their ships from our shores." His mouth tightened. "I underestimated the depth of Bel's hatred. Of his hunger for Elthas. For Lyla."

The name landed like a stone in a pool; eyes slid to me, then back to him.

"I misread the board," he went on. "I thought I was choosing the path that spared our people months of blood. Instead I walked into a god's theater. There was no reasoning to be had—only spectacle and pain. Juniper..." His voice thinned, then steadied by force. "Her death is Bel's doing. But the road to it began with my choice. I won't hide from that."

Silence, save for the faint tick of cooling wax.

"I did learn what we could not have learned from a council table," he said, not pleading, only stating. "Bel will use any chain to reach Lyla. That is the enemy we face—not a rival court, but a predator who feeds on death."

Luther's mouth twitched, readying a retort. Spencer didn't give him the space.

"What will not happen again is this: I will not act alone. Not like that. Offensive plans—if we make them—will be made with this council and Crystalford, under command and with time enough to stack the odds in our favor. If you require that as decree, draft it and I will sign my name to it." He let the words hang, then added, quieter, "Hold me to it."

He sat back, but the fire in him didn't dim. "Bel wants us fractured. He wants me reckless and you contemptuous. He wants Lyla isolated. I'll not give him that."

Greenhow's chin dipped once, a sober nod. Emberly's pen paused over her notes. Across from us, Luther's eyes flickered before he cleared his throat with a rasp.

"Very well," Luther said at last, words clipped. "We will take your assurances... for now. See that you keep them."

Spencer didn't flinch. "I intend to." He slid his hand to mine beneath the table, warm and steady. "I'll do whatever it takes to win this together."

Lord Greenhow broke the silence with a slow incline of his head, his voice carrying weight rather than sharpness.

"Your Majesty, I accept your words. It takes more courage to admit miscalculation than to cling to pride. I will hold you to your promise, as you asked—and I will stand with you in it."

A low murmur circled the table, but Greenhow pressed on, folding his hands atop the parchment before him.

"Now, to the matter at hand. Crystalford's troops will reach Tathlamar by tomorrow. Five thousand men, well-trained. We must decide where to place them. How many will go to the coastal towns, and how many will concentrate here at the capital?"

I could almost feel the energy in the room shift—the scrape of quills against parchment, the shuffling of maps, councilors leaning in. Spencer straightened, already framing a suggestion. My lips parted to offer my own.

The doors slammed open.

A scout stumbled in, his cloak half-torn, sea-salt still clinging to him. His voice cracked as he blurted the words, breathless.

"Scoria Bay ships—crossed the sound. They're sitting just beyond range of our batteries." He gulped, eyes darting over the table. "A dozen of them, maybe more. They're holding the bay, blocking passage. Our fleet, Crystalford's fleet—they're trapped inside the river mouth."

Gasps, curses, a chair scraping against stone. My pulse pounded like a war drum.

My voice cut into the silence, sharper than I intended. "Go. The courtyard. Bring Captain Nymbria and her first mate here at once."

He bowed and fled, boots clattering across the floor until the doors slammed shut again.

The chamber held its breath. I braced myself for the protest I expected—Luther's sneer, someone's muttered remark about bringing pirates into the king's council. But none came. The councilors' faces were drawn tight with worry, not disdain. Their silence was a kind of acquiescence, a signal that even here, in the sanctum of Elthas's power, they were willing to place trust in her.

And through her, in me.

That realization settled in my chest, steadier than I deserved.

Maps shifted across the table, parchment edges curling under nervous hands. Greenhow muttered about troop dispersal, another lord spoke of river batteries, voices rising with clipped urgency. But all I could hear was the pounding of my heart, the knowledge that twelve Scoria Bay ships sat across our waters like wolves on the edge of a flock.

The doors opened again.

Nymbria strode in, salt-streaked coat swinging around her boots, Finn close behind with the quiet weight of someone who carried steel and knew how to use it. The air itself seemed to steady when they entered, the babble of councilors dimming into order.

My shoulders loosened before I even noticed the tension

they held. Nymbria and her crew had pulled me through Bel's dungeon, through fire and loss. If anyone could help me carve a path through this, it was them.

And yet, beneath the relief, fear gnawed at me. Dread curled in my gut. This was no mere blockade. This was Bel's hand tightening around us. His trap, his timing. He was drawing me out, making sure there was no retreat.

I clenched my fists beneath the table, wishing for one more day, one more week—enough time to train until my magic didn't stutter when fear crawled through me. Enough to learn how to look at him without the terror that had frozen me before.

But time was a luxury Bel would never give.

CHAPTER 31

The gates of Tathlamar groaned open, the iron hinges shrieking like old wounds torn fresh. Beyond, a river of Crystalford steel poured in, rows upon rows of soldiers in crisp formation, their banners snapping in the cold wind. Armor gleamed beneath the pale morning light, polished so sharp it hurt to look at.

At their head rode Frederick. His helm was tucked under his arm, his golden hair damp with frost, his jaw set in that way of his that made him look equal parts kingly and weary. When he saw me standing with the welcoming party, his expression softened. For the briefest moment, his shoulders eased, and I almost believed he was glad to see me.

I stepped forward, ignoring the cold bite of stone under my slippers, ignoring the eyes of half the city watching from the walls above. "Prince Frederick," I said, and bowed my head just enough.

He swung from his saddle in one fluid motion, boots striking the ground with a soldier's weight, not a prince's. He clasped my hand as he bowed, his grip firm, eyes catching mine with unspoken words.

"Your Majesty," he murmured, a flicker of warmth beneath the frost.

The cheers of the crowd filled the silence for us, a roar of gratitude that nearly drowned out my thoughts. Nearly. Because as I walked beside him, back through the gates and into the city, a question lodged like a thorn in my mind.

What would he have done, in Spencer's position?

It only took a heartbeat to know the answer. He had already shown me. Frederick had charged his kingdom into war for me, with Crystalford's fleet now standing between Elthas and annihilation. But as we moved through the streets, the memory of the meeting on Lummi Island rose—the stiffness in his posture when he looked at Nymbria, the awkward weight in the air between them.

Was this truly for me? Or had he come to fight for her?

We crossed the courtyard on our way to the castle, the winter sun casting sharp lines across the stone. The air smelled faintly of singed earth and salt—familiar now, the scents of training. Nymbria stood at the center, arms lifted, water swirling around her in ribbons that caught the light like molten glass. Mina watched from the edge, her head cocked, sharp eyes following every movement.

Frederick slowed. His boots scuffed against the stone, his pace faltering as though the sight struck him somewhere deeper than armor could guard. His gaze fixed on Nymbria, studying the curve of her shoulders and the way her hair whipped against her cheek as the current obeyed her command. Regret flickered in his eyes, plain enough that I almost pitied him.

"You know I'm aware of your history with her," I said softly, watching his expression.

A rueful smile tugged at his mouth. "Of course you do. You always were too perceptive." His hand flexed at his side, the leather of his gloves creaking. "I only wish things had been different."

"She surprised you, didn't she?" I pressed. "Being there, at the meeting."

He exhaled, a breath heavy with years. "More than you know. It's been... gods, years. She did everything in her power to avoid Crystalford since she left." His eyes didn't leave her, even as we resumed walking. "And yet here she stands."

We reached the far edge of the yard when he angled a glance at me. "Tell me truthfully, Lyla. That man at her side—the first mate. Are they…?" He trailed off, the question hanging awkwardly between us.

I couldn't stop the laugh that burst out. "Nymbria and Finn? No. They act like brothers, not lovers. Trust me, if you've built that particular nightmare in your head, you can put it to rest."

Something eased in his shoulders. The shift in his expression was subtle, but unmistakably showing the faintest flare of hope. His eyes went back to her, softer now.

I almost warned him, almost told him not to let hope take root. The words died before I could speak them, because he was already speaking, voice low and certain.

"Nymbria's the one who got away, Lyla. She always has been." His voice was low, but it throbbed with something old and unhealed. "I know it was an arrangement, the match our fathers wanted. But I was the one who asked for it. I'd seen her long before that. She was this beautiful, wild, defiant girl who slipped away from lessons and courtiers, who ran down to the piers without a care for what anyone thought. She was fearless. Untamed. And gods help me, I loved her for it. I didn't want to steal that fire from her, I wanted to guard it."

His throat bobbed as he swallowed hard. "I would have told her that if she'd let me. That I wanted her free, wanted her fierce, wanted her just as she was. But she never believed me. She thought binding herself to me would be a cage. She thought I'd trap her."

He dragged a hand over his jaw, shaking his head. "The truth is, I would have given up crown, country, even my name itself, if it meant she could keep that wild joy and still let me have a chance to love her."

His words pressed into me, raw and unguarded, and for a moment I could only stare. I had known Frederick as steady, dutiful, sometimes stiff in his diplomacy—but this? This was him stripped bare. A man who had carried a love so fierce it had outlasted years, borders, and silence. The depth of it melted something in me. My chest ached with compassion for him, for the boy who had once begged his father for her hand not out of duty, but out of wonder at the wild girl who belonged to the sea.

And yet unease crept in alongside it. Nymbria was not a girl anymore. She was a captain, a goddess reborn, a woman whose heart was her own—and the thought of speaking on her behalf made me wary. Admiration for his steadfast love warred with the sharp reminder that even devotion could become a chain if placed carelessly.

"Frederick…" My voice cracked before I steadied it. "She would be moved, hearing this. Anyone would. It's… beautiful."

His eyes lit with hope, fragile and bright, and he leaned in, almost boyish in his plea. "Then talk to her for me. Please. Tell her what I should have said back then. I don't think it's too late, Lyla. Not if she only knew."

I almost promised. Saints, I wanted to. But the image of Nymbria standing in the courtyard earlier—focused, shoulders squared against a war that could consume us all—rose up before me.

"I'll think about it," I said gently. "After the war. For now, she needs her attention undivided. None of us can afford distractions while Bel is coming for these gates."

His face tightened with restraint, hope dimming though it didn't die. He nodded once, the weight of both longing and understanding settling heavy between us.

"We had planned for you to take time to rest today, if you need it," I said, shifting topics. "There is a war council meeting in about thirty minutes. I've set you up with these quarters," I gestured to the door next to us, "and the meeting will be down the hall, third door on the right. Would you like to be there?"

Frederick nodded, "I will make sure my general and admiral are there too." He said stiffly.

❄

The council chamber felt more like an arena than a meeting hall. Maps sprawled across the table, markers jutted like half-buried blades, and already voices clashed loud enough to rattle the panes.

Luther slammed his palm against the map. "They've bottled us in, plain and simple. A dozen ships sitting fat and content just beyond our reach. We can't touch them without leaving ourselves exposed, and they know it. The answer is obvious—fortify the river. Hold the capital. Keep the queen locked away where she belongs until this storm passes."

I bristled, but Greenhow's voice cut across before mine could. He leaned forward, weathered fingers pressing the edge of the map. "That's hardly wise. With respect, Lord Luther, your plan cedes the sea entirely. Scoria Bay's fleet has already severed our supply lines. If we turtle up here, they starve us into surrender. Our people will wither before they even march on the walls."

The scrape of metal rang out as Frederick's general dragged a marker across the coastline, jaw set like carved stone. "Both of you miss the heart of it. The fleet is stronger, faster, better armed. We won't break their blockade by brute force, nor by hiding behind stone. The only hope we have is to concentrate what ships you do possess with our reinforcements. One decisive strike, break a flank, and the rest will fall. If it fails, at least we'll die fighting, not rotting."

Luther scoffed, folding his arms. "Bold words, General, but reckless. One strike? And if Bel himself stands on their decks? We cannot gamble the kingdom on a single attack."

The room rippled with mutters, half the council nodding with him, the others shifting uneasily.

My fists tightened against the wood. "You speak as though this is a mere squabble between kingdoms. He is a God, Luther. He won't be beaten while I'm sitting in these walls pretending he can't reach. If Bel is out there, then I need to be there."

A silence followed, taut as a bowstring. Luther's face purpled, but before he could bark again, Greenhow lifted a hand, calm but firm. "She's right. If Bel is their spearhead, then walls mean nothing. We must plan for his presence, not just his army's. And that means Her Majesty cannot be hidden away." His gaze shifted to me, and there was steel beneath his gentleness. "If we don't allow her to meet this threat head-on, we may as well surrender now."

The debate flared again, Luther shouting of risk, the general arguing for glory, Greenhow pleading for balance. Their words tangled, sharp and useless, until they blurred into noise. I sat back, jaw tight, letting them wear themselves hoarse. No argument of mine would pierce the egos clashing around me.

Still, a chill threaded through me as I listened to Luther thunder about retreat and walls. His plan made no sense—surrendering the seas when the blockade already strangled us. It would doom Elthas to fall without a single battle fought. Foolishness... or something darker. I bit back the thought, forcing it back into the crevice it escaped from. This was not the time to lay suspicion bare.

By the time voices grew ragged and fists slowed their pounding, the bones of a plan had formed. A push at the river choke, Crystalford's fleet concentrated for one strike, the capital fortified as best as it could be. Good enough to satisfy them. Nymbria gave her nod; neither of us could find fatal flaws.

But when it came to my place in it, the shouting began anew, each man arguing to pen me inside the castle like a gilded bird. They would never understand. Not until they saw Bel themselves.

I rose to my feet, the scrape of the chair legs cutting through their bickering like a blade. The noise faltered, eyes shifting toward me.

"At the end of the day," I said, my voice carrying, low but sharp, "none of you have the power to dictate where I will be. Not one of you understands Bel as I do. Not one of you hears him whisper in your head. I will not sit hidden behind these walls while he devours my kingdom."

Luther slammed a fist on the table. "Your Majesty, this is madness—"

I turned on him, glare like steel drawn from the forge. His

words caught in his throat. For once, he shut his mouth, cowed by nothing more than my eyes.

I swept my gaze across the chamber. "My place will remain fluid. When Bel strikes, I will meet him—wherever that may be. And none of you, not a single one of you, will stand in my way. If you want to serve your queen, then clear the path between him and me, so that fewer men die needlessly between us. Do not waste lives trying to protect me from what cannot be avoided."

The silence that followed was heavy, almost reverent.

Greenhow's weathered face softened, his voice almost pleading. "Then at least allow a queen's guard—ten of our best—to remain at your side. If not to shield you, then to carry your word where it must be heard."

I considered him, the earnestness in his eyes, the weight of his plea. At last I inclined my head. "Ten. But they answer to me alone. My command above any of yours, above any general's. If I am to face Bel, then those I bring with me must be mine to direct."

He bowed, relief flickering across his features. "So be it."

With that, the meeting dissolved. Papers gathered, chairs scraped, and the councilors shuffled out with their mutters trailing after them. My hands trembled as I set them on the table, though I held my chin high. I had won this fight, but the greater war loomed still.

Dinner awaited, but my appetite felt like ash.

That evening the hall blazed with firelight, the long tables groaning under the weight of roasted game, glazed roots, and sweet breads steaming in their baskets. Musicians played from the balcony, their lilting strings half-drowned by the hum of hundreds of voices. At the head of it all, the dais had been stretched to twice its usual length—Amyra's idea—so that Crystalford's leaders might sit beside us, a show of unity for all to see.

From my place between Spencer and Amyra, the arrangement reminded me of those long tournament dinners. Frederick sat across from Nymbria, Finn beside her, Ethan and Ivy a touch further down. Laughter and chatter rolled easily across the table, wine passing freely, but my eyes kept catching on the undercurrent between two of them.

Frederick's gaze lingered, steady and unblinking, every stolen glance at Nymbria threaded with something deeper than mere curiosity. And Nymbria—gods, she saw him, of course she did—but she anchored herself to her cup, to Finn's murmured jokes, to anywhere but Frederick's eyes. Her smile was sharp, her posture easy, but the deliberate way she never looked his way told its own story.

I pressed my lips together, sipping my wine. Whatever history lay between them, it hung like smoke above the feast, invisible to most but impossible to miss once you'd breathed it in.

The food was rich, the firelight warm, and for a moment the hall could almost have been any other gathering, not a war council in disguise. Conversation at our table skipped like stones across calm water.

"...and then the fisherman had the audacity to tell me," Ethan was saying, his hand cutting through the air as though still affronted, "'No, sire, I can't sell you this one. It looks too much like you.'"

Amyra nearly choked on her wine, laughter bubbling. "What kind of fish was it?"

"A salmon," Ethan replied gravely. "Big eyes. Pink cheeks. Stared at me like it knew me."

Finn barked a laugh, leaning back in his chair. "So the fisherman thought a salmon was your long-lost twin? Gods above, I hope he charged extra for the resemblance."

Nymbria arched a brow, swirling the wine in her cup. "Or refused outright, for the dignity of the royal family."

That earned a ripple of chuckles, even from Spencer, who shook his head. "You all laugh, but now I can't stop picturing Ethan's face on a salmon's body."

"Don't give the bards any ideas," Ivy said with mock sternness, though her lips curved. "We'll never hear the end of the Ballad of the Salmon Prince."

Frederick, who'd been quieter than most, leaned in with just enough dryness to make it land: "I'd pay good coin to see that sketched on a tavern wall." His gaze flicked—unintended, perhaps—toward Nymbria. She caught it, her expression unreadable, before she returned to breaking bread as though nothing had happened.

The laughter rose again, chasing away the heaviness that had clung to us since returning from Scoria Bay.

Finn, quick as ever, pounded the table in rhythm and broke into song, voice carrying above the laughter.

> "Oh the Salmon Prince with cheeks so fair,
> Swims upstream with royal air…"

THE HALL ERUPTED, some joining the rhythm with their mugs, others howling with laughter as Ethan dropped his face into his hands, shaking his head.

The table rocked with laughter, tankards thumping in time to Finn's mock-shanty. Even Ethan cracked a smile, though he tried—and failed—to glare the pirate into silence. The sound of it all swelled, spilling into the rest of the hall. For a little while, the weight of the blockade, of Bel, of war itself, thinned beneath the roar of voices and clatter of dishes.

The evening blurred into an easy rhythm of food and wine, conversation darting from story to story, the kind that kept heads thrown back in laughter and cheeks warm with drink. For the first time in weeks, it almost felt like living instead of surviving.

When the feast finally waned and the last platters were cleared, we rose from the table. I caught sight of Frederick lingering just behind Nymbria and Finn as they slipped into the corridor, the three of them heading together toward her quarters. His posture betrayed a quiet hope, his gaze flicking once more to her as the crowd thinned around us.

Meanwhile, Amyra looped her arm through mine, her eyes glinting with something playful beneath the torchlight. "You look far too serious for someone who just survived a hall of drunken sailors singing about salmon," she teased, brushing her shoulder against mine.

Spencer came up on my other side, his hand finding the small of my back. "She's serious because she knows what's waiting when we get back to our chambers." His voice was low, warm against my ear.

Heat rose in my cheeks, though my smile betrayed me. "Maybe I'm serious because I know I deserve nothing of what either of you are promising me right now."

Amyra gasped in mock offense, her pale eyes dancing. "Then we'll just have to convince you otherwise, won't we?"

Spencer's chuckle rumbled deep in his chest as his arm tightened briefly around me. "Careful, love. Between the two of us, you don't stand a chance of holding out."

My laughter slipped free, soft but full, as the three of us turned down the familiar corridor. I actually felt free when I realized I didn't care if the guards saw the way our steps quickened, or the way Amyra's hand lingered at my hip while Spencer's brushed against mine. Whatever waited tomorrow, tonight would be ours.

CHAPTER 32

The pounding rattled the chamber door hard enough to shake me from the warm fog of sleep. I cracked one eye open. The room was still black with night, only the faintest wash of starlight pressing at the shutters. For a heartbeat, I almost let myself sink back down, convinced it was some half-dream noise.

Then the door crashed wide, a flood of torchlight spilling in, and Ivy's voice split the air. "Lyla! Hurry—now!"

I jolted upright, the sudden chill raising gooseflesh across bare skin. Amyra stirred at my side with a groan, while Spencer tightened his arm instinctively around my waist, still half-asleep.

Ivy was already across the room before I could find words, arms full of trousers and tunics she must have snatched straight from the wardrobe. "Get dressed, quickly," she urged, tossing one pile toward Amyra, another toward me. Her braid had half unraveled, strands of dark hair still plastered to her face with dried sweat.

Only then did her wide eyes flick to the tangle we made on the bed. She froze, color rising high on her cheeks. "Oh—gods, I'm sorry," she blurted, the words tumbling over themselves. "Spencer, I didn't mean— I'll just—" She spun half a step, then thought better of it, clutching a tunic tighter to her chest. "No time. Truly, forgive me, but there's no time for modesty."

Amyra was already fumbling into the tunic Ivy had thrown her way, muttering curses as the fabric twisted the wrong way. Spencer finally sat up, rubbing his face, still dazed, while I yanked the sheet higher, half shield and half comfort. My pulse thundered too loud to let me speak.

"What's happened?" I managed at last, voice rough, though Ivy's panicked eyes told me before she even answered.

"The guards are sounding the alarm for invasion," Ivy said, breathless, fear flickering in her eyes.

None of us lingered another heartbeat. I threw the sheets aside, skin prickling in the cold air as I snatched the bundle of clothes from her arms. The stale scent of sweat and sex clung to me, a reminder of the night we'd stolen, but there was no time. A basin, a cloth, a pause to clean myself... every second could cost lives. I shoved the thought away and forced myself into the gown, fingers clumsy but fast.

"Ivy, you and Ethan, go down to the cellars. Please. You two need to—" I choked on the words, knowing that I was plotting for my own death.

Ivy nodded. "He's already on the way, and I'll be taking the servants' stairs down as soon as you're on your way."

We were dressed and at the door in record time. Outside, ten armored guards stood shoulder to shoulder in the hall, shields gleaming in the torchlight, spears angled. The narrow corridor was choked with steel and bodies. I grimaced, half gratitude, half claustrophobia. "Where was the breach? How long ago?" My voice came sharper than I intended.

"Western walls. Just fifteen minutes past," one reported, helm shadowing his face.

I blinked, trying to grasp it. "You all got into your armor and posted here in fifteen minutes?"

Another guard gave a curt nod. "We train for that, Your Majesty. We are here to protect you."

My jaw tightened. "No. You're here to help me reach Bel."

That earned a ripple of unease. One of the younger guards frowned, confusion plain even beneath his helm. "Begging pardon, Majesty, but... who is Bel?"

Before I could answer, Spencer's voice came from just behind me, dry as sand. "The tall, angry demon. Can't really miss him."

The tension in my chest eased for the briefest moment. I reached my hand back without turning, and found his. His fingers closed tight, warm and steady, grounding me. His other hand settled on my shoulder, the pressure firm, reassuring. I clung to that small tether of touch, drawing strength from it as the weight of what lay ahead pressed in.

"Move out," I snapped at the guards, voice ringing sharper than steel. "Either lead me there or clear the hall."

Half the line surged ahead, shields up, boots pounding the stone in unison. The rest fell behind, the weight of their steps echoing like a drumbeat as Spencer, Amyra, and I pressed forward in the center.

The torches streaked past us, shadows racing with us down the passage. My pulse hammered in my ears, but another sound pressed tighter—their footsteps, the two people I loved most in this world, keeping pace when they shouldn't.

"You should stay," I said, forcing the words out between breaths. "Both of you. Bel will be looking for me, not you. If you stay, you live. If you follow—"

"No." Spencer's voice cut me off, steady and low. "You ran through hell to pull me back from death itself. Do you think for a second I'd let you walk into it alone?"

Amyra's hand brushed mine as we turned a corner, her pale eyes hard with defiance. "And I've loved you since that night under the northern lights. If death wants you, Lyla, it'll have to get through me first."

I opened my mouth to argue, to command them as their queen, but the words died in my throat. They had already chosen.

So instead I slowed just enough to glance at them both, letting the fire inside me soften for a heartbeat. "Spencer, you're the strength I never knew I needed, and somehow still gentle. And Amyra…" My throat tightened, but I forced it through. "You've always been the light I measure myself against, and the warmth that keeps me alive."

The air thickened around us, heavy with the weight of everything we hadn't said, everything we couldn't afford to lose.

"I love you both," I said, clear and unshaken this time. "So if I fall, promise me you'll carry that love forward. Promise me it won't die here."

Amyra squeezed my fingers. Spencer pressed his shoulder against mine. Neither gave their word, but I could feel their promise in their touch, fierce and unbreakable.

The doors slammed open beneath our push, and the world outside roared at us. The western military training fields were awash in chaos. Steel rang against steel, a hundred voices shouting orders and screams alike. Smoke curled from the rooftops beyond the wall, dark plumes twisting against the half-light. The stench of fire and scorched wood hit me first, then the faint, acrid tang that meant flesh had already burned.

I froze on the threshold. My eyes dragged across familiar stone now streaked in soot, across bodies I couldn't yet tell were friend or foe. The ground was churned, scarred by fire and bootprints, stained dark where blood had already spilled. This was home. These were my people. And Bel had turned it into a battlefield.

A thousand thoughts clawed at me in the same instant—how many lives had already been lost, how many more would be before this ended. My chest ached with the weight of it, a devastation so sharp it nearly rooted me where I stood. For one ragged heartbeat, I couldn't breathe.

Spencer's hand pressed against the small of my back, steady and firm. "Eyes forward, Lyla," he said softly, but with that quiet steel in his tone. "They need their queen right now."

Amyra's fingers brushed mine, a silent tether, pulling me out of the hollow of despair and into motion again.

I forced my feet to move, stepping out onto the stone with the guards fanning ahead. But the crack of fire and the clash of blades lingered in my bones, each sound a reminder that every heartbeat cost us another innocent life.

We ran hard across the yard, boots slapping stone slick with ash. My lungs burned with smoke and cold air alike, but I didn't stop. Not until the wall loomed above us. I seized the ladder and climbed, hauling myself up rung by rung, the din of battle rising with me.

The sun was just breaching the horizon behind us, its light spilling gold over the rooftops of Tathlamar. It caught on the smoke, turning the haze into molten ribbons that drifted above the carnage. At least with dawn came vision—the night no longer cloaked our enemies, even if it revealed every wound my city has already endured.

I reached the parapet, heart pounding, only to have two of my guards close in at once, shields angled so tight around me that I could see nothing but the inside of their steel.

"Move," I snapped, trying to crane past them.

"Forgive us, Majesty," one said, his voice taut with strain. "We can't. Arrows are thick out here. Drop the shield, and you'll be a mark before you blink."

The truth of it stung worse than the smoke in my throat. I pressed my lips together, fighting the urge to shove past them. Instead, I exhaled, long and low. "Fine. Then take me to the nearest merlon tower. If I can't see over, I'll look through the slits like the archers do."

They exchanged a quick look, then nodded. "North, just ahead. Keep low."

We moved as a cluster, shields still braced around me, our pace angled toward the squat shadow of the tower that jutted from the wall—stone thick enough to shrug off fire, narrow windows cut just wide enough for an arrow's aim.

The merlon tower yawned open before us, its archway spilling into a narrow chamber that smelled of smoke and sweat. Archers lined the slits, loosing shafts with practiced rhythm, the twang of bowstrings sharp as snapped bones.

One of the guards motioned me forward, easing me toward an open slit between two bowmen. The stone was cool beneath my palms as I braced against it, forcing myself to lean close enough to peer outside.

The world beyond reeled into view.

Fields that had once been golden with winter wheat now writhed under fire, curling black smoke into the sky. The river, swollen with morning tide, churned with burning wreckage—bits of timber from ships and docks, bobbing like corpses too charred to name. Closer, the western quarter of Tathlamar was a snarl of collapsed roofs and broken walls. I caught glimpses of neighbors I'd known since childhood sprinting through the streets, clutching children, screaming for kin already lost.

The sound hit next. A clash of steel on steel, the thunder of boots on stone, the guttural roar of men cut down mid-breath. A war-drum of violence that vibrated up my arms until I had to clutch the stone tighter, knuckles whitening. My head swam with it, a dizziness curling hot behind my eyes.

Everywhere I looked, chaos. Flames licking skyward, arrows blotting out the dawn, bodies both rising and falling with every heartbeat.

But not him. Not the monster I knew must be here.

I dragged my gaze across the carnage again, hunting for that towering figure, those black eyes, that living wall of muscle and hate. Nothing. Only soldiers. Only blood.

I pressed my forehead to the stone, trying to steady my breath. Bel was nowhere to be seen—yet every scream, every fire, felt like his shadow stretching long over the city.

My breath hitched, fogging the stone as I pressed closer to the slit. And then—

'Looking for me, little one?'

The voice coiled through my skull, tinny and grating, like rusted metal dragged across glass. My stomach lurched at the sound, bile threatening the back of my throat.

'Where are you?' I hissed inside my mind, my fingers biting into the stone sill. *'Why hide behind all this destruction?'*

The laughter that answered was low, guttural, reverberating in the marrow of my bones. It wasn't heard so much as felt, slithering into the hollows of my chest.

'Hide? No, child. I feast. Every scream, every flame, every fresh corpse

—' his voice purred, jagged and smug, '—*feeds me. Strengthens me.*'

My stomach turned violently, the air sour with smoke and charred flesh. I clutched the wall harder, fighting the wave of nausea that rose hot into my mouth. The battlefield blurred before my eyes, not from smoke but from the sickness in my chest.

I gritted my teeth, forcing the nausea down. '*Enough games. Show yourself. Where are you, Bel? Where will you stand when I tear you down?*'

The laugh cut short, sharp as a blade snapped in half. Silence slammed into my skull, leaving only the pounding of my heart.

I reached outward, desperate. '*Mina?*'

Her reply came swift, her tone unshaken, cryptic as always. '*Go to the docks.*'

I spun from the window. "The docks," I ordered, my voice raw but steady. The guards didn't hesitate. Shields lifted, they fell into formation, and we barreled down the stairwell into the training fields below.

Spencer and Amyra were close behind, but our pace faltered as the ground told its own story—bodies scattered across the grass, guards and townsfolk both. We had to weave around them, boots sliding on blood-slick stone, the stench of iron heavy in the air. Every step forward felt stolen from the dead.

Northward we pressed, lungs burning, the smoke thickening with every breath. The battle's roar dulled beneath the growing thunder of the sea.

And then—just as the salt wind struck my face—black smoke erupted ahead, curling upward in a choking plume. It thickened, twisted, and in the space between castle and sea, Bel took form.

He loomed from the smoke, monstrous and towering, the ground itself seeming to shudder beneath him. His eyes burned that endless void, and the scowl twisting his face promised nothing but ruin.

Amyra gasped sharply beside me, a hand flying to her

mouth, her wide eyes fixed on the sheer scale of him.

Spencer froze. His body went rigid, shoulders locked, breaths coming shallow and fast. His eyes glazed over as he surely must be recalling Spencer's chains in memory, to the phantom wounds Bel had carved into him. His hands trembled where they hovered near his sides, not reaching for a weapon, only curling into fists that couldn't close all the way. The sound of his breath, too quick, too ragged, cut me worse than Bel's laughter ever could.

"Spencer," I turned to him, grabbing his arm, pulling his focus to me. His eyes were glassy, distant. "It's all right. Stay back. Reach for Mina. Beg her to come if you have to. I'll go." My chest burned as I said it, but I meant it—I couldn't lose him to this again.

He dragged in one breath, then another, then another—like a drowning man forcing himself to break the surface. His jaw clenched. He gave a sharp shake of his head.

"No," he rasped, voice raw but steadying. "I swore I would stand with you, and I meant it. No matter what." His trembling stilled, his hand finding mine in a grip so fierce it was almost painful. His eyes, still wet, locked on mine. "I will not leave you to face him alone."

I swallowed hard, my heart lurching between fear and pride. Amyra's hand found my other side, her touch electric with resolve even as her body still shook.

I turned to the line of guards at my back next. Their armor caught the smoke-stained light, shields raised, spears trembling just enough that I noticed.

"You may be brave," I said, voice ringing louder than I felt, "the best fighters Elthas has to offer. But that—" I pointed toward the towering figure waiting in the black smoke— "that is the God of Death. And he's intent on killing me." My throat tightened, but I forced the words out. "If you charge in with me, you need to know he wields fire like you wield your swords. If you choose not to go, I understand. Your families need you too."

For a moment, silence. I saw fear flash across their faces—

one man's lip trembling, another's grip tightening white-knuckled on his spear. But then their spines straightened, their shoulders squaring, their gazes hardening like steel forged under heat.

One stepped forward, fist striking his chest plate with a clang. "We swore our oaths, Your Majesty. We'll follow you wherever you go." The others echoed the vow, a low murmur that rose like thunder.

I nodded, heart aching with gratitude, but I held my ground. "Then hear my command. You will not face Bel. He is mine. What I need from you is to ensure no others come near me while I fight him."

The largest of them, broad-shouldered and scarred, gave me a look that might have been disbelief—or fear that I'd lost my mind. "Alone, Majesty?"

I lifted my hand, conjuring a small flame in my palm, the fire dancing steady despite the nerves I held. "We're more evenly matched than it seems."

The guard stared at the flame, then back at me, his jaw working. Slowly, he gave a sharp nod. He turned to the others, voice like a war drum. "Form the line. Nothing reaches her but the god himself."

Shields shifted, boots stamped into the dirt, and in their eyes I saw it: terror, yes—but also devotion, and the raw courage of men willing to stand between their queen and the world's end.

The guards locked their formation, shields overlapping, spears braced. Smoke curled from the scorched cobbles where Bel stood, massive and motionless, waiting.

Then the sound slithered into my head—a sharp, mocking tsk tsk, rattling like metal scraping bone.

'Still playing queen, little flame?' Bel's voice oozed through me, scratchy and tinny, every syllable burning like acid on my nerves. *'All this posturing, all these speeches... when you could simply come meet your end. I am waiting. Stop pretending you have a choice.'*

The flame in my palm sputtered once as nausea rolled through me, but I closed my fist around it, forcing the heat back into my veins.

I said nothing. I let Bel's words coil inside my skull like smoke, refused to give them breath. One step, then another, my boots striking stone in rhythm with the pounding of my heart. The air thickened as I closed the distance, sulfur biting at the back of my throat. His grin stretched wider with each stride I took, a predator savoring the moment prey walks willingly into its jaws.

Doubt gnawed at me. Every instinct screamed trap, screamed turn back, but my legs carried me forward until only ten feet of scorched ground yawned between us. I stopped, chest tight, flame prickling at my fingertips.

Past the haze, to his left, a shape caught my eye. Nymbria was poised at the rail of her ship, sails half-drawn as though she'd been ready to slip away but had halted to watch. Her silver-blue eyes fixed on us, on me. Relief welled so sharp it almost broke me. I wasn't alone.

Bel's head tilted, the gleam in his black eyes cutting sideways. He lifted one massive hand, almost lazily, and pointed.

I followed the gesture—and my breath caught. To the right, a tide of Scoria Bay soldiers surged forward, shields flashing, blades catching the morning sun. Fifty men, at least, thundering down on us.

My pulse roared in my ears. I spun left—another wave. Fifty more, pouring from the smoke, the ground trembling under their boots. The air split with their battle cries.

For a heartbeat, terror gripped me. I could almost feel the walls closing in, two jaws ready to snap shut around me and everyone I loved.

But then I forced myself back to him, back to the towering demon who was the true threat. My shoulders squared, my chin lifted. "End it now!" I shouted, the words ripping from my chest, raw and defiant. "No more games. End it all now!"

The fear still knotted in my stomach, my magic quivering at the edge of release. But I held, praying against all sense that somehow words might cut deeper than fire. That maybe, just maybe, this could stop before the world drowned in blood.

Bel only shrugged, the motion casual, almost bored—yet

steeped in mockery. "Suit yourself," he purred.

His arm swept up, faster than thought, and a spear of fire ripped across the space between us. It seared past, the heat blistering against my cheek and arm. I staggered, heart hammering, staring down at my sleeve where the cloth smoldered. Confusion wiped through my head, how did he miss?

The scream split the air. Spencer's scream.

My blood turned to ice. I whirled, eyes wide, and saw him crumpled on the ground behind me, writhing, clutching his side where the flames had struck. My breath locked in my chest.

Bel hadn't aimed for me at all. He never meant to.

No—he was aiming for Spencer. Always Spencer.

My stomach hollowed out, horror carving it wide. I could see it in Bel's expression, the slow curl of satisfaction on his monstrous face. He hadn't come here to kill me outright. He'd come to make me watch, to tear Spencer from me piece by piece, to punish me for daring to win against him before.

The world narrowed, every thought boiling down to one: he's going to take him from me.

I dropped to my knees so hard the stone bit into them, scrambling to his side just as Amyra slid in opposite me. Spencer lay sprawled on the ground, the fire still licking faintly along his skin before guttering out.

"Spencer—Spencer—" His name tore from my throat again and again, a broken chant, as though sheer repetition might tether him here.

Amyra's hands were already glowing, pressed desperately to the scorched flesh at his ribs. "Stay with me, please stay with me," she whispered, voice cracking as the light surged through her fingers.

His body arched once, a strangled breath shuddering out of him before his head lolled back. Unconscious. My vision blurred with tears as I grabbed his hand, shaking it, clutching it, my sobs choking his name over and over.

Amyra's glow grew brighter, searing, sweat breaking across her brow and dripping into her lashes. "It's not enough," she gasped, the words ragged, panicked. "Gods, why isn't it enough?"

The smell of burned flesh clung heavy in the air, acrid and sickening, while my heart thrashed like a trapped bird. I could not lose him—not after everything, not after dragging him back from Bel's clutches only to watch him die in mine.

I pressed my forehead to his shoulder, my tears streaking down over the raw skin as my magic jittered under my skin, begging to be unleashed, but useless against wounds like this. "Please," I begged hoarsely. "Not him. Not now. Please."

CHAPTER 33

Amyra's hands trembled as she pressed them to Spencer's chest, light flickering weakly from her palms. "Stay with me, stay with me, gods Spencer, just stay with me."

Her voice cracked, breaking on the edge of sobs. She lifted her face to me, her pale eyes locking onto mine, and I nearly crumbled under the despair written there.

Fear.

Helplessness.

The dawning truth that even her magic, steady as the tide, might not be enough.

Something inside me broke.

I couldn't watch. He was slipping away, and she breaking under it. Rage roared up, blistering, consuming, all teeth and fire. I slammed my palm into the ground, the stone cracking under the blow. Heat erupted in my chest, demanding release. I surged to my feet, ready to burn the world down around Bel, to make him choke on every ounce of suffering he had ever carved into mine.

But before I could unleash it, before flame even reached my fingertips, the world tore itself away.

Sound died first. One heartbeat, Amyra's desperate cries filled the air, Spencer's ragged breaths rattling in his throat. The next, silence swallowed everything. Not quiet, but pure silence, absolute, suffocating, so thick it pressed against my skull until my ears rang.

The smells followed. Blood, sweat, smoke, brine—all snuffed out. Only my own scent lingered, sharp and bitter with fear, like iron scorched on hot coals.

Then the world itself dissolved.

The docks, the water, Bel—gone. Only blackness remained. I spun in place, wild, searching for anything to anchor myself. The emptiness was so total I almost doubted I still had a body. My fire burst free at last, flames ripping from my hands in searing arcs. They roared bright and violent, but they found nothing. No walls. No air. No ground. My magic vanished into the void, swallowed whole, leaving not even an echo of heat.

A scream ripped from me, raw and wordless, the only sound in that endless dark. I screamed again, until my throat tore, until I felt like my very soul was trying to claw its way out.

And then, light.

A single star pricked the void, so faint I thought my tears had made it. But it pulsed, steady, patient, alive. I stilled, chest heaving, eyes fixed on that trembling glow.

The pulse quickened. Thump. Thump-thump. Thump-thump-thump. It wasn't random—it was a rhythm. A message. I felt it inside me, reverberating like a heartbeat that wasn't mine.

I blinked hard, and the pattern etched itself into my mind, each flash carving meaning deeper and deeper until I wasn't just seeing it—I was understanding. The star wasn't just light. It was speaking.

The pulsing star grew brighter, steadying into a rhythm that burrowed into me until it was no longer just light but language, thought, truth.

You have reached the final threshold.

The words weren't spoken, but I felt them vibrate in my bones, as though my blood itself carried the message. My breath caught.

Before you take the last step, you must understand who you will be if you succeed.

The glow swelled, filling the black with silver-gold light, and in it I saw myself—not a queen in jeweled crown, not a girl clutching at fire with trembling hands, but something larger. Vast. Terrible. Beautiful.

You are Balance. You are Magic. If you ascend, you will awaken the pantheon, and restore harmony to the fractured human lands. It will be your sacred charge.

My lips parted, questions tumbling to the edge of my tongue. What does that mean? How? What will it cost? But the star dimmed, refusing me, its silence sharper than any answer.

When it pulsed again, the light felt heavier, like it was warning me.

But know this: there are consequences. If you lean too far, if you tilt the scales in any single direction, the world will pay the price. Your power lies in the demand for harmony.

I scoffed, bitterness twisting my throat. "And Bel? He's tipped the scales until the world is drowning in shadow. He's abused his role for centuries. Where were his consequences?" My voice cracked through the silence, swallowed instantly by the dark.

The star flared, piercing, merciless. *He is facing them. You are his reckoning. His consequence. His end.*

The words seared through me, hotter than flame, sweeter than breath. I gasped, clutching the revelation to my chest. I am his end.

The void shattered.

The star's words still thundered in my chest as the world bled back into being. The crackle of fire, the stench of charred flesh, the frantic sob of Amyra's voice—everything struck sharper, louder, as though the void had stripped away all softness.

Time dragged like honey. Spencer was still sprawled in the dirt, his chest rising in shallow jolts under Amyra's trembling hands. Her face was slick with sweat, lips moving in desperate whispers as if sheer will could knit him back together.

Beyond her, the royal physician hobbled toward us, his gray robes flaring as he ran. My stomach sank as I saw his truth. He would never make it. The arrows hissing through the air would shred him before he reached Spencer's side.

My gaze snapped back to Bel. He loomed just as he had before the void claimed me—unaware, unprepared. Time had not moved for him. But for me, everything had changed.

Heat surged through my veins, molten and relentless. I thought of Spencer's scream, of Juniper's last battle cry, of Amyra's tears spilling over his broken body. Rage rose up, vast as the sea, and I stopped fighting it.

I let it consume me.

Flame erupted from my hands—not the gold-red burn of before, but a fire so hot it seared the very air into blue-white brilliance. The ground blackened beneath me as I poured it forward, a single stream of pure destruction lancing into Bel's chest.

His head snapped back, his roar rattling the docks. The blast drove him off his feet, staggering him like a struck titan. His skin blistered and split beneath the blaze, and the fire clung, gnawing at him as he tumbled backward into the water with a scream that shook the shoreline.

I stumbled forward, breath ragged, my steps dragging me to the edge. My eyes locked on the boiling surface, refusing to blink, refusing to let him rise again.

The sea heaved—then stilled.

I looked up and caught sight of Nymbria as she stood on the deck of her ship, her hands raised high, water coiling around her like living chains. With a final thrust, she cast it down, pulling him under with the strength of the ocean itself.

Our gazes caught across the distance, her power folding back into her even as mine guttered inside me. For a heartbeat, we stood as one, the flame and the tide.

Then she broke the moment. Nymbria vaulted off the rail of her ship, sprinting down the gangway, racing not toward me but toward Spencer.

Nymbria hit the ground in a skid, her boots grinding against splintered boards as she threw herself beside Spencer. Water shimmered in her palms before her knees even touched the earth, spilling in silver streams that hissed as they met the scorched flesh of his chest.

"Come back to us," she pleaded, her voice low but commanding, as if sheer conviction could tether him. "Stay here. Be with us."

Her words echoed Amyra's. Amyra's trembling hands were still pressed to him, her magic flickering unsteady, tears streaking down her pale cheeks. "Stay, Spencer. Please—don't you dare leave us."

I dropped at his head, my knees hitting stone hard enough to bruise, but I barely felt it. My fingers found his hair, damp with sweat and ash, and I bent close enough to breathe his ragged exhales. "Come back," I whispered. "Stay here. Be with us." The mantra rolled from me, over and over, not words anymore but a plea that bled from my very bones.

And slowly—impossibly—it began to work.

His chest lifted, steadier now. The shallow, stuttering gasps deepened into something closer to breath. The angry blisters across his skin dulled, hardening into blackened scars. His fists, which had been clenched in rigid agony, eased open, fingers curling lax against the ground. The rigid line of his body slackened, the torment melting out of him like smoke.

Amyra's breath hitched in a sob. My own tears spilled hot down my cheeks, blurring my vision.

"He's—" Amyra's voice cracked. "He's coming back."

Nymbria's hands hovered still, glowing faintly as the last of the magic sank into him. His breathing was even now. His chest rose and fell like the tide.

I pressed my forehead against his temple, tears soaking into his skin. "You'll make it," I choked. "You're going to make it."

And for the first time since Bel's fire struck him, I believed it.

Amyra's sob broke free, mine followed, the two of us crying over him, not in despair now but in sheer, shuddering relief.

Spencer was alive. He would live.

I lifted my head at last, my tears still falling hot across Spencer's soot-marked skin. The air around us felt strange—too still.

The clash of steel was gone. No more screams, no more arrows thudding into stone. Only the soft lapping of the tide against the pilings, the shallow rasp of Spencer's breath beneath my hand, and my own heartbeat crashing in my ears.

Slowly, I raised my gaze.

Across the yards, through the haze of smoke and ash, the battlefield lay eerily hushed. Our guards stood motionless, blades lowered but still drawn. And opposite them, where a tide of Scoria Bay men had surged moments before, there was no charge, no chaos.

They were on their knees.

Dozens of them, heads hanging, weapons slipping from slackened grips to clatter against the stone. Their faces were pale, bewildered, eyes darting like men roused from a nightmare they couldn't quite recall. Some blinked rapidly, as if trying to clear fog from their minds; others touched the ground in front of them, steadying themselves, confusion written in every line of their posture.

It wasn't surrender, not exactly. It was as though Bel's fall had snapped something inside them, some leash they hadn't even known bound them.

A shiver tore down my spine.

Bel was gone, dragged beneath the water's depths. And without him, his army had broken—not in defiance, but in disorientation, like sleepwalkers waking to find themselves on a battlefield.

My throat tightened. For a moment, I didn't know if I could breathe. My hand stayed tangled in Spencer's hair as though anchoring myself to him, but my eyes stayed locked on that impossible sight.

The God of Death had vanished, and his men were staring at me as though seeing me for the first time.

CHAPTER 34

The infirmary smelled of boiled herbs and saltwater poultices, a sharpness that clung to my tongue and refused to leave. Spencer lay propped against thin pillows, color returning slowly to his face. His breathing was steady now, but I still found myself counting each rise and fall of his chest as though any moment it might falter again.

Amyra sat curled against him, one hand wrapped around his wrist, the other smoothing over his chest as though she could keep him tethered here by touch alone. She hadn't let go of either of us since we'd carried him in. I could feel the ache radiating from her—grief and terror carved into her shoulders, a weight I had forced her to carry by letting her stand in the fire with me.

I wished I knew how to ease it, how to undo what she'd seen and felt. Instead, all I could do was sit across from them, hands useless in my lap, and drown in the guilt that her bright spirit now carried scars I couldn't heal.

The royal physician's oldest apprentice moved briskly around the cot, eyes sharp but voice calm. He checked Spencer's pulse, pressed his palms gently along ribs and limbs, then leaned back with a sigh. "The orders are simple, Your Majesty. Rest. Hydration. Don't push yourself to exhaustion." His gaze flicked between the three of us before softening. "That said... the truth is, Captain Nymbria's magic closed every wound. Bone and flesh are whole. What remains is weakness from blood loss, and the toll trauma takes on the mind. Physically, you are fine."

Amyra let out a shaky laugh, but her grip didn't loosen. Spencer met her eyes, then mine, and I saw how hard he fought to project steadiness, even as shadows lingered behind his gaze.

When the apprentice finally dismissed us, we moved together—Amyra and I each bracing an arm as Spencer swung his legs from the cot. He muttered something about being perfectly capable, but his weight sagged between us all the same.

We left the sharp smells of the infirmary behind and stepped into the corridor. The air was warmer here, touched with the aromas of roasting meats and fresh bread drifting from the kitchens. My stomach growled, startling me with its insistence, and for the first time in days the thought of food didn't turn my throat sour.

In the dining hall, the clatter of cutlery and low hum of voices met us before we even stepped inside. At the doorway, we nearly collided with Frederick, Nymbria, and Finn.

Frederick's face was flushed from the cold, but his eyes lit with relief at seeing Spencer upright. He clasped my arm in greeting, his grip lingering. "You three have missed quite the morning of reports."

Nymbria folded her arms, expression grim but steadier than the night before. "It seems every last Scoria Bay soldier was under Bel's spell. When he fell, the tether snapped. They looked like men waking from nightmares."

Finn leaned forward, his voice low and edged with disbelief. "Some dropped their swords mid-charge, swearing they didn't even remember drawing them. Others begged forgiveness. The commanders have already met with our generals. They swear not just to withdraw, but to help rebuild what they've destroyed."

Frederick nodded, jaw tightening as though he still couldn't quite believe it. "They've promised their king will send word directly to you, Lyla. An offer of truce. Perhaps more."

The words should have been balm, but a strange chill slid through me. Peace, from a country that had nearly razed us under Bel's shadow.

Amyra leaned closer, whispering against my arm as if sensing my unease. "If the spell broke with him, then maybe... maybe it really is over."

I wanted to believe her. I wanted to breathe in that hope and let it fill every crack. But I could still feel the echo of Bel's laugh in my bones, a memory that refused to fade.

The six of us gathered at the long table, dishes already laid in abundance—platters of venison glazed with honey, bowls of steaming root vegetables, fresh bread still fragrant with the oven's warmth. Servants refilled cups as if they couldn't keep up, but the laughter, the sharp exclamations, the overlapping voices carried the true feast.

Spencer sat propped between Amyra and me, still pale, but more himself as he listened to Finn embellish every detail of the fighting. "—and then Lyla just stood there, hand blazing like the sun itself, and the whole dock erupted blue. I swear to you, Bel stumbled like a drunk who'd had too many tankards, straight off the pier."

Nymbria groaned, though there was no hiding the proud curve of her mouth. "You make it sound like she set fire to the sea itself."

"Didn't she?" Finn grinned, tearing into a hunk of bread. "I'll be telling that story until the grave."

Frederick leaned forward, eyes shining with awe. "And I'll swear my loyalty to you until mine, Lyla. Elthas has my ships, my sword, my—"

I didn't meet his gaze. My hand pushed at the rim of my plate, circling crumbs, while his words drifted past like smoke. The star's voice hummed louder in my memory than any oath he could offer. *If you ascend, you will awaken the pantheon, and restore harmony to the fractured human lands. It will be your sacred charge.*

Sacred charge. The words rang like iron chains.

I reached out for Mina, more desperate than I cared to admit. Her voice snapped back instantly, warm and too-casual.

'Congrats, babe. Goddess unlocked. When you're ready for the deep dive, I'll be in your room. Bring questions. I'll bring answers..'

My throat tightened.

Finn was halfway through acting out a sword swing with a dinner knife when I scraped back my chair. The sound cut sharper than I meant it to. All eyes turned to me.

"I have somewhere I need to be," I said simply, already standing.

A flicker of confusion crossed their faces, until Nymbria's voice rose smooth and easy, corralling the silence. "She has some loose ends to wrap up, it'll make sense later." She redirected the table with practiced ease, teasing Finn for exaggerating.

It was her way of shielding me, even here, of telling me that she suspected where I was going—and why.

I slipped from the hall, the hum of laughter dimming behind me, and walked toward the path I already knew I couldn't avoid.

I knocked once, knuckles grazing the painted wood, and her voice called, "Come in."

The door swung open, and I stepped into a world I barely recognized. It struck me, with a pang, that I hadn't been in here since those first weeks in Elthas—half a year ago now. Back then it had been spare, almost monastic. Now… it breathed Mina.

Above the bed, a cocoon of pink gauze shimmered in the lantern light, suspended from a single hook in the ceiling and cascading down in gossamer folds. It caught every flicker, scattering it into soft glimmers, like I was standing inside the heart of a seashell.

The walls, though, stole my breath. Canvas after canvas covered them, layered close, every one an explosion of color and shape—no clear figures, but emotions made visible.

A storm of deep sea blues crashing against each other.

A canvas swallowed whole by shades of black, textured so thick it seemed to pull me in.

Streaks of violent red, jagged as lightning.

Greens and browns woven together until I could almost smell moss, hear branches groan.

Pink upon scarlet, a heartbeat in paint, throbbing with love.

Midnight speckled with silver dots, a sky I might fall into.

A calm, endless expanse of summer blue sky, so soft it made my throat ache.

One canvas where muddy browns and sharp reds met at the center, bursting outward into arcs of rainbow.

And finally, one almost bare—layered whites, creams, and beige, a quiet peace that felt louder the longer I stared.

I almost understood. The collection teased at meaning, like a riddle I should know the answer to. But the harder I tried to name it, the further it slipped from my grasp.

Mina, watching me take it all in, only smiled knowingly and gestured toward a small round table in the corner. Two chairs, close enough that knees might brush.

I sank into one of the chairs, still dizzy from the crush of colors around me.

"You did it, my Nivara," Mina said softly.

The name hit me like a bell rung too close to my ear. My breath caught. "I did… didn't I?"

Her lips curved, playful at first, then tempered with something heavier. "Well. Mostly."

I snapped my gaze to her, searching her face. "What does that mean?"

"He's not dead," she said simply, almost gently, "but you knocked him out. He's down, hurting, and thanks to Nymbria, he's caged. That's more than anyone's managed in a thousand years."

"Not… dead?" The word fell thin from my lips. I wanted to drag the truth out of her with my bare hands.

Mina only shook her head, her smile sad now, her golden eyes dimmed.

The air left me in a whisper. "What do I need to do? To finish it?"

"You already know." Her tone wasn't unkind, but it landed like a teacher reminding a student of homework.

I pressed, voice breaking. "Awaken the pantheon?"

Mina nodded once.

"But how?" My hands trembled against the table.

She leaned back, shrugging, almost infuriatingly casual. "That part isn't my lane. If it's like my gift, it'll come naturally once you connect to your gift. You just have to find the tether and walk the path."

I let out a bitter laugh, scrubbing at my damp eyes. "So vague. So impossibly vague."

"Welcome to godhood, babe." Mina's grin softened the sting, but didn't erase it.

I stared at our joined hands, voice cracking. "This is only the beginning, isn't it?"

Mina didn't flinch from the truth. She nodded.

The tears came hot, unwanted. "I can't be the queen Elthas needs and do this. Can I?"

Her hands closed tighter around mine, warm and steady. "Ethan is ready. Ivy already knows more than she realizes."

I dropped my head, tears dripping onto her fingers. And for once, Mina didn't tease, didn't prod. She just held me there, letting the silence say what she couldn't.

I pulled my hands from Mina's and rose, the chair scraping softly against the floor. The room felt too heavy, too close. I crossed to the window and pressed my palms to the cool stone ledge, needing air, needing space.

The courtyard below stretched quiet in the afternoon light. At its center, where winter's frost still clung to the edges of the garden beds, a single bloom had forced its way open. A purple iris—tall, bold, impossibly early. Its petals curled like flame caught in stillness, the first sign of spring daring to defy the season.

Too soon, I thought, a couple weeks at least. Unless it wasn't chance at all. Maybe the star, whatever it was representing, had sent it as its own message to me.

I blinked the tears from my eyes and straightened, my chest lifting with resolve. "Enough weeping," I said, voice raw but steady. "I have a kingdom to fix, after I've spent the last nine months breaking it."

When I turned back, Mina was still at the table, her fingers drumming lightly against the wood. Her smile didn't reach her eyes. There was something else there—uncertainty, maybe even pity. As though she wasn't sure the choice I'd just made was the right one.

CHAPTER 35

I had timed this meeting carefully—knew Ivy would be buried in the tasks I'd set for her, knew Spencer and Amyra were busy enough to give me and my brother this space alone. Ethan's chambers carried his usual sense of order—maps aligned in neat stacks, ledgers squared on the desk, a fire banked low to keep the room warm without waste. But the moment I sat down to have our chat, I saw the cracks in that composure. His grin was waiting for me, stretching wide before he even spoke.

"We've begun the planning, Lyla. Ivy and I." He practically leaned forward in his chair, words tumbling out too fast to restrain. "We've already chosen the colors—sage and lavender. My favorites. The florists promised it'll be breathtaking, arrangements overflowing in both shades. And the chef—gods, you should have seen him. He's been pulling out recipes he's hoarded for years, swearing he can make the perfect feast. He already has the courses set, and I can tell you, it will be flawless." His eyes were bright, boyish in their joy. "Ivy will glow in it, Lyla. I want her day to feel... worthy of her."

His enthusiasm was so genuine, I found myself smiling despite the ache pressing into my ribs.

And then he said, almost carefully, "We thought perhaps the summer solstice. Would you allow it?"

The air caught in my throat. The solstice. The day our mother didn't wake, the day she was taken from us, the day that Bel started his war path against me. The memory hit sharp, like an old wound reopening. My first instinct was to recoil, to say no, not that day, not when the pain was etched into it.

But I saw Ethan's eyes, wide and waiting, hope hanging on my answer.

I breathed slowly, weighing it. Perhaps it wasn't desecration at all. Perhaps it was reclamation.

At last, I nodded. "Yes. She would have approved of Ivy. And maybe it's right—that her day be remembered for joy instead of only grief. A way to honor her, and the choices she made for us."

Relief washed over his face, bright as sunlight, and his grin returned with force. "Thank you, Lyla. I wanted to have her there for me, to let her know she's still in our thoughts."

I nodded, my composure too unsteady to reply. She would know. She had always said Ivy was like her second daughter. She loved her almost as much as me, almost as much as Ethan does now. She would have been more excited than any of us, I would think.

When the excitement settled into a gentler silence, I leaned forward, twisting my hands together. "Have you thought about what I asked you?"

Ethan's grin faltered. His eyes slid away, finding the grain of the desk instead of me. But he nodded once, stiffly.

I gave him time, the quiet stretching between us like taut thread. Finally, I asked softly, "Do you have an answer?"

He looked up then, and my chest tightened. His eyes were glassy, a sheen of unshed tears threatening to spill. "Is it truly the only way?"

My throat closed. Words refused me, so I only nodded.

He rose abruptly, crossing the room in a few strides, snatching a handkerchief from the side table. He pressed it into my hand with a kind of fierce tenderness. I tried for a smile, but it landed thin, brittle, not reaching my eyes.

He let out a shaky laugh, scrubbing a hand down his face.

"I'd be a horrible big brother—and an even worse royal—if I didn't agree to your request."

Hot tears broke free before I could stop them, streaming down my cheeks. I stood quickly, needing to leave before I crumbled.

"Lyla," he called after me. I froze at the door.

His voice cracked, but his words carried a crooked grin. "Could you... do it in a way that makes me look half as cool as you did?"

A startled laugh broke from me, unguarded. Not what I expected. "Yes," I promised, wiping my eyes. "I'd be proud to give you that."

I headed to my office. We still needed to repair relations with Scoria Bay. Part of me wanted to wait until they came crawling back, but a week had passed since the battle and no word had come. If Elthas was to move forward, I had to be the one to clear the path.

I sat at my desk, the parchment crisp beneath my hand, and began to write.

To His Highness, Prince Egan of Scoria Bay,

In the interest of securing a lasting peace between our realms, I extend to you, or to a delegate of your choosing, an invitation to meet with me at Tathlamar. It is my hope that through dialogue we may lay down enmity, seek common cause, and build the foundations of stability our peoples so greatly deserve.

I await your reply with due anticipation.

With regard,

Lyla, Queen of Elthas

I sealed the letter with wax, pressing my signet deep until the crest cooled hard. As I held it, I weighed the means of its journey. Magic could carry it swiftly, true, but would it reach him? While I knew where that office in the fortress was, it had felt half-abandoned, more grave than dwelling. Better the surety of a courier than the risk of silence.

I rose, letter in hand, and carried it myself down to the postal room, unwilling to leave this first step to anyone else.

The air in the postal office smelled of stale beeswax and dust, a far cry from the perfumed halls I was used to. A lone clerk looked up from his ledger, quill dangling between his fingers. His eyes went wide under his bushy brows, and he scrambled to his feet so quickly the stool clattered over behind him. He looked torn between bowing to me and reaching to fix his stool. I had to bite my lip to hold back my smirk.

"Y–Your Majesty!" he stammered, voice cracking. "I—I didn't expect—well, I mean, we never—no one said—"

I set the letter gently on the counter, sparing him further suffering. "This is to be delivered to Scoria Bay. It requires your most trusted courier."

His throat bobbed as he swallowed, fingers twitching as though afraid to touch the sealed missive. "O–of course, my Queen. Immediately. I'll—yes, I'll see it arranged at once."

"Thank you," I said simply. His face reddened as he tried to bow and snatch up the letter at the same time. I left him to sort the clutter he made of his work station, and headed back up the stairs.

Nymbria was striding into the corridor as I emerged. Salt clung to her still, like she carried the sea with her wherever she went.

"What now?" I asked, slowing to match her step. "The war's done, the kingdom no longer needs your fleet at its beck and call. Do you already have your course plotted?"

Her mouth pulled into a wry smile, but the shadows in her eyes betrayed her. "We tried. Yesterday. Had everything stowed and ready to cast off. But the tug hit me harder with every order to prepare to leave the docks. Like claws in my chest. We stopped before I tore myself in half trying to leave."

I studied her for a beat, then let a grin tug at my lips. "Good thing you paused. I might have a suggestion."

Nymbria's jaw tightened, as though bracing herself for

whatever I was about to propose, but before I could say more, the sound of boots echoed in the hall behind us.

We both turned to find Finn rounding the corner with a casual ease, swagger in every step, and came to rest against the stone arch near us as though it had been waiting for him. Arms folded, grin slanted, he drawled, "Well, well. Plotting without me again?"

"Talking," Nymbria corrected flatly, though a faint flush betrayed her.

Finn pushed off the wall and slid into step beside us as though he'd been invited. "Talking, plotting, scheming—call it what you like. With the two of you, it always sounds dangerous." His grin sharpened, eyes glittering with mischief. "But if you're looking for a better way to spend the evening… my quarters are also large enough for three. Wine's already open."

"Finn," Nymbria sighed, the corner of her mouth twitching. "You do realize charm loses its edge when you use it like a hammer?"

I rolled my eyes, a laugh slipping out before I could stop it. "Do you ever quit?"

He spun to walk backward a few steps, spreading his arms like the answer was obvious. "Why would I, when it keeps working?"

"Only in your head," Nymbria shot back smoothly, though the warmth in her tone softened the bite.

His wink was pure trouble, grin the picture of unrepentant charm.

I shook my head at them both, unable to keep the smile off my face. "Gods, the two of you. If this is how you're going to keep bickering, maybe I'll take the wine for myself and leave you to it."

Nymbria snorted, Finn laughed outright, and for a heartbeat, it was just the three of us, easy and unguarded, and it felt surprisingly comfortable.

CHAPTER 36

I had almost everything in place. Almost. The one thing left was the hardest, telling Spencer and Amyra about what I had to do. I knew them well enough to picture their faces even before I spoke—Amyra's eyes lighting with eager devotion, Spencer's jaw setting in quiet determination. They'd insist on following me anywhere, even into ruin, and I couldn't let them. Not this time.

I'd prepared the room for it, as if setting the stage might somehow ease the words. Dinner laid out on the low table, candles casting soft light across the walls, a fire burning steady in the hearth. No friends, no staff, no interruptions. Just us. I had even given Ivy the evening off. I told her to go spend time with Ethan, to polish her plans until they gleamed. She'd beamed at me, already rattling off a list of ladies-in-waiting who might fill her duties once she was married to my brother. Always so precise, always so thorough. If only she knew that soon that list would be for her choices instead.

The quiet stretched until I heard them—two familiar voices rising from the corridor. Spencer's deep timbre, warm as ever, and Amyra's brighter lilt twining through his words. Laughter spilled between them, careless, unburdened. The sound should have steadied me, should have reminded me why I was doing this. Instead, my stomach knotted and my palms dampened, as panic set in.

I sat frozen by the fire as their steps drew closer, heart pounding in time with their cheerful chatter. For the first time in a long while, I wished for one more delay, one more reprieve. But the door handle turned, and there was no turning back.

The door swung open, and they both stopped short. The table gleamed with silver and polished glass, steam curling from covered dishes, firelight painting everything gold.

Amyra's hand flew to her mouth. "Oh, Lyla…" Her eyes shone as she turned to Spencer. "Look at this. She did all of this for us."

Spencer's gaze swept the room, and then he grinned at me —boyish, disarming. "Gods, love, you outdid yourself. You're spoiling us."

Heat rushed to my cheeks. I forced a smile, though my pulse thudded like a war drum. If only they knew. "I just wanted us to have a quiet night."

Amyra was already crossing the room to kiss my cheek, her fingers brushing lightly over my arm. "It's perfect."

Spencer leaned down to kiss my temple, his hand warm on my back. "Best surprise I've had in weeks."

I smiled again, sharper this time, hoping it passed for real. My tongue itched with words I couldn't yet bring myself to say. Instead, I let them drift toward the bathing room, listening to their lighthearted banter echo off the stone.

When they came back, faces damp and hair smoothed, the mood was easy, tender. They sank onto the cushions around the table, reaching for goblets as though this were nothing more than another night in our chambers.

Amyra brushed a stray curl behind her ear, eyes bright with pride. "I helped in the infirmary today. The physician is teaching me how to grind and mix herbs for poultices—comfrey and willow bark, for burns and fevers. I want to know what to do when my magic isn't enough." She smiled at me, glowing with quiet determination.

Spencer chuckled softly. "And I spent my morning with

Lord Greenhow. He really is the nicest man I've ever met. He told me three stories about Amyra as a child before I could even get a word in." His grin softened into something almost bashful. "Feels good, calling him my father-in-law. Like it's real."

Amyra laughed, swatting his arm. "It is real, you goose."

They both turned to me then, radiant in the firelight, and my chest squeezed so tight I thought I might shatter before I got the words out.

I cleared my throat. "I'm glad you both had a good day," I managed instead, smiling weakly as I folded my napkin, unfolded it, then folded it again.

Amyra's smile faded. She tilted her head, studying me with that uncanny way she had of peeling back every layer. Her goblet clicked softly against the table as she set it aside, then her hand slid across to catch mine. "Lyla. What's wrong?"

The warmth of her palm anchored me, but it also made the truth heavier. My gaze dropped to the untouched plate in front of me, steam curling upward, the scent of roasted herbs and butter suddenly cloying.

I drew in a deep breath, chest tight. "I have to leave." The words scraped out, small but irrevocable.

Spencer shifted beside Amyra, brows knitting, but I pressed forward before courage failed me. My throat closed, but I forced it open. "I need to go with Nymbria."

The silence that followed felt like the whole world holding its breath.

Spencer was the first to move. His chair scraped back an inch, the muscles in his jaw twitching as he stared at me like I'd just struck him. "With Nymbria?" The words snapped sharp, too loud for the quiet chamber. "After everything—after I nearly —" He cut himself off, breath ragged, fists curling on the table. The flicker of jealousy in his eyes burned hotter than the candles between us.

Amyra's hand tightened around mine, softer but no less urgent. "Lyla… I don't understand." Her brows pinched, lips trembling as if she couldn't quite shape the question. "What do you mean, leave? You can't just—" She broke off, shaking her head as though the pieces wouldn't fit together.

My vision blurred, tears pressing hard at the corners of my eyes. The words swelled in my chest, aching to be spoken, and yet my throat closed against them.

My hand trembled as I lifted the cup, the wine sharp and cool as it slid down my throat. I drained half of it in one pull, hoping it would steady me. It didn't. Setting it back down, I dragged in a breath, willing my voice not to shake.

"It's not like that," I began, eyes flicking between them. "It's not that I'm in love with her. It's that... our job isn't done. When I thought Bel had—when I thought that you were—" My voice cracked, and I pressed my lips together until I could go on. "When that despair hit me, that I might have lost my husband, something broke open inside. I finally channeled the power I've carried all this time. And with it came... a duty. The stars came to me, they paused everything and explained to me that I still had something to do. I can't stay here and complete it. Not if I'm meant to become what they demand."

For a heartbeat, silence stretched taut across the table. Then Amyra's fingers clutched mine, so tight it almost hurt. She shook her head, tears already brimming. "Then I'll go with you," she said fiercely, no hesitation, no doubt.

Spencer's jaw worked, his eyes still storm-dark, but he gave a sharp nod. "And so do I."

The jealousy still lingered in his face, a shadow he couldn't quite banish. But that flicker, raw and human, made my chest ache with love for him all the more. Even in his anger, he was choosing me.

I squeezed Amyra's hand, then pulled back, shaking my head. "No. You can't. Neither of you. This... this isn't a journey across borders or a march into battle. I don't even know where I'll go, or how, or what I'll face when I get there. It could be anything. It could be worse than Bel. I won't drag you into that."

Amyra's chin lifted, stubborn fire in her pale eyes. "You

don't get to decide that for me. For us. You're my heart, Lyla. My place is with you, wherever that leads."

Spencer leaned forward, his voice low but firm, the edge of command slipping into it. "And you're my queen, but more than that—you're my wife. I swore I'd stand at your side no matter what. Do you really think I'd let you walk into whatever this is alone?"

I pressed my hands to my temples, a tear sliding free despite my effort to hold it back. "You don't understand—"

"We understand enough," Spencer cut in.

Amyra nodded, her fingers reclaiming mine. "We're not asking, Lyla. We're telling you. You won't be alone in this."

For a long moment I stared at them both, love and terror warring in me. My chest felt too tight, my breath too shallow. Finally, I exhaled, slow and shaky, and gave a small nod. "Fine. You can come. But you have to promise me—both of you—that the moment it becomes too dangerous, you go home. You don't argue, you don't hesitate, you go."

Neither looked happy with it, but after a pause, they both nodded.

Relief and grief tangled in me until I couldn't hold back anymore. I leaned across the table, pressing my forehead against Amyra's, reaching for Spencer with my free hand. His palm closed over mine at once, warm and steady, and Amyra's breath shivered against my cheek. For a moment, all the fear quieted, replaced by the steady pulse of us three, bound tighter than vows or crowns could ever make us.

"I love you both more than I can ever say," I whispered, voice raw. "That's why I need to try to keep you safe. But... I don't know if I can do this without you."

Amyra's lips brushed my temple in a soft, reverent kiss. "You'll never have to."

Spencer squeezed my hand harder, then pulled back just enough to look at me. His expression was softer now, the jealousy dimmed into something closer to protectiveness, though the shadow of it still lingered in his eyes. "I need to know," he said, voice steady but edged. "How does Nymbria fit into all this? What's her part in what you're being called to do?"

I swallowed, my thumb brushing against the back of Spencer's hand. "I don't know," I admitted, the words tasting bitter for how little they offered. "All I know is that our connection is still strong. Whatever fate or the stars or the gods themselves are weaving, she's part of it."

Amyra's brows drew tight, but she didn't let go of me. Spencer just waited, gaze steady, as if he could will me to give him more than I had.

"She told me," I went on, "that when she tried to sail away a few days ago, she couldn't. The further her ship prepared to cast off, the worse it got—like some tether yanking her back. She said it wasn't just strong, it was painful."

Amyra's lips parted in a soft gasp. Spencer's jaw worked, but he didn't speak, his silence somehow heavier than any words.

"It means something," I said quietly. "Even if I can't see what yet."

Spencer's brow furrowed, his voice low but edged. "So what then? You're just supposed to go traipsing across the world with her? Aimlessly wandering until fate decides to drop an adventure in your lap?"

The words stung sharper than I expected. My shoulders stiffened, and I pulled back just enough that the warmth of his hand felt foreign instead of steadying.

"I don't exactly have a guidebook," I snapped, the frustration breaking through before I could soften it. "There isn't a neat little manual for how to become a goddess of balance—or for what it means to wake the Gelid Pantheon and put the world back in order." My voice caught, then steadied into something sharper. "So if I'm fumbling my way forward, I'd appreciate a little faith in my ability to find the path. To navigate this. To not lose myself—or us—along the way."

Silence stretched between us, heavy as the air before a storm, until Spencer pushed back his chair. He rose without a word, circling the table. My breath caught when he dropped to one knee beside me, his hands clasped and placed in my lap as if they belonged there.

"Lyla..." His voice was rough, stripped of its usual steadiness. "I'm sorry. I don't mean to doubt you. I just—" He swallowed hard, eyes lowered. "I don't know what to expect anymore. I don't know what tomorrow looks like for us. And that terrifies me."

My heart softened even as my throat tightened. I lifted one hand from his, tracing my fingers along the line of his cheek. His head tilted up at the touch, blue eyes meeting mine, vulnerable and pleading.

"You don't have to know what tomorrow looks like," I whispered, thumb brushing against the edge of his jaw. "You just have to be with me for it."

He exhaled, shaky but relieved, leaning into my touch. The apology was in his eyes, the forgiveness in mine.

Amyra's fingers tightened around mine, her voice slipping into that blend of gentleness and teasing she wielded like a blade.

"Gods, you two are dramatic," she said, lips quirking. "One of you ready to fling yourself into despair, the other into divinity. And meanwhile, I'm just trying to enjoy dinner with my spouses."

A startled laugh broke from me, catching on the edge of tears, and Spencer let out a low chuckle too, the tension easing from his shoulders.

Her hand stayed clasped in mine, warm and unshaken, the anchor I hadn't realized I'd been clinging to. I felt a weight lift, as Spencer moved back to his seat, and we settled into the meal.

CHAPTER 37

The reception hall shimmered with candlelight, laughter and music weaving through the air like ribbons of light. Yet beneath the warmth of it all, the day's weight pressed hard on my chest. The summer solstice had always carried meaning in Elthas, but this one bore too much at once. The first anniversary of my mother's death. The wedding of my brother to my dearest friend. And the last sunset I would see in Elthas for who knew how long.

Spencer stood beside me in a sage suit that sharpened the green of his eyes until they gleamed like cut emeralds. Amyra's lavender dress matched my own, simple but elegant, the fabric catching light as she moved. Standing between them, my hands in theirs, I felt almost complete—almost steady. I watched the dancers spin across the floor, and caught Ethan glancing at us from the dais, where he and Ivy sat, their faces lit with a joy so unshakable, it burned through any grief that welled up today.

The ceremony already blurred in my memory, dreamlike, though pieces stayed sharp. Ethan's voice catching as he promised Ivy forever. Ivy clutching his hand like she'd never release it. The cheer of the crowd when their vows sealed. And then, as if summoned by the words themselves, the clouds parting to let sunlight blaze down upon them—golden and fierce, a blessing from above.

Now, as the hall rang with celebration, I blinked against the sting in my eyes, caught between joy and sorrow, past and future. Tonight belonged to Ethan and Ivy. But Ethan and I had one more surprise planned for the crowd still gathered.

Across the tables and flickering candles, Ethan's gaze found mine. He gave the smallest nod, steady and sure. My heart leapt. I squeezed Spencer's and Amyra's hands once more, then let them go and slipped into a back room I had prepared.

Waiting for me there were the items I had selected for this moment. Mina had been teaching me how to use my magic in ways that weren't about survival or battle, and tonight, for the first time, I wanted to share that with my people.

I drew in a breath, focused, and willed the air around me to shimmer. When I stepped forward, I did not walk—I winnowed. A sparkling cloud burst across the dais, stardust and smoke curling together, and I emerged from it. Gasps rippled through the hall, followed by a hush so sudden it pressed against my ears.

Light clung to me like a second skin, a soft glow that made the lavender of my dress gleam as though lit from within. I let my magic carry my voice, lifting it clear above the silence, each word thrumming through the chamber.

"My people," I said, and my voice carried like wind across water, soft yet unignorable. "I stand before you no longer only as your queen, but as what I was always meant to become—the newest member of the Gelid pantheon."

Gasps broke the silence, quickly swallowed as I raised my hand. "The goddess of balance," I continued, "keeper of harmony between forces too easily broken. Where chaos overwhelms order, I restore. Where cruelty outweighs mercy, I right the scales. It is not a throne I sought, but a sacred duty entrusted by the stars themselves."

The glow deepened, casting the hall in soft radiance as I drew a breath. "Because of this, I can no longer reign in Elthas. To serve balance, I must walk where the world is fractured, not remain bound to one crown."

A murmur stirred, trembling with both awe and fear, but I

pressed forward, my words as certain as the fire burning in my chest. "And so, tonight, in this hall of joy, I anoint new rulers to guide you through what lies ahead. Ethan and Ivy, whose love binds two families, whose strength will bind this kingdom. By my hand, by my magic, by the stars themselves, I name you King and Queen of Elthas."

The light around me flared, dazzling bright, before settling into a warm glow that lingered.

The silence that followed was not empty but brimming, as though the hall itself held its breath. Then it shifted—not into cheers or shouts, but into something quieter, deeper. A murmur of awe, the sound of people kneeling, the creak of benches as men and women bent their heads. Tears gleamed on faces lit by the glow still radiating from me. No one reached for cups or called out, as might happen in a feast; this was not celebration, but consecration.

I turned, and with a sweep of my hand, light coalesced between my palms. It shimmered, molten and radiant, until it hardened into two crowns, heavy and intricate, the finest pieces of our treasury. Both were lined with deep blue velvet, the golden filigree curling in delicate, ornate patterns. Gems in every shade of the rainbow caught the glow of my magic, scattering shards of light across the hall.

I set the first crown on Ethan's head. Its square, angular strength was no less dazzling than the delicate filigree of the one I used to wear. As I lowered it onto his brow, the jewels flared with color, catching every torch and candle. "Rise, Ethan of Elthas," I intoned, my voice still edged with the resonance of power. "My brother. My king."

Then I turned to Ivy. She knelt before me, hands pressed to her heart, tears shining unchecked on her cheeks. I raised the crown that had once graced my head—its design soft, petals poised to bloom, delicate and radiant as she herself. As it settled against her dark hair, she drew in a shaking breath, her eyes closing as though to let the weight of it sink into her bones. "Rise, Ivy of Elthas," I said. "My sister. My queen."

Together, side by side, they stood crowned. And the hall

seemed to exhale in relief, reverence, and the first fragile bloom of hope.

As Ethan and Ivy turned to face the hall, crowned, radiant, their hands instinctively finding each other's, I felt the tension I had carried for so long unspool from my chest. For the first time since I was thrust into this throne, the weight was no longer mine to bear. Relief coursed through me, sharp and sweet, like a deep breath after surfacing from too long underwater.

Elthas would be safe in their hands. Ethan, with his steady heart and innate sense of fairness. Ivy, with her brilliance and warmth, her ability to see ten steps ahead without losing sight of the people right before her. Together they could give this kingdom what I no longer could—focus, stability, devotion to its every need.

But the relief tangled with something heavier. As I looked at them, their crowns glinting in the light, I knew this was the moment everything changed. The life I had built here, filled with the council halls, the training fields, the long nights tangled with Amyra and Spencer, the roots I had sunk deep into this soil, it was all about to shift into something unrecognizable.

My lips curved in a smile, but my throat tightened around it. Joy for them. Pride in what we'd endured to reach this day. And beneath it, sorrow like an undertow, tugging at me with the knowledge that the only life I'd ever known was already becoming memory.

The Goddess of Balance. That was who I was now. And balance demanded letting go.

AFTERWORD

When I first stepped back into this world, I thought I understood the shape of Lyla's path. I thought I knew what she would carry, what she would lose, and what she would become.

But writing *Toll of the Crowned Flame* taught me that stories grow the same way people do—through fracture and through defiance, through love that keeps choosing itself even when the world demands pain and sacrifice.

I wrote this book in the aftermath of a life that had dropped out from under me entirely. There was no steady ground, only the shock of free fall and the slow work of finding my footing again. I'm still unlearning the false sense of safety built on keeping me quiet, still naming harms I was taught to endure, still tracing the thin, persistent threads of healing as they appear. That path is only just beginning. And in the middle of it, I found a truth I hadn't trusted in years: beginnings don't wait for certainty. They rise out of collapse, and choosing one—again and again—is its own act of survival.

Lyla learned what it meant to hold power without losing her softness.

Spencer learned what it meant to protect without possessing.

Amyra learned what it meant to love fiercely while refusing to shrink.

AFTERWORD

And Ethan, well, he learned that fear isn't a warning to turn back. It's the doorway you walk through to become someone braver.

Writing them through grief, war, devotion, jealousy, magic, and triumph changed me. These characters carried me as much as I carried them, and if they met you somewhere along your own journey, if they offered you a breath, a spark, a reminder that you deserve joy without permission, then this story has done the work I hoped it would.

Thank you for walking with them. Thank you for trusting me with your time and your heart. This world continues because you keep turning its pages.

And though Lyla has found her place, the tides are still shifting. There is another story rising from the deep.

A woman who fled a crown.
A pirate who carved her own freedom.
A goddess whose magic was once stolen.
A heartbeat that calls to the ocean itself.

When you're ready, come with me to chase the waves.

Nymbria's story is calling.

ABOUT THE AUTHOR

OLIVIA TILDON (they/she) writes queer romantasy for rebels with soft hearts—readers who crave defiant love, layered magic, and characters who change the world by choosing themselves. A mother of twins navigating a military divorce, Olivia rediscovered writing during a season of upheaval, solitude, and impossible choices. Without a budget or a blueprint, she taught herself to publish and poured everything she had into stories that reflect the quiet power of authenticity.

A queer author drawn to stories about chosen family, forbidden love, and becoming who you were never allowed to be, Olivia builds worlds where identity is power and love is an act of defiance. Without a budget or a blueprint, she taught herself how to publish and built a career from the ground up, pouring that grit and vulnerability into every page.

Her work is driven by the belief that small, brave choices can be revolutionary—and that stories still have the power to heal, awaken, and set us free.

Want more magic?

Download *The First Spark*, a free prequel to *Iris of the Crowned Flame*, by signing up for the newsletter. Get early access to new books and behind-the-scenes lore, and join a growing rebellion of romantasy readers.

Find Olivia online at www.oliviatildon.com and on social media @olivia.tildon

ALSO BY OLIVIA TILDON

The *Oracles of the Gelid* series
Iris of the Crowned Flame (Book 1)

The next book in this series is coming soon, and will follow Nymbria's story.

www.ingramcontent.com/pod-product-compliance
Lightning Source LLC
LaVergne TN
LVHW091717070526
838199LV00050B/2427